**"What do you want,
Why are you here?"**

"I'm applying for the job."

"You think you could handle it? Handle me?"

"That all depends on whether you're a gentleman or not."

He took another step, until his chest brushed her arm. "I'm not."

The cold air behind her and the heat in front met inside her, brewing up one hell of a storm. It wasn't enough he had that rugged cowboy thing going on, but he also oozed bad-boy sexy, which wasn't the least bit fair.

His hand lifted and he touched her hair. Just her hair. And she nearly dropped her soda. She needed to make her mouth work. For words to form. But that seemed way too difficult as his fingers brushed her cheek. "I don't think this is such a good idea."

"What?"

"You touching me."

"I'll stop if you want me to."

She closed her eyes. His thumb, callused and thick, followed the curve of her jaw all the way to her chin. "Stop." Her voice sounded weak, soft.

"You're old enough to know better," he whispered.

"Better than what?"

"That you shouldn't play with fire if you don't want to get burned."

Dear Reader,

Welcome to Trueblood, Texas!

Here's what I want to know—how come, when I lived in Texas for five years, I never met a man like Cole Bishop? That doesn't seem fair, does it? I know there are men like Cole—rough and stern on the outside, passionate and loving in private. I just haven't met my Cole...yet.

Here's the other thing I want to know—how come I can't be more like Lily Garrett? She's a pistol, that Lily, and I do admire a woman who isn't afraid to say what's on her mind.... Oh, wait. My friend (who's reading over my shoulder) tells me I shouldn't lie to my nice readers. I do say what's on my mind. In fact, no one can stop me from sharing my two cents. That's true, I guess, but Lily has such class, such flair, and she's so darn quick! I usually think of the perfect thing to say about two hours after the conversation is over.

Here's what I know for sure—there's magic involved in writing a novel. Oh, there's plot and character and dialogue and all the usual stuff, but sometimes, if I've been very, very good, the book will take wing and soar, and all I have to do is hang on for the ride. *The Cowboy Wants a Baby* was like that. It will always have a special place in my heart, and I hope, dear readers, that it will be a special book for you, too.

I love to hear from readers! http://www.joleigh.com.

Jo Leigh

TRUEBLOOD, TEXAS

The Cowboy Wants a Baby

Jo Leigh

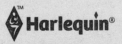

Harlequin®

TORONTO NEW YORK LONDON
AMSTERDAM PARIS SYDNEY HAMBURG
STOCKHOLM ATHENS TOKYO MILAN MADRID
PRAGUE WARSAW BUDAPEST AUCKLAND

Jo Leigh is acknowledged as the author of this work.

To my friends at Army Street with all my affection, and to Marsha for having such faith.

Recycling programs
for this product may
not exist in your area.

ISBN-13: 978-0-373-36583-8

THE COWBOY WANTS A BABY

Copyright © 2001 by Harlequin Books S.A.

For questions and comments about the quality of this book please contact us at Customer_eCare@Harlequin.ca.

www.Harlequin.com

Printed in U.S.A.

TRUEBLOOD, TEXAS

THE TRUEBLOOD LEGACY

THE YEAR WAS 1918, and the Great War in Europe still raged, but Esau Porter was heading home to Texas.

The young sergeant arrived at his parents' ranch northwest of San Antonio on a Sunday night, only the celebration didn't go off as planned. Most of the townsfolk of Carmelita had come out to welcome Esau home, but when they saw the sorry condition of the boy, they gave their respects quickly and left.

The fever got so bad so fast that Mrs. Porter hardly knew what to do. By Monday night, before the doctor from San Antonio made it into town, Esau was dead.

The Porter family grieved. How could their son have survived the German peril, only to burn up and die in his own bed? It wasn't much of a surprise when Mrs. Porter took to her bed on Wednesday. But it was a hell of a shock when half the residents of Carmelita came down with the horrible illness. House after house was hit by death, and all the townspeople could do was pray for salvation.

None came. By the end of the year, over one hundred souls had perished. The influenza virus took those in the prime of life, leaving behind an unprecedented number of orphans. And the virus knew no boundaries. By the time the threat had passed, more than thirty-seven million people had succumbed worldwide.

But in one house, there was still hope.

Isabella Trueblood had come to Carmelita in the late 1800s with her father, blacksmith Saul Trueblood, and her mother, Teresa Collier Trueblood. The family had traveled from Indiana, leaving their Quaker roots behind.

Young Isabella grew up to be an intelligent woman who had a gift for healing and storytelling. Her dreams centered on the boy next door, Foster Carter, the son of Chester and Grace.

Just before the bad times came in 1918, Foster asked Isabella to be his wife, and the future of the Carter spread was secured. It was a happy union, and the future looked bright for the young couple.

Two years later, not one of their relatives was alive. How the young couple had survived was a miracle. And during the epidemic, Isabella and Foster had taken in more than twenty-two orphaned children from all over the county. They fed them, clothed them, taught them as if they were blood kin.

Then Isabella became pregnant, but there were complications. Love for her handsome son, Josiah, born in 1920, wasn't enough to stop her from growing weaker by the day. Knowing she couldn't leave her husband to tend to all the children if she died, she set out to find families for each one of her orphaned charges.

And so the Trueblood Foundation was born. Named in memory of Isabella's parents, it would become famous all over Texas. Some of the orphaned children went to strangers, but many were reunited with their families. After reading notices in newspapers and church bulletins, aunts, uncles, cousins and grandparents rushed to Carmelita to find the young ones they'd given up for dead.

Toward the end of Isabella's life, she'd brought together more than thirty families, and not just her orphans. Many others, old and young, made their way to her doorstep, and Isabella turned no one away.

At her death, the town's name was changed to Trueblood, in her honor. For years to come, her simple grave was adorned with flowers on the anniversary of her death, grateful tokens of appreciation from the families she had brought together.

Isabella's son, Josiah, grew into a fine rancher and married Rebecca Montgomery in 1938. They had a daughter, Elizabeth Trueblood Carter, in 1940. Elizabeth married her neighbor William Garrett in 1965, and gave birth to twins Lily and Dylan in 1971, and daughter Ashley a few years later. Home was the Double G ranch, about ten miles from Trueblood proper, and the Garrett children grew up listening to stories of their famous great-grandmother, Isabella. Because they were Truebloods, they knew that they, too, had a sacred duty to carry on the tradition passed down to them: finding lost souls and reuniting loved ones.

PROLOGUE

THE YEAR WAS 1918, and the great war in Europe still raged, but Esau Porter was heading home to Texas.

The young sergeant arrived at his parents' ranch northwest of San Antonio on a Sunday night, only the celebration didn't go off as planned. Most of the townsfolk of Carmelita had come out to welcome Esau home, but when they saw the sorry condition of the boy, they gave their respects quickly and left.

The fever got so bad so fast that Mrs. Porter hardly knew what to do. By Monday night, before the doctor from San Antonio made it into town, Esau was dead.

The Porter family grieved. How could their son have survived the German peril, only to burn up and die in his own bed? It wasn't much of a surprise when Mrs. Porter took to her bed on Wednesday. But it was a hell of a shock when half the residents of Carmelita came down with the horrible illness. House after house was hit by death, and all the townspeople could do was pray for salvation.

None came. By the end of the year, over one hundred souls had perished. The influenza virus took those in the prime of life, leaving behind an unprecedented number of orphans. And the virus knew no boundaries. By the time the threat had passed, more than thirty-seven million people had succumbed worldwide.

But in one house, there still remained hope.

Isabella Trueblood had come to Carmelita in the late 1800s with her father, blacksmith Saul Trueblood, and her mother, Teresa Collier Trueblood. The family had traveled from Indiana, and left their Quaker roots behind.

Young Isabella grew up to be an intelligent woman who had a gift for healing and storytelling. Her dreams centered on the boy next door, Foster Carter, the son of Chester and Grace.

Just before the bad times came in 1918, Foster asked Isabella to be his wife, and the future of the Carter spread was secured. It was a happy union, and the future looked bright for the young couple.

Two years later, not one of their relatives was alive. How the young couple had survived was a miracle. And during the epidemic, Isabella and Foster had taken in more than twenty-two orphaned children from all over the county. They fed them, clothed them, taught them as if they were blood kin.

Then Isabella became pregnant, but there were complications. Love for her handsome son Josiah, born in 1920, wasn't enough to stop her from growing weaker by the day. Knowing she couldn't leave her husband to tend to all the children if she died, she set out to find families for each one of her orphaned charges.

And so the Trueblood Foundation was born. Named in memory of Isabella's parents, it would become famous all over Texas. Some of the orphaned children went to strangers, but many were reunited with their families. After reading notices in newspapers and church bulletins, aunts, uncles, cousins and grandparents rushed to Carmelita to find the young ones they'd given up for dead.

Toward the end of Isabella's life, she'd brought together more than thirty families, and not just her orphans. Many others, old and young, made their way to her doorstep, and Isabella turned no one away.

At her death, the town's name was changed to Trueblood, in her honor. For years to come, her simple grave was adorned with flowers on the anniversary of her death, grateful tokens of appreciation from the families she had brought together.

Isabella's son, Josiah, grew into a fine rancher and married Rebecca Montgomery in 1938. They had a daughter, Carrie Trueblood Carter, in 1940. Carrie married her neighbor William Garrett in 1965 and gave birth to Lily and Dylan in 1971, and daughter Ashley a few years later. Home was the Double G ranch, about ten miles from Trueblood proper, and the Garrett children grew up listening to stories of their famous great-grandmother Isabella. Because they were Truebloods, they knew that they, too, had a sacred duty to carry on the tradition passed down to them: finding lost souls and reuniting loved ones.

CHAPTER ONE

THE MANTEL OF the massive stone fireplace in the great room of the Double G ranch overflowed with calla lilies. The elegant white flowers had been placed with care just below the portrait of great-grandmother Isabella Trueblood, and Lily Garrett knew who was behind the sentimental gesture.

She turned to face her loved ones, and her gaze landed on her father, William. "I can't believe you did this, Daddy. You know they're my favorite. You're trying to make me cry, aren't you?"

"Nothing wrong with a tear now and again." With a smile that made him seem much younger than his sixty-one years, William leaned over and kissed her on the forehead. "There's nothing I wouldn't give you, darlin'," he whispered.

"I know, Daddy. Thank you." Before Lily let the moment disarm her further, she looked over at the couch. Her brother, Dylan, sat perched on the arm. "Hey, get over here. It's your birthday, too."

He shook his head. "I'm fine right where I am."

"You coward."

He shrugged. "That's me."

She sighed, even though she wasn't really upset. Dylan was shy about this kind of thing, which was peculiar, since he wasn't shy about anything else. But she didn't mind taking the spotlight for her twin.

"I'm only letting you off the hook because I'm so much older."

"Ha," he said. "By all of eight minutes."

"Quiet, you young whippersnapper." She smiled, really looking at him, appreciating him. He had the light-brown hair and blue eyes of their father, while Lily had inherited her mother's wavy black hair and green eyes, but they were well and truly twins. The bond between them... Well, sometimes even she didn't understand the connection.

Her gaze moved to the rest of the family. Her sister, Ashley, who looked disgustingly young and perky in her tennis whites. Six years Lily's junior, Ashley had taken time from her busy schedule at the ad agency to be at the birthday party.

Max was there, too. Although not related by blood, he was family in all the ways that were important. He'd grown up on the Double G, just as his father had before him. As ranch foreman, Max played a large part in making the horse and cattle ranch profitable. As a friend, he was even more important. Only five years older than Lily, he'd been a playmate, a tease, a strong shoulder to lean on.

"So are you going to open the presents or what?" Ashley checked her watch impatiently. "I've got a game at four."

"Your game can wait." William walked over to the big leather couch and eased down, a contented sigh escaping the moment he was off his feet. "It's not often we have the two of them home on this special occasion."

"They're going to live here forever now," Ashley said. "We'll have hundreds more birthdays to celebrate."

"But none like this." Lily took Ashley's arm and maneuvered her to the couch, next to their father.

Now that she had everyone's attention, Lily cleared her throat. "This isn't an ordinary day. Aside from it being our thirtieth birthday—which, by the way, I feel is totally unbelievable since I don't feel twenty-five, let alone thirty—today marks a new beginning for me."

Her brother's right brow arched in a silent question.

"You've all had to put up with a lot from me for the last seven months. I want you to know that I appreciate your patience and your generosity."

Ashley's eyes widened. "*You* appreciate *us?* It's a rare day indeed."

"Hush, Ashley, and let me finish." Lily moved to the center of the room and glanced up at the second floor for a moment. She cleared her throat, then went on with the speech she'd prepared that morning. "The construction on the new offices is nearing completion, which should be a relief to everyone."

Ashley clapped, prompting Lily into giving her younger sibling one of her better glares.

"Finders Keepers is well on its way to becoming the success we knew it would be," Lily went on. "There's a need for what we're doing. Too many people are lost and lonely, longing for what we have in abundance in this very room. It's a cold world out there without someone who loves you. Someone to love. And it's part of our legacy to help." She hesitated, wondering if she had the nerve to say the rest. But then she looked into her father's eyes.

"I also want to let you guys know that as of this day, I won't be griping about Jason Gill anymore. In fact, I won't even bring up his name."

Ashley's phony choking earned her a pinch from Dylan. Lily didn't let the episode shake her.

"I'm finished with that," she continued. "My entire focus is going to be on the agency and nothing else. But I will say one last thing. I know there's a lesson in this. There's a reason I fell for the rotten son of a bitch, and a reason I didn't know he was married. Unfortunately, I have no clue what that reason is. But I figure if it wasn't for endings, there wouldn't be new beginnings, right?"

Tears came to her eyes, but she blinked them back. The speech, the sentiment, were totally unlike her. She prided herself on her no-nonsense approach to life. Maybe it was turning thirty. Maybe it was the heat. She had no idea what had prompted her to get all mushy. But enough of that. She pushed her shoulders back, took a deep cleansing breath, then made the mistake of looking at Dylan.

His eyes seemed focused on something far away. She had a good idea what he was thinking about. Last year had been tough for him, too. He'd lost a part of himself while he'd been in Dallas. She wished with all her heart that she could take away his pain as well as her own. At least they were home, where they could rebuild their lives and find some peace.

"This is what's important," she said, mostly to Dylan, but to herself as well. "Being here with the people we love, and who love us. That's the best present of all."

"Uh, Lily?"

She was almost afraid to respond. "Yes, Ashley?"

"Does that mean you won't be wanting the sweater I got you?"

Laughter shifted the mood, and when Lily walked

over to strangle her little sister, things got even live-
lier. Although she didn't hurt Ashley, she did pluck
her gift from the pile on the coffee table. "Sweater,
eh?"

Nearly tearing off the white bandage on her hand,
a reminder not to save feral puppies without thick
gloves, Lily ripped into the purple-and-white package
that Ashley most assuredly had paid someone to
wrap. Lily flipped open the box underneath. But there
was no sweater. Instead, she pulled out a Sherlock
Holmes hat, a meerschaum pipe, and a magnifying
glass.

Dylan cracked up and Ashley's cheeks turned pink.

"This is so cool!" Lily plopped the hat on her head
and stuck the pipe in her mouth, then turned to her
brother. "Watson, bring me my violin."

Dylan got up off his perch on the side of the couch
and approached her, a sly smile tugging the corners
of his mouth. "Watson?" He swiped the hat from her
head. "I don't think so."

She reached to grab it, but Dylan held it too high.
"Give that back. It's mine!"

"Finders keepers," he said, dangling the woolen
cap tauntingly in front of her.

"I've got your finders keepers right here, buddy."
She jumped for the hat and caught the bill. They
tugged back and forth, causing much hooting and
laughter from Ashley and Max, until, at William's
urging, Dylan gave up. Lily put the hat on, grinning
at her victory. They hadn't tussled in years. It reminded her of their childhood. There had been lots of
roughhousing, but very little ill will. Well, except for
the time he'd broken into her diary. But since that

had happened fifteen years ago, she might be ready to forgive him.

"It's my turn," Dylan said, taking the second of the purple-and-white packages. He, unlike Lily, took his time opening the gift. First the ribbon, then each piece of tape. It was maddening. Finally, though, he hit a box. He opened it and grinned as he pulled out a mahogany door plaque that read Finders Keepers in beautiful gold script.

"For the new office," Ashley said.

"It's a knockout, Ash." Dylan passed the plaque to Lily, then kissed his little sister on the cheek. "You did good."

"Was there any doubt?"

Lily didn't respond. She was too busy admiring the beautiful workmanship on the plaque. The investigative agency was as real as the wood in her hands. Their intervention had brought three couples together and reunited two mothers and their children—everything Dylan and she had talked about when they'd decided to carry on the Trueblood legacy.

She couldn't wait until the offices were finished. Maybe she'd even open a bottle of champagne when they put this plaque on the door.

Max cleared his throat, getting her attention. He nodded at the other presents on the table. She plucked a pink bag from the pile and read the card first. It was from her father, and the message was as sweet and corny as he was. Inside she found a jewelry box.

She could sense, even before opening the lid, that she needed to sit down for this one. She settled on the couch, forcing Ashley to squeeze against the arm. When she opened the box, her heart stopped. She recognized the necklace instantly. It had been her mother's.

"We thought you ought to have that when you turned thirty." William squeezed her hand. "She'd be so proud of you."

Lily lifted the elegant teardrop diamond on the slim gold chain. She'd seen her mother wear this on the most special of occasions. It had been her pride and joy. "Help me?" she asked, turning her back to her father and lifting her hair. His fingers trembled slightly as he struggled with the catch, but she didn't mind the wait. It gave her time to settle her own emotions. She still missed her mother so much.

"There you go, darlin'."

She let her hair loose and rose to look in the hallway mirror. The diamond hung beautifully on her neck, just below the hollow. It was stunning, but the importance wasn't in the perfect three-carat stone. It was in the memories. And in the future. She'd give her daughter the necklace, and with it, all the stories of Lily's mother, and her mother before her.... All the proud heritage of the Truebloods, who'd risen from the ashes of the worst epidemic the world had ever known, only to plunge into the work of reuniting families, finding lost loved ones, creating hope from despair.

"Come back, Lily. Dylan's opening the next one!"

She left the mirror, but not before she said a silent thanks to her mother.

Dylan had nearly finished his painstaking unwrapping by the time she sat back down on the couch. He got a jewelry box, too. Her father's watch. The one William had been given by the Ranchers' Association. The one he'd worn each time their mother had donned the necklace.

"Dad, I—"

"It's your time, son. I'm just glad I'm here to see you wear it."

Dylan didn't speak. He took off his own battered watch and put on the heavy silver timepiece. It looked right on his arm. As if it had always been there.

"There's only two more," Ashley said impatiently. "So, would you guys please open them together? And, Dylan, I swear to God, if you don't rip the paper like a normal human being, I'll whack you with my racket."

"You try, little sister, and you won't sit down for a week."

"Why? You'd take away the chairs?"

"Very amusing." Dylan stood tall, reaching his full six-feet-one-inch and folding his muscular arms across his chest. "Amusing, and yet highly annoying."

"Just open the damn present."

"Ashley, language."

"Sorry, Dad."

Lily interceded by grabbing the next gift. Inside the bag was the most beautiful journal. It had her name inscribed on the outside, and inside was page after crisp white page, just ready for her favorite purple pen and her most private thoughts. "Max."

He nodded. "I remember you saying you were reaching the end of your last one."

"Handsome *and* smart. What a combination."

He blushed, which had been her intention, and she stood to give him a thank-you kiss on the cheek. But as she turned, her attention was diverted. Sebastian

Cooper stood in the doorway, his face ashen and his eyes dark and terrible. She hadn't seen him much since his wife had disappeared. He looked like he'd been chewed up and spit out.

She got Dylan's attention and motioned toward the door. She heard a small gasp as he turned to see his best friend. Which meant Sebastian's condition had worsened very recently.

Dylan rushed around the couch and reached Sebastian's side at the same time Lily did.

"What is it?" Dylan's hands formed fists, something he'd done his whole life when he was terribly scared.

"I'm sorry. I should have called."

"What's wrong? Is it Julie?"

Sebastian shook his head. "It's not that. Or maybe it is, I don't know. All I'm sure of is the San Antonio cops couldn't find the River Walk without a guide. It's been seven months—"

Lily winced at his obvious pain. It must be torture. Julie had vanished early in January, the apparent victim of a car-jacking. So far the police had no leads, and Dylan had only been able to do so much investigating without tipping his hand. He hadn't wanted to push his services on Sebastian, but it had been impossible for him to sit by and do nothing. Julie and Sebastian meant too much to him.

When Lily had asked Dylan why he didn't just insist on heading the case, he'd talked to her about friendship and loyalty and male pride. She hadn't completely understood, but he remained adamant that before he could pull out all the stops, Sebastian needed to ask for his help.

It appeared he just had.

DYLAN GOT OUT the Johnnie Walker Black and poured Sebastian two fingers. The family had dispersed until dinner, so Dylan joined his friend at the kitchen table, handing him the glass. "Tell me what you know." Dylan probably knew as much as Sebastian did about the case, but he had the feeling his friend needed to talk about it.

Sebastian's hand shook as he held the amber liquid. "The only evidence they found was some blood on the back seat of the car. Julie's blood."

Dylan made sure he didn't react at all to the bald words. At least not outwardly. Sebastian needed him to be strong now. But it was damn hard.

Julie and Sebastian meant more to him than anyone outside his family. Hell, he'd grown up with Sebastian, the two of them riding the rodeo circuit all through high school. They'd even gone to college together, and that's when Julie had entered the picture. Beautiful Julie. Who had called him her white knight, but married Sebastian. Dylan couldn't bear to think of her hurt, or worse.

"They traced the last few hours before her disappearance. She'd been to the bank—to the safe deposit box."

"What did she do there?"

Sebastian shrugged. "Not much. Got some papers, I think. But someone must have seen her there. Assumed she'd gotten valuables."

"And followed her."

Sebastian knocked back his drink, shuddering as the scotch went down. "Followed her and took her." He stared at Dylan, his eyes filled with more pain than any man should have. "The nights are the worst. I can't sleep. I keep thinking about what she's going through."

"We'll find her, Sebastian. I swear on my life, we'll find her."

"I kept thinking the police would find her. That it had to be something simple, a misunderstanding, that she'd left because I'd said something thoughtless, but she would have called. She isn't cruel. Dammit, I should have come to you first."

"It's good that the police are involved. But they have too many other cases. I swear to you, Sebastian, I'll find her."

Sebastian nodded. "I know." He swallowed hard, then tried to smile. "Remember Christmas?"

"Of course."

"She was so happy about the locket. So thrilled that I'd had the stones replaced."

"It meant a lot to her."

Sebastian leaned across the big oak dining table. "I keep thinking that's what the bastard saw. That the necklace drew his attention. If I hadn't given it to her—"

"Stop it. You didn't do this. It's not your fault."

"How do you know?"

"I know this—when she gets back, she's going to need you. If you rake yourself over the coals like this, you won't be any good for her."

He leaned back, nodding. "Right. I need to be strong for her."

"Let the detective in charge know you've hired us. I'll need to see their reports."

"I will."

Dylan nodded at the scotch bottle. "Need another?"

"Yeah. But I'm not going to. If I start drinking now, I don't think I'll be able to stop."

"Right. So why don't you kick back. Take a swim or something. We're having dinner in a couple of hours."

"I can't, Dylan. I wish I could."

"You don't have to see anyone. I could arrange that."

Sebastian stood. "I have to go. I'm grateful to you, buddy. And listen." He swallowed again, his Adam's apple too visible. He'd lost weight. "Whatever happens—"

"We'll find her."

Sebastian turned away. A lock of his hair fell over his eye. Julie would have pushed it back, then she would have kissed him. It was something she did without fail. She'd been a sucker for Sebastian since day one. Dylan was glad she'd found happiness. Now all he had to do was bring her back to the arms of the man she loved.

Failing wasn't an option.

Lily raised her soda glass. "To us."

The rest of the family joined her in the impromptu toast. "To us."

They drank their assorted beverages and went on with the birthday dinner. Max and her father were already deep in discussion about the new paddock. Ashley, still in her tennis outfit, ate as if calories didn't exist. Dylan hardly touched his food.

She knew Julie's kidnapping weighed heavily on him—even more so now that he'd agreed to take the case. She wondered again if Dylan knew he was still in love with Julie. It had broken his heart when she married Sebastian, but good old Dylan hadn't said a word. He'd just stood there as best man and watched his one true love marry his closest friend.

So much of what had happened to Dylan was connected to that moment. His decision to leave San Antonio and work for the Dallas P.D. His undercover work infiltrating J. B. Crowe's mob family. The fateful error that had blown his cover.

Most people wouldn't tie all those events together, but most people didn't know Dylan the way she did. Sometimes—she wouldn't swear on a bible or anything—but sometimes she felt absolutely sure that she could read his mind. And that he could read hers. More than that, she felt his pain. Not to the degree he felt it, but it was there. A dull ache that told her Dylan was in trouble. It didn't seem to matter how far away he was, she always knew.

The ache was strong tonight. She wasn't at all sure he should have taken the case. If he failed...

And even if he didn't, the outcome was probably going to devastate him. The odds of Julie being alive after seven months were slim.

Dylan shoved some food around on his plate. She reached over and touched his hand. Startled, he looked at her.

"It's going to be okay," she whispered.

"I don't know."

"I do. Because you're going to do everything possible. You're the best man for the job and there's not going to be one stone left unturned. If anyone on earth can find her, it's you."

He nodded slowly, unconvinced, she thought.

"Little brother."

The appellation always made him smile. Eight

minutes didn't make him her "little" anything. But his smile failed to appear this time.

"Dylan, I know it's hard, but for Dad's sake, try. Eat something, just a little. Smile, even if you don't mean it."

He sighed. "I am pretty good at appearing to be something I'm not. And right now that means being in the mood to celebrate."

"After dinner, why don't we sit down and talk about what we know so far, and what's next."

He smiled, and damned if she didn't believe the transformation. "Good idea, Lily." He ate some steak, drank some iced tea, laughed at something Ashley said.

But the ache was still heavy in Lily's chest. The ache that told her Dylan was dying inside.

CHAPTER TWO

LILY'S FIRST VIEW of Eve Bishop's mansion came after almost a mile of winding road, flanked on each side with huge chinquapin oaks she'd give a pretty penny to see in the fall. The trees cast shimmering shadows on the road and her car in a windblown ballet.

The house itself was equally awe inspiring. Two-story Victorian, it was registered with the historic society as one of the original German mansions built in the late 1800s. As she drove closer, Lily could see the facade wasn't quite up to snuff. It needed paint and the garden was overgrown. But then Eve was in her seventies, and Lily had grown increasingly alarmed over the woman's frail health.

She'd met Eve while volunteering for the Texas Fund for Children, a large charitable organization that provided funding for a children's hospital and rehabilitative center, staff for the two largest orphanages in the state and many other educational and health programs. The whole shebang had been started by Eve and her late husband, and Eve had worked hands-on to build the foundation for over twenty years.

Lily parked the car in the circular drive and stepped out into the brutal July sun. With a high in the hundreds and the air thick with humidity, it wasn't a pleasant place to dawdle. But she did. She lingered in the garden for a moment, her mind's eye seeing what the grounds were meant to be when tended properly.

At the massive front door, she hesitated once more. Eve had asked her to come by, but had been quite mysterious about her reasons. Lily hoped it wasn't because she was ill. Aside from admiring Eve for her philanthropy, she liked the woman very much and considered her a real friend.

She rang the doorbell, hearing its echo inside, then waited. The house was so large, easily ten thousand square feet, that unless Eve had help, it was going to take her a while to get to the door. To Lily's surprise it was opened almost immediately by a young woman with a welcoming smile.

"I'm Lily Garrett. Here to see Eve."

"She's expecting you," the woman said as she pulled the door open further. She was in her twenties, Lily guessed, and of Hispanic heritage. Her dark hair had been pinned up, and she wore shorts and a T-shirt, completing the ensemble with bare feet.

"Please, come this way." Her accent was slight, lilting. She led Lily through the broad foyer, her bare soles slapping the white marble floor, then stopped at a door just a few feet down the hallway. She knocked twice but didn't wait for a response. Lily nodded her thanks as she stepped inside.

The room captivated her instantly. Very Victorian in style, decorated in different hues of pink and white, it was made perfect by the elegant tea cart holding a silver service. Eve sat on an overstuffed chair, her petite body dwarfed by the chair's velvet wings.

"Lily. I've made tea."

"I see. It looks wonderful."

Eve patted the cushion of the love seat next to her chair. "Come. And tell me if you prefer milk or lemon."

"Milk, I think."

For the next few moments, Eve went through the slow ritual of afternoon tea, complete with tiny crustless watercress sandwiches, pink petits fours with icing that matched the color of the walls exactly, and little lumps of sugar doled out with silver tongs.

Lily took advantage of the lull to study the decor. Lush bouquets of fresh flowers were on the mantel and an end table. A white upright piano was the centerpiece of the far wall, and a brick fireplace flanked by bookshelves did the honors on the wall to her left. Antique dolls stared wide-eyed from various perches throughout the room, their bright curls adding a bit of life to the old-fashioned library.

Above the fireplace was a portrait, and Lily knew instantly that it was of Eve. She'd been much younger then, her now silver curls a deep coppery red. Her skin was smooth, her long neck arched and coy. The artist had captured her spirit, especially in her eyes. But the vivid blue in the picture had faded on the older woman.

Eve handed Lily a plate and a teacup, waited for her to take a sip, then sighed.

"What is it, Eve? Is something wrong?"

The old woman's hand trembled as she put her cup on the tea cart. "Several things, in fact."

"Is there something I can do?"

"I dearly hope so."

Lily took another sip of tea, but she hardly tasted it, her curiosity was so great.

"The simple fact is that I'm dying."

Lily nearly dropped her cup at the stark words. "Oh, no. Please, not that."

Eve nodded. "I don't mind very much. Honestly. I've had a rich and full life. My days now are mostly about pain, feeling it, treating it, ignoring it. My hands have become traitors and my eyes, well, maybe it's not so terrible to see the world in shadow."

"Is it really that bad?"

"Sometimes. But nothing hurts as much as the heaviness in my heart. And that's why I've called you."

"How can I help?"

Eve leaned back in her chair as if the effort of sitting upright had become too much for her. "I have a grandson."

"You've never mentioned him."

"I haven't. Because I haven't seen him in five years. I haven't spoken to him or heard about him. My son, his father, died four months ago. He had a heart attack. He hadn't spoken to Cole in five years, either."

"Why?"

"That's not important," she said, her brow furrowed with the effort of the conversation. "What is important is that I see my grandson before I die. I won't be able to rest until I do. Can you understand?"

"Of course. You love him."

"More than he'll ever know."

"Do you know where he lives?"

She shook her head slowly. "The last I heard, he was in Houston. But that probably isn't where he is now."

"Do you have any idea what he does?"

"No. Business, perhaps ranching. I don't know."

"I see."

"You don't. But you don't have to. Lily, I trust you. I know you'll bring him back. I'll pay twice your normal fee if you'll abandon all other cases to concentrate on this one."

"You don't have to do that."

"I don't have to do anything. But I'm a rich old woman whose shopping sprees are over."

Lily had no intention of arguing with her. She'd send an appropriate bill when the job was done. If, in fact, it ended satisfactorily. "I'd like to take this job, Eve, but I have to make something clear. I won't bring him back against his will. We reunite families that want to be reunited."

"Fine. Then I'll trust you to make him want to come home."

"Fair enough. I'll do my best."

"I know that, Lily. That's why I called you. I've done a little research of my own. I'm impressed with this new company of yours. But believe me when I say it was only because I'd met you and seen how you operate that I considered hiring you. Finding my grandson is the most important thing in my life. And that life, if one believes the doctors, will end in approximately six months."

"Please don't say that. Anything can happen. Miracles."

Eve's smile changed her face. The beauty of the portrait was still there despite the ravagement of years. "There are no miracles. Only things to regret. I don't want to go that way, you see. I don't want to die with this terrible regret."

"I do understand, Eve. I do."

Eve's pale-blue gaze met Lily's and held it steady.

The determination there was like steel. "Find him. Do whatever you have to do to bring him home. He's my only heir. He'll inherit it all. Make sure he understands that."

Lily nodded.

"Now drink your tea. It's probably cold by now."

MAX SANTANA yearned for a shower. A long, cold one. Riding out to the far pasture hadn't bothered him, but hauling that big mother cow out of a muddy bog had worn him to the bone. It was the heat. Normally San Antonio was in the high eighties this time in July. But a heat wave had settled across the state, shooting the temperature and the humidity to record levels.

He loved everything about this place except the high heat. Days like this, he had to keep his mind occupied on cool things. Iced tea. Snow. A long swim in a chilly pool.

The only thing Max wanted more than a dip in the pool was a woman.

As he rounded the corner of the big house, he bumped into something soft and sweet. Lily.

"Hey, Max."

"Sorry about that."

She waved the small accident away.

Lily was a woman all right, but to him she was practically a sister. What he needed was a stranger with loose morals. Yes, indeed. But he'd think about that in the shower. "Dylan's looking for you."

"Pardon?"

"You know. Your brother. He's looking for you."

"I've been out." She sounded distracted, her voice was softer than normal. And she hadn't smiled once.

"What's wrong?"

She didn't answer him.

"It's not that son of a bitch Jason Gill, is it? 'Cause I know where he lives and I've got vacation time coming."

"No, no. It's nothing like that."

He folded his arms across his chest and frowned at her. He wanted to look down his nose at her, but with her being five foot nine and him six-one, his scowl wasn't nearly as effective as it should have been. The more he studied her, the more he knew something was wrong. Lily had her hair up in some sort of tortoise-shell contraption, but a long strand had escaped captivity and hung down past the middle of her back. Lily didn't miss things like that unless she was preoccupied or worried.

"Max, calm down. It's a new case, that's all."

"What kind of case?"

"I need to find a missing heir."

He grinned. "How much is at stake? I could sure use an inheritance."

"You could, huh? And what would you do with your millions, Mr. Santana?"

"I'd buy the O'Neill place."

She smiled, finally. "You are the most predictable man. So why don't you tell me where my little brother is?"

"He's in the office, and I'm going to tell him you called him that."

"You do, and I'll tell that O'Neill girl you've got the hots for her." The O'Neill girl was about fifty, and ornery as hell.

"Lily, don't threaten me. You know I can be vindictive as hell."

She slugged him in the shoulder, and for a skinny girl like her, she made it hurt. "You don't have a vindictive bone in your body. But you sure need a shower." She waved her hand in front of her nose and made a face at him. "You smell like wet cow."

He grunted, then headed off again. After his shower, he'd dive in the pool so fast he'd hardly feel the splash. Oh, yeah.

DYLAN WAS IN the makeshift office, actually a spare bedroom in the old part of the house. They'd moved in two desks and a filing cabinet, then loaded the place with electronic equipment: fax, computers, printers, phones, scanner, all of which would be transferred to the upstairs offices as soon as they were ready. For an interim space, the bedroom wasn't bad. Just small.

Lily put her purse in her bottom drawer then waited while Dylan finished his phone call. From his tone, she gathered it was business, and as she shamelessly eavesdropped, she realized he was talking to Bill Richardson, one of the homicide detectives working on Julie Cooper's case.

Searching for Cole Bishop was going to prevent her from assisting Dylan, but given the circumstances, it couldn't be helped. With Eve so ill, there wasn't a moment to waste. Besides, Dylan on his own was quite formidable, and she had no doubt that he'd do everything possible to find Julie. She just hoped he wouldn't get hurt. Either physically or emotionally. So much was at stake.

"I'll get back to you," Dylan said as he acknowledged her with a nod. "And see what you can do about those files, huh?" He listened for another few moments, said his goodbye and hung up. His attention was focused on her now, but she could see the strain of the morning's work on his face.

"How goes it?"

He shrugged. "Just trying to get up to speed. What was your meeting about?"

"I've got a case."

"Now?"

She nodded. "I'm sorry. I know how important it is to concentrate on finding Julie, but this is something of an emergency." She explained about Eve's request, and about the ticking clock. Dylan had met Eve on several occasions and his concern for her was immediate.

"Okay, I can do this on my own, but I think we need to get an assistant now instead of waiting for the offices to be finished."

"I agree. Any suggestions?"

He shook his head. "I'll make some calls in the morning."

Lily turned on her computer, ready to start the search for Cole Bishop. She heard Dylan curse softly, and when she looked up, he was staring at his notepad, his face a mask of frustration.

"What's wrong?"

He shook his head. "Things aren't adding up right."

"What do you mean?"

"Nothing concrete. It's more gut feeling than anything else. Something's eating at me."

"Well, then, you'd better pay attention. I don't know anyone who has better gut instincts than you."

He gave her a sardonic grin. "Not always."

She hadn't meant for the conversation to go there.

Dylan had been on an undercover assignment in Dallas the previous year. His gut instincts had taken him into the very heart of J. B. Crowe's mob family, but last October, he'd made one mistake—and that was all it took in his line of work. His cover had been blown, and he barely made it out of there alive. "Come on, Dylan. Did we or didn't we agree not to wallow in the past?"

"We agreed. But as I recall, it was after you ate an entire pint of Ben & Jerry's as you rehashed some memories I'm too much of a gentleman to bring up."

"Subtle. Like a sledgehammer."

"All I'm saying is the things we went through are a part of us. I don't think we can forget about them."

"But we don't have to beat ourselves up over and over, do we? Frankly, I don't want to live like that."

He leaned back in his chair and linked his hands behind his neck. "So why don't you find someone new? Someone who isn't married?"

"Date? Me? No. No way."

"Why not? You planning on becoming a nun?"

"Knock it off. Of course not. But I'm certainly not going to get myself involved this soon after— I mean, anything I would do now would be a rebound thing, right? I don't trust rebound things."

"Yeah, I suppose. But that doesn't mean you can't go out. There's such a thing as dating for fun."

"Which you would know about how?"

"Point taken."

"I think, for us, for now, we need to focus on the agency. In a year or so, we can rethink things, but now? Let's just be detectives."

"Right. Good answer."

She sighed. "So quit bugging me. I have work to do."

He didn't say anything, but about two minutes later, a rubber band hit her in the shoulder. Being so much older and more mature than Dylan, she let it pass.

WHEN LILY LEFT the office, it was almost eight. Dylan was hungry—he hadn't eaten since noon—but the idea of joining the family for dinner didn't sit well. He didn't want to make small talk, and he certainly didn't want to discuss his progress on the case.

Progress. As if he'd made any. The police were cooperating, to a degree, but that was only because he'd been part of the brotherhood. The evidence was sketchy as hell. Would car-jackers be sophisticated enough to wear gloves? Why else would there be no fingerprints in the car? Did they simply hold a gun to her head and force her out? Then why was there blood on the back seat?

It didn't make sense, and Dylan's instinct told him it wasn't a car-jacking. And yet, there was no ransom note. No demands. There had to be something else, some third possibility he couldn't see yet. She could have taken off, of course, but that wasn't Julie's style. He'd just keep digging until he figured it out.

His gaze shifted to a framed photograph on the wall behind the credenza. In it, he was with Julie and Sebastian, all smiles. Sebastian's arm was around Julie's waist and Julie's head rested on his shoulder. They were the picture of connubial bliss. Although they'd spent the day on the ranch, they'd been AWOL for about an hour after lunch, and Dylan knew exactly what they'd been doing.

He'd tried like hell not to let his imagination run wild, but he should have known better. With Julie, he had no willpower, no control. She came to him in dreams, while he was out riding, during business meetings. He'd thought by now he would have accepted that she'd chosen Sebastian. He'd been wrong.

He opened his bottom drawer and took out the bottle of aged scotch he kept there. But he didn't pour any. Instead, his gaze moved back to the photograph. To the necklace Julie wore with such pride. It was a silver heart that opened to reveal a small picture of the happy couple. It had been her mother's locket and Sebastian had scored major points for fixing it up like he had.

Dylan had given her earrings. But she wasn't wearing those in the photo. Just the necklace. Which was appropriate, of course. But he'd wished…

Screw that. It was over. Over and done, and Julie was with Sebastian. If Julie was alive, that is. If he could find her.

Although he wasn't a man who ordinarily prayed, he closed his eyes and repeated the desperate bargain that had become almost a mantra in the last six months. "God, please keep her safe. Bring her home. If you do that, I swear I'll stop loving her."

CHAPTER THREE

LILY TURNED UP the music as she merged onto U.S. 87. Another few hours and she'd reach Abilene. She'd found Cole Bishop easily enough. Now came the hard part. Getting him to come back with her.

Thanks to the Internet, she'd actually learned a good deal about his work. He had a successful mid-size ranch—the Circle B—just outside the small city of Jessup where he raised prize-winning Black Angus cattle. He had an excellent breeding program, but what he was most noted for was the way he managed the ranch. His techniques had been written up in *The Cattlemen* and the *High Plains Journal,* two big trade magazines. His approach to ranching was modern and cost-effective. Clearly, he was a smart cookie.

What she didn't find was anything about the man himself. No personal information at all. She couldn't find any pictures, either.

It occurred to her that perhaps Mr. Bishop wanted to connect with Eve again, but that he didn't know how. Men, especially ranchers, could be stubborn as mules. So maybe her appearance would be just the excuse he needed to mend his fences and go back into the fold.

But somehow she doubted it. Why? She couldn't say. Like her brother, she trusted her gut instincts. They'd always been alike that way. Most of her insights had been about Dylan; it was a twin thing, which she'd discovered wasn't uncommon at all. But when she'd moved out of the house, other events seemed to trigger that sixth sense of hers. It wasn't as if she had ESP or anything. Just that from time to time her radar would go off.

It had gone off with Jason Gill, but she'd ignored it. There had been that small worried voice in the back of her head when he'd asked her to leave New York and transfer to the Dallas office. But had she listened? Oh, no. She'd moved, lock, stock and barrel. Once she'd turned off her receiver, it had stayed off. She'd believed every honeyed lie, and she'd fallen hard. She still got monthly issues of *Bride* magazine at the house. Instead of canceling the damn subscription, she preferred to stack the magazines in a pile by her bed. A towering reminder to heed her intuition.

Of course, sometimes listening to the quiet voice inside led to things that were hard to deal with. As a forensics specialist working for the FBI, she'd learned how to go by the book. Except that one time. The small voice had led her to discover that the death of a pregnant teenager and the child inside her had not occurred in a drive-by shooting, as the police believed, but at the hands of her own father.

She'd realized then that forensics wasn't where she belonged. It wasn't all bad. But the case of the teenager, and of course the whole Jason mess, convinced her to leave Dallas and come home. That, at least, had been a positive thing.

The memories had shattered her good mood, and that wasn't acceptable. She turned up the radio until the car vibrated with Reba singing "Fancy." Lily sang along, not caring that her voice was terrible, and that she only hit some of the notes some of the time. She loved singing in the car, and she didn't give a hoot who saw her doing it. She had a long road ahead, and nothing like good old country music to help her along the way.

By the time she reached the tiny town of Jessup, Texas, she was sung out, rung out and starving. The town looked like a hundred others in South Texas. The biggest single store was the grain and feed. Then a Wells Fargo branch. There was an antique store next to a gun shop, and next to that Pete's Dry Cleaning. Then she spied a little diner, Josie's, and she pulled around back to the parking lot. She'd purposely waited to eat until she arrived in Cole Bishop's town. Waitresses in small-town diners could be a wealth of information.

She peeled herself off the seat then shut the door; her car looked a little worse for wear, but that wasn't because of this trip. It had only taken six hours to get here from the ranch. The sports car was almost ten years old, and the Texas weather had beaten down the old broad. But there were some good years left in her. At least, Lily hoped so.

She ran her fingers through her hair, straightened her blouse and skirt and headed inside.

It took her a moment to adjust to the dim light after so much bright sunshine. But once she did, she felt as if she'd been there before. It was a familiar setup, typical of diners all over the country. Four or five booths, a few tables, a counter, a small soda fountain. The waitresses wore jeans and T-shirts with white aprons slung low on their hips. The other truly Texas touch was the preponderance of Stetsons on the clientele.

Lily headed to the middle seat at the counter, between a wiry old cowboy who looked as if he slept in his boots and a middle-aged woman eating a salad, her paperback book open behind her plate.

The waitress, Ginny, according to her name tag came to Lily with a menu and a smile. "Afternoon."

"Hi."

"You headin' to Fort Worth?"

Lily shook her head. "Nope. But maybe you can help me?"

"I'll do what I can."

"First, I need some chicken-fried steak."

"Smart girl. There's none better in the county."

"Excellent. And I'll have an iced tea, please."

Ginny wrote the order, then turned and put it on a clip in the window opening to the kitchen. She poured the tea, gave the cowboy some fresh coffee and came back to Lily. "So what else can I help you with?"

Lily guessed her age at about forty, give or take. Her short cropped hair had some gray in it, her eyes had laugh wrinkles and so did her smile. It was obvious she liked the idea of a stranger in town, with all new stories to tell. Lily sent up a mental thank-you to the patron saint of private detectives, if there was one. "I'm looking for someone. His name is Cole Bishop."

Ginny's pencil slipped from her fingers. The woman to Lily's right snapped her book shut. The cowboy pushed back his Stetson. The reactions were startling, to say the least.

"Are you here for the job?"

Lily had no idea what the job might be, but it seemed a likely avenue to pursue. She couldn't imagine what could cause such a stir. "Yeah. You know anything about it?"

Ginny glanced meaningfully at the woman with the book. The best Lily could figure, the waitress was either scandalized or jealous, or else she had an upset stomach. Finally looking back at Lily, Ginny shook her head. "I don't know that much about it."

Right. "Whatever you can tell me would be great. I'm not sure I got all the details."

The woman shrugged a what-the-hell. "I'll tell you one thing. He's a stunner."

"A stunner?"

"Best-looking man I've ever seen in the flesh."

"I see," she said, although of course, she didn't. What did his looks have to do with the job? Dammit, she shouldn't have said she was going after the job. Now it was impossible to ask straight out what it was.

"And Lord knows he could have any woman he wanted just by crooking his little finger."

The woman next to Lily nodded her agreement. "You'd think he'd want to do things the regular way, wouldn't you?"

Have any woman? The regular way?

"So, tell me something, sweetie," Ginny asked, lowering her voice. "Why on earth would a beautiful young woman like you want to do it?"

It? What was it? "Uh, you know. The usual reasons."

"Usual? I don't know where you're from, child, but in this part of the world, there ain't no usual in what Cole Bishop's up to."

Shit! "Well, that's the thing. I was hoping to learn more about it before I went to see him. *If* I go to see him."

Ginny leaned forward and opened her mouth, but the little bell from the kitchen drew her away before she could say one word. It ended up being Lily's lunch that was ready, and once Ginny retrieved it, she seemed ready to spill the beans. To make sure the waitress knew she had the floor, Lily quickly cut a big slice of the meat and shoved it in her mouth. What she should have done first was make sure it wasn't scorching hot. But she just smiled through the pain as she chewed.

Ginny opened her mouth again, but for the second time, she was interrupted.

"I heard that Stephanie Davidson went by his place about two weeks ago." The woman to Lily's right leaned forward. "She said he was a regular son of a you-know-what."

"I do, Patsy, I do." Ginny shook her head and frowned. "He 'bout bit my head off a couple days back. Just because his coffee wasn't hot enough."

"That's Cole Bishop for you."

"And yet the women fall at his feet. Except for, you know. That's just plum crazy." Ginny realized what she'd said, and shot Lily an embarrassed glance. "No offense meant."

"None taken." Lily smiled, but her imagination was going hog-wild. Was the man a deviant? A pervert? A talk-show host? Maybe Eve wouldn't want him back in her life. Maybe Lily should get in her car and head on home. *What in hell was this job?*

"I don't know." Patsy took a swallow of her iced tea, probably just to add to the drama of the moment. Even after she put down her glass, she hesitated. "I think what the man needs is a good woman. Someone who can turn him around."

"Wait a minute. Are you saying he's gay?"

Ginny shook her head at Lily's question. "Not so's you'd notice. He sees a waitress out at Hastings from time to time. And don't she like to brag about it. According to her, he's got the biggest—"

The kitchen bell rang, and Ginny hustled to the window before she finished the sentence. Lily figured she knew what was so big about Mr. Bishop, but in cattle country one could never be quite sure.

"Manny sure does speak highly of him, though," Patsy said the moment Ginny returned from her waitressing duties.

"Who's Manny?" Lily asked.

"He works for Bishop. Young man, real polite. He's got a girl, Rita Borrego is her name, and she works at the Millers' place. She's a cook and pretty as a petunia."

Lily didn't care about petunias. She wanted to know what was going on with Cole. It was a nightmare version of twenty questions, and Lily's turn was about up. "So, about this job..."

"Jessica Tanksley," Patsy said, as if Lily hadn't spoken. "She's my sister's boyfriend's cousin. She went out there." Patsy looked up to heaven for a moment, then back down. "He looked her over like he was buying a prize heifer. Asked her about a million questions. Real personal, if you get my meaning. But she must have answered wrong. The man never did call her."

This was getting weirder by the second. Not to mention more frustrating. What kind of a job was this? He'd looked the woman over like a cow? Asked personal questions? "What about family?" Lily asked, deciding to approach things from a different angle. "His, I mean."

Ginny's brow rose. "The last person who asked Cole Bishop about his family came down with a sudden case of broken nose and cracked ribs."

"Oh, my."

"My aunt Maureen says he's got a closet full of skeletons." Patsy lowered her voice. "She heard he killed a man."

Lily's mouth dropped open. She hadn't considered that he might be a cold-blooded killer. On the other hand, murder was a damn hard thing to hide. If he'd—

"I'm not saying it's true. But that's what she heard. That he killed a man in cold blood and never gave it another thought."

"Forgive me, Patsy, but your aunt Maureen's crazy as a bedbug."

"She's only been in the hospital that once."

Ginny's hands went to her hips. "It just ain't natural, that's all." She gave Lily a probing look. "And even though it's none of my business, I think you should get in that car of yours and keep on driving. Go on to Fort Worth. Get yourself a real job and find yourself a nice man. Girl like you doesn't need to be messing with the likes of Cole Bishop."

Lily was tempted to do just that. All this talk of unnatural acts had given her the willies. But the willies had never stopped her before. Besides, she knew a thing or two about small-town gossip. Most of what she'd heard this afternoon was probably hogwash. She'd feel a lot better, however, knowing which parts were true. *Just what in hell was this job?*

DYLAN CHECKED OUT a tall blond beauty as she walked down Crockett. He had his sunglasses on, so his perusal was private. As she crossed the street, he jerked his mind back to the business at hand. Sebastian was probably waiting for him downstairs.

He headed toward a huge wooden pushcart with the famous green awning. Perk at the Park, an outdoor coffee bar on the River Walk. Sure enough, there was Sebastian sitting in his usual spot under the brown umbrella. He looked like hell.

Dylan stopped at the pushcart and waited for Kelly Adams, the owner of Perk, to finish her last order. She looked pretty this afternoon, but then she always looked pretty. Maybe it was time for him to do something about his social life. Going out with Kelly would be fun. They'd known each other for a long time, and he felt comfortable with her. She was no Julie but—

He nipped that thought in the bud. Julie's husband sat waiting for him, and the poor guy was nearly out of his mind with worry. Sebastian needed his friendship now. And his total concentration.

"What'll it be, Dylan? The usual?"

He shook his head. "Iced coffee, if you've got some fresh."

"Of course I do. Heavens." She wiped her hands on her apron and turned to fetch his drink.

From the back, Dylan could see her jeans and the small T-shirt she wore. She really was attractive. Maybe, when he'd found Julie, when his life wasn't so crazy...

"Here you go." She handed him the tall plastic cup. "And do me a favor? Cheer up your buddy there, huh? He's got me worried."

"Me, too." He handed her a five. "Thanks, Kelly."

"Hey, your change."

"Keep it," he said over his shoulder.

Sebastian glanced up at him with worried eyes. His hair, usually meticulous, looked as if he hadn't put a comb to it. His smile was a pitiful attempt.

"Hey, ya bastard." Dylan used the old greeting, but it didn't change Sebastian's expression.

"Anything new?"

Dylan shook his head. "Have you slept at all?"

Sebastian shrugged. "I don't sleep through the night anymore. Not like I used to. I end up watching the damn weather channel all night. Go ahead, ask me about tomorrow's high."

"Man, you've got to do something. Have you seen a doctor? Maybe he can give you a sleeping pill."

"Nope. I've thought of it, but it would be too tempting to get dependent on them. I'm not drinking much, either. I need to be clear about things. On my toes."

"Well, I think a couple nights' good sleep would go a long way."

Sebastian looked at the river for a long moment. He sipped his coffee, then put the cup down. "I found a note from Julie last night."

Dylan sat up straight, his heart lurching in his chest. "A note?"

"Don't get too excited. It wasn't a recent note. It was from Christmas. She'd written me a little thank-you for her gift and stuck it in my sock drawer. Except it got caught in the back, and I only saw it today because I yanked the damn drawer out by mistake."

"What did it say?"

He leaned to his right and pulled his leather wallet out of his back pocket. With agonizing slowness, he opened the billfold and brought out a small piece of paper. He put his wallet back, then unfolded the paper. It was all Dylan could do not to rip it out of his hands.

It turned out, he didn't need to. Sebastian handed him the note.

Her handwriting jolted him. He hadn't realized how well he'd known the beautiful script. "Sebastian," the note read. "I love you so. The locket is worth everything to me. I'll never take it off. Never."

Dylan folded the small piece of paper and handed it to his friend. "Son of a bitch."

Sebastian turned to him, his gaze hard and cold. "You have no idea."

"It's not your fault. I know you want it to be, but it's not."

His friend's laugh sent a chill down Dylan's back. There was such self-hatred, such mockery in the hollow tone.

"I should have been with her."

"You were at work."

"It doesn't matter. I should have been with her and I should have protected her. I wanted her to get a gun, but she wouldn't hear of it. She said she'd probably end up shooting herself. I told her we'd go to the range so she could learn how to use a pistol, but then, I don't know, I got busy. I got a new client... I never brought it up again."

"Sebastian, you have to stop this. It's going to drive you insane."

"What's wrong with that?"

"Nothing. Except Julie's coming back. She is. Do

you want to be here when she does? Or in the nut-house?''

"How can you be so certain?"

"Remember when we were in Houston at that rodeo? The one where you got the wild bull—what the hell was his name?"

"Goliath?"

"Yeah. Goliath. And I told you to change your gloves?"

Sebastian nodded. "I didn't listen."

"And the gloves tore."

"The rope ripped my hand to shreds."

"Well, like I knew about the rope, I know about Julie."

"You are one weird bastard, you know that, Garrett?"

Dylan nodded. "Why else would I hang out with you?"

Sebastian smiled. And for the first time since Julie's disappearance, Dylan felt it was real. But it was gone all too soon, and the cloud of darkness resettled over his best friend.

"I want to go over everything again." Dylan got a small notepad from his back pocket. "Step by step."

"I've told you everything I know."

"Then tell me again."

Sebastian sighed. Closed his eyes. And started from the beginning.

CHAPTER FOUR

LILY SLOWED the car as she drove up Cole Bishop's drive. The two-story ranch house reminded her of her cousin Ted's in Waco. The wide front porch had room for a swing or a rocking chair, but it was bare. Painted white, the house itself seemed relatively new, a plain canvas with nothing to distinguish itself.

The lawn was the same. Rye grass, green even in this heat. No flower beds, no hedges. A big oak saved the view from being nondescript.

She wondered if she shouldn't just write him a letter. It wasn't easy to admit, but the conversation from the diner had her a little spooked.

Of course, her dilemma might be solved with a knock on the door. He probably wasn't home. She hoped he wasn't home.

As soon as she opened her car door, she could hear cattle lowing in the distance. It was a familiar sound, one she'd lived around her whole life. Some people would comment on the odor, but she didn't mind it. Folks from cattle country were exposed early to the downside of ranching. It was only the city folk who balked.

She got out, shut the door behind her and opened her purse. After a fresh coat of lipstick, she ran a brush through her hair and popped a mint in her mouth.

As she turned toward the front door, something else familiar, a feeling, not a scent, hit her in the solar plexus. Ever since she'd joined the FBI she'd learned about the combination of fear and excitement that came with a new case. She felt in no personal danger. It wasn't like some of her assignments in the Bureau. But there were high stakes, and she'd have to be alert and aware of everything. Cole Bishop was an unknown, and from the descriptions she'd heard in the diner, he could be anything from Wild Bill Hickok to Hannibal Lecter.

Well, she could be as macho as the next ex-FBI agent. After one last look at her car and safety, she headed toward the porch. No boards squeaked, another sign that they hadn't been here long.

She rang the doorbell and waited, taking calming breaths as she did so. A moment later, the door swung open and Cole Bishop stood before her. It had to be him.

He was on a cell phone, and after giving her a quick once-over, he waved her inside. As she walked past him she was instantly aware of the man's size. And something more. He wasn't just tall, he was powerful. Her gaze went to his biceps, and even beneath his white shirt she could see his arms were thick and corded. Not like a bodybuilder's, though. Like a man at the peak of physical perfection.

He didn't smell half bad, either.

She walked into a sparse living room. Bare white walls, hardwood floor, a leather couch and matching club chairs. The coffee table didn't even have a magazine on it. It was odd, as if Bishop rented the place.

"I don't think that's such a good idea."

His voice startled her and she whirled around, wondering what she'd done wrong. But he wasn't talking to her. Still on the phone, he paced across the floor in his cowboy boots, worn button-fly jeans, his white shirtsleeves rolled up past his elbows. Power. In the way he strode, in his posture, in the way his voice flowed deep and smooth as fine whiskey. She felt a little shiver as he eyed her before turning back to his conversation.

Ginny had said he was the best-looking man she'd ever seen in the flesh, and Lily concurred. Over six feet tall, he had to weigh almost two hundred pounds, all muscle. His tousled brown hair hung over his collar, and when he stepped in front of the window she could see streaks of sun-dyed blond. He had the face of a Marlboro Man, a real cowboy, tough and masculine from the inside out. Even his ocean-blue eyes had a hint of steel in them.

Her gaze moved to his chest and she wondered how he'd look without his shirt on. It took her a moment to realize he'd finished his conversation and put the phone down.

He narrowed his focus to her and only her. Unabashed and brazen as hell, he looked her over from the top of her head to the tips of her toes, taking a little extra time when he got to the chest area. Just as she opened her mouth to protest, he walked behind her.

She tried to swing around, but his hand on her arm stopped her still. Her natural instinct was to jerk away, to defend herself, but she held back. She didn't want to blow this in the first five minutes. But if he didn't let her go in about two seconds, she was going to make sure he understood what gelding was all about.

"How old are you?"

"Pardon me?"

"I said, how old are you?"

That's when it dawned on her that he must have assumed she was here about the position. *The job,* whatever it might be. In that split second she decided to play along, at least for now. At least until she figured out if he was truly dangerous. "I'm thirty."

"Bit old to start having children, isn't it?"

Having children? "No, I don't think so." Her voice sounded normal, she felt sure. Well, almost normal.

"What about illnesses. You have any?"

"None."

"You sure?"

"Of course I'm sure."

"What about your hand?"

She touched her bandage. "A bite. Nothing serious. Just a frightened dog, that's all."

He came around in front of her again, and this time he studied her face. But not in the usual sense. His eyes narrowed as he examined her inch by inch, like a plastic surgeon looking for flaws. Heat warmed her cheeks, but she kept her expression neutral. The thing that frightened her most was that she wanted him to like what he saw.

"How about your teeth?"

This was getting ridiculous. "How about yours?"

"That's not relevant."

"Why not?"

"Because I'm the one with the checkbook."

"But—"

"But nothing. If I decide you're the right one to

have my child, then you can ask me questions. I'll decide then if I want to answer you.''

''Your child?'' she whispered.

''Make no mistake about it. Even though you'll be the child's mother, that role will be temporary. He's going to be my son, and I alone will make all the decisions affecting his future. The marriage will be for his sake, so he won't be born a bastard, but trust me, you will not be my wife.''

Dear Lord...

''So...?'' he queried.

''Huh?''

He lowered his head, but not his gaze, and it made him look like a professor addressing a backward student. ''Your teeth.''

''They're great. My dentist sends me fan letters.''

He coughed, but she didn't care. If she'd gotten it right, he wanted to hire a woman to get married, have his child, then leave. My God. He was a loon. Or worse.

''What about—''

She held up a hand. ''Hold it.''

Impatience drew his brows together.

''You're not the only one who has some decisions to make here, buster.''

''Buster?''

She nodded. ''Yeah. This will be my kid, after all. And even though you'll have custody, there's nothing you can do to take away my part in this. Besides, anything could happen to you. You could get shot by an irate female, and then where would I be?''

''You—''

''I'd be raising the kid, that's where. Therefore, I'll

need to make sure you're not swimming in the shallow end of the gene pool.''

He didn't say anything, but there was a glimpse of something that might have been a smile. Or a murderous gleam. Whatever it was lasted about one hot second and was replaced by a scowl, which seemed to be his natural mien.

"Do you work out regularly?" he asked, as if she hadn't just finished her tirade.

"I keep fit."

He nodded, his gaze moving to her hips. "Any history of mental illness in your family?"

"Just the usual. An agoraphobic aunt. A cousin who prefers cats to people, which is becoming more understandable every second."

No reaction. At least his gaze moved back to her face. "Did you bring your medical records?"

"Whoa. Not so fast. We're not even close to the medical records portion of this deal. I've got some questions of my own now."

His mouth pressed into a thin line. But he nodded. Once.

She took advantage of the opportunity and gave him a slow perusal, purposefully lingering when she reached his fly. She shook her head a little and creased her brow, as if he hadn't met her standards. She took her time walking around him, touched his upper arm, nodded. Then, to make sure he understood who he was dealing with, she patted his butt.

"Hey." He spun around to face her.

"Just checking."

He took a deep breath, and she could see him struggle to calm down. The crazy thing about this was that he didn't look crazy. Or dangerous. In a bad mood, yes, but that wasn't illegal in Texas. He seemed like a normal, if too good-looking, man. So why in hell did he need to buy a wife and child?

This was getting really interesting.

Bishop shook his head and stepped away. "This interview is over."

Dammit. She couldn't lose him this fast. Eve would be heartsick. No way could Lily live with that kind of guilt. And no way could she leave without getting to the bottom of this very odd situation. "Don't dismiss me just because I've got an attitude. In my experience, it comes in real handy."

"What kind of experience would that be?"

She relaxed, but not much. "I haven't had a lot of luck with men. In fact, I've pretty much had it with the whole gender. What I'm looking for is something with no complications. I want to write, and I want to be left alone. But I need to eat, too."

"Write what?"

"Novels."

He nodded. "How did you hear about me?"

Okay, she'd gotten her reprieve. Now she had to hang on to it. "Ginny at the diner told my aunt and she told me."

Bishop checked his watch, then looked out the window. At what, Lily couldn't see.

"Come sit down." There was no politeness in his statement, no niceties about the man at all as far as she could tell. He led her to a large kitchen, which was just as blah as the living room. Of course he didn't hold her chair for her. The only thing he did that was the least bit courteous was nod at the fridge. "There are drinks in there."

"Thank you for your gracious offer, but I'm fine."

She winced at her stupid big mouth. This was no time to antagonize the man.

He ignored the jab. He just grabbed a thick file from the sideboard. It had no markings on the outside, but she gathered it was his Child Bearer folder.

"This is the deal." He didn't open the file. He just looked her right in the eyes as he laid it out. "I don't want a wife. I want a child. My child. The only reason a woman has to be involved at all is to bear the child and care for him until he's old enough for me to tend him. I've decided to marry the woman I choose, but there will be no married life. I want my son to have every opportunity. And no strikes against him out of the gate."

"And if it's a daughter?"

"That's okay, too. None of this is negotiable. Trust me, the financial arrangement will allow you to do all the writing you want. The only thing is, when the child is old enough, you leave."

"What about visitation?"

He turned away for a moment, and she saw his jaw flex. "I haven't decided about that yet."

"Is it my turn?"

"Go ahead."

"First, how do you plan on me conceiving this child?"

"I have a doctor lined up for in-vitro fertilization."

"You'll pay for everything? Insurance? Clothes?"

He nodded.

"What about spending money?"

"You don't have to worry about that. I'll make sure you want for nothing."

"No offense, but how do I know you have enough

money to back up that offer? Your spread is no King Ranch.''

"If it gets to that point, I'll give you access to my financial statements.''

She eyed him long and hard, still amazed at the proposition. Now she understood why Ginny and Patsy had been so alarmed. It would have been better if she hadn't needed to lie, but given the circumstances, she forgave herself. This was the most bizarre arrangement she'd ever heard of. Naturally, she wanted to bring Cole home to Eve, but, her own curiosity was now so great it would take a crowbar to pry her out of here. "I'll stay for a week.''

"Excuse me?''

"I said, I'll stay. But only on a trial basis. I'm not walking in here without knowing you better, and that's final. This is a major decision for me.''

"How do you know I'm even considering you for the job?''

She smiled. "How many other women have gotten to this stage of the interview process?''

"Several.''

"And how many told you that you were out of your ever-loving mind?''

He flipped open his file and the jaw twitched again. "We'll try it for three days. If you check out.''

"If I check out how?''

"I'm going to investigate you, Ms.…'' His brows creased and his nostrils flared. "What the hell is your name?''

"I thought you'd never ask. It's Lily. Lily Garrett.''

He handed her a job application form. "Fill out the personal information.''

"Fine. But I need to make a phone call. If I'm staying, I have to let certain people know."

He handed her his cell phone.

She flipped it open and dialed all but one number, then gave him a pointed look. "Do you mind?"

"No."

"Fine." She got up and headed for the living room. At least Bishop didn't follow her. Dylan answered on the second ring.

"Listen," she said, making sure Bishop couldn't hear her. "I'll explain later, but someone's going to be doing a check on me. Make me sound like I'm your flaky sister, and your secretary. Bad secretary. Tell them I want to be a writer. Say I earn about fifteen grand a year, and if it gets real chatty, say I've had a couple of lousy relationships."

"What in hell—"

"I'll call you. Bye." She clicked off the connection and turned to find Cole on his feet, halfway to her. "All done," she said, holding out the phone for him.

"Who was that?"

"Not that it's any of your business, but it was my brother. I told him I'd be gone a week."

He took his phone back. "I'll show you to your room."

She smiled at him. Her most dazzling grin. But he just turned around and walked toward the hall.

COLE KNEW he was making a grievous error even as he led the woman toward the back of the house. First, she had a mouth on her, and he sure as hell didn't need that. But her attitude wasn't half as disturbing as the effect she had on his libido.

She was too attractive. While that should be a plus

in her favor, it presented some significant issues. If he chose her, she'd live here for several years. They were sure to run into each other, even though he'd make absolutely certain they didn't get personally involved on any level.

If he could have raised an infant by himself, this wouldn't even be an issue. He'd thought about hiring a nanny, but he'd read too much about the initial mother-child bond to want to risk that with his child. Besides, he needed to have someone with a vested interest in sticking around. His last five housekeepers had quit in rapid succession, and so had the last three cooks. It was so damn hard to get good help these days.

He heard her behind him as he opened the door to the guest room. Unfortunately, he made the mistake of being a "gentleman" and let her pass while he held the door. Her scent hit him hard. Flowers. Flowers and female, that's what she smelled like. The female part was far more interesting than the flowers.

"This will do."

She stood in the middle of the room, her arms folded as she checked out her living quarters. He took the opportunity to look at her—this time, not as a potential mother, but as a woman.

Her height was good. He guessed she was five eight or nine. A real Thoroughbred, too, her long slender legs shown off well by her fitted skirt. Her blouse wasn't form fitting, and yet he could see the shape and size of her breasts. He liked what he saw. Not too large. Just right.

He had to admit he liked the hair, too. Long, almost to her waist, and black as the midnight sky. But the worst of his problems was her face.

She had the kind of beauty that could make a man do foolish things. Her clear green eyes were intelligent and observant. Her lips, full and lush, seemed poised to break into a smile. He could guess what her skin felt like. Pure silk. Stunning looks and that smart-ass attitude of hers—he could see why she'd had trouble with men. Most men would want to possess a woman like her. Most men wouldn't stand a chance.

"Who's your decorator?" she asked. Now she was by the armoire, opening the drawers one by one.

"No decorator. I furnished the place."

She gave him a mocking glance. "Really?"

"I haven't had the time for anything but the necessities."

"Right. Because of your vast financial empire. I forgot."

"Look, if you don't—"

"Wait." She held up her hands. "I didn't mean that. It was very rude of me. I guess I'm just tired, that's all. I've been on the road all day."

"From?"

"Just outside San Antonio."

"You work there?"

She nodded. "For my brother's small private investigation firm. Finders Keepers. I take care of the office. You know, filing, computer work, that sort of thing."

"You don't like it?"

"I do. But it's a full-time job that doesn't pay a hell of a lot."

The alarm on his wristwatch went off, and he silenced it with a quick flick of his finger. He didn't want to leave. He wanted to find out more about Lily Garrett. A great deal more.

But there wasn't time now. "You brought your things with you?"

"They're in the car."

He nodded, turned and headed back down the hall, leaving the scent of the woman behind him. He'd let her stay, at least for tonight, but she wasn't going to work out. Which was too damn bad, because he didn't have another prospect in sight.

The plan was sound. He'd get everything he wanted. A child. A woman he'd control with his checkbook. No complications. What he hadn't counted on was how difficult his search for the right woman would be. Most of the applicants had been completely unacceptable. Those who came close either hadn't passed the background check or clearly wanted the marriage to be a traditional one.

At least Lily hadn't balked at his proposition. Maybe it would have been better if she had.

He passed through the kitchen and went out the back door. The heat hit him like a slap in the face, but he just kept walking. One of the bulls had hurt his leg yesterday, and the vet was due. After that, he needed to talk to Manny and find out how the new feed was working out.

Halfway to the paddock, he found himself thinking about the woman. The curve of her breasts, the way her legs went on and on. An ache came over him. It had been too long since he'd had a woman. Which was another reason he shouldn't have let her stay.

If there was one thing on earth he wished for more than a son, it was to stop feeling this need. Most times, he could push the desire out of his head, and when he couldn't, there were some willing waitresses in Jessup and Hastings to ease the pain.

But he hated that part of himself. It made him weak. Vulnerable. He never wanted to be vulnerable around a woman again. When he was hard, his head got soft. He got stupid.

Not this time. If he didn't stop thinking about her, he'd tell her to leave tonight.

CHAPTER FIVE

LILY CLOSED the bedroom door, took a peek out the window to make sure no one was lurking outside, and called Dylan on her cell phone. He picked up before the phone rang.

"Lily?"

"Yeah." She didn't bother to ask him how he'd known. This little magic trick had happened before.

"What the hell was that last call about?"

"Okay." She sank down on the bed, happily discovering it was firm, but not too. "You're never going to believe this." She went on to tell him about Cole Bishop's proposition, pausing only to let Dylan ask a question here and there. By the time the whole story was out, she was back on her feet, at the bedroom's other door. She rapped softly, and when no one answered, she opened it slowly, somehow expecting to see Rochester's wife or a reasonable facsimile.

"Lily?"

"Hang on." She peeked behind the door then sighed with relief. "How interesting."

"Excuse me? Do I need to be on the phone for this?"

"Yes. I just found the nursery."

"Boy, he's a positive thinker, isn't he?"

"I'll say. And here's the really fascinating part."

She walked over to the gorgeous antique crib. "The room is completely decorated. Murals on the wall, pictures, cute little puppy lamps and sheets and curtains."

"Why is that so fascinating?"

"No other room in the house is done. Not like this. I mean it. There isn't one picture on a wall, not one tchotchke at all. Zippo."

"Maybe the decorator hasn't finished yet."

"He doesn't have one. He told me."

"So, it's clear this guy is willing to go to some pretty serious lengths to have a child. What worries me is why."

She shook her head as she ran a hand over a huge stuffed tiger propped in the corner. "That worries me, too. So how about you do a little digging on him while he's doing a little digging on me?"

Dylan sighed. "Sure, why not."

"Uh-oh. Things not going well with Julie's case?"

"You could say that. I swear, Lily, the woman just vanished off the face of the earth. I know it doesn't seem possible, but I'm hitting my head against brick wall after brick wall."

"Nothing in the police reports?"

"Not that I've seen. And remember Eddy Baskin?"

"The cop from Dallas?"

"He's down here now, and he gave me the real scoop. Truth is, the PD isn't doing any better."

"I have faith in you, Dylan. If anyone can find her—"

"That's the problem. Can she be found? I don't know."

"It's too soon for that kind of attitude, little brother."

"I'm okay. It's Sebastian I'm concerned about. He looks like hell."

"Well, then that makes it even more important for you to think positively. You have to believe you're going to find her, Dylan. She needs you, and so does Sebastian."

"Right."

"You know what?"

"What?"

"There are baby clothes in the drawers."

"Who *is* this guy?"

"Got me. But we're going to find out, aren't we?"

"You be careful, huh? If he's a creep—"

"I've met creeps before, Dylan. And I know how to handle myself."

"Of course you do. But it's a brother's prerogative to worry. Oh, I told Dad you'd be gone for a few days."

"Thanks. Hey, have you called about an assistant yet?"

"Nope. But I will if you stop talking."

"Bye." She hung up and continued her investigation of the nursery. It truly was a lovely room. The walls, the palest blue, were bordered in the puppy motif, which was completely adorable. The carpet the same eggshell color as in the rest of the house, but in here, the pile was twice as thick.

He'd gone to a lot of trouble to make this room perfect. She'd never seen a man want a child like this. Not a man alone, at least.

Her friend Irene and her husband Don had been trying to have a child for three years. Last time they'd talked, Don had broken down completely. He felt utterly desperate and was talking about going to a sperm bank, but it was clear the idea humiliated him. He wanted a baby like this. Like Cole.

She could only hope that Cole's intentions were honorable. But the truth was, she'd seen too much in her FBI days to think all people were motivated by high standards and morals. Especially devilishly handsome men.

Dylan would find out if there was anything hinky about Cole. Any criminal record or a hint of impropriety. Even though it was prudent to think this unorthodox arrangement wasn't kosher, Lily had a feeling about Cole. He was odd, that was for certain, but she knew somehow he wasn't doing anything illegal.

After she'd retrieved her suitcase from the car, she went back into her room. She'd brought clothes for a week, but she couldn't imagine being here that long. Heck, she might be gone by tonight. Especially if she kept goading him the way she had. The smart thing to do would be to shut up and agree with the man, whatever he said. But she could have sworn she'd seen something in his eyes when they were sparring. A hint of interest, of curiosity. Her intuition was telling her that Cole needed a challenge. She'd give him one. Unfortunately, there was a fine line between a challenge and a pain in the ass. She'd just have to feel her way because she needed to find out a few things about Mr. Bishop. Eve was counting on her.

He'd thank her in the end. She knew that, too. It was getting to the end that was tricky.

She took out her journal and put it in the drawer of the bedside table along with her favorite purple pen. Next to them went her antibiotics, her birth control pills—which she could not believe she was still taking, except that they were good for her complexion—and a big juicy novel. Since there was no television in the room, she was happy she'd brought something to read. Of course, she could go exploring. Find out where the television was.

She slammed the drawer shut and headed off to see what she could see.

THE BULL was going to make it. He'd hobble for a week or two in his splint, but there was no serious damage. Not that animals with broken legs were killed anymore. But caring for the monster wouldn't be easy. He was a mean SOB, and Cole and the vet had used some mighty powerful tranquilizers on him before they got close. He was one of the prime studs on the ranch, an award winner with an impeccable lineage.

Cole needed to meet Manny. Then he had correspondence to catch up on and a few phone calls to make. Work enough to last until dinner. But the woman was on his mind.

He stared up at the house as Doc Scott's van spewed dust on its way out. He'd been out here nearly an hour. Too long. He didn't know her. She could be anything. A thief. A con artist. It was foolish to leave her alone.

Manny would have to wait. Besides, he had to fax her information to the private detective he'd hired to do background checks. Just to be on the safe side, though, he'd stay in the house for the rest of the night. His work could wait.

As he neared the back porch, he wondered what

he'd find her doing. Resting? Reading? Maybe taking a shower?

Bad thought. Because with the thought came images. Moving pictures in living color. The steam, her naked body, his mouth on her—

He stopped, took his Stetson off his head and wiped his brow. It was too damn hot. Summer in Jessup was five degrees from hell. The sun beat down from a pale-blue sky with not a tree or a cloud to soften the blow. But Cole didn't mind working up a sweat. Not doing honest work. What he wouldn't do was get himself crazy over a woman—even a woman like Lily Garrett. No matter that her hair glistened or her eyes sparked with intelligence. He wasn't about to let his guard down.

He knew too well how cunning women could be. How sly and manipulative. Oh, he wasn't foolish enough to think all women were like that. He knew there were just as many honest, straightforward women as men. The problem was, he couldn't tell the difference.

He could read a man. Tell a lot about him from his handshake. From his eyes. From the tone of his voice. But he was helpless around the female of the species. Not a feeling he liked.

This woman, this Lily Garrett, was even more dangerous. Half his mind was occupied thinking about that hair of hers. Those legs. She could be selling him the Brooklyn Bridge and he wouldn't know it.

So what in hell was he doing, letting her stay? Was he that desperate, or just stupid?

Dammit, he hadn't thought his life would turn out like this. He'd had it good. The world on a silver platter. But then...

All he wanted was his own little family. Him and his baby. The two of them would build an empire, standing side by side. He'd be what a father should be. Cole Junior would never have to worry about his old man doing him dirt. But first, Cole Senior had to find a woman.

He'd thought about this long and hard, and while it might not be a solution for another man, it suited him. He would be in complete control. His son would look to Cole to see how to grow up. To see what was right and wrong.

Cole headed on again, and this time he wasn't going to be distracted. He needed to find out everything he could about the woman inside, and he needed to do it fast. The rest of his life, and his son's life, depended on him doing this right.

LILY TURNED the page of her journal and continued writing in that frenzied way of hers. When she got like this, when her mind spun twice as fast as her hand could write, her heart pounded and her breathing grew shallow, as if she would die if she didn't get it all on paper. As if her thoughts would disappear unless they were in purple ink.

It was her seventeenth volume. Everything from schoolwork to being a twin, to first love and betrayal was in her journals. She thought of them as her essence, and more than that, her teacher. Putting it all down in writing had helped her in more ways than she could ever say.

Now, sitting cross-legged on this strange bed, her feet curled under her, her hair tied back and her journal on page six, she felt safe. She felt in control. She would bring Cole back to Eve. They would reconcile. She knew it.

"He's got something to hide," she wrote. "Something that ripped him away from his old family and twisted his vision of a new family. It's all tied together. He doesn't want a child so much as he wants someone—family—to love."

Of course, Lily would never share these impressions with anyone else. But it was important not to dismiss them out of hand.

She paused, stretched her neck, gnawed on the end of her pen. Then she shifted her focus back to the present. But instead of thinking about Cole Bishop's dark secret, her thoughts strayed to the breadth of his shoulders. The streaks of blonde in his hair. That cruel mouth... What would it be like to kiss a man like him? So hard. So demanding.

A shiver took her by surprise, and an ache she'd banished came back and settled in down below.

"Oh, no," she said aloud. "No way. I'm not interested in Cole Bishop. Or any man. Not yet."

She turned back to her journal and scribbled furiously, listing all the reasons she had no business thinking about shoulders or kisses. There were a dozen reasons, maybe more. But only one that mattered. She wasn't healed yet. Not by a long shot. To make another mistake might be fatal. Well, maybe not *fatal* fatal. But there were several women she knew well who had been so damaged they'd thrown in the towel. Given up on men completely. She didn't want that for herself.

Someday, she planned to marry. Before she was forty, preferably. This year would be about finding out what she wanted. Who she was. Learning why things had gone so badly in Dallas.

She paused, thinking about how her criteria had changed as she'd gotten older. When she was in her early twenties, the number one thing she wanted was someone gorgeous. The inside of the package hadn't mattered at all. She wanted someone cool and sexy and a little bit dangerous. Then she'd gone through her "deep" phase, where her entire focus was on intellectuals. What a disaster that had been.

In her late twenties, she'd gone for humor. That had been fun, but ultimately unsatisfying. The man she'd been with had been a riot, but his humor was a shield she'd never gotten past.

Then there'd been her married-FBI-agent phase. No, that wasn't fair. She hadn't known. He'd been so right in so many other ways. Funny, intelligent, sexy as hell. The missing ingredients were honesty, obviously, and kindness.

Kindness hadn't been on her list until lately, but now it was right up there at the top. She wanted a man with a good heart. Someone who thought of her first. Just like she'd think of him first.

Who knew? Miracles happened. She might find him. Someday. Certainly not here or now. Good grief. Cole Bishop might be a lot of things, but kind? Highly doubtful.

She heard something. A door shut.

He was back.

She closed her journal and uncurled her legs, disturbingly aware that her pulse had quickened. It probably wasn't anything. Just nerves about the case. She had a lot to find out in a short period of time. And she had to find the right moment to tell Cole the truth about why she was here.

After two deep, slow breaths, she got up, put her journal underneath her underwear in the top drawer of the armoire, then headed out to see Cole.

He was in the kitchen, drinking a tall glass of water. With his head back, his neck caught her attention, and as he swallowed, his Adam's apple rose and fell in such a dramatically masculine way it was only natural that a little shiver would race up her spine. It didn't mean anything.

When he brought the glass down, he wiped his mouth with the back of his arm. Oh, mama, but he was a fine-looking specimen. Purely from an aesthetic perspective, of course.

He stared at her blatantly, not saying a word. His gaze moved over her again, a patient inspection of a different sort from the one a few hours ago. There was heat in his gaze. Almost a hunger, as if he wanted to drink her like that glass of water.

She blinked first. The tension inside her was too strong. "Did you finish your business?"

"Not all of it."

"Are you leaving again?"

He shook his head.

"Why not?"

"I don't want to leave you alone here."

"It's all right. I can amuse myself."

"I don't care about that."

"You don't?"

Again, he gave that slow shake of his head, his gaze never moving an inch.

"What do you care about?"

He swallowed. Looked down her body again, then back to her eyes. "You're a stranger."

"True."

"You might have an agenda I don't know about."

She felt her face heat, and she headed for the refrigerator before he could see her. "What do you mean?" Purposely standing with her back to him, she opened the fridge and searched for a cold drink.

"For all I know, you're a world-class con artist. Maybe you mean to steal me blind."

"I'll forgive the conjecture, but only because you said 'world-class.'"

He moved closer to her. She could feel him behind her, so close it made the hairs on the back of her neck stand up. What did he know? Had her cover already been blown?

"Did anyone ever tell you that flippant attitude of yours could get you in trouble?"

That whiskey voice of his slipped inside her, making her hand tremble as she pulled out a can of soda. He was too close to her. And she was too aware of him. "Everyone's told me that. From my parents to my bosses to my next-door neighbor."

"And you keep it up?"

It was hell trying to focus on this silly conversation while her hormones were going bonkers. What was this? Some kind of a joke? It was as if she'd never been near a man before. She wished she could climb in the vegetable crisper and close the door behind her. But she had to face him. This was business. A tricky business at that. When she did turn, she was immediately sorry to have given up the crisper idea so quickly.

He towered over her, even though he wasn't that

much taller. It was the whole package of the man that made him seem so large. So strong. As if he could snap her like a twig. But that same power suggested something else, something she was a fool to think about. What would it be like to have sex with him? To have him inside her?

She popped open the soda and the noise made her jump. He didn't even blink. He just kept staring at her, his eyes raw with flat-out want.

She lifted the can to her parched lips and took a sip. He watched her mouth, his own lips parting. She'd never seen such a mouth on a man before. His lips were just full enough to make the idea of kissing him alluring, but they were also slender and hard; made for sliding over a woman's curves.

"What do you want, Lily Garrett? Why are you here?"

"I'm applying for the job."

"You think you could handle it? Handle me?"

"That all depends on whether you're a gentleman or not."

He took another step, until his chest brushed her arm. "I'm not."

The cold air behind her and the heat in front met inside her, brewing up one hell of a storm. It wasn't enough he had that rugged cowboy thing going on, but he also oozed bad-boy sexy, which wasn't the least bit fair.

His hand lifted and he touched her hair. Just her hair. And she nearly dropped her soda.

"You're old enough to know better," he whispered.

"Better than what?"

"That you shouldn't play with fire if you don't want to get burned."

She needed to make her mouth work. For words to form. But that seemed way too difficult as his fingers brushed her cheek. "I don't think this is such a good idea."

"What?"

"You touching me."

"I'll stop if you want me to."

She closed her eyes. His thumb, callused and thick, followed the curve of her jaw all the way to her chin. "Stop." Her voice sounded weak, soft.

"Stop this?" he asked. "Or this?" He leaned forward that small bit and kissed her.

It wasn't the hard edge she expected. His lips barely touched hers. His breath slipped inside her as he moved his head back and forth, rubbing her in that one spot. It was maddening and electrifying.

Finally, she couldn't stand it. She leaned in. But at that very second, he stepped back, and when she opened her eyes, his face wore that damned granite mask. As if he hadn't touched her. Hadn't made her crazy inside.

"This isn't going to work," he said, his voice tinged with anger.

She looked down, breaking the connection between them. It had been a test. A stupid— "I don't appreciate being played for a fool, Mr. Bishop."

"I don't think you're a fool."

"No? Then what was all that about? Were you trying to get me to kiss you? To slap you?"

"I wasn't trying anything. If you stay, we're going to be in close quarters. You understand? In the same house, in the same room."

"So what? Do you find me so irresistibly attractive that you're afraid I'll drive you wild? That you won't be able to control yourself when I'm near?"

Finally, his mask cracked. A half smile changed his face, but not for long. He pulled himself together. Almost. He had to take a few steps back to make the shift complete. "I do find you attractive. And that's a problem."

"Well, there's only one answer to that, Cole Bishop."

"What?"

"Get the hell over it."

CHAPTER SIX

COLE BLINKED. It wasn't the response he'd expected. She wasn't what he expected. By now, she should have been packed and halfway to the door. Instead, she stood toe to toe with him, her eyes challenging him to do his worst.

What she didn't understand was what his worst was. And he couldn't tell her. Because his brilliant little plan had backfired. Instead of scaring her away, he'd just put the fear of God in himself.

He'd wanted to kiss her. Hell, he still wanted to kiss her. He wanted to bring her into his arms, and he wanted to touch every inch of that long, lean body. He wanted those legs wrapped around his waist.

She stepped neatly around him, leaving the refrigerator door open. "What time is dinner?"

He should just tell her to go. What was the point in her staying? She'd never work out.

"Dinner?" she prompted. "You know, the meal after lunch?"

"Six-thirty."

"Thanks. See you then."

He closed the fridge, and by the time he'd turned around, she was gone. He leaned back, wondering how things had gotten so out of hand so quickly.

He knew his size intimidated people, and he'd

learned to use it effectively. Sure, Lily was tall, but when he stood close, she must have felt vulnerable.

He also knew his stare unnerved even the most secure individuals if he wanted it to. And he had. But Lily had kept her cool. At least, for the most part. There had been a few moments there…

Shit. He needed his head examined. In the meantime, he had a couple of things to do. Fax her application to the detective, and then take a long, cool shower.

LILY CLOSED her bedroom door, then slumped against it, her heart beating frenziedly against her chest. "I am in *so* much trouble here. And I've only known him three hours."

She pushed off the door and flung herself across the bed. That little tango in the kitchen had nearly done her in. The jerk had some nerve testing her like that. For all he knew, she was going to be the mother of his child. It wasn't nice and it wasn't fair, and oh, my God, how she'd flunked.

This attraction to him was something outside of her experience. It made her feel foolish about Jason, which was perhaps the most damning evidence. In all the time she'd been with Jason, including that heady rush at the beginning, her body had never reacted like it just had with Cole.

She turned over and looked down at her boobs. "Bad body," she scolded. But there were no immediate apologies. Maybe she should call Dylan and talk it over with him. No. This was not something she wished to discuss with her brother. Ashley? Uh-uh. Somehow, somewhere, it would come back and bite her on the butt.

The other options were her two closest girlfriends, Denise and Sandy, but Denise was in Europe on a business trip and Sandy was too much in love with Paul, her babe du jour, to give sensible advice.

What a pickle. The intelligent thing would be to march out there, tell Cole that she was a private detective, that she'd been sent by Eve, yada, yada, yada. Then he'd tell her exactly what she could do with Finders Keepers, and she'd be staying at the Jessup Motel.

Plan B? Keep her wits about her, find out all she could about Cole, and when the time was right, explain the situation if it seemed prudent. If he really was a nutball, she didn't want to turn him on Eve.

And then there was Plan C. Which was forget about the case, forget about her vow to stay chaste until she was completely over Jason, and attack Cole in the middle of the night. Make love until the paramedics were called, then spring her true mission on him when he was too weak to argue.

Plan C had some merit. She just wished she'd paid attention when Sandy had talked about rebound guys. There was something every woman should know about meeting men right after a big breakup, but for the life of her, Lily couldn't remember what it was. Sleep with them? Don't sleep with them? It was one of the two.

My goodness, but this was not how she thought her day was going to go. However, there was a little part of her that was unapologetically excited. Curious as hell about what was going to happen next. She honestly didn't know. Would he make another move? Would he ignore her?

She had the feeling if he really meant to kick her

out she would have been kicked by now. No, despite
the Granite Man demeanor, the guy was probably as
confused as she was.

Wanting to hire a wife. For heaven's sake. What a
dumb thing to do. Maybe she was supposed to be here
to knock some sense into the big guy. Show him that
he couldn't be in control of everything. And that
money and the love of a mother didn't mix.

Sighing, she sat up, looked at the clock. Another
forty minutes and it would be dinner. She was definitely hungry. But there was time to shower, to cool
herself down and gather her composure. Assuming,
that is, that she could stop thinking about those shoulders.

FROM THE VOICES, she guessed there were about five
people in the dining room. Five men, to be more precise. One of them, presumably, was Cole Bishop.

Maybe she should go back and change into her
dress. And her Manolo strappy sandals. She'd learned
in the last few years that she had a powerful weapon
in her body. Not that she was Rachel Ravishing or
anything, but when she played it right, her body could
be downright distracting. It wasn't surprising, really.
Men had very little willpower when it came to the
promise, no matter how remote, of sex. So why
shouldn't she use that fact to her advantage?

She turned back, then stopped. It wasn't necessary
to play the game on that level. Sure, he'd gotten to
her with that almost-kiss, but that didn't mean she
had to pay him back in kind. She had a job to do,
and nothing in her mission required showing a little
thigh.

Besides, it wasn't clothes that made the woman,

right? It was attitude. Confidence. Since she'd decided to stick with Plan B, she needed to forget about everything but doing the job. Getting what she wanted quickly and efficiently. He could only intimidate her if she let him. She straightened her shoulders, undid one more button on her blouse, and walked into the dining room like she was Cindy friggin' Crawford.

It was a stunner of an entrance. She hadn't needed the dress at all. With her hair down, her makeup just right, the hint of décolleté, she owned the damn room. All conversation ceased. A man in a stained white hat let go of his spoon. Several jaws dropped. Someone swore just under his breath. The only problem was, Cole wasn't there to see it.

She pasted on a smile as she walked up to the closest cowboy and extended her hand. "I'm Lily Garrett."

The man was older, perhaps in his early sixties, with a thick head of white hair. He wore glasses and he looked at her through the lower part of his lenses. "Pleased to meet ya," he said, his Texas accent as thick as spring mud. The hand she shook felt rough and warm. His jeans and shirt were both dusty, as were his boots. But the huge rectangular belt buckle around his waist was so shiny she needed sunglasses.

"I'm Chigger," he said. "I'm the stockman here." He nodded to the cowboy on his right. "This here is John. He works with the bull breeding."

"Nice to meet you."

John touched the tip of his hat with his fingers and gave her a friendly nod.

"Manny, come on over here. Meet Lily Garrett. You too, Spence."

Both men obeyed. They were years younger than

Chigger. Manny, an absolutely adorable Latino, looked to be in his early twenties, and Spence, a solemn gent in the only baseball cap in the room, was around her age.

They both said "Hey," and then the whole group of them got real quiet. They didn't stop looking at her, though, and she said a silent thanks that she hadn't put on the dress.

Spence cleared his throat. "Excuse me, miss, but are you the new cook?"

"Me? Oh, no."

The men sighed. Heavily. The hunger in their eyes dulled, and she realized they hadn't been thinking she was a hot mama at all. So much for the powerful weapon of her body. "You don't have a cook?"

"Not since Ellie quit." Chigger hitched up his pants. "She made the best roast chicken I ever ate."

The others nodded. Manny, whose name she remembered from the diner, frowned. "Anything's better than J.T.'s cooking."

"I heard that," a man said from the kitchen. "And you, Manny Peres, are not having any dessert tonight."

"I don't like your lumpy pudding anyway."

"We're not having pudding." The kitchen guy stuck his head out. "We're having ice cream. Everybody but you."

Manny rolled his eyes. "He's full of—"

Chigger coughed, but she still heard the curse word. Not that she hadn't heard it before. She was a rancher's daughter after all. But it was sort of gallant that the old gentleman wanted to protect her delicate ears.

"Now, Lily Garrett." Chigger shoved Manny toward the dining room table. It was sort of set. The silverware was in a jumble in the middle of the table, napkins in a big pile next to that, and plates stacked on the other side. "Just who might you be?" He leaned in close and lowered his voice. "You're not applying for the, uh, other job, are you?"

"Mind your own business, old man."

She whirled around to find Cole standing behind her. His scowl didn't bother her this time. But his nearness did. Her tummy did that strange tightening thing again, and her fingers went to the hollow of her neck.

"You respect your elders," Chigger said, but he didn't press Lily for more information.

Cole had changed clothes. Showered. His hair was still damp, and if she wasn't mistaken, his face freshly shaved. Interesting. Or did he always shower before dinner?

He'd donned another pair of jeans and his slim hips made her think evil thoughts. When her gaze moved up to his chest, things went from bad to worse. She forced herself to turn and look at the other men.

They stood silent and still, gazes moving from Cole to her and back again. It was as if they were on hold, waiting to see what they should do, how they should react.

She understood. It seemed natural to take Cole's emotional temperature and prudent to act accordingly. He wasn't someone you'd want to cross. The only one who was relaxed was Chigger.

"Well, are we gonna stand here all night gawkin' at each other?" the old man asked. "Or are we gonna eat?"

That pushed everyone into motion again. Everyone but her. Cole headed toward her, moving his gaze slowly down her body, then up again. He didn't react, except for rhythmically fisting and loosening his right hand.

She turned her back on him and smiled at the men. "I don't know about anyone else, but I'm famished. Is there something I can do to help with dinner?"

"Cook it," Manny mumbled.

Chigger put his hand on her arm and led her to the table. With a courtly bow, he held the chair for her. "You're our guest, and just because some of us were raised by wolves, that doesn't mean all of us were. What can I get you to drink, young lady?"

"Thank you, sir. I'd love a glass of ice water, if that wouldn't be too much trouble."

"Not at all."

She heard Cole snort from halfway across the room. But she didn't care. It was nice to be treated like a lady. It didn't mean she couldn't put any one of them in a headlock if she had to, but common courtesy was always welcome.

Manny sat down on her right, and Spence hurried to take the seat on her left. She reached for a napkin and some silverware, and then the others followed suit. A few moments later, J.T. came out of the kitchen holding a steaming pot. Stew, with thick chunks of meat and potatoes. A little heavy for this time of year, but it smelled okay.

Chigger showed up behind her and set down her water. Bread—two loaves, store bought—completed the menu. Everyone had taken a seat except Cole.

Another power trip. She recognized it from her

days at the academy. He waited until the silence returned and then, when every eye was upon him, sat at the head of the table.

"I'm reminded of a story," she said, and the focus of the room switched to her. "In France, during the time of Napoleon, it was an incredible breech of etiquette to sit down before the emperor. In fact, being that he was a megalomaniac and a dictator, there were actual protocols written, explaining that the bottoms of the visitors should not touch a chair until the bottom of the emperor touched his. Only Napoleon was a restless sort. So people at his dinner parties kept jumping up and down all night, deathly afraid to have their bottoms in contact with anything inappropriate lest the wrath of the emperor should come down upon them."

No one laughed. They all just looked at Cole again. It was like a tennis match with the score forty-love.

"Pass the lady the stew," Cole said finally.

That broke the ice. The pot was passed as they all grudgingly filled their plates.

"I had a stew once," Manny said wistfully, "made with lamb and fresh-picked carrots and potatoes. Man, that was some stew."

Spence nodded as he looked at the lumpy concoction on his plate. "Remember that roast what's-her-name—the one with the glasses—made?"

The men, except Cole of course, nodded.

"She was a good one," Chigger said. "Mary. That's right. She made those pies, too." He gave Cole a disapproving scowl. "She would have stayed, too. She liked it here."

"She liked the liquor cabinet," Cole said.

Lily decided it was time to try the food. It couldn't be that bad. Stew wasn't that difficult. But the moment she had it in her mouth, she understood all. It was terrible. Not just bland, but actively awful. She just smiled and chewed, not wanting to hurt J.T.'s feelings.

The men beside her had no such qualms. J.T. took their abuse manfully. In fact, he seemed just as displeased with the meal as the others.

Only Cole ate silently. She'd managed to avoid his glare through most of the meal. Finally, she couldn't stand it any longer. She let her gaze slide over to him as he ate. He didn't acknowledge her at all, didn't even realize she was looking his way. At least, so she thought. But a moment later, his hand moved to his chest, and, in a gesture familiar to all history buffs, he slipped it inside the front of his shirt.

She burst out laughing. Once more, the conversation halted. But when the men looked at Cole, his hand was on the table, his expression slightly puzzled, as if he didn't understand her outburst, either. The sly dog.

"YOU STAYING the night?"

As Lily turned to Spence with a smile, Cole swallowed the last of his bread. He hadn't been the least bit hungry, but he'd eaten every bite of the horrible meal. At least the ice cream was good. The dinner had shown him, as if he still needed reasons, just how unsuitable she was for the job. She talked too much, for one thing. And she distracted the men, for another. What he needed was an old-fashioned ranching wife. The kind who knew how to work hard, have kids and keep her opinions to herself.

That jab about Napoleon still rankled. Cole might be a lot of things, but a megalomaniac wasn't one of them. He was something of a dictator, but only because that's what running a ranch required. He was proud of his spread and of the way his men respected him. He never asked them to do anything he wouldn't do himself.

But she'd walked in and tipped the scales, and that wasn't going to work at all. Not even for a night.

"Yes," she said, her smile making Spence blush. "I'm staying for a few days. Cole and I are trying to see if we want to work together."

"Doing what?"

"Oh, he wants to pay me to have his baby."

Spence spit his soda across the table. Cole put his spoon down, harder than he'd intended. No one spoke. They just turned to stare at him. Dammit, when she said it like that, it sounded terrible. Not at all like the sensible course he'd outlined. "It's more complicated than that."

She nodded. "Right. He also wants to pay me to be the child's mother, but only for a year or two, right, Cole?"

He should escort her to the door right now. Put an end to this before she caused any more havoc. Instead of answering her, he pushed back his chair and stood up. "I'm sure you gentlemen will excuse us. The lady and I have things to discuss."

Five chairs scraped, and five men tipped their hats in her direction before beating a hasty retreat. Half their ice cream lay melting in their bowls.

"That wasn't nice."

"I don't need to be nice. This is my ranch. We do things my way here."

"I know."

"We like it that way."

"Is that the royal *We?*"

His hands flexed in his desire to wring her pretty neck. Why the hell didn't she button her blouse properly? If she thought she'd get a reaction out of him, well...

She'd be right.

Dinner had been hell. He hadn't wanted a woman so much in years. Maybe ever. She made him furious, but she also made him hard. She'd be something in bed. A wild filly meant to be tamed.

But that wasn't the point. "Look, Ms. Garrett, I don't think—"

She got up from her chair and headed his way. He fought the urge to run, more worried about the look in her eyes than the sway of her hips. She moved real close. Near enough for him to get a whiff of her perfume.

"I know what you're going to say," she said, her voice softer than it had any reason to be. "You're going to say this isn't going to work. But I don't think you're right."

"No?"

Her mane of hair shimmered as she shook her head. "Something tells me I should stay. For a little while longer, at least. I feel this compelling need to understand what's going on here. Not just the fact that you want to do what you want to do, but that I'm considering doing it with you. That's a puzzle, don't you think?''

He wanted to smile. She'd given her speech with such seriousness, and shockingly enough, he'd understood her. But he was going to disappoint her. She wasn't the right woman for the job. Not at all.

''You're still thinking I'm not the right woman for the job, aren't you?''

He blinked at his own transparency. He'd trained himself never to give anything away by expression or posture. In fact, he'd probably have made a great poker player.

''It may turn out that I'm not,'' she went on. ''But I think we ought to wait a little longer. It's only the first day, after all. Besides, there's something you don't know about me.''

''What?''

''I'm a terrific cook.''

''We don't need a cook.''

She cocked an eyebrow. Even he couldn't let that lie stand. ''Okay. We do, but it's not going to be you.''

''Why not? I'm here. I need the work. The men need the nourishment.''

He looked at her long and hard. She didn't flinch, didn't blush. She was a piece of work, that's for sure. Her children would probably inherit that cocky attitude, that willingness to step up to the plate.

''All right,'' he said, knowing he was going to regret the decision. ''But just for a couple of days until I find a new full-time cook.''

She nodded. ''Good. I think that will give us plenty of time to decide if we want to have a baby together.''

She'd done it again. Made it sound foolish. But he knew better. His plan was a good one, dammit. It would give him everything he wanted. Well, almost everything.

CHAPTER SEVEN

LILY STOOD UP, feeling slightly less than triumphant. This was not easy. Cole was not easy. If only she could be certain things would work out the way she wanted them to. Eve had become a good friend, and in her heart Lily knew that whatever was ailing Mr. Granite would be helped by mending some old fences.

More than most people, Lily understood how important it was to nurture family connections. Her whole history—the Trueblood side of her family— was all about that. Reconciliation. Finding love when all seemed hopeless. It wasn't by accident that she and Dylan had come to form Finders Keepers. It was destiny. And bringing Cole and Eve together was destiny, too.

Cole folded his napkin and put it on the table. "Do you want to start tonight?"

"Start what?"

"Your cooking duties."

"Why, you didn't get enough to eat?"

He cocked his head slightly to the right. "I meant the clean up. Around here, if you cook, you clean."

She smiled. "Sorry, wrong answer, but thanks for playing."

"What?"

God, he was good-looking when he was bewildered. "I'll cook three meals a day, and I'll clean up after breakfast and lunch, but dinner is out of the question."

"Why?"

"Because I don't clean up after dinner."

His lips pressed together in a hard line for a few seconds, but then his shoulders relaxed. "Is there something wrong with you? Are you ill?"

"Nope."

"Is there some religious significance to the dinner meal?"

"Only on Christmas."

"And yet, you don't—"

"Clean up—"

"After dinner."

She nodded.

"I see. Then I'm afraid —"

"You know what my specialty is?" she said, interrupting him with the voice she used to get special favors. "Barbecued ribs that fall off the bone. Biscuits so light they practically float to the ceiling. And the best damn peach pie in five counties. No brag, just fact. And that's just for starters."

It worked. She could see it in his eyes. That he actually licked his lower lip was something of a clue, too, but the proof of the pudding was in his eyes. Sex and food. Men could be made to do practically anything for both, if used correctly. Why more women didn't utilize this potent combination, she wasn't sure. But growing up on a ranch with a whole herd of men around, she'd learned to cook early and well. As for the sex part? She could win a few blue ribbons at that, too, if she did say so herself.

"I'll make it easy on you," she said. "Call the guys. Let's see if they're willing to do it my way."

"You know they are. They'd build you a house if they thought it would mean three good squares a day."

"Then it's all settled."

"I don't like it."

She patted his hand. "I know, honey. But don't worry. It's all going to work out. I promise."

He didn't seem to believe her. Hell, she didn't know if she believed herself. But she wasn't about to stop now. She'd learned a few things in the FBI. First, if you wanted to get the job done, it was better to apologize later than ask permission now. Second, once a course was decided, it was vital to be committed and stay committed. It was the doubt that got you into hot water.

So she was going to be a cook, at least for a little while. About that, there had been no lies told. She was a great cook. She'd learned from her parents, both of whom were talented in the kitchen, and knew that good dishes came from the best ingredients. If J.T. had been doing the shopping as well as the cooking, she might be going to the store tonight.

Leaving Cole and his perpetual scowl, she went into the kitchen, prepared for an ungodly mess. But it wasn't bad at all. Good for J.T. Unfortunately, her luck didn't hold when she opened the fridge. Although she'd looked inside earlier when she'd gotten a soda, she hadn't been concerned with potential ingredients or lack thereof. There was a gallon of milk, three tubs of butter, and enough beer to sink a battleship. The vegetable crisper contained a bag of unopened mini carrots, the fruit bin was barren, and although there was meat in the freezer, she could hardly tell what it was for the freezer burn.

She closed the door and nearly leaped out of her skin to see Cole standing right there, only inches from her, a repeat of that afternoon. The man needed a bell around his neck. Well, around some part of his body. She grinned at the image, which seemed to upset him.

"What is that about?" he asked, meaning her smile. Maybe "growled" was more accurate.

"Nothing. I need to go shopping."

"When?"

"Before breakfast."

He snorted. Not a disgusting snort. Just one of those I knew all along this was going to be a pain in the ass snorts.

"You don't have to go with me," she said.

"No? Can you cover the cost?"

She could, with her trusty gold American Express card, but he didn't need to know that. "Well…"

"I thought not."

"You could always give me your credit card."

The look he gave her was what she expected. *Not in this lifetime, babe.*

"Have it your way," she said. "I'm ready when you are."

"I have to work tonight."

"Go right ahead. I'm sure no one will mind oatmeal tomorrow morning instead of the eggs, bacon and pancakes I was going to make."

He looked at her for another long minute, his granite facade not quite so solid, then turned on his heel and headed for the door.

"Excuse me."

He didn't stop.

"Excuse me!"

He paused at the door.

"Does this mean you'd like to go shopping now?" she asked.

"Yes."

"Okay. Only I have to get my purse. And make a list of the things we'll need. So you just wait right there." She headed toward the hallway, walking quickly past him toward her room.

"Ms. Garrett."

She didn't stop.

"Lily!"

That did it. She turned. Smiled sweetly. "Yes?"

"How long is this going to take?"

"The shopping? Or the getting ready to shop?"

"The getting ready."

"About half an hour."

"Tell you what. You do what you need to do, and I'll be in my office, waiting."

"Perfect."

As he walked away, she heard him sigh. She recognized the sound very well. She'd heard it all her life. From her father and Dylan to her professors and her bosses. Half the conversations she'd had since puberty had ended with the other party sighing. She used to take it personally. Not anymore. In fact, she was rather proud of her ability to confound. In this situation in particular it was wise to keep Cole Bishop off-balance. He was too darned used to being in control. She'd just have to see about that.

COLE HAD NEVER been keen on shopping. Not for clothes, not for gifts, not for anything. But of all the shopping he disliked, food shopping was the worst.

Lily, on the other hand, looked as if she was here for the duration. Her list in one hand, her pen in the other, she went aisle by slow aisle, with him being the good little houseboy, pushing the cart.

"I wonder if there's any whole wheat flour in the pantry. I forgot to look." She turned to him as if he'd know.

"I have no idea."

"You eat, don't you?"

"But I hire people to cook for me."

Her hands went to her hips and her brows lifted. "That's right. You do. So how much am I going to get?"

"Not a cent."

"No?"

"You volunteered, remember?"

"So that means it's not worth anything? Hogwash."

"I didn't say it wasn't worth—" Again, he stopped himself. He wasn't completely certain how she got to him like this, but she did. Consistently. Dammit, people were intimidated by him. Didn't she know that? Exasperating woman. Her child would probably inherit that lip. That sass. Who wanted a smart-aleck kid? Nobody, that's who.

His gaze went to the shopping cart. A big old leg of lamb stared up at him, and the thought of what J.T.—or any of the men—would do to that perfect piece of meat gave him pause. As soon as he found another cook, the situation would right itself. "I'll pay you a hundred a day."

"You'll pay me one hundred dollars?" Her voice seemed particularly loud in the cramped cereal aisle.

He looked at her again and felt a knot in his stomach at her satisfied grin. Damn it. She'd done it to him again. "Only if you're worth it."

"Oh, honey. For a hundred dollars a day, I'll make you and all the men so happy you won't know how to thank me."

Behind him, Cole heard a feminine gasp. He turned to see Julianne Roberts, the mayor's wife, staring at him, righteous indignation making her nostrils flare. It took him a second to realize what was up. That she'd overheard that last bit of conversation and gotten the wrong idea. "No," he began, "you don't understand...."

He reached out, but Mrs. Roberts jerked back. "Excuse me." Then she pushed her cart down the aisle so fast she knocked into a display of laundry detergent, starting an avalanche of blue boxes that spread into the pet food aisle.

"Hey, nice neighbors you got here."

Whirling on Lily, he froze her with a stare. "That was not amusing."

The left corner of Lily's lip curled up. "Actually, it was."

"You have a very sick sense of humor."

"Yeah. I know. But come on. Did you see her face? The way her nose was twitching, she looked like an indignant bunny rabbit."

Cole bit the inside of his cheek. The image, however, didn't disappear with the pain. He shifted his gaze to her hand. "What's next on the list?"

She shook her head and sighed, but didn't belabor the point. She just headed toward the produce section.

Cole stayed silent for the rest of the trip, despite the fact that Lily did everything under the sun to get a reaction from him. He remained stoic, silent, unflinching. Except when she wasn't looking. Then he cursed himself for the fool he was. For the trouble he had let himself in for. For the way he ached with wanting her.

LILY PUT the last of the vegetables in the crisper, then proceeded to fold the paper bags from the store. She'd had to explore a bit to find out where things were kept, but now she had the kitchen logistics down. She'd get the coffee ready tonight, and in the morning she'd make her mother's famous buttermilk pancakes. The men would be happy.

But that still left the rest of tonight to get through. It was only nine-thirty. Cole had retreated to his office, the coward. The rest of the men were already in the bunkhouse.

Maybe Cole would like something to drink. That would be a nice thing, wouldn't it? Considerate. He was probably thirsty by now.

Oh, dammit, she needed to lay off. Leave him be. If only the urge to needle him wasn't quite so powerful. But the way he struggled to keep his control was something to behold. She wanted him to laugh. Really laugh. The kind that cleansed the soul. She had a feeling he hadn't done that in a long, long time.

She sat down at the kitchen table, listening for signs of life. Nothing but the buzz of the fridge. Her thoughts went directly to this afternoon. When he'd kissed her. When he'd held all the cards, every one. And yet he'd pulled back.

It was a form of control, she understood that. Despite his denial, it had been a test, but *she* hadn't been the subject. The physical pull between them was real enough, but then, his whole plan was designed to eliminate such base urges. He didn't want to need anyone, not physically, not emotionally.

But that wasn't the whole story. Not that she was a psychologist or anything, but she knew something about human nature. And what she knew about Cole was that there was someone inside that fortress of his. Someone who wanted to be challenged, who wanted to laugh, and who wanted to care. The key to unleashing that part of him was getting him to connect to his past. He didn't know it, but she was going to save his life. By bringing him back to Eve, she would smash down the walls around his heart.

She hadn't made a conscious decision to be a smart-ass with him, but now that she thought about it, her instincts had been right on the money. He needed someone like her. Someone who didn't cower at that scowl of his.

This was going to work. She'd bring him back to his family, bring laughter into his brooding silence, get him to abandon this dumb idea to buy a kid. Dylan would say she was being a might optimistic, but she didn't think so.

She was here for a reason, and it wasn't just so Finders Keepers would earn its fee. She was here to do a much bigger job. After all, she was a Trueblood.

COLE TURNED OFF his computer and stared at the blank screen. He'd gotten nothing done. Well, except for stringing about fifty paper clips together. Which was crazy. This was the part of his work he liked. The books, the projections, the budgets. All the things a rancher was supposed to hate. Not him. He belonged at his desk—thinking, planning. But tonight, he'd been useless. Lily wouldn't leave him be.

Knowing she was just down the hall was torture. It didn't help when he told himself it was purely physical. That he wanted her because she was the most interesting and frustrating woman he'd met in years.

That was the problem. She was beautiful, strong, willful, determined and witty. All the things he appreciated in a woman. All the things that made him stop thinking clearly.

He truly didn't understand women. Yeah, lots of men said that, but in his case it was achingly true. They bewildered him, confused him, made him question himself. It was easier all the way around if he just avoided them, as if he were allergic to them. Oh, the occasional meeting didn't stir any symptoms, not even when that meeting was in the Jessup Motel. But long exposure wasn't smart.

He should tell her to leave. That would be safe. On the other hand, what man in his right mind wouldn't want her as the mother of his child? All those qualities of hers were exactly what he'd hoped for.

The other women he'd interviewed had shown him how rare it was to find someone like Lily. But would a woman like Lily really settle for the arrangement he had proposed?

Nice little paradox.

One he wasn't going to settle tonight. He turned off the computer, threw the paper clip chain in the top drawer and headed for the kitchen.

She wasn't there. Which was fine, except he'd wanted her to be. He'd actually found himself looking forward to sparring with her. Yet another warning sign.

He got himself a Corona and unscrewed the cap. It was nearly eleven, and he liked to get to sleep before midnight so he could start the day early. No way was he going to fall asleep anytime soon. Not when he was keyed up like this.

He took a long drink, then headed out for the back porch. It was still hot—this was Texas after all—but comforting in an odd way. The sultry air carried the scent of night-blooming jasmine, a smell that reminded him of his first girlfriend. He'd been fifteen, and she'd been fourteen, and he used to sneak out of his bedroom window in the middle of the night and run to her house, where she'd be waiting in the garden. They'd kissed. Not very well, actually. He hadn't heard of French kissing back then, and neither had she. But the passion in those closed-mouth clinches had been undeniable.

His gaze moved up to the sky and a million stars. Cicadas sang a loud chorus, and still Cole couldn't relax. He'd never been what you could call laid-back, but in the last few years, especially since he'd decided on his future, he'd found some respite. If she stayed, he probably wouldn't feel calm again. Not until she left. Could he tolerate a couple of years of this tension? For himself, no. But was anything too much to ask for his child?

"Are you going to speak to me or just howl at the moon?"

Cole jerked back, nearly dropping his beer. He found her sitting on the chair, alone on the porch. She seemed to meld with the night, be part of it. Even now that he knew she was there, she wasn't easy to see.

"Didn't mean to scare you."

"I didn't know you were out here."

"It's okay. I wasn't sure whether to stay quiet or

not. You looked like you were pretty deep in thought. But then, I figured if you tried to sit down, you'd probably have a coronary or something, and I haven't brushed up on my CPR lately.''

"Thanks. I think.''

"I'd offer you a chair, but there isn't one.''

"I've been meaning to get some.''

"Yeah. Ruling an empire is hell.''

He was glad it was so dark. He didn't want her to see his smile. No use making her any cockier than she already was.

"Hey, Cole?''

"Yes?''

"Now that I'm an employee and all, why don't you tell me something about yourself.''

"I don't like talking about myself.''

"Do you have something to hide?''

He hesitated. Not because he didn't want to answer her, but because he didn't necessarily want to give her his usual answer. If things were going to work out between them, if she was going to be the mother of his kid, she had a right to know some things. Not everything. But some.

"You're not an ax murderer or anything, are you?''

"No.''

"So what's the big deal? Everybody has a lousy past. Everybody has stuff they regret. It doesn't mean anything unless you let it.''

He bristled at the pop psychology. What she considered lousy and he considered lousy were two very different things. "There are no medical risks, I promise you that.''

"Nope. Not good enough.''

"What is it you need to know?''

She stood, walked over to him. "You stay right there. Don't move." Then she hurried into the house.

A few moments later, she came out holding one of the dining room chairs. She set it down opposite the old wooden porch rocker, then took her place once more. "Sit."

"I—"

"Oh, don't give me excuses, just sit for heaven's sake."

He opened his mouth, then realized he really had only two choices. Sit, or go inside. Inside was safe. But outside had Lily. He walked over to the chair and sat, his knees just a couple of inches from her.

"Thank you." She patted his knee, a perfectly innocent gesture that made his pulse go crazy.

"Now we can talk. What I want to know about is you. Where you grew up, what you were like as a kid, what brought you to this place in your life."

"There's really no need for you to know all that."

"Yes, there is."

"Why? I told you all the important details. There's no medical risk. No criminal past. Nothing that would have an impact on you getting pregnant."

"But I need to know."

"Why?"

Her head tilted slightly, but he couldn't see the details of her face. Or her eyes. "Because it matters. If you're serious about this, and I think you are, you must know there's an inherent flaw in your plan. You want a mother's love to help mold and shape your child, but the child isn't going to want to stop being loved just because the timer goes off. You may be able to have a marriage that's a business arrangement. Of that, I'm pretty sure. It can work, too. I think it happens more often than anyone thinks. But the kid issue is something else entirely.''

''You don't understand.''

''Then help me. Tell me about you, Cole. Let me understand.''

He almost said no. He'd tried like hell to forget his past. But her words had a ring of truth to them, even though he wasn't about to alter his plan now. For his son's sake, he'd talk.

CHAPTER EIGHT

LILY DIDN'T press him. In fact, she remained completely still, hardly daring to breathe. It was like being inches from a wild buck who could bolt at any second.

She wished she could see him more clearly. The stars were bright, but the moon was a crescent. His body language told her several things. His arms were relaxed, not folded across his chest or anything, yet he had one hell of a grip on his beer bottle. He leaned slightly forward, which was an indication that he was willing to share, but he wouldn't look at her.

As the seconds ticked by, she marveled at her own audacity. She'd met this man today, and here she was asking him to share his secrets. Yet it made its own kind of sense. Something she'd learned in her years in law enforcement was that most folks will reveal more to a total stranger than someone in their immediate circle, especially if what they had to say was painful. Why that should be so, she didn't know, but she'd seen it time and time again.

She'd discussed it once with a professor, and he'd theorized that the need to talk, to unburden, was hardwired—one of the ways human beings stayed connected as part of a community. But such honesty also made us vulnerable, so it was better to let it all out with someone who could do you no harm.

Cole's gaze was on her. She didn't remember him looking up, but he must have when she was so lost in thought. His expression, what she could see of it, didn't seem terribly open. Oh, well. It had been worth a shot. Maybe in a day or so, she'd try again. See if she could get him to trust her a little more.

She started to get up, but stopped when he cleared his throat.

"I was raised in San Antonio. In the King William district. My parents married too young. My mother was only sixteen, and my father was eighteen. I was born shortly after the wedding. We lived with my grandparents for a long time."

"Your father's parents?"

He nodded. "They had this huge place, with acres of land. I was an only child, but I was never bored. There was always something to do, and my mother was almost a playmate."

He took a long drink from his beer, then leaned forward so his elbows were on his thighs. "My father was gone a lot. He traveled for business. I worshipped him. He used to bring me things from all over the world. One time it was an electric scooter from Germany. Camping gear from Alaska. A kite from Japan. But I didn't see him very often."

"That must have been hard."

"It was okay. I got along fine. My mother was there. And we took care of each other. She had no one. Her parents had died when she was four, and she'd been raised by her aunt. But her aunt had gone into a home the year before my mother and father met."

"Oh, my. She must have doted on you."

He nodded. "For a while."

"What do you mean?"

He stood up and walked over to the railing, where he leaned forward, staring into the darkness. "There was this Saturday I was supposed to go to a basketball game with my dad. We had our own place by then. The Spurs were playing that day, and I was a huge fan. Only, my dad couldn't make it. He said he had to work. My mom saw how disappointed I was, and she ended up taking me, even though she didn't like sports. During the second quarter, the camera scanned the crowd, you know, where the pictures come up on the giant screen. And there was my father. He had his arm around this woman's shoulders, and she was laughing and she buried her head in his neck when she saw the camera was on them. And then, this kid— he was about my age at the time—climbed up on my dad's lap and waved. Like *he* was his son, not me."

"Who were they?"

"I didn't know for a long time. My mother took me to my grandmother's for a while. I didn't see either of my parents for almost a month. But then my mother came and got me. Everything had changed. She wasn't the same anymore. My father never talked about that woman or that kid. Finally, when I was about fifteen, I found out that the woman was his mistress and the boy was his son. My half brother."

"Did you discuss it with your father?"

"Nope. And I never met them, either. Never even tried."

"What a jackass."

Cole turned. "Excuse me?"

"Not you. Your father. He was a jerk."

Cole smiled. She could see it clearly, even in the dim moonlight. "Yeah. He was."

"But your grandmother. She was there for you, wasn't she? She took care of you?"

He nodded as he walked back to the chair. He didn't sit, though. He just put one of his strong hands on the back. "She did. She made sure I had everything. A good education, a car when I got my driver's license."

"But...?"

He opened his mouth, but only to finish off his beer. When he brought the bottle down, he shrugged slightly. "It's late. It's been a long day."

"That it has." She stood, wanting to move closer to him. Knowing it wasn't the time. "When does everyone show up for breakfast?"

"Six-thirty."

"It'll be ready."

"You have everything you need in your room?"

"Yep."

"Okay, then."

She smiled.

He didn't move. He just stood there.

"Is there something else?" she asked, taking a tentative step toward him.

"No. It's just that—"

"What?"

"I haven't thought about some things for a long time."

"I didn't mean to stir up bad memories."

"That's just it. I'm remembering some good things, too. My mom was real pretty. And she had the nicest voice. She used to sing me Beatles' songs. And she had this yellow dress."

"Where is she now?"

"She died eleven years ago."

"I'm sorry."

"Yeah. Me, too." With that, he walked to the porch steps and headed off somewhere, maybe the barn. Maybe just a private place.

It was time to turn in. She just hoped she could get some sleep. There was so much to think about. Not the least of which was the way she wanted to comfort him. To hold him, pet his hair, tell him it was going to be all right.

It was kind of scary, when she got right down to it. She wasn't supposed to feel anything for him. He was a case, that's all. She needed to be objective. Impartial.

Man, was she in trouble.

DYLAN GLANCED at the clock and winced at the hour. It was nearly 4:00 a.m., so what in hell was he doing in his office? Torturing himself, that's what. He'd pulled out an old box of letters, one he hadn't even known he'd saved. In fact, he had a suspicion *he* hadn't been the one to stow them. The box had Lily's fingerprints all over it. She was a firm believer in the written word, and it was beyond her why everyone in the world didn't keep a journal.

He never was that comfortable with a pen, or even a keyboard. It felt too risky to write about the real stuff. But there had been a few years when he'd followed Lily's example. Only he hadn't written in a diary. He'd written to Julie.

The top envelope was made out to him. Julie's pretty handwriting was as familiar to him as his own. He pulled the note from inside and looked at the date.

March 18, 1989. He hadn't known her long. But he'd already fallen in love with her. The part he couldn't recall was whether he'd admitted the fact to himself at that point. Probably not. He wasn't the brightest kid on the block when it came to matters of the heart.

Dear Dylan,

If I get through economics without killing myself, we'll have to celebrate. Maybe pizza and a bottle of wine? But none of those awful anchovies! Did I tell you I put your buckle on the wall? I even framed it. The other girls in the dorm are all jealous, and oh, Carol Lacey really likes you and wants to ask you out. But I just love the way the buckle shines, and I'm so proud of you for winning at the national rodeo! I know Sebastian was green with envy. But that's okay. He'll get over it. He wants us to go see *Batman,* but I just can't picture Michael Keaton in it, can you? I do like Jack Nicholson, though. Will you come with us? I have a little secret to tell you. I had a dream about you last night. It was, well, it was pretty risqué.

He crumpled the paper in his hand, unable to read another word. She'd dreamed about him once. She'd lived in his dreams, coming to him again and again, only in his dreams she loved him, which was the cruelest part of all. Because he'd wake up every morning and remember it wasn't true.

She was still alive. He knew it with absolute certainty. Something would have died inside him if she wasn't. But where was she? *Where?*

COLE TURNED OVER and punched his pillow, trying to find a comfortable position. It was past four, and he'd only slept in bits and snatches, awakened time and again by nightmares. Not about monsters or falling into dark voids or things that go bump in the night. His nightmares were all about one thing—Lily.

She'd done something to him. Put a hex or a curse on his head. He never talked about his family. Not to anyone. Not even his closest friends.

Huh. His closest friends were Chigger and Manny. There was no one from the old days, from his past. And he wanted it that way. For him, everything that had come before the ranch was dead and buried. His real life had started five years ago.

So why had he dredged up those memories tonight? Just because she'd asked? That was ridiculous. And true.

Dammit, why was this so complicated? If he'd been a woman, he could have gotten pregnant any damn time he wanted, and that would have been that. The father wouldn't have had to know a thing. So why in hell didn't he just adopt?

He turned over, his sleep-deprived brain cutting right to the chase. His ego, that's why. He had no desire to raise some other man's child. He wanted this done his way.

Lily had a lot of things going for her. But she had even more against. No way could they go through with this. He wouldn't be able to keep his hands off her. Not that he would do anything against her will, but there was no denying the two of them had chemistry.

She'd be a pain. She'd want to be part of his son's life forever. She'd drive him crazy.

She already had.

If only she didn't have that hair. Or those legs, or that mouth, or those eyes… Hell, it was the package that appealed, not the parts.

She was something. Sassy and bright, infuriating and intriguing. But then, he didn't really know her, did he? He'd proven to himself that he wasn't a good judge of women, so why was he jumping to conclusions now? He had a feeling it had more to do with sex than with wisdom.

He ached from want. All the way to his bones. And she was the cure.

Okay, so maybe she wasn't the right woman for the job, but maybe she could be right in another way. Maybe she'd be amenable to a different kind of arrangement. One that didn't have lasting repercussions.

He sighed, wishing he could turn off his thoughts and get to sleep. Tomorrow would be hell. He wasn't one who could go without sleep easily. Not like Chigger, who only needed about four hours a night.

The best thing to do was just forget about her and think of something else. Work. Right. That journalist for *The Cattlemen* was coming tomorrow. No, not for a couple of days. Dammit, he didn't even know what day it was. All because of her.

WORD MUST have gotten around. It was the only explanation she could come up with. The hands arrived a little after six. No one she knew on a ranch ever got up earlier than they needed to. Thank goodness the coffee was ready. The men, after asking if there was anything she needed them for, were at the dining room table drinking coffee, lying through their teeth and laughing it up.

All except Cole.

Lily tested the griddle. The temperature was perfect, and she ladled out the first batch of hotcakes. The big pan of scrambled eggs would be ready at the same time, as would the bacon. She had the feeling there wouldn't be any leftovers.

As she cooked, she wondered about the rest of the day. Of course, there were two more meals to prepare, but that wasn't going to take all her time. She'd like to go for a ride, if Cole would lend her a horse. She'd also like to nap and catch up on the sleep she'd missed last night.

Normally, she slept like a baby anywhere. Nothing fazed her. Except thoughts of this case. And Cole. She'd ended up turning on the light at three and scribbling in her journal. Unfortunately, all she'd written were questions, no answers. What was it about him that made her so…itchy? And why in hell did she want him to scratch that itch when she knew perfectly well that it was completely inappropriate and stupid?

She was on the rebound, which accounted for a lot, but not all. Something else was at work here. Unfortunately, she had no idea what.

She turned the pancakes, and for the next fifteen minutes concentrated on nothing but the meal. When it was done, she went to the kitchen door and called for a little help. Of course, the first one she looked for was Cole, but his seat was still empty. All the other guys jumped up, which was sweet. She nodded at Spence and Manny. They helped her carry the food to the table.

Everything looked great. And smelled better. She'd even brought out another pot of coffee and a pitcher of orange juice. So why was everyone sitting there with empty plates in front of them?

"Infant, I won't buy that one. You'd better set up your stand on another corner."

"Meaning?"

"Meaning you have a motive. And motives transform love into a dirty word."

She laughed again. She was clearly enjoying herself.

"Peter. Dear Peter! For once in a lifetime, the boot's on the other foot. *I* am the hungry aggressor; you, the prospective victim of violation. So, don't call me a whore, not even by implication. Not that the word offends me; it simply doesn't fit. Tonight, *I* am buying. How much do you usually get?"

He grinned at her, said:

"Would you like a *pitillo?*"

"Yes," she said; "why yes, of course."

He took out his cigarette case, opened it. Lit the cigarette for her. Snapped the case shut.

"Don't you smoke?" she said.

"No," he said. "I told you last night I didn't. These are bait."

"Meaning?"

"Meaning, my dear little girl baby playing grown-up sophisticate, that you are the finest actress I ever met."

"Oh, come now, Peter!"

"I'll prove it to you. All night long, you've played a role foreign to every aspect of your training—even, I'll wager, to your true personality. For instance, I've spent a good part of my life in Spain. So I know that Madrileñas of good family never—"

"And who, may I ask, is a Madrileña of good family?"

"You," Peter said.

"Now really, Peter! I am a native Costa Verdian."

"A native Costa Verdian who knew instantly what I meant when I said *pitillo* instead of *cigarrillo?* Who, for our first date, invited me to meet her on the Street of the Theenko de Mayo, instead of the *Seenko* de Mayo? Who always says Theeoodad Villalonga, instead of *Seeoodad* Villalonga?"

"Bravo, Peter! My clever, clever Peter! Yet, you are

wrong. I was born here in Ciudad Villalonga, however you pronounce it. I will concede you your point, though. From age eight to eighteen, I was educated in Spain. So?"

"So this. Spanish girls of your social class or Costa Verdians are the same. They don't proposition a man. They'd die first."

"Of—unsatiated lust, Peter—or of shame? Or of a combination of both?"

"That's my question, Niña. And the answer to it is, in your case, neither. Now, I'll ask you one: What the hell ever gave you the idea that I'd consent to being used?"

Her eyes were very bleak.

"I was too busy looking at your shoulders; the set of your jaw that I didn't study—your mouth, sufficiently, Peter. Nor your eyes—"

"Oh, hell" he said. "This isn't getting either of us anywhere, so . . ."

He stood up.

"Don't go, Peter," she said. And then he saw the tears were there, hot and bright and sudden on her face.

"That's better," he said. "That's much better."

And sank down beside her once again.

9.

"Peter."

"*Muñeca?*"

"Tell me about—her."

"Oh, hell! Tell you what about her, Niña?"

"Is she as beautiful as her pictures?"

"More. She is absolutely breathtaking."

"Oh!"

"Why *Oh, Muñeca?*"

"I don't know. No, that isn't true. I'm afraid I do know."

"Then say it."

"Not now. Later, perhaps. Peter—do you—do you love her so very much?"

He turned away. Turned back again.

"You want the truth, Infant?"

"Yes, Peter."

"Very well. The truth is that I don't love her at all."

She looked at him. Her gaze explored his face.

"Are you trying to comfort me now?" she said.

"No. I haven't any comfort to offer anyone, *Muñeca.* All I've got left in me is—pain."

"And some capacity for pity, I hope. Tell me, why don't you love her? You said she is beautiful . . ."

"Beauty is a state of mind. To me, you are the most beautiful thing that ever drew breath. I was meant to love a girl like you. That's part of it. The rest is too long, too dreary, too hurtful. Say that my love was a long day dying. Say it was bled out of me by watching from the sidelines what she let happen to her. What she seized, welcomed, embraced. Say it was killed little by little by—disgust. By utter nausea. That when, finally, pity gave me my heart's desire, I found it too-too hideously scarred by all too many brief encounters; that the image I'd worshiped so long was dead. Leaving—"

"What, Peter?"

"A ghost. A Pavlovian bitch going through the conditioned reflexes of passion. You ring that bell, and my Judy gives. Oh, I am sorry! That was a lousy thing to say."

She bent her head. Averted her face for a long, breath-stopped moment. Then she lifted it, said:

"Isn't the truth nearly always rotten? Peter—"

"Yes, Infant?"

"I'll take you home now. You've won."

"I've won what?"

"Your moral victory. I-I won't risk your contempt. You were right. I was playing a game. A great and terrible game which I have lost now. Totally. In so many, many ways—"

"Meaning?"

"How do I know what I mean? Say that what I'd planned to do was less sacrifice than sin. That the nobility I was giving myself credit for was—all, or nearly all—a lie. A pitiful thing, to lie to oneself, no? But now, I have stopped doing it, I think. . . . Come. When we're outside in the car—"

"What car, Infant?"

"Mine. She has probably sent it back by now. I told her to. When we're outside and in the car, I shall say a thing to you. Will you please not look at me when I say it?"

"Not looking at you, *Muñeca,* calls for will power. But if you insist—"

"I do insist."

"Then, tell me why?"

"Because it will be the truth. For the first time tonight. No! I-I've told you the truth many times tonight, Peter. Without knowing it. Believing that I lied. Now, come."

He got up. Put out his hand to her. She took it. Then, watching her face all the time, he drew her very slowly, quietly, into his arms. Kissed her mouth, gently, tenderly, with what was less passion than an aching sense of loss; less desire than pain.

She drew back, looked at him; and her eyes were crystalline, light-filled.

"Now," she said, "I don't have to wait until we are outside. Now I do not even have to hide my face. I love you, Peter. Do you hear? I love you!"

"And I—" he began, but she put her hand over his mouth.

"Don't say it!" she said. "It is enough that I love you. Because tomorrow, when you learn my name and begin to hate me, you will wish those words unsaid. Oh, Peter, *Cielo,* I—"

The telephone guillotined her voice.

He released her. She went to the instrument, picked it up. Said:

"Speak?" Then:

"*Ay, no!* Do not tell me this, Doña Elena! Oh, Holy Mother of God! Oh, Infant Jesus! Oh— What? *Ay, no!* No, Doña

Elena—of course I sound strange! I am not Marisol! I am Alicia. Marisol is not here. She is saved! By now she is almost to New York! Yes. Doña Elena—yes, I do know that. But it is not my fault. It is not my fault, I tell you! Yes—yes! He is a monster. Yes, perhaps you are right. Perhaps we are all monsters in my family. Because, even to save your daughter-in-law, this night I would have done a monstrous thing. That God pardon me! *Adios! Adios . . .*"

She turned away from the phone.

"Peter," she said. "He is dead. The comedy would have been futile in any case. Roberto, the husband of Mari, is already dead. I-I should have sinned for nothing, but for you! And I—"

"Alicia," he said. "That's your name, isn't it? What a lovely name!"

But she went on speaking very slowly and clearly in the flat-toned, deceptive calm of pure hysteria.

"And now I am sorry that I did not. That I did not take you into my body, into my life. Make even with you a child in your image. But then, who knows? I might have cursed it with my own—with this filthy blood I bear!"

"Alicia *mía*," he said. "Alicia what? Tell me the rest of your name."

She shook her head, wildly.

"No, Peter," she said.

"Why not?"

"Because you would hate me. And that would be too much. On top of all the rest, Love, that simply could not be borne!"

"Infant, nothing could make me hate you. Nothing in this world."

Her gaze flickered over his face. He could almost feel her gaze.

"Tell me."

She did not answer.

"Tell me, Alicia."

She turned her face away. The lamp was behind her. He could see that crystalline spill outlining her profile in a wash of light.

She turned back again. Faced him.

"It is Alicia Villalonga," she said.

He stood there, blessing his knees for not having given way beneath him. He took a step forward. Another. Put out his arms to her.

Wonderingly, she came to him. He lifted her chin. Kissed her throat. Her mouth. Kissed away the glitter, the salt, the wet. She clung to him, weeping.

And from every point of the compass, the sirens shrilled.

She looked up at him. But he was not looking at her. Gently he pushed her away. Walked over to the wall above the sofa. Took down quietly and carefully the ancient breastplate of a conquistador. Stood there a long moment, staring at the fine pair of almost invisible wires trailing down the wall. At the round, black, obscene mouth of the microphone.

He heard the pitiful, sobbing intake of her breath. Put up his hand and tore the microphone from the wall.

"*Ay!*" she moaned. "Now I have murdered you, too! Now I have caused your death!"

He grinned at her.

"Let's get out of here, Infant," he said. "Don't think the night air's healthy in this neighborhood. Come on! Let's go!"

"Where?" she whispered. "Where can we, Peter? Where in the world that he—"

"*Muñeca*, when necessary, I can play rough, too. Now come on!"

10.

The first thing they saw when they came out of the house was the white convertible. It was parked directly in front of the door. The top was down and music was blaring. Peter leaned over and cut the switch. The music stopped.

The man who lay across the seat sat up, rubbing his eyes. He was dressed in a green-gray uniform with red collar, cuffs, and epaulettes. They could see all that because the sun was already up. On his chest was a badge. It read *Aeropuerto:Estacionamiento—Airport: Parking.*

"*Buenas días,* Guardia," Peter said.

"*Ay, Señor!* I fell asleep. The little blonde Señorita—how pretty she was!—gave me the keys to this enormous vehicle and told me I must bring it to this address. Whereupon, she said, the Señor would reward me . . ."

"She was right. But why did you not ring the bell?"

"Because," the parking attendant grinned, "the little blondie said I was not to. She said that since it was very late, the Señora and the Señor would prefer not to be disturbed. She said, however, to inform the Señores that she had got safely aboard the four-motor of reaction for New York."

"Your friend," Peter said to Alicia, "is not as innocent as she looks."

"Peter!" Alicia said. "We must go! Jesus y María! How can you be so tranquil?"

"Haven't seen anything very frightening yet. Come on, *Muñeca,* get in." He helped her into the car. Turned to the guard. "Here," he said, "is your reward, friend."

The guard stood there holding the thousand-peso note

between his hands. They shook. It was more money than he ever made in a month. Before he could get his mouth closed enough to say thank you, Peter had slipped under the wheel, kicked the Lincoln into life. They moved off, down the street.

"Where are you taking me, Peter?" Alicia said.

"My place," Peter said.

"Your place! Dear God!"

"Yes. The last place they'd think we'd go. There's things there we'll need. A gun. Camera. Rough clothes. A sleeping bag."

"For two?" she said.

"For one. For you. I'll sleep on the ground. I'm used to it."

"But, Peter—"

" 'Licia, you think we could get across a frontier?"

"No, Peter."

"Neither do I. So we head for the Sierras. Join the Castristas."

"But the Castristas are dead, Peter."

"One band. There are others. Many others."

"Peter, *Cielo*, we'll never reach the Sierras."

"We'll try," he said, and bent the Lincoln around a tight turn into his street.

"Ohhh!" Alicia said.

"*Muñeca*," he said, "believe me, that was the sweetest lifetime any guy ever used up in one night."

The armed police were already out of their jeep, walking toward the white convertible with their Bren guns pointing. Another jeep screeched around the corner and pulled up behind him. Every window in the building where he lived was open. All his neighbors were hanging out of them. Except for Concha, la Portera. She was out on the sidewalk. For a scandal like this one, she'd risk getting shot.

They sat there, waiting. Suddenly, Alicia turned to him. She put her arms around his neck, tilted her face sidewise and kissed him. A long time. A very long time.

Concha dropped to her knees. Crossed herself. Started praying. "God forgive her!" she said.

"Get out!" the Captain in charge of the Armed Police barked. He had a Mauser pistol in his hand.

Peter opened the door; Alicia opened the door on her side, too.

"No, Doña Alicia," the Captain said. "Not Your Excellency. Only this lecherous brute of a Yanqui who has abducted the illustrious lady."

"So?" Alicia's voice was clear, ringing, carrying from one side of the street to the other. "That is your story, my Captain? You have been misinformed. I was not abducted. I went with my lover willingly. I declare this before God and in the presence of all these witnesses! And if it is your intention to save my reputation—"

"Alicia!" Peter said.

"I further declare that I spent all night in his arms. Which may be a sin, but it is no crime. So now, put up those guns!"

"Doña Alicia," the Captain said, "I am very sorry; but my orders are from your Illustrious Brother, His Supreme Excellency, the Head of the State."

"Who is an assassin, a pervert, and a murderous swine. This, too, I declare before witnesses."

The Captain turned to the Sergeant.

"Arrest the people in those houses. All of them. Shoot any who resist."

"Oh, God!" Alicia said. She bent her head and wept.

"Get out, Gringo!" the Captain said to Peter.

Peter got out of the car. He looked at the Captain. Said:

"Tell me, my Captain, when you go to the *excusado*, do you also jerk out a pistol and order your bowels to move?"

The Captain brought his knee up into the pit of Peter's stomach. Clubbed him with the flat of the pistol as he doubled. Kicked him after he was down. It was a beautiful job. Very expert. The worst of it was to be taken like that, having had Ranger-Commando training himself.

Then Alicia was out of the car and upon the Captain. Ten years under the Carmelite nuns of Madrid disappeared. Eight centuries vanished. Every drop of Castilian blood, leaving only Gypsy, Moorish, Tluscola. It took four policemen to get her off the Captain. What her nails did to his face wasn't pretty.

The policemen came out of the houses, herding the people before them. They did their work with enthusiasm. With zest. They used their rifle butts, rubber truncheons, their feet. One old man fell. They encouraged him in various ways to get up. But not even reddening their bayonet points in his skinny old buttocks was effective. He wanted to cooperate, but he couldn't. The blood that was coming out of his mouth and nose was choking him. They kept on encouraging him until he turned his head to one side and vomited up his breakfast. It was mixed with blood, too, from where they'd kicked him in the stomach.

The Captain nodded. They dragged the old man to the corner. Shot him in the back of the head. Stuffed him head down into a garbage can with his feet sticking out.

After that, they didn't have to encourage the others any more.

They slung Peter into the jeep face down. Five policemen sat on him. From time to time they hit him with the rubber truncheons. A sergeant and three policemen got into the Lincoln with Alicia. The Marias Negras came, those big black closed trucks that could pack prisoners in on a raid, drive slowly around town in the heat of the day and arrive at the jail with most of the captives dead of asphyxiation, thus saving the Everlasting State much trouble and expense. They loaded the people into them.

Then the procession started off, down the street.

Peter sat there, staring into the spotlight. He had been staring into that spotlight on and off for the better part of three days.

"Now, will you sign it?" the Captain said.

"No," Peter said.

The Captain nodded. The Sergeant hit Peter in the face with his fist.

"Now?" the Captain said.

"Look, my Captain," Peter said. "I have a thing to say."

"Then say it!" the Captain said.

"If I sign this literary masterpiece, confessing to the crimes of abduction and rape, I will have conceded guilt to acts for which the punishment is death even in many civilized countries."

"You mean we are not civilized?" the Sergeant said.

"My dear Sergeant, in a civilized country, you would be in a cage. In the Zoological Gardens. And the children would feed you peanuts."

The Sergeant hit him again. So hard the chair crashed over.

"Pick him up, fool," the Captain said. "You break his skull before he signs this and we'll all be shot!"

The Sergeant picked Peter up, chair and all.

Peter grinned at the Sergeant. His lips were like two blood puddings, but he managed that grin.

"I was mistaken, Sergeant," he said. "You are a very pretty boy. So pretty that I think—"

"What?"

"That Miguelito has enlarged your anal orifice for you."

The Sergeant's fist came back.

"Stop it!" the Captain said. "You were saying, Reynolds?"

"That goon squads are always defeated by a certain lack of logic."

"Meaning?" the Captain said.

"I sign this, and I am executed. I don't sign it and I am assassinated. Either way, I die."

"True, but by signing this you die very quickly upon the *garrote vil;* which merely breaks your neck when the Executioner turns the wheel. Whereas, if you do not sign it, I shudder to contemplate how you will die. In fact, I shall not contemplate it. I should, I fear, lose my lunch."

Peter grinned once more.

"My dear Captain," he said. "There is one other element in this equation—"

"Which is?"

"Marisol Talaveda, wife of Roberto Ruiz Mateos. No. I beg pardon: Widow of Ruiz Mateos."

The Captain stared at him.

"Who is already in New York. With a document signed by me. With certain photographs taken by me. The document is addressed to my government. It says, in brief: No matter how expertly they fake it, even if they blow me up in an airplane with fifty-three others as they did Emilio Duarte y Marin, or in a jeep crash, suspiciously close to the correction centers, as happened to Roberto Ruiz Mateos; no matter what confession I may sign, my death in la Republica de Costa Verde is *ipso facto* murder. Please take the proper steps."

"You lie!" the Captain said.

Peter grinned. It was a very tired grin, but authentic, for all that.

"Of course I lie," he said; "under these circumstances, wouldn't you? But, before we commence the waltz again, dear Captain—are you willing to gamble upon the certitude or lack of it of what I have said?"

The Captain sat there. The sweat popped out on his forehead and ran down the furrows Alicia had clawed in his face.

"Shall I hit him again?" the Sergeant said.

"No—wait. I must think—" the Captain began; but with no interval at all, the door opened, and another policeman stepped through it. This one was a Colonel—a rank existing in the Costa Verdian police because in the Glorious Republic they were a part of the Army, like the SS.

"Release him," the Colonel said.

"What!" the Captain said.

"You heard me! Release him. Don Luis wants to talk to him."

"So!" Peter said. "Even *this* joint is bugged!"

"What do you mean?" the Colonel said.

"Bugged. Implanted with various microphones which enable his superiors to hear every time the Captain scratches his balls. Or breaks wind. Or makes love to the pretty Sergeant," Peter said.

"Begging Colonel Lopez' pardon, the Colonel did appear

with much suddenness at a strangely appropriate moment," the Captain said.

"That is none of your business," Colonel Lopez said. "Release him!"

"Don't just stand there!" the Captain said to the Sergeant. "You heard the Colonel! Release him!"

The Sergeant bent and fitted a key into the handcuffs holding Peter's arms to the chair. Then he knelt down and unlocked the cuffs holding Peter's ankles to the legs of the chair.

"Can you stand, Don Pedro?" he said—promoting Peter thus to the aristocracy, giving him that upper-class title of *Don*, seizing with a lackey's instinct upon flattery as a means to defend himself, to defend the absolutely indefensible: the hired thug that he was.

Peter sat there rubbing his wrists, his ankles.

"I think so," he said; "just give me a minute, Sergeant."

The Sergeant stood there. So did Colonel Lopez. The Captain still sat behind the desk.

Peter put his hands down on the arms of the chair and pushed. Came up, very, very slowly. Stood there swaying like an axed oak. Bent forward. Farther. Gathered speed. Measured his length upon the floor.

"Pick him up," Colonel Lopez said.

The Sergeant bent, put his two arms under Peter's armpits. Stopped, seeing how Peter was looking into his eyes.

"Take your hands off me," Peter said. Saying that, his voice wasn't even loud.

"But, Don Pedro," the Sergeant said.

"Take your hands off me," Peter said.

The Sergeant looked at Colonel Lopez.

"Leave him alone," the Colonel said.

Peter put his own two hands down, and pushed. They were swollen to the size of a pair of small hams. They were about that color, too. He went on pushing, while the sweat jetted out of his pores. It plowed furrows through the dirt and blood on his face. And now he was on his hands and knees, shaking his head, so that the drops of sweat and blood made a splatter on the floor. Again the Sergeant bent to help him.

"Don't touch me!" Peter said.

He came upright now. Hung there. Put his two massacred hands down on the Captain's desk, and stared into the Captain's face.

"Look, Reynolds—" the Captain said.

"I know. You were only following orders. So was the Sergeant. I hold you no ill will, either of you."

"That's damned handsome of you, Reynolds," Colonel Lopez said.

"So," Peter went on, "when I, personally, take care of both of you, it will be on behalf of the poor bastard you shot in the back of the head; the women you beat and kicked; the children you slapped around while following orders. Entirely without malice, gentlemen. As a demonstration of what a free man is."

"And what is he, my dear Reynolds?" Colonel Lopez said.

"One who never follows orders. Not from the Devil. Not from God. A guy you've got to kill. Because break him is the one thing you can't do. Well, Colonel, shall we go?"

The Colonel smiled.

"Yes—Don Pedro. The indestructible Don Pedro; we might as well," he said.

Colonel Lopez did not take Peter directly to the office of the Head of the Secret Police. Rather, he took him to his own quarters. There on the bed was a complete change of clothes, from the skin out. When Peter came reeling out of the Colonel's shower, still groggy but beginning to feel remotely human again, he found that the clothes fitted him perfectly. Then he saw why. They were his own. He looked at Colonel Lopez. The Colonel smiled.

"It became obvious to me two hours ago that Doña Alicia was winning her battle with Don Luis. Which didn't surprise me, Mr. Reynolds. Her brother's known weakness for her makes her difficult to oppose. So I had your clothes brought here. I hope you will permit me one indiscreet question— which is not inquisitiveness on my part, but simply a prudent desire to be able to trim my sails closer to the prevailing winds, if such an excessively nautical term may be allowed a soldier . . ."

"All right," Peter said. "What do you want to know?"

"You are not actually married to the lovely motion picture actress, are you?"

"No," Peter said.

"Then my tactics were correct," Colonel Lopez said. "I may even boast a bit of my skill as a strategist. May I offer you a brandy, Mr. Reynolds?"

"Yes," Peter said.

"Carlos Primero? Veterano? 103 Black Label? Or—Remy Martin? Bisquit? Heine? Courvoisier?"

"Carlos Primero," Peter said.

The Colonel poured a snifter for Peter and another for himself. Big snifters.

"What was your strategy, Colonel?" Peter said.

"To dissociate myself from your interrogation from the outset. Those who have offended the future brother-in-law of the Head of the State are going to regret it," Colonel Lopez said.

Peter sipped the brandy. It was a good brandy. The best of all the Spanish brandies. Better even than most of the French.

"You, Colonel, are an optimist," he said.

This office was different from the Captain's. Possibly because it obviously was not designed to be used for the interrogation of prisoners. It was paneled in caoba and teak. The furniture was upholstered in top-grain calfskin. The only picture was a photograph of El Indominable. Life-size. Looking at it had the usual effect upon Peter. He felt faintly sick. But he went on looking at it. And getting sicker. Because, studied well, with due allowances made for the puffiness of lifelong dissipation; the down sag and twist of utter depravity, Miguel Villalonga did look like Alicia. When it came to the mouth, in him gone past her mouth's warm tenderness into a sado-masochistic leer, the resemblance was remarkable. There was something to be said for that "blood of monsters" remark after all.

The man behind the desk watched what was going on in Peter's face. It seemed to amuse him. He made no effort to interrupt Peter's study of El Líder Glorioso's portrait. He said:

"Why yes, Mr. Reynolds, they are full brother and sister, not half. Carlos Villalonga acknowledged them both. And since I have often had the privilege of swimming with our Great Leader, I can tell you that he, too, has a blue-moon birthmark under his left breast."

"So?" Peter said, and looked at the man behind the desk. He was dressed in civilian clothes, a perfectly cut suit of raw Italian silk. Peter had never seen him before, but he knew who he was: Miguel Villalonga's personal assistant and Head of the Secret Police, known throughout the Republic of Costa Verde as Luis Sinnombre, for the two excellent reasons that, having started life as an orphan and a foundling, Don Luis actually hadn't any name and because, without stretching the point too far, the phrase *sin nombre* could also be held to mean unspeakable, which Don Luis indisputably was.

He smiled at Peter out of what an American lady journalist had been pleased to call his jaguar mouth and turned his —phrase also the lady's—antique Toltec eyes toward one of the heavy, upholstered chairs.

"Have the goodness to sit, Don Pedro," he said. That was another of the Costa Verdian oddities. In no other country in South America are the ancient Spanish forms of courtesy —reserved, of course, to the upper class—*Don* and *Doña* used. But in Costa Verde, they come almost as naturally to the tongue as they do in Spain.

Peter sat.

Luis Sinnombre looked at his face, and made little clacking noises of sympathy.

"I fear some of the minor police have been overzealous again!" he said. "If you will give me a description of the offenders, I shall see that they are severely punished."

"No," Peter said. "I fell down the front stairs while in a state of intoxication."

Don Luis laughed.

"You know who I am?" he said.

"Yes," Peter said. "I once met a friend of yours in New York. Grace Matthews."

"So?" Luis said. "And how is dear Grace?"

"As well as can be expected," Peter said.

"What am I to imply from this curious phrase?" Luis said.

"What you will," Peter said.

"Then I shall permit myself to think that all is not well with the little Grace . . ."

"You have permitted yourself a thought of remarkable accuracy," Peter said.

"Would the great Don Pedro, journalist extraordinary, care to elaborate?"

"I don't suppose it matters. The last time I saw Grace she was in an insane asylum. Her middle-class American background had never ceased to war against the curious and unusual desires that had been instilled in her—where, and by whom, it is superfluous to say. In the war which her prim Midwestern conscience fought against the filthy, nauseous, and even painful sexual perversions she had learned to enjoy, it was her reason that lost. The psychiatrists say her case is as much without hope as its cause was—without name."

Luis Sinnombre threw back his head and laughed aloud.

"What a pleasure it is to hear a Gringo employ the Spanish language with such precision. Even to the play upon words! Don Pedro, tell me: What are your true feelings toward that skinny little she-monkey of an Alicia?"

Peter looked at him. Smiled.

"Whatever they are, they remain my affair," he said.

"And hers?" Luis said.

"Perhaps. Why don't you ask her?"

"I have."

"And what did she say?"

Luis shrugged.

"What one might expect. With her looks—which I, for one, find oddly attractive; exotic, rather—"

"That makes two of us," Peter said.

"Ah, so? Good! I shouldn't want the poor little thing to pine away of unrequited passion. In any event, I think you'll understand that the little Alicia isn't every man's cup of tea, that here tastes are rather conventional, we prefer the Goyaesque female, *Maja Desnuda* type. Or to use a totally intranslatable phrase of ours, *metida en carnes*. Do you know what that means?"

"Stacked," Peter said. "All the usual feminine equipment, but applied with a certain generosity in certain places."

"Right! What an apt translation of it! So, the poor little thing has been lonely. Her position as sister of our Glorious Leader doesn't help, either. Frightens the more desirable types away. Attracts the undesirable—the overly ambitious with no merits of their own. So, naturally, when you were a little kind to her, she rather seized upon that kindness; you, a foreigner, with obviously no desire to inherit the Presidency of Costa Verde—"

"Obviously," Peter said.

"The trouble is, Reynolds, that you've put yourself—and me—in quite a spot. Due to the excellent training that the lovely Miss Lovell has bestowed upon you—"

"I don't know what you're talking about," Peter said.

"Ah? Oh, I see—the Anglo-Saxon conception of gallantry! Touching. Oh, quite. But actually, my dear Reynolds, I was referring to the exquisite knowledge of feminine psychology you displayed, not anything more intimate—"

"I still don't know what you're talking about," Peter said.

"Oh come now, Reynolds! Your performance was masterly! All that mid-Victorian reluctance to letting yourself be seduced, on the score of abstract morality, or again, on the score of your loyalty to dear Judith, and lastly, out of your doubt as to the lady's sincerity—so put that those doubts became a sort of modesty on your part on the one hand and a delicately implied exhibition of respect for the lady herself on the other. Oh, yes, masterly is the word!"

"Thanks," Peter said.

"Took me all night to decide what your game was. Incidentally, your refusal to mention her name added quite a fillip to the performance. Had I known it was merely our Alicia, your resistance would have been much less impressive. Poor 'Licia, easy to resist, isn't she?"

"I may have been more tempted at another time in my life," Peter said, "but, offhand, I can't remember when."

"Now, Reynolds!"

"I mean it," Peter said.

"All right. Then let me put it to you fairly: What, actually, is your feeling toward Doña Alicia Villalonga, Widow of Duarte y Marin?"

Peter looked at Luis. Studied him.

"I love the ground she walks on," he said.

He heard the door crash open. Alicia came through it in one long blinding rush. Hurled herself upon him, curled with boneless grace into his lap, her arms around his neck almost strangling him. Then she turned him loose. Put up her slim hand and ran her fingertips over his face, his mouth, so lightly that almost they didn't touch. Even so, they made him wince.

"*Ay!*" she wailed. "*Ay yai!* How they have hurt you!" She whirled, would have leaped across the desk if Peter had not held her. "Beast!" she screamed. "Animal! Pig! Dog and son of dogs! Ay, I will kill you, Luis! I will! I will! I will!"

"Infant," Peter said, "gentle down, will you?"

She turned and started kissing all the bruises and the cuts and the cigarette burns upon his face.

"*Muñeca*," Peter said, "even that hurts."

"Oh!" she said, and buried her small face in the hollow of his throat.

"My dear Reynolds," Luis Sinnombre said, "either you are the cleverest man alive, or the luckiest. Perhaps even both. They go together, don't they?"

"You mean?" Peter said.

"That you, of course, did not know or even guess that I had the little Alicia concealed behind that door?"

"Of course not," Peter said.

Luis sighed.

"My intention was good, Reynolds. I wanted to demonstrate to my beloved little sister—"

"My God!" Peter said. "You mean that you—?"

"That I am her brother, too? I think so. But we do not know, really. The ever-generous Isabel brought me up. At various times, in various moods, and in various stages of drunkenness, she tells various tales. Usually I am the son of a dear, dear friend of hers, who died. A fellow worker—"

"You mean a fellow whore?" Peter said.

"That sort of bravado is cheap, Reynolds. Besides, the truth does not insult me. My mother—if I had a mother—was either a street whore or the great Isabel herself. Which is a difference in class, merely. At times, dear Isabel—who is much woman, Reynolds, and for whom my admiration and my gratitude are genuine—says I am hers, and that my father was an exiled Mexican, or Colombian, or Chilean, or Peruvian—or any other republic that comes to her mind—statesman. At other times, she declares that my mother's name was Teresa, or Pilar, or Rosario, or Mercedes, or Maruja—and that my father was a billygoat. Or a monkey. Or a big black buck nigger they imported from Cuba because of his sexual prowess. Which didn't—and doesn't—matter. What does matter is whoever my parents were, they seem to have endowed me with brains. Which inheritance—my only one, I assure you—Isabel furthered by sending me to one of your greatest, most liberal universities. . . . Oh, no; don't ask me which one! The authorities at my Alma Mater have been trying to hide the fact that my name rightfully belongs on their roster of graduates—and with honors, my dear Reynolds—ever since. An amusing point is that she used money she had blackmailed out of Carlos Villalonga for Miguel's education to send me along, as well, with the additional irony that I graduated with honors while Miguel was expelled for failing his classes and general roistering. But where were we before we entered into this detour through my personal history?"

"You were attempting to demonstrate to Alicia—"

"That, despite all my warnings, and her own exemplary behavior up until now, she has at last allowed herself to fall into the hands of a mercenary adventurer. But you have endured three really rough days and persist in saying that you love her. Almost you convince me that you actually are sincere."

"Frankly, Don Luis," Peter said, "I don't give a damn if you're convinced or not. So long as Alicia is. Are you, Nena?"

"Peter—" Alicia whispered.

"Yes, Nena?" He used that word because it suited her. Both it and *niña* mean little girl, except that *nena* is generally applied to littler girls, and is tenderer somehow.

"How can you love me? I am ugly—"

"Lord!" Peter said.

"And depraved and of a family of utter vileness. You are kind, I know; but this is too difficult to believe . . ."

"My dear Alicia," Luis laughed, "may I suggest that the smell of money surrounding you is sufficient to perfume away the odor of your family, even if you are generous enough to include me?"

"And may I suggest that you take all that money and shove it?" Peter said.

"Oh, come now, my dear Reynolds, everyone knows how you Yanquis are!"

"And everyone forgets that we are the people who have given away more money than any other in the history of the world. Say we did it selfishly. All right. But who else ever has, even selfishly? Skip that. It leads to politics and politics give me a pain in the gut. Put it this way: If it were possible for me to marry Alicia, I should insist that she use every *centavo* of her fortune to build an orphanage exclusively for the children of the people murdered by you and Miguelito. That she take off her clothes and burn them. That she come to me absolutely unadorned, and uncontaminated by anything that that money, which stinks of blood and putrefaction and has the echoes of screaming about it, has ever bought. *Only* on those conditions would I accept her as my wife. Point number two: I earn between twenty-five and forty thousand dollars a year, which works out to enough millions of your pesos to make the question of fortune-hunting on my part academic. Point number three: Miguelito would have a hemorrhage of fecal matter, faint, and fall into it, before he would permit his sister to marry a Gringo. Am I not right?"

"Perfectly. Except that Miguel knows absolutely nothing about this—so far."

"Ha!" Peter said. "You mean he missed the chance to listen in on a bugged passage at arms?"

"I mean that you, my dear Peter, would not be alive now if he had heard that tape."

"You heard it, didn't you?"

"Oh yes. And found it vastly entertaining. I gather you wonder why *I* have not had you killed? My dear Peter, Miguel and I don't see eye to eye about a great many things."

"All right. But just tell me: Why didn't he listen to it? I thought that was one of his favorite amusements."

"It is. Only, last night, his leg—you know about the attempt on his life some years ago?"

"Yes. You flew him to the Mayo Brothers' Clinic. Saved his life. Touching example of fraternal devotion. He came back and built Our Lady of the Remedies Hospital. Fine job. One of the best hospitals I've ever seen."

"Thank you. The point is, my dear Peter, that the doctors at the Mayo Clinic gave him three choices: a paralyzed, dragging leg; no leg at all, except, of course, one of the marvels of your Yanqui ingenuity, an articulated metal limb; and third, a leg which functions almost normally, but at the cost of a slow dull pain from the damaged nerves all the time, and even, some of the time, an absolutely insupportable ache. He chose number three, which was courageous but hardly intelligent, no? It accounts, I think, for the badness of his temper. Additionally, his violence and his excesses have weakened his heart. Doctor Gomez insists that he spend much of the time resting—"

"I know," Peter said. "Vince told me. An injection that puts him out for twelve hours."

"Which he hates and refuses to accept most of the time. But that night, the pain was so great, that he gave up even the keenly anticipated pleasure of determining whether even so powerful a chap as you are would be able to thaw out dear Marisol's deep-frozen little tail. Which is why I say your luck is astonishing, Reynolds. He was asleep during the festivities. My second act, after listening to that touching curtain speech of Alicia's—noble of you, my dearest; but oh so foolish, no?—was to give Miguel another shot of the sedative, after, of course, sending the police to apprehend so dangerously convincing a lover. Incidentally, that medicine is another of Padre Pío's discoveries; he has compiled a whole new *Materia Medica* from the pharmacopoeia of the Tluscolan witch doctors."

"The little Padre cured me of a tropical fever in one day," Peter said, "but I still think he did it with prayer."

"Ah, so? Charming thought. Look, Peter, I find myself forced to trust you. What's more, inclined to do so. You are a sentimentalist. I even believe you mean it when you say you have no interest in Alicia's money; the more so since my investigations show that the Reynolds of Charlestown, Massachusetts, are not exactly poor."

"My father's dough. Belongs to him while he lives. And when he dies, he can do what he pleases with it. Bury it with him, if he wants to. I make my own."

"Sturdy Yanqui independence! But your father *is* a wealthy man?"

"You could call him that. The point's irrelevant. I love Alicia. I should love her equally if she hadn't a *centavo*. I categorically refuse to accept even a real, a sol, or if you have any smaller coins, one of them of that money. I'm sentimentalist enough to believe it would damn us forever. On the other hand, if she too seriously cares whether I have money or not, she can go to hell. As much as I love her, she can. Do you, Nena?"

"Peter! You know I would scrub floors for you. Or"—

and a flash of pure mischief lighted her eyes—"sell myself to other men and bring my earnings home to you. Would you like that, *Cielo?*"

"I'd break every bone in your lovely little body," Peter said. "Get on with it, Luis."

"All right. There is no point in my trying to convince you of my great love for the sovereign people. I sprang from their loins, as it were; I had to endure their manners, and their stench, far too long. Until Isabel rescued me. There's nothing ennobling about poverty, Reynolds—quite the contrary. The people are, you know, if you're not totally a fool, a disgusting conglomeration of exceedingly filthy and stupid animals. But, despite that, I fear me that Miguel's oppressively totalitarian state is an anachronism which cannot long survive."

"You've got something there," Peter said.

"So now, you, my dear Peter, offer me an out. I present Miguel, when he returns, with a *fait accompli.*"

"Returns?" Alicia said. "Returns from *where,* Luis?"

"The high seas, my dear Alicia. You know he has been threatening to leave Costa Verde to go to hell and go fishing as he does every year about this time. So when he awakens aboard *la Flor del Mar,* he will be told that I personally brought him aboard, which is true; and that he, in a moment of lucidity between profound dreams, ordered me to do so, which is not so."

"Oh!" Alicia said.

"The point is, he is unlikely to return until the fishing palls upon him. Which depends upon how the marlin and the sailfish are running. If his luck—and ours—is good, he'll stay away for two months, maybe three. Time enough for me to get you two safely entangled in the bonds of holy wedlock."

"Good God!" Peter said.

"You *are* of our faith, aren't you, Reynolds?"

"Yes," Peter said.

"Simplifies matters. Wait—I'll explain. The only way for the Republic to survive is to make an opening toward the Liberal Center, if not toward the Left. We push the happy couple forward. Under the liberalizing influence of our new Gringo brother-in-law, we slacken off a bit; let the *canalla* breathe—if they haven't forgotten how. Peter and Alicia—the popular young lovebirds: opening orphanages, dedicating schools, visiting the peasants with gifts of fertilizer and a tractor or two, say. Having babies. Oh, swarms of babies! Starting housing projects—low-rent, of course. The new public image, until the *muchedumbre*, which is as dumb as it is much, forgets. Neat, don't you think?"

"And," Peter said, "closing the Centers of Moral Correction and Social Re-education? Taking away all arms except maybe their truncheons from your goons?"

"Hard bargainer, aren't you, Reynolds? If you insist, even that."

"Good. But I don't insist. I can't."

"Meaning?"

"That I cannot marry Alicia."

Alicia sat up suddenly, staring into his face.

"Sorry, Nena; but it has to be said. I can't marry you. As much as I'd love to, I can't."

Her mouth was visibly trembling now.

"Because of—*her?*" she said.

"No. Not because of her."

"Then why, Peter?"

"Because on June Second, 1954, I married a Miss Constance Buckleigh in Our Lady of Mercy Church in Boston, Massachusetts. That the lady later left my bed and board in the company of an advertising executive who could have bought and sold me three times over even with my father's money thrown in, and who had, additionally, a position that allowed him to come home every night, which was the chief objection that Connie had to me, has nothing to do with it. Nor that she later obtained a Nevada divorce and, at least as far as civil law is concerned, legalized her position. Nor that she has since presented him with three splendid children. Canon law is explicit: So long as Miss Buckleigh lives, she remains my wife. And in la Republica de Costa Verde, there isn't any other kind."

Luis Sinnombre sat there. Then, very slowly, he smiled.

"A formidable obstacle, I'll admit. But not insurmountable," he said.

"And how do you propose to surmount it?" Peter said.

"Leave that to me, Peter! Alicia, you may take him home, if you like. Even bundle with him a bit more, if either of you feels up to it. Betimes, I shall pay a call on the Archbishop in the Ecclesiastical Palace. Clever old boy, the Archbishop. Expert on Canon law. Might come up with a fancy new grounds for an annulment, say—"

"Oh!" Alicia said.

"Now, dearest, you run along. Take your new fiancé home. Your Perhaps Brother will fix things up so you can marry him. But please, Dear, one thing—"

"Yes, Luis?" Alicia said.

"Try not to get too obviously pregnant too far ahead of time. You know how archbishops are. Stubborn old chaps. Always dreaming of picking up that final Cape and Mitre in Eternal Rome—"

"Good God!" Peter said.

"Don't worry about it, Reynolds. By the way, Alicia, I've already ordered all those people released, just as you requested. Except, of course, the old boy who tripped and fell into the garbage can. The garbage truck took him away by mistake. We'll compensate his family, of course. . . . What are you waiting for? Miguel is completely out of the way, unreachable except by radio; which is to say totally unreachable in this affair, since all telecommunications are controlled by the police, which I head. So run along. Divert yourselves hugely, with the proper precautions, of course. However little you may be disposed to trust me, you can trust my desire to stay alive and in power. So we have a community of interests: you want your sex bouts legalized and sanctified before God and man. So do I. What does it matter that our motivations differ? You heard me, go ahead!"

Peter stared at him.

"And, Amigo Peter—the Captain who conducted that inquisition has as of now been transferred to a highly unpleasant post in the South. The Sergeant has been broken to the ranks. They, believe me, exceeded their instructions by far—"

Peter went on looking at him. Then: "Thanks for nothing, Luis," he said.

Riding in the big car toward his flat, Peter didn't say anything. Alicia didn't either. From time to time he looked at her profile, studying it, trying to capture its unique quality. He supposed that, if you wanted to be strict about it, you could call her a homely little soul. Only he couldn't be strict about it; he was past being strict about anything so far as she was concerned. But·one thing was beyond argument: he had seen men go to the firing squad with more cheerful expressions on their faces than the one on Alicia's now. He went on watching her. She went on driving. Pulled the big Lincoln up before his door. Said:

"Good-by, Peter." She said it in Spanish, using *Adios!*— "To God."

"You mean 'till later on,' don't you? Or 'till tomorrow'?" Peter said. Those forms—*hasta luego* and *hasta mañana*— are a lot less final than *Adios!*, especially the way Alicia said it then. He didn't like the way she said it at all.

"No, I mean good-by, Peter," Alicia said.

"*Muñeca*—" Peter said.

"Good-by, Peter. *Adios!* Because there are some things I know. You see, they forced Emilio to marry me, too. Oh, not what you're thinking! I came virgin to my marriage bed. They have other means of persuasion, and the situation where I could justify to myself my she-goat's blood didn't exist then. I couldn't delude myself into thinking I was trying to save a life."

"Angel," Peter said.

"Angel! Don't blaspheme, Peter! Call me what I am, my mother's daughter. Your little bitch. In any case, Luis has spoiled it now. Again. I won't watch your eyes grow weary, trying to avoid mine, as Emilio's did. I won't go through that again, Peter. I-I used to try to invent—stratagems to—to force him to lie with me—to get me with the child I wanted with all my heart. He was all man, Peter. During our three years of marriage, he worked his way through the entire chorus line of el Teatro de la Comedia! But, when he started in on La Luna Azul, I—"

"You what, *Muñeca?*"

"Screamed and cursed him and threw one of my Latin women's vile temper tantrums. He sat there looking at me until I had no more breath left, or any tears. Then he said, he said—Ohhh, Peter!"

"He didn't say 'Ohhh, Peter!' I'm sure of that, Nena."

"No. He said very quietly: 'My dear Alicia, I gave you my name, which was to sully it enough. I have no intention of begetting monsters.' Then he walked out and left me there."

"He was a fool!" Peter said.

"No, *Cielo*, it is you who are a fool. If you had any sense, you'd leave me, too."

"Alicia, if you don't cut this out, I'm going to do more than that. I'm going to beat the very hell out of you!"

"Go ahead," she said; "I wouldn't care."

"Baby—" Peter said.

"No, Peter. Luis has spoiled it now. You were—beginning to love me a little, weren't you? Lies! Deception! Tricks! Always manipulating everyone. Or murdering those whom he cannot manipulate. So hear me well, Peter!"

"Yes, Alicia?"

"I will not marry you. No matter what Luis forces that poor old frightened man in the Ecclesiastical Palace to do or say. Not because I do not love you; but because I do—"

"Nena, Bébé, Infant!"

"You won't be forced to take me, Love. You won't be tied to this—this outcast and garbage of the world! This ugly little witch and daughter of witches! No! No! I can't, I won't, I won't!"

"All right. Romance is all over. Thanks for a lovely evening, Nena. And a few more scars."

"Ohhh, Peter!" she wailed.

"Putting aside for the moment my own feeling about the matter, answer me one thing, Angel."

"Don't call me Angel! What thing, Love?"

"Now that our wedding has become an affair of state to Luis, how do you propose to stop him, 'Licia?"

She looked at him.

"Do you not have another razor you can lend me?" she said. "Alicia!"

"No—that's her style—isn't it? So cheap, somehow. So mundane. No, Peter, *Cielo*, I—I shall enter the Carmelites. Peaceful, what? No fear. No hate. No—no *maldito* men!"

He grinned at her, suddenly.

"Nena," he said, "I wasn't going to, but now I think I'd better invite you to come upstairs with me."

She shook her head so violently that the tears jetted from her eyes in a semicircular spray.

"Upstairs," she whispered, "where *she* has been all these weeks? In *her* bed, Peter? I may be a Villalonga. I do have Isabela Cienmil's blood in my veins. But this species of vile vileness I am not, Love. Oh, Peter, can't you see there's no hope for us? That it's wrong? All wrong? *Ay, Jesus y Maria!* I—"

But he took her small face between his two hands and kissed her mouth.

She tore her face away from his. Said:

"And when she comes out of the hospital, what will you do, Peter? Tell me! What will you?"

"*Muñeca*, we'll cross that bridge when we get to it."

"No, *Cielo*. We have crossed it already. Now get out! Leave me in peace! *Leeeeve meeeee!*"

But he put his arms around her and drew her to him. His mouth hurt like hell, but he went on kissing her until she curled up against him, clinging to him and crying, and Concha, la Portera, came out of the house and stood beside the car.

"Doña Alicia," Concha said.

Alicia straightened up, blinking at Concha out of those enormous doe's eyes.

"*Sí*, Señora?" she said.

Concha dropped to her knees before the car. Her fat face

was flooded. She knelt there blubbering like a bleached whale. Then she put out her two fat red paws in a gesture that must have cost her more than charging into enemy fire costs a soldier. She grabbed Alicia's little hand and covered it with great slobbering kisses.

Alicia looked from Concha to Peter, her warm mouth making a jungle orchid, blooming into a perfectly rounded *Oh!* of pure astonishment.

"But, Señora, I do not comprehend—what is it that passes with you?"

"*Ay,* Doña Alicia!" Concha sobbed. "You are good! You are so good!" And Peter could measure the degree of Concha's emotion by the very forms of her speech. For not only did la Portera forget that a woman of the humble classes should have addressed so distinguished a lady in the third person, saying "The Lady is so good!" but she swept past the second degree of politeness and instead of calling Alicia *Usted,* just barely acceptable in a female concierge, called her *tú.*

Peter, who had summered and wintered with the Hispano-American aristocracy, held his breath. But Concha rushed heedlessly on: "You are so good, Doña Alicia! All the world loves you, for you have saved us all!"

Then Peter saw what there was in Alicia's face now; radiance. She put out her other hand and tugged Concha upward. La Portera lumbered to her feet. Then Doña Alicia Villalonga, Widow of Duarte y Marin, did a thing that had never been seen in Costa Verde from the day when, according to a completely lying tradition, Cristóbal Colón came ashore and unfurled the banner of Their Catholic Majesties before a group of stark-naked fisher Indians: she leaned out of the car and planted two soft, warm kisses on Concha's fat cheeks.

Concha clapped her two hands to her face. Swayed there. Then she whirled and ran back into the house. From every window on that street, the great shouted *Vivas!* roared.

"Long live Doña Alicia!" the people cried. "Long live our good, kind lady! Long live the Patroness of the Poor! Long live our Protectress!"

And now truly that warm, mobile, wonderful face was dissolved, was melted. She hid her face against Peter's chest, and lay there, crying, while the people made the heavens ring.

"Nena, I don't know whether you know it, but you've just won the revolution," Peter said.

11.

"Peter!" Judith said. "Your face!"

"Lord, Judy, I forgot," Peter said. "Should have left it home, shouldn't I?"

"I knew Vince was lying. I knew it. He swore that a big story had broken, down in the South, somewhere, and you ——Peter, tell me: What was her name?"

"What was whose name, Judy?"

"The dear little creature you got your countenance pushed into that meat grinder over."

"That, baby, is a long story."

"But not a true one. Peter, if you're going to lie to me, skip it. I knew damn well that if they kept me in here another week, you'd start in to investigate the local talent! But, Lover Boy, couldn't you have picked a single gal? From the way you look, this one must be married to King Kong!"

"Judy, baby, about dames, down here they shoot a guy. This lesson was purely political. I got caught accidental, like a dragnet-type raid. And Miguelito's Boy Scouts thought I was refusing to answer questions I didn't know the answer to. Hell, I didn't even understand the questions. This morning they released me with apologies. Risks of the profession, girl friend."

"Peter—how much of the truth are you telling me now?"

"About twenty-five per cent, Judy. The other seventy-five, I'd just as soon you didn't know in case they start getting inquisitive again. When it comes to politics, all that Latin gallantry sort of takes a holiday. Whatever else they may do to this pan of mine falls under the heading of gilding the lily by now; but nobody ever taught these goons they shouldn't play rough with girls—"

"Peter, is it true that they automatically rape all the women prisoners?"

"So I've heard."

"Oh, good! Look, Lover, if you don't get me out of this den of chastity right away, I'm going to commit a political offense —like screaming 'Down with The Leader!' at the top of my lungs."

"Judy, for God's sake!"

"Oh, Peter—just think! All those big, strong policemen!"

"Sorry, baby; but my sense of humor's way off today. I grant you that, for a healthy girl, being raped isn't all that godawful. But these types are graduate sadists. I don't think even your definition of fun and games includes having your nipples burned with cigarette butts, or your vaginal tract packed with broken glass."

"Judas!" Judith said.

"I've been trying to get into one of those correction centers to try to see if I couldn't sneak a few shots so that later on I'll be able to prove what goes on down here. But so far, no good. Latin America is one of the world's worst beats, Judy. Down here the choice isn't between good and bad, but between bad and worse. No, between worse and worst. You have a perfect demonstration of Malthusian principles, under a religious hierarchy which makes any effective birth control program impossible. You have a wealthy upper class —in Costa Verde, twenty-five families own seventy-two per cent of the arable land—whose response not only to the legitimate demands of the lower orders, but also to any slight amelioration whatsoever, is, 'Screw you, Jack!' Who, while keeping not two, but three sets of books, and managing to escape paying taxes entirely, swear at us because our contribution to their welfare isn't greater. You have no effective middle class. You have not rich and poor, but plutocrats and the starving. And, on the other hand, you have the Commies. Who promise the moon and the stars, and deliver rocket bases and the rationing of even those miserable foodstuffs formerly available to the hungry. Who, after liquidating the poor, goddam noble, deluded kids they've sucked in by their propaganda and used as cannon fodder to gain their ends—like Juan and Pepe and Federico, and even that poor bastard Jacinto—will substitute for the crude job those gorillas did to my face a subtler kind of torture, one that gets down to where a man lives, to the ultimate question: Just what the hell am I?"

"Peter," Judith whispered, "those coppers have discouraged you, haven't they?"

"Not just them. Human nature discourages me. Let's change this subject. When does Vince say I can bail you out of this Saintly Atmosphere?"

"Friday. Day after tomorrow. Peter, darling, are you in good shape?"

"Middling, Judy. Middling. Miguelito's playmates don't leave a guy feeling like the power and the glory."

"Peter—"

"Yes, Judy?"

"Kiss me. Then go home. Go to bed. Alone. Get some sleep. Eat lots and lots—of eggs. It's eggs that little boys are supposed to eat to build them up, isn't it? And oysters. Eat two dozen oysters. Because, Lover Boy, you're going to need your strength!"

When he came out of the hospital, he found Tim O'Rourke waiting for him, sitting behind a big black cigar in a rented car.

"Peter," he said, "how much of it is true, and even if it is, what sense does it make?"

Peter looked at him.

"None—to both questions," he said.

"I was going home this Monday. And then this breaks. Carloads of uniformed throwbacks arresting a whole streetful of people. And why? Our *Pe-tah's* been busy again! *Hayzus,* as they say down here, why don't you keep still, boy?"

"I do," Peter said. "Just like a mouse."

"Yeah. I'll bet. The kind of mouse that has dames screaming and pulling up their skirts. And from the looks of what's left of your manly beauty, the cats down here play awful rough when they catch friend mouse up to his mousie tricks. Look, Pete, I don't know how, or why, or with what you do it; but tell me: Is it true?"

"Is what true, Tim?"

"*His* sister! *His!* Cute little monkey-faced babe with lips that would keep her out of the University of Alabama. That one? True or false?"

"Tim," Peter said, "you'd better change your brand."

"Don't know why; but she sends me, brother! Just like Judy does. No, more. Is it that great minds move in similar channels?"

"Could be," Peter said.

"Then you admit—"

"I admit nothing, friend."

"You wouldn't!" Tim grinned. "But, Peter the Mouse—or rather Brother Rat—just look what's coming around the corner!"

Peter looked in the rear-view mirror of the rented Ford. The white Lincoln pulled up behind him, so close that its front bumpers almost touched the Ford's rear ones.

"Oh, hell!" Peter said.

Alicia got out of the Lincoln. She had on a white sharkskin suit. The suit was another little marvel. With her in it, it made two marvels. At least two. Maybe more. Her heels clicked decisively on the sidewalk as she headed toward the door of the building in which Peter lived.

Tim put his head out of the window.

"Señora de Duarte!" he called.

Alicia stopped; turned.

"Pardon me, Señora," Tim said, in his quite good Spanish, "but if you're looking for Peter the Rat, here he is!"

Alicia came toward the Ford. Tim got out of it at once. So did Peter. He came around the other side to meet Alicia. Put out his hand to her; but she didn't take it. She went up on tiptoe and kissed his mouth.

"Oh, Peter, *Cielo*, I have been so worried," she said. "I have been calling you all day—"

"Alicia," Peter said, "may I present a friend?"

"But of course!" Alicia said; then, seeing Tim's red, Irish face, she switched at once into English, which she spoke in musical little trills and bursts, and—probably because she had learned it in Madrid—with a marked British accent. "I am so sorry, Señor. It was not my intention to be rude; but I was so preoccupied with the *asunto*—affaire, no?—of Peter, that . . ."

"I noticed that, Señora," Tim said.

"This," Peter said, "is the Señor Timothy O'Rourke. He is Irish-American. A reporter, like me. But since he now has first cousins in the White House, he's got all the advantages."

Alicia's dark eyes widened.

"Oh, then he can help us, *Cielo!*" she said. "If he is a first cousin of your President, why—"

"Niña," Peter said, "I made a joke. A bad joke."

"Not so fast, *Cielo!*" Tim said. "Oh, brother, just wait till I tell the types on your night desk that the babes down here call you Heaven. Old Heavenly Pete!"

"You want me to laugh? Comic? Ha! I just laughed. You got something to say, say it."

"Seriously, Peter, maybe I *could* help you lovebirds. I'm going home next week. I could get a message out, if that's what you need."

Alicia looked at Peter.

"Yes," Peter said. "One can trust Tim."

"Then, *Cielo*, may we not ascend to your flat, all three of us, where we can talk?"

Peter stopped.

"I think they may have hung a few microphones in strategic locations by now," he said.

"No," Alicia said. "Colonel Lopez gave the order that you were to be removed from close surveillance. And I have an enormous desire to see your flat."

Tim looked at them both.

"Doña Alicia," he said, "are you sure you're being wise? In any country such as this, the arming of scandals necessitates very little—"

Alicia smiled. But that smile was the saddest thing in the whole world.

"The scandal has already been armed, Don Timoteo. And of reputation, I no longer have any left to lose. So let us go very quickly up the stairs so that *quiza* we may prevent crime from being added to what so far is merely the minor sin of evil thoughts."

"Crime?" Peter said.

"Yes, Love. Now come that we may speak of it."

"Wait a minute," Tim said. "Doña Alicia, don't you think it would be wise to put up the top of your car, and lock it, before we go? Why, you've even left the keys in the ignition—"

"I always do leave them thus," Alicia said, "in order to evade having to search for them amid ten thousand other useless things in my handbag. There is absolutely no danger, Don Timoteo; this car is too well known. Who would be so ungrateful as to steal the automobile of the sister of the Ever Generous Benefactor of the People of Costa Verde? Besides, in this *barrio* at least, the people love me. Don't they, *Cielo*?"

"Yes," Peter said.

He opened the door for them. Alicia walked straight across the room and picked up Judith's photograph from where it stood on Peter's desk. She stood there studying it, a long, long time. When she put it down and turned to him, Peter could see the tears in her eyes.

"Now, Nena—" he said.

"It is all right," she said; "a weakness, no? I should not

have come up here. I have no right even to—to this stupid
jealousy I cannot dominate. Don Timoteo, the women of
your country are not so foolish, are they? No matter. I love
Peter. I have no shame of that. But to share him with this
faded *viciosa* upon terms of equality—one concubine is as
good as another, no?—that is too shameful. And yet—and
yet I am here to prevent a thing from happening that would
make it possible for him to marry me and take away my
shame."

"Would your brother consent to such a marriage, Doña
Alicia?" Tim said.

"No. But Luis thinks to arrange it before he returns. And
afterwards to convince Miguel—wrongly I am sure—that
through Peter he can influence the attitude of your country
toward ours—"

"Now I get it!" Tim said. "Your Old Man still pulls a lot of
weight around the State Department, doesn't he?"

"I don't think you do. It's a very complicated oversimpli-
fication," Peter said.

"Peter," Alicia said, "do you know the address of your-
your wife?"

"Oh, brother!" Tim said. "So you've been holding out on
me again, Peter Pan! Not only has the guy got a harem down
here, but—"

"If you mean my ex-wife, yes," Peter said.

"A wife can never be *ex*, Peter. Or very rarely. Then there
are special circumstances which permit an annulment. Beyond that, no. That she left you, played the whore, is a
matter for her conscience; but it does not dissolve your
bonds, as you know very well. There is only one way that
you can be free of her. The way with which Luis is occupy-
ing himself now."

"Good God!" Peter said.

"Amen!" Alicia said, and crossed herself. "Yes, Peter,
Love; Luis has thought of that. You see, the Archbishop has
proved difficult. He is an old man and tired and afraid. But
now he has Padre Pío once more at his side, which makes a
difference. Because of that, Luis has had to forego his dream

that the Archbishop would grant you an annulment of your marriage. And you—"

"And I?" Peter said.

"Must give to Don Timoteo here, the address of your faithless wife. So that he may warn her, and him who calls himself her husband, and also the police of the state or province wherein she resides. Or else—"

"Nena, don't you think you exaggerate a bit?"

"Do you remember the case of Professor Hernandez?"

"Good God!" Peter said again.

"Hernandez? Hernandez?" Tim said. "Rings a bell. Saay! Wasn't he a refugee from down here, who was teaching Spanish at City College, and sort of wound up missing?"

"He," Alicia said, "was flown to Ciudad Villalonga in an airplane. After he had been taken by two thugs in the very mouth of the Metro—the Subway—on one of your busiest streets. He was drugged, brought to Flushing Meadows Airport in an ambulance. The pilot of the aircraft filed a false flight plan, telling the authorities that he was taking the sick man to a clinic in Massachusetts. Instead, he flew south. Brought the poor man here. It is said that Dr. Hernandez could be heard—screaming—for days—before they grew tired and let him die."

"Who told you that?" Peter said.

"My mother. She witnessed it." She opened her bag. Took out a pack of cigarettes—Players. Peter lit her cigarette for her.

"And where is your mother now?" he said.

"She is a prisoner. In a luxurious flat she is not allowed to leave—since this of her drunkenness and vile behavior at your embassy. Please, Peter, give him the address."

"All right," Peter said. He took out his pen. Tore a sheet of paper from his address book, and wrote on it. Passed the paper to Tim.

Tim looked at it. Folded it; put it in his pocket. Turned to Alicia.

"You don't even know her," he said; "and yet—"

"I know Peter," Alicia said; "which is enough."

"Meaning?" Peter said.

"That I will not have you look at me with accusing eyes. Or see in them speculation over what sort of monsters I may bear you, fruits of a marriage based upon a murdered woman's blood. No, Peter—all that is possible between us is sin. Sin I shall one day have strength enough, grace enough to give up. But now—"

"Now?" Peter said.

She turned her face toward Tim.

"Don Timoteo," she said, "would you think too ill of me if I asked you to leave us here—alone?"

"Not at all," Tim said, and stood up.

"Tim, boy," Peter said. "I——"

"You've got it rough, son," Tim said. "Don't worry; I'll do what I can—"

She lay there on the sofa in his arms. Put up her hands and touched his battered face. Then her little head lifted. Her nostrils flared. She got up. Walked through the door into his bedroom. Stood there staring at all those flasks and jars. Pulled open a drawer. Lifted a handful of gossamer. Of silken cobwebs and mists and air. Let them fall. Turned to the closet. Jerked wide the door. The rich, insidious odor of Judith's special *Peut'être* perfume came out from the rows and rows of dresses hanging there.

"Ohhhh!" Alicia said, and bolted for the door. In it, she stopped, without even turning her face:

"Peter—"

"*Muñeca?*"

"Come with me?"

"Where?"

"Oh, I do not know. To the forest, to the swamps. To a wild place where you can take me like an animal upon the ground. But not—not here! Not in this little flat that smells of her. Not where her presence moves between us like a ghost. Oh, Peter, *amor, Cielo,* I——"

Peter got up. Took her arm. Quietly they went back down the stairs.

From where they were now, they could see the volcano. It jetted fire. The clouds above it were angry, red.

"The old gods," Alicia said. "There are times, Peter, that I believe in them."

"Do you?" Peter said.

"Sí. It is sinful of me, I know. But I have too much Tluscola in my veins. Zopo is amused. Now he is chuckling to himself at the sins and follies of men. One night he will laugh. And his laughter will destroy the world."

Peter looked up at the volcano.

"You just might have something there," he said.

"Peter—" Alicia said.

"Yes, Nena?"

"I-I pray for you—for us. Which is a kind of blasphemy, no? For how can one pray while in a state of sin? For to want you as I do is a sin. And such a sin for which forgiveness is not possible, since to be pardoned one must repent. And how can I repent of loving you? Oh, Peter, *Cielo*, I—"

"Don't cry, Nena. This is a great thing that you have. I envy you."

"You envy me? Why, Peter?"

"Because you have this simplicity. As though there had been neither time nor history. As though the world had stopped six hundred years ago. I envy you these wondrous, childlike things you have: Sin. And remorse. And repentance."

She stared at him.

"You have them not?"

"No, Nena."

"But, Peter—"

"Let us not speak of it. There are no words. Or too many. What they add up to is vacancy. A universe from which all gods have fled. Except perhaps Shiva."

"Shiva?" she said.

"A monster of a Hindu god. With many arms. Dancing upon the prostrate world. The Destroyer."

"Oh!" she said.

"Hell," he said. "I talk rot. Nena!"

"Yes, Peter?"

"Shall I take you back now?"

"Yes. Because it is spoiled, no? Our night. Because I cannot get the smell of that scent of hers out of my nostrils. How is it called, Peter?"

"*Peut'être.*"

"*Peut'être?*"

"Yes. *Peut'être*, which means *tal vez*, which means *quiza*, which means perhaps, which means maybe. Like life."

"Oh," she said, "if I had a perfume made, it would be for you. And I would call it *Siempre.*"

"*Siempre*—Forever. Or *Jamás*—Never?"

"Oh, Peter, *Cielo*, you are in a mood! I am sorry. Do you want me to-to—If you desire it, I . . ."

"No, Nena."

"Oh!" she said.

"Let's just sit here and look at the volcano. For one thing, I'm tired; for another—Hell, Nena; can't we just be?"

"Yes," she whispered, "only——"

But he reached out suddenly and gripped her wrist. Because something rose-white and enormous was rising behind them. It filled the rear-view mirror completely, shutting out the dark.

"Pe—" she began; but he clamped his other hand over her mouth. Turned her loose, laying a warning finger across his own lips. Opened the door. Got out. Saw that what had risen behind them was the Lincoln's trunk lid. But, by then, it was too late.

"No," the voice said; "the time for being is over. Comrade."

"Ohhh!" Alicia said.

"The time for many things is over. You disappoint me, Comrade Reporter. I had the intention to wait until you were mounted, in the saddle, and then remove you. Take your place. Let you divert yourself by watching—"

"As you did with the Indian girl, Jacinto?" Peter said.

"Oh, I'm cured of that, Amigo! Twenty nights in The Blue Moon cured me. But now there is no time. The pretty Alicia will pardon my lack of gallantry. I will teach her the delights of love another day. Tonight, there are more important things to do."

"Such as?" Peter said.

"Later. First, do you feel heroic tonight, Comrade?"

"Hell, no! And point that burp gun some other way, won't you? It makes me nervous."

"Good. Then I shall not have to make the so-very-pretty Alicia twice a widow, and only once a bride?"

"No," Peter said.

"Good, again. From the looks of your face, Peter—you should be more inclined to cooperate with me by now."

"With the murderer of Pepe? Why should I trust you, Jacinto?"

"I have much sorrow of that," Jacinto said; "but trust me —you must, or die. Now listen to me carefully—"

"Wait," Peter said; "tell me one thing, Jacinto: How the devil did you get into the trunk of this car?"

"Oh, Peter!" Alicia said, "the keys! Just as Don Timoteo said, I should have—"

"Do not blame yourself, little Monkeyface," Jacinto laughed; "you did nothing more than save me five minutes. The five minutes it would have taken me to open the trunk in any event. And, before I forget, if you cooperate with me, upon your return you will find the spare tire in the hall of your building. I put it there. I needed the space."

"I see," Peter said. "Go on, Jacinto. What do you want of us?"

"You will get in the car and drive to the military air base. But slowly, Amigo. You have already given me heart failure more than three times on the way here. Of course, most of the stuff I put into the trunk of your car is plastic, which requires fire to explode. But I have not too much security about the pins of those Czech-fabricated grenades. They never fail to fire; but often they go off ahead of time—"

"*Dios mío!*" Alicia said.

"God does not exist, Comrade Sister of the Dictator. Now

listen to me, while I explain it. You, Peter, will drive straight for the gate of the military airport."

"And?" Peter said.

"When the guard stops you, you, Doña Alicia, will lean out."

"And?" Peter said again.

"She will say that you, her fiancé, has expressed a desire to see the aircraft."

"At this hour?"

"At this hour. The great are always whimsical, no?"

"All right," Peter said.

"You will drive the car onto the base. Park it by one of the hangars. Get out. I shall remain hidden between the seats. But you will remember that this Sten gun can cut through the backs of the seats quite easily."

"Then?" Peter said.

"The aviators will gallantly show you about the base. If you are wise, you will accept their invitation to drink with them. You will behave quite normally; and say nothing of my presence, here. You will leave the air base in the car. By then, neither I nor the explosives will be in it. This, if you are wise."

"And if I am stupid?"

"You will betray me. And I shall die. But the results will be the same. I shall still destroy that base. There will be only one difference."

"And that is?"

"I shall shoot Doña Alicia. I make this choice now, because I know from experience you are willing to risk your life, Peter. Somehow, I do not believe you will risk hers."

"You've got something there, chum," Peter said.

Peter looked at Alicia where she sat, surrounded by the pilots. They weren't all there, of course. Only one of the four aces who flew the pursuit planes, and nine of the sixteen others who piloted the lumbering transports which also served Miguel Villalonga as bombers were present. The rest were out on the town. Which was just as well.

"Nena," he said, "excuse yourself for a moment. I have a thing to say to you."

She came to him at once. He took her hand, led her to the door.

"We stay," he said. "There is an enormous risk; but it is better that we run it than to accept the certainty that we will be connected with the events if they occur after we have departed. When the shooting starts, fall to the floor. I do not think Jacinto can shoot us all; but—"

"Now look, Don Pedro!" one of the pilots called out, "Time! You're being damned selfish, y'know. After all, you have her company all the time."

"Should we tell them?" Alicia said.

"No. Your kind-hearted brother has bombed too many poor villages of innocent Indians with these aircraft now. Let him lose them! Why—"

"Time, Don Pedro; time!" the pilots called.

Smiling, Peter released her arm. She went back toward the group of pilots. The way she walked was something to see.

The lone pursuit pilot came up to Peter. He was smiling.

"It seems I owe you an apology, Don Pedro," he said.

"I'm sure I don't know for what," Peter said.

"Not too long ago," the pilot said, "I bombed and strafed two horsemen on a mountain road . . ."

Peter looked at him.

"Great sport, wasn't it?" he said.

"Well, of course, I can appreciate that from your end it might—"

"And I can appreciate it from yours," Peter said, smiling still. "I didn't, before. Throughout the Korean War, I was an infantryman. Saw things too close up. Since then, I've learned to fly. I hold a limited commercial ticket now. So I know how it is upstairs, Amigo. A man doesn't look human, does he? Even on horseback. The perspective plays tricks. The height, the speed. At five hundred kilometers an hour, it isn't possible to see the precise details. Only—"

"Only what, Don Pedro?"

"I was an infantryman, so I remember them. The shredded flesh. The pink coils of guts. How Juan screamed—because he had a name, you see; his mother called him Juan—and went on screaming almost until he died. I remember the spinning human insects at the vortex of a small-sized hell of napalm. I, Captain, have seen—quite recently—manflesh bubble and char and stink while that black, blistering dummy of tar twisting in the middle of your chemical holocaust had still air enough in his lungs to scream his guts out with. I know, I know; you get yours, too; you young, Jovian riders of thunderbolts. But it's over very fast for you—even when you light the day with flame. And to scribe one's end across half of heaven is different in quality from puking up one's life into the mud. Such an end is glorious, don't you think?"

"The fortunes of war, Don Pedro. I think you're being unfair to us, actually. You came out alive, so you shouldn't have any complaints . . ."

"While you do?" Peter said.

"Yes! If we only had jets! I do not see why your government is so stingy with us, Reynolds. After all, we are the number-one anti-Communist force in Latin America. And Castro has his MIGs!"

Peter turned to the window. The four pursuits stood on the tarmac. The Republic P-47 was closest to him. Then the Mustang. Then the two Corsairs. The DC 3s were in the hangars.

Peter saw the tiny figure come running out of the hangar. He turned back to the pilot.

"I beg your pardon?" he said. "I don't follow that argument. There is no quarrel between Costa Verde and Cuba."

"No quarrel!" the pilot said. "Why—"

And all the night roared. Vomited flame.

The pilots rushed through the door.

Peter raced toward Alicia.

"Get down!" he said. "On the floor! Flat!"

"Peter!" she wailed.

He caught her by the waist. Threw her down. Fell beside her.

Just outside the door the Sten gun stuttered. They could hear the pilots scream. The windows crashed in. Dissolved into powdered glass. A line of splinters plowed itself across the floor, marching toward them. Peter gripped Alicia to him, hard, rolled with her, putting his body between her and that burst. She moaned a little. The next burst went over them, clipped clods of plaster from the walls. Then there was silence.

Peter crawled toward the window. Raised his head. Saw Jacinto lob a grenade into the open hatch of the Thunderbolt. Another. The fat-bellied pursuit lifted from the tarmac. Came down in two halves. Blazed. And now the Mustang split itself down the fuselage, spewed around, trailing flame. The two crank-winged Vought Corsairs dissolved into fire. The flames stood straight up three hundred meters. The tarmac was like day.

Black figures poured out of the blazing hangars. Then the burning gasoline got to the wing guns of the wrecked planes. The fifty-caliber Brownings started talking, chuckling to one another with mindless, murderous laughter. The tracers were beautiful. They cut down the running men as though they had been aimed.

Peter crawled back to Alicia.

"Scratch one air force!" he said. "Viva Jacinto!"

She didn't answer him.

"Come on, Nena!" he said. "We'd better get out of here!"

He heard her voice. It was curiously faint.

"*Cielo*—" she said

"Yes, Infant?"

"Kiss me?"

"Lord God, Alicia!"

Her hand came away from her side. She held it out to him. He saw now what it was filled with. What dripped between her fingers.

"Alicia!" he screamed.

"Kiss me?" she said again.

He kissed her mouth. It was very cold.

"Infant, Nena, Bébé," he wept. "Oh, Christ! Oh God, Oh Jesus—why? God damn it, why?"

"Peter——"

"Nena?"

"They laughed. The old gods. They—"

But he was up by then, had her in his arms, was racing for the door, jumping the sprawl of bodies that lay in it, pounding through that firelit hell to the Lincoln. Got to it. Saw it hadn't any windshield. The front seat was snowy with powdered glass. A line of black holes were stitched along its side. But he got into it anyhow. Laid her down beside him, her head resting on his lap. Turned the key. The motor caught.

He bent the Lincoln around in a screaming turn, racing for the gates. He saw the sentries standing there firing at the car. He ducked as low as he could and slammed the accelerator to the floor. Barreled through the wildly leaping sentries, through that gate out onto the road. Sitting there now, his eyes flooded, blind, he snaked the big car through turns it was never made to take at the speed it was going now.

She lay there looking up at him, her eyes wide, smiling a little.

By the time he got to the hospital there were four police jeeps behind him and two motorcycle police at his side. When he slammed the Lincoln to a stop, they surrounded him, pistols drawn.

He ignored them; bent and picked Alicia up. They fell back, staring at the dark, exotic flower, blooming through the white sharkskin suit at the level of her waist. Then they came roaring in. Her voice stopped them.

"No!" she said. "It is nothing—a scratch. Let us alone! Oh, Peter, Love—"

Then she fainted.

Peter was borne through the doors of the hospital on the crest of a green-clad wave. Hands came out of a white blur and took Alicia away from him. Other hands reached out and pinioned his wrists. Then one of them, an officer from his voice, said:

"Do not be fools! Look at his face!"

They stared at him. Turned him loose. Fell back. It was like the movements of a satanic ballet.

"Don Pedro," one of them said, "pardon. We did not think—"

" 'Sall right," Peter said.

He sat down, suddenly. He had to. He sat there with the tears on his face for three eons and one eternity. Then Vicente Gomez came through the door, said:

"Peter—she's all right. A bullet plowed along her side. Made a furrow. Bloody mess, but not dangerous. Snap out of it, will you?"

"Thanks, Vince," Peter said. But he didn't stop crying. He couldn't.

Vince bent over him.

"Sister!" he called.

"Yes, Doctor?" the nursing sister said.

"Prepare a room. He's in shock. I'm going to give him a shot. One that will put him out until day after tomorrow."

"Thanks, Vince," Peter said again.

12.

Leaving the hospital with Judith in a taxi, Peter saw that all the streets were crawling with uniformed policemen. They were stopped four times in three blocks, and the identity cards which were *de rigueur* for any foreigner remaining more than three weeks in Costa Verde carefully examined. But the fourth time, the officer commanding the Security Police was the Colonel Lopez who had kept apart from Peter's interrogation.

"Look, Colonel," Peter said, "we really would like to get home before night, you know."

The Colonel smiled. Took a large piece of paper from his brief case. It had the Costa Verdian shield on it. Seals. Stamps. Ribbons. It was as official-looking as all hell. He scribbled on it briefly. Took out a roll of Scotch tape and stuck it onto the inside of the windshield of the taxi.

"There, Don Pedro," he said; "you won't be stopped any more. Just remember to make the *taxista* give you back that permit when you leave the cab. Remind him that if he doesn't, he'll be shot. *Adios!*"

"*Adios!*" Peter said. "Many thanks, Colonel . . ."

"This," Judith said, "is one hell of a joint, isn't it? What are they all so jumpy about?"

"They've got troubles, Judy—now more than ever."

And now, as the taxi moved off, purring past one roadblock after another, slowing just enough for the police to see all those ribbons, stamps, and seals shining through the windshield, Peter could feel the stiff square of cardboard in his inside coat pocket. The sister had brought it to the room in the hospital in which he lay, fighting to wake from that little death Vince Gomez had slipped into his veins. Only it had been in an envelope then. He had torn open the envelope and a note had fallen out of it, first. He picked up the note and read.

"For you. I did not dare give it to you last night. Your Alicia."

It was a post-card-size photograph of her. It hadn't been retouched at all, which meant, if anything, that she had finally convinced herself that he actually did like the way she looked. And, for that very reason, the photographer had produced a little masterpiece. Given the materials he had to work with: Alicia's peculiarly exquisite sculptural quality; her lack of a line-blurring excess of flesh; the haunting purity of the planes, angles, shadow-catching hollows of her tribal fetish of a face, dramatically bisected by the startling warm-soft contradiction of her mouth—and add to all that the simple fact that the essential ingredient of any masterpiece is the truth, the photographer could hardly have missed. And hadn't. Those eyes of Nefertiti, Astarte, almond-shaped, doe-tender, effortlessly resolving the antithesis of utter blackness and total luminosity, caressing his face out of that light-transformed gelatinous mass of silver salts; that imperial lily stalk of a throat swaying toward him; that regal, queenly little head, fixed in an attitude of total attention under that saucy, mocking little-bad-boy's cut of hair—all these unlive counterparts of things that, living, he loved, would, he knew, so long as sight and sense and memory dwelt in him, be able to stop his mind, his heart.

Across the bottom, she had scrawled in a tall, angular Gothic script that somehow defined her *Siempre, tu Alicia* —"Forever, your Alicia." And he had the feeling that that was nothing less than true; but instead of exalting him, it made him feel like dirt.

He could see Judith's absolutely perfect profile against the window of the taxi. He said, under his breath: "Oh, god-dam!"

Judith turned toward him.

"What did you say, Peter?" she said.

"Nothing," Peter said.

"Peter—"

"Yes, Judy?"

"You have such rotten luck, don't you?"

"Judy baby, you've lost me already. Climb down off that oblique tangent, will you?"

"I lost you a long time ago, Peter. When I first started in to make a career of being a bitch."

He looked at her.

"Baby, can't we talk about something else?"

"No. It has to be said. You have such rotten luck, my poor old battered darling. Just think—if I had died, you'd have been rid of me. Left with a first-class memory: Judith Lovell died for me. Killed herself because I wasn't there—"

"Baby."

"Yes, Peter?"

"That won't wash."

"I know it won't. The truth is always nasty, brutish, and short. Who said that?"

"Hobbes. Hume. One of the two; I can never remember which. Only he wasn't talking about the truth. He was replying to Jean-Jacques Rousseau's Noble Savage concept. The exact quotation is, I believe: 'Man in a state of nature is nasty, brutish, and short.'"

"He had something there. The truth in my case is that I've tried to kill myself several times. Usually for the same reason: Life had started to taste like vomit again. That nothing anybody did or said had any sense to it, any meaning. That everything I did ended with me puking my guts up. That waking up with a hangover, or with the screaming meemies from having smoked half a pack of reefers, or with some hairy stinking naked ape beside me all produced the same effect: that this was always where I came in on the goddam picture. The fornicating merry-go-round. The life is circular. That 'the future is only the past again, entered through another gate . . .' Who said that, Peter?"

"Oscar Wilde."

"*He* would. I even tried that, once."

"Tried what once?"

"Sleeping with another dame. No goddam good. Nothing she could do that a sixteen-year-old boy couldn't do better, not to mention a man. Only, Peter, darling, will you permit me a slightly less unpleasant truth?"

"Yes, Judy."

"The only time I ever tried to kill myself, meaning it, was *this* time."

"Oh!" Peter said.

"Oh, what?" Judith said.

"Oh, hell."

"Amen. The other times, I scratched my wrists. Or took sleeping pills. But this time I picked up that cool, sweet blade and really dug it in where it'd do some good."

"Judy, please!"

"And even then, it didn't work out. I missed the big artery. I didn't die. So you're stuck with me again."

"You hear me screaming?"

"No. You're too goddam sweet. Too good. Oh, Peter, I—"

"Now, Judy—"

"When you came into my room this morning to take me home, it—Say, Peter! I know what it is I've been meaning to ask you! What *was* all that uproar last night? People yelling their heads off over some Doña Alicia? Who is Doña Alicia? And what the hell were they saying? I heard something about Don Pedro, too. And *foo seel lah do. Tee rah tay ohs.* What the devil was all that? And policemen all over everything this morning. Why, darling?"

"Judy baby, do me a favor?"

"What kind, Lover?"

"Never learn Spanish. Promise me?"

"Oh!" she said. "Pedro—Peter. You!"

"Baby, there are hundreds of guys named Pedro down here."

"Peter—what did happen? The truth, now."

"Somebody took a shot at His Nibs' sister. Wounded her slightly. That's all I know."

"*Foo seel lah do.* From *fusil*—a gun! That was it. And that other word?"

"*Tirateos*—a volley of shots. Crossfire."

"And Don Pedro?"

"You'd better ask the lady that, if you ever meet her. I wouldn't know."

"All right. It sounds like the truth. Not very likely for you to get mixed up with the Boss' sister. The girlies at The Blue Moon and creatures like me are more your style."

"Gee, Toots, thanks!" Peter said.

"Because you're a softie. You don't know how to say no. Instead of telling us '*Screw you*, Jill!' you go ahead and do it for us—so sweetly, nicely, tenderly, that we never got over it. Ever since Madrid I've known that. Remember what I did when I got off the plane in Mexico City, after you'd stuck your neck in a sling for me again?"

"Yes, you cried."

"Do you know why I cried, Peter?"

"No," Peter said. "Besides, you're going to tell me anyhow; and at some length—"

"Right. Peter, tell him to drive around a while. I don't feel like going home yet. I do want to tell you things. All the things I've never been able to say before. Only, I'm back from the Valley of the Shadow now, so maybe I can."

"All right," Peter said, and instructed the driver, who grinned at him, said:

"Of course, Señor! With this permit we can go anywhere!"

"Now where were we?" Peter said.

"The reason why I cried. You. There you were outside the Customs stall. So big. Rock-solid, steady. So good. So goddam good. Standing up there amid all the rubble—"

He looked at her.

"What rubble?" he said.

"My rubble. The years, Peter. You know, all the wasted years. All the time I've spent helling around, collecting bodies, faces. Funny how they all run together, now. But yours never did. Maybe because you look like a bulldog or a prizefighter. So ugly. Did I ever tell you how ugly you are?"

"No," Peter said, "you never did."

"You are. Horrid. A mug to frighten children. But such nice eyes. Brown. Warm. Kind."

"Is this the latest technique, Judy?" Peter said.

"No. Or if so, it's awful. What I'm trying to say is the same thing I couldn't say when I got off that plane in Mexico two months ago, now. Still can't say it. I've misused those particular words too often. Taken all the shine off them. And now that I mean them, honestly and truly and awfully mean them, they choke me."

"What words, Judy?" Peter said.

"I can't. They sound so goddam phony. All right. When I came out that door of the Customs in Mexico, it hit me. For the first time, I mean. Harder than now. By now, I'm almost used to it. I stood there with my heart in my hand —my battered, vagrant, shopworn heart—and tears in my eyes—real ones, not glycerine—and was literally sick with the realization that all I've been doing all these years was trying to find an adequate substitute for you. A stand-in. A double. A replica. A replacement. Only there aren't any. And as phony, fake, incredible as it sounds, even to me, what I wanted to say to you in Mexico and couldn't, because I didn't think I could put the bit across convincingly is: 'I love you, Peter.' You know, L-O-V-E. The emotion that the ingenue feels for the hero. And you don't spell it S-E-X. At least not all the time. When that detail came around like a rabbit punch, I went into shock a little, I think. So now, finally, I've said it. And please forgive me for being so presumptuous . . ."

Peter didn't say anything. There was, at that moment, nothing to be said. He could feel Alicia's photo in his jacket pocket. It was growing. In a little while it was going to burst through the cloth. Through his heart.

But Judith was talking again.

"It hit me and I cried. The contrast. After all the phonies and the creeps, you. Just like I remembered you. No better. A little uglier, a little more battered. But aged so beautifully like a good no-frills Burgundy. Did Dekov tell you how much time I spent talking about you?"

"Yes," Peter said.

"He called you my point of no return. My life's fatal divergence. Oh, Peter, why didn't you just beat the hell out of me in Madrid that time and make me stay? I wanted to! I wanted to so goddam bad . . ."

"You didn't act like it," Peter said.

"I know. I never do. If I acted the way I should, or the way I really want to— Funny. They're always the same. Did you know that? I don't *want* to do the perfectly dreadful things I do. I want—"

"What, Judy?"

"To be kept warm and safe. Protected. Told what to do. I love you, darling. Only you spell it *need*. Oh, Peter! That really takes the shine off, doesn't it? I'm being honest again. Bad habit, being honest."

"No," Peter said. "It's a good one, Judy."

"Peter—"

"Yes, Judith?"

"Take me home, now. And Peter—"

"Yes, baby?"

"When we get there, *don't* make love to me. Even if I ask you to."

"All right, Judy. But out of plain curiosity: *Why?*"

"Hard to explain, darling. Say I want to be with you. Stay with you. Literally. As in *Webster's.* To remain. To be near. Close to you. There. So that I can—love you. *You.* Peter Reynolds; you big ugly paleolithic throwback, but with such a lovely, lovely soul. Oh, Peter, why can't one say these things any more? Why does it sound so fake to say what's simply true? That you're good! That I love your goodness. That there are other things about you far more important than your abilities as a bedmate; that—"

"In other words, my soul?"

"Yes, goddamnit; and don't call it a semantic irrelevant, either!"

"I wasn't going to. I was thinking about a line from a popular Spanish song of some years back, 'Julio Romero de Torres.' That line is *'Con alma negra y con pena . . .'* "

"Meaning?"

"Meaning a soul black and with pain."

"No! That's not true! Not at all—"

But Peter had leaned forward and was touching the *taxista* on the shoulder.

"Stop the car!" he said.

"Peter," Judith said, "what on earth did I do or say—"

"You? Nothing, baby. It's that boat tied up to the quay there."

"That pretty white one?"

"Yes."

"What's wrong with it?"

"Nothing. Except that it shouldn't be there. And that it's got the wrong name painted on it."

Judith leaned out of the taxi.

"*La Flor del Mar,*" she read. "*The Flower of the Sea,* right?"

"Right," Peter said.

"And what should it be called?"

"Let's skip that bit, Judy. If I'm wrong, it won't make any difference; if I'm right, it'll make even less. Just wait here for me like a good girl," Peter said.

He got out. Walked toward the quay. At once, an armed policeman barred his path.

"The yacht of His Excellency," Peter said, "when did it return?"

"This morning," the policeman said. "Why?"

"I'm a reporter," Peter said; "the doings of His Excellency are always news."

"Your papers!" the policeman said.

Peter showed them to him.

"Pay tayrrr Rrrraynolddds. Ay, sí! The celebrated Don Pedro who some say is the fiancé of—I am very sorry, Sir; but it is prohibited to allow anyone aboard without a special order from His Excellency or Don Luis; but if the Señor will wait a minute, I'll see what I can do."

"Don't want to go aboard. Just want to know why they came back. Usually when the Head of the State goes fishing—"

"He stays for weeks. But this time—tell me, Don Pedro, were you not a witness of what happened last night? I heard . . ."

"Yes, I was," Peter said.

"Then I can tell you. The explosions could be heard out to sea. And the flames from the aircraft and the hangars burning could be seen even from the distance at which the yacht of His Excellency cruised. So—"

"I see. Thank you, Guardia," Peter said.

He walked back to the taxi. Got in. Gave the driver their address.

"Peter—" Judy said.

"Not now, Judy; I've got thinking to do," he said.

The taxi drew up before the building.

"Wait here, Judy," Peter said.

"But, Peter—"

"Wait here, Judy. There's no time. All I'm going to bring down is your passport, and mine. Not even baggage. So, if we are stopped, I can say we were simply going to have a drink on the airport terrace. Just you smile sweetly and say nothing, catch?"

He found the passports at once. But he stayed upstairs long enough to write:

"It is still perhaps, *Muñeca*. And even though hope is a game for fools, I cannot accept that *never*." He signed it simply *Peter*; added his New York address and phone number, sealed it in an envelope, and wrote her name on it. Then he went downstairs to give it to Concha.

Concha was already outside talking to Judith. The fact that Judy got one word in ten troubled la Portera not at all. With delighted malice she was telling the story of how Doña Alicia, who loves much Don Pedro, had saved all the people on the street from being shot, when Peter came up to her. He smiled at her broadly.

"If," he said in Spanish, "you don't keep your fat, silly mouth shut, I personally shall see that you are not only shot, but tortured to death. Now take this, and give it to the lady whose name you have already mentioned too frequently, the next time she comes here. Have you understood, Concha?"

"Sí, Señor!" Concha said, and fled back into the hall.

"Peter—" Judith said.

"To the airport," Peter said to the taxi driver.

They moved off.

"Peter—"

"Judy, couldn't we just skip it?" Peter said.

"Oh, no, my beamish boy! Because that Don Pedro isn't two hundred other guys, he's you. Now tell me, what's she like?"

"What's who like?" Peter said.

"Doña Alicia," Judith said.

"Cute," Peter said.

"Come on, Great Lover, give!"

"Judy, do you mind if I save what little breath I've got left? Because much as I hate to tell you, if I don't get onto a plane damned soon, the guy who's going to be *fusilado* is me. And however you spell it or pronounce it, it comes out meaning dead."

"Oh!" Judith whispered. "Peter—"

"Yes, baby?"

"Because of her?"

"No, Judy; not because of her."

"Then why, darling? Please tell me."

"Because His Nibs and Luis Sinnombre don't see eye to eye on certain delicate matters. And I got caught in the middle. Judy baby, don't ask me questions. Let's just go eat some cherry cheesecake at Lindy's, shall we?"

"Oh—all right. Let's," Judy said.

The girl at the reception desk was stunning. But when Peter asked her for two one-way tickets to New York, she stopped smiling.

"Your passports, please!" she said.

Peter passed them over. What she was looking for took her two seconds to find. Or rather not to find.

"But you have no exit visas!" she said.

"Now look, *Cielito Lindo*," Peter said, "we're United States citizens, remember? I know that to get out of this free and liberal organic democracy, Costa Verdians have to have exit visas with a certificate from the local police precinct that they haven't spoken out of turn in the last six months. But not us. The tickets, please, like a nice little girl?"

"Sorry," the receptionist said.

"Why not?"

"National emergency. There were—well—certain acts of sabotage."

"The military air base was blown up. All the aircraft therein contained were destroyed. Several pilots, merchants, and other personnel were killed. The assassin escaped. After shooting, among others, Doña Alicia Villalonga, Widow of Duarte, Sister of the Head of the State. Which events I witnessed and have already filed with my newspaper by carrier pigeon. So keeping us here is ridiculous. Come on, Maja Vestida—give!"

"I am sorry, Señor; but I have my orders. You have to file a petition for an exit visa ten days ahead of time just like everyone else. With the police of the *barrio* of your residence. As of this morning, foreigners are no longer exempt from this ruling."

"I see," Peter said. "Thank you, Señorita."

"Don't mention it," the receptionist said.

"I won't," Peter said; "and Señorita—"

"Yes, Señor?"

"Be my guest. At my funeral, that is," Peter said.

"Oh, Peter! Peter!" Judith said.

"Gentle down, Judy. Just you sit in the waiting room while I do some telephoning."

"Peter, for God's sake!"

"Judy, let God take care of Himself for the moment. Right now I'm trying to take care of Peter and Judy. I'm going to try to get through to Don Luis. Convince him that perforated hides aren't being worn this year. Definitely unhealthy. Drafty, what?"

"Peter, if you don't stop being so goddam bright, I'm going to scream!"

"Baby, do it for both of us, will you? Now sit there," Peter said, and was gone.

He called the hospital first. But they wouldn't put him through to Alicia's room. They insisted that she had gone home. So he asked to speak to Vince, who confirmed what the sister had said.

"Why, yes, Peter; she's gone home. I tried to point out to her that it was inadvisable, but she simply wouldn't stay. And one doesn't say no to Doña Alicia, you know. I don't suppose it matters. I've got her wrapped up like a mummy. And if she moves about too much, it'll hurt enough to make her lie down. What's that? Why no, Peter—no one's been here asking for you. Right. I'll call you tonight."

He had no trouble getting through to Don Luis. The conversation was brief. Don Luis politely suggested that Peter drop in to see him at his office. He seemed neither troubled nor annoyed.

Peter took Judith home first. That was easy enough. What took some doing was getting her to stay there.

"My dear Peter," Don Luis said, "if you will help me by answering truthfully a few questions, I think we can smooth the whole thing over. First of all, how did those Commandos get into the airport?"

"Commando, not Commandos," Peter said. "Just one. If they had a few more like him, they'd be sitting in that chair right now, asking *you* questions."

"Don't doubt it. How did he, Peter?"

"Hidden between the seats of Alicia's car," Peter said.

"I thought so. Why?"

"He was awfully persuasive. His persuasion could run through a twenty-five shot clip in three seconds flat."

"Again, all right. I'd already assumed you were under duress. But what is going to be dreadfully hard to explain away is why, after he'd left you and Alicia in the officers' club, you didn't report what was going on."

"He said he'd shoot Alicia if I did. *Alicia*, Luis, not me. He figured that I might be willing to risk my neck. But not hers. He was right. Damned right. The proof of what I'm saying is that the bastard, thinking I had talked, did shoot Alicia. Fortunately, his aim wasn't any too good."

Very slowly, Luis Sinnombre smiled.

"You, my dear Peter, are either the world's finest liar or you are telling the truth. Which is it?"

"The truth," Peter said.

Luis went on smiling.

"In any event, it doesn't matter. Miguel has been informed that Alicia is in love with you. I pointed out to him that having a fatal heart attack would make sure that you would end up married to her, and thus stopped him from roaring like an infuriated bull. He has not been informed that you were even in a position to consummate this great love of yours and Alicia's. By the way, if—as she stubbornly insists—you haven't attended to that detail, it might not be a bad idea to do so. A little bundle from heaven on his way might make excellent life insurance for you. In any event, don't worry. Miguel is not overly bright. He tried to insist that if she hadn't been out with you, she never would have been in danger. To which I could easily reply that since he has always been exceedingly permissive about her comings and goings out of the idiotic idea that she could be trusted, she might have been in much greater danger alone; and add to that the fact that by driving that shot-up wreck of a Lincoln like a madman, you very probably saved her life. So now, he has subsided into the sulks, muttered grumbles, and ridiculous threats to beat her half to death once she has that bandage off."

"You tell him for me—"

"One moment, Peter! Let me handle Miguel. I'm good at it. All I want from you is a bit of cooperation."

"Such as?"

"First of all that you refrain from pulling any more silly stunts like attempting to leave the country as you did this morning."

"All right," Peter said. "And—?"

"You take dear Judith night-clubbing tonight. May I suggest the Obsidian Room of the Verdian Hilton?"

"All right again. Why?"

"Special performance for Miguel's benefit. He sees you being most attentive to dear Judith, who is certainly the world's most tasty dish, he'll be comfortably reassured that you have no serious intentions toward that skinny little she-monkey of a sister of his. Or maybe ours. Even he has no illusions about her looks."

"Only I do. What happens when he tells her about the performance?"

"He won't have to. She'll be there."

"Look, Luis. She's been shot. Even a grazing wound like that one hurts like hell."

"I know. But it's not my idea, Peter. It's hers."

"Oh," Peter said.

"The thought being to prevent Miguel from being nasty to you. Or finding some capricious excuse for murder. Of course, she's sure to get her tender little heart slightly broken. Sorry, but that can't be avoided. You can repair it, oh so sweetly, later."

"I'm not so sure I like this—"

"My dear Peter, I'm trying to keep you alive and functioning. I base my future on this romance of Alicia's. And Miguel is damned unpredictable. For Alicia's sake he just might risk ruining the country for the simple pleasure of having you shot. One never can tell with him. His mind functions in odd ways. I'd advise you to cooperate."

Peter looked at him.

"Luis, you just sold me a bill of goods," he said.

When he opened the door to his flat, Judith didn't come running to meet him. Instead she came very slowly, and her face was strained and white.

"Well?" she said.

"Shooting's off," Peter said. "I may be target for tomorrow; but tonight—Peace—it's wonderful. So we celebrate. City's flossiest nightspot. The Obsidian Room."

"Peter, I don't think I . . ."

"Judy, we have to. Semi-command."

"Oh!" Judith said.

"Don't I even get a small-sized kiss?" Peter said.

"No. Yes. But first close your eyes, and put out your hands."

He closed his eyes. Put his hands out. She poured something into them. Something light and powdery and dry. He opened his eyes. Looked down at his two hands. They had cigarette butts in them. Lipstick stained.

"I don't think I need to remind the Great Lover that I don't smoke Players," Judith said.

"Oh, hell!" he said.

"She also pawed my lingerie, the jealous bitch," Judith said.

Peter didn't say anything.

"All right," Judith whispered. "No scene, darling. What right have I? Peter—one question: You want me to get lost?"

"No," Peter said.

"You mean that, darling?"

"I mean it."

"Don't worry; I'm not going to ask you why you mean it. I know better than to look a gift horse in the mouth. Peter—"

"Judy?"

"I think maybe you had better make love to me, now. I know I told you not to. But, oh Judas! Now I need comforting. Please?"

"Oh, all right, baby," Peter said.

13.

The walls of the Obsidian Room were of black glass. The lights were concealed behind plaster cupids. The orchestra members were dressed in white tuxedos with silver lapels. The instruments were white, too. The trick was to cut all the lights except a couple of ultraviolet rays. Then the instruments seemed to be floating in midair held by white suits with nothing in them. Even the girl singer disappeared, leaving only her vastly overstuffed white-spangled dress wiggling in the dark without any visible means of support.

"Big deal," Peter snorted.

The waiter guided them to the table with the aid of a

flashlight. Slapped the menu down on the table. Disappeared. The lights came up again. Things grew edges. Tables blossomed all around them. People.

Peter began to relax. Then he saw what was standing around the walls. Behind all the columns. He said: "Ugh!"

"Why *ugh*, darling?" Judith said.

"Ever notice that apes in tuxedos look more like apes than they do in the raw?" Peter said.

"Oh!" Judith said. "Peter, why are they here? Following you?"

"No. Means that some bigwig is going to put in his appearance. The situation is a trifle uncertain since the Commies washed out the Costa Verdian Air Force. The Minister of War is already in Washington, pleading for jets. Their pitch is that Fidel is all set to invade."

"Is he?"

"No. He's got troubles enough in Havana. Don't know why, but I enjoy seeing these types sweat. Remember how the streets were crawling with coppers this morning? Everybody watching everybody else?"

"Your order, Sir?" the waiter said.

"Champagne," Peter said. "Piper-Heidsieck, Forty-three."

"I'm sorry, Sir; but—"

"Veuve Clicquot. Same year. Or Mumm. Brut. Or any goddam thing. As long as it's not pink or sweet."

"Very well, Sir," the waiter said.

"Peter!" Judith said. "Just look who just came in!"

"No," Peter said, "I don't want to. I can't. Not so soon. Not without a drink in me."

"But, darling, it's Doctor Vince. With a girl. A very pretty girl. Probably his wife. He does have a wife, doesn't he?"

"Yes. But as a general rule, one doesn't go pubcrawling with one's own *frau* in Costa Verde—"

"Oh," Judith said. "Peter—I do think they're coming over here!"

"Oh, God!" Peter said.

"But why, darling? I thought you liked him?"

"Judy, tonight I don't even like me."

Vince was standing by the table, smiling at them. Peter got up.

"Peter," Vince said, "may I present my blushing bride? That is, she used to blush. By now, she's forgot how. Paloma love, this is Peter Reynolds."

"Enchanted," Peter said; "and this—"

"Oh, I know who she is!" Paloma Gomez said. "She's why we're here. I insisted brazenly that Vince bring me. I was just dying to meet her. Am I forgiven, Miss Lovell?"

"Of course," Judith said, "though I fail to see what you've done that requires forgiveness. I like being flattered!"

"Join us?" Peter said.

"Try and stop us," Vince said. He signaled to the waiter. The waiter came flying, followed by a busboy with two more chairs.

"Vince," Peter said, "how'd you know?"

Vince leaned close. Dropped his voice. "That you two were going to be here tonight?" he said. "Simple. Luis called me. We're window dressing. My Dove doesn't know that, though."

"Oh," Peter said.

"You're in a spot, Peter. But anything I can do to help, I will."

"Son, you got your sewing basket with you?"

"Lord, Peter; why?"

"To put the pieces back together," Peter said.

"I've seen all your pictures," Paloma was saying to Judith. "I don't think I've missed even one—"

"How could you stand 'em?" Judith said.

"Now really, Judith," Vince said, "you've done some fine things."

"Yes," Judith said, "two. One was to leave Hollywood. The other was to come crawling on my knees to Peter. Only things I've done in my life that made any sense—"

"Judy," Peter said, "drink your champagne. Generally speaking, people cry into their cups after, not before."

The trouble was, she took him at his word. But instead of making her morose, it made her gay. Peter stopped holding his breath after a while. Because, now, clearly, she had set out to please. And, when Judy deliberately decided to be charming, what happened to the people around her was worth watching. They melted. Under the hypnotic, loving, tender, total attention of her gaze, the soft, liquid caress of her voice, they turned wax, helplessly waiting to be molded into the shape of her whimsical heart's desire. There was something a little terrifying about it. Because you never could be sure she wouldn't suddenly whirl and rend the creatures she had made. All the time she spun yarns about the motion picture industry—already moribund and half a ghost by the time she had come to it, so that her career had mounted upon the great final wave of its dissolution—Peter kept watching her out of the corner of his eye, listening to her voice playfully combining lies, damned lies, and god-damned lies for Paloma's especial benefit with such stark, utterly simple sincerity that even knowing how most of it had really been, he found himself half-believing her.

"So," she was saying, "all I had on was about five pounds of beads—you know, the costume department's concept of how a Byzantine Empress dressed—"

"You mean their concept of how to titillate the suckers," Peter said.

"Right, darling! Right as rain! But anyhow, Paloma dearest, I was supposed to wear a few things under all that dime-store jewelry. The essentials—Peter, can I tell her this? You know Spanish girls are so modest . . ."

"Now you've got to!" Paloma said.

"All right. So along with the beads they gave me a sort of half-bra and a *cache-sexe*. That sounds nicer than a G-string, doesn't it, Peter darling?"

"Judy, for God's sake!"

"Anyhow, it was ohhh so ohh hot in Madrid. I went to sleep in my dressing room. So when they called me, I jumped up, put on the beads, and forgot the essentials. I thought that the cameraman and the grips were sort of staring at me; but in that costume, they would have anyhow. Besides, all I had to do in that scene was to sit on a throne. I suppose everything would have been just fine and dandy if Peter hadn't chosen that moment to drop in. I hadn't seen him in years. And, of course, I've been in love with him all my life—"

"Judy, please!" Peter said.

"Oh, leave her be, Peter," Vince said.

"So I got up from there, and ran to meet him. Well, one smart cameraman kept right on shooting. Made himself a fortune selling bootlegged copies of that take!"

"How awful!" Paloma said.

"You've got something there, my dear," Peter said. "It was even worse than that. You want to hear the really horrible part?"

"Of course!" Paloma said.

"The real lowdown is that not one word of this yarn of Judy's is true," Peter said.

"Now *Pe-tah!*" Judy said.

"She had on a thing like a Mother Hubbard. Acres and acres of cloth. Gold lamé shawl. A crown. She was so damned covered up that—"

"Peter," Judith said, and her voice made him stop dead; "just who *is* that girl?"

"What girl?" he said.

"That one. That little dark creature. Stunning. Looks like she belongs on a barge on the Nile."

Peter didn't turn.

"Why?" he said.

"Well, from the way she's staring at you," Judith said, "I'd say that all she needs to make her perfectly happy would be a knife and a fork. And you on the plate, darling. That gleam in her eye is positively cannibalistic."

"Judy," Peter said, "you're imagining things again."

"No, I'm not. Peter, darling, would it be badly seen in polite Costa Verdian society if I went there and belted her one?"

Vince laughed.

"I'm afraid, Judith, that if you belted that particular little creature one, you'd end up in front of a firing squad. That little girl happens to be the sister of the Head of the State."

"Not Doña Alicia!" Judith said.

"The same," Vince said.

"*Pe-tah*—" Judith said.

"Oh, Lord," Peter said.

"Now, darling—all I wanted to ask you was: Do you think the orchestra knows 'Frankie and Johnny'?"

"Hell, no!" Peter said.

"Why, Judy?" Vince said.

"Want to sing it. To celebrate being done dirt to. Or by. Really give out with that punch line, 'He was my m-a-a-a-a-n; but he done me wrong!' "

"Now, Judy," Peter said.

"Well, haven't you?"

"No," Peter said.

"Then you're a fool. She might have taught you something new. With hot sauce and chili peppers on it. Vince, which one is His Nibs?"

"The one on her left," Vince said.

"Oh!" Judith said.

"You're among friends, Judy," Vince said. "Speak your piece. I'm curious."

"He'd set a new style in heavies," Judy said. "Subtle. Delicately cruel. The kind who'd have to have a violin sonata played to him while he watched a man being tortured to death. Right?"

"Absolutely," Vince said.

"Look how listless he is. Bored. Like Nero or Caligula. No, Nero's better. Caligula was just plain nuts. But this one is crazy in devious ways. Twisted. He'd kill his own mother for amusement. Say, Doctor Vince, who is the other one?"

"Luis Sinnombre," Vince said.

"Hmmm," Judith said; "that I like. That I'd buy a portion of. He looks like—he looks like—Paloma, please forgive me; but he looks like horizontal fun!"

"Judy," Peter said, "I've the damnedest feeling that the one who's going to get belted is you, Baby. And by *me*, if you don't cut this line of chatter out."

"He looks as lower-depths as a slum brothel," Judith said. "Appeals to all the ways I'm not a good girl, darling. You know, Peter, you're so goddam wholesome. But that Luis! Oh, brother!"

"You know," Vince said, "it's curious what a chasm separates the sexes. Women never have the faintest idea why we find certain little creatures exciting. Nor vice versa. I know that Luis is enormously successful with the girls, but I'll be damned if I can see why. Dreadful-looking creature, isn't he?"

"That Toltec eye," Peter said, "that jaguar mouth."

"Why, Peter! What a poet you are!" Paloma said.

"I," Judith said, "do see what *you* see in *her,* darling."

"That hot sauce and chili pepper?" Paloma said. "You know, Judith, we *Hispano-Americanas* get a bit tired of that conception you Nordicas have of us. We aren't at all—"

"I wasn't being serious, Paloma," Judith said; "I was only plaguing Peter. Fact is, I don't know that at all. I think she's cute. Ugly cute. But interesting. Such a soulful face. She probably wouldn't be worth a damn in bed, but—"

The champagne Peter was drinking went down the wrong way. He choked.

Judith looked at him.

"So," she whispered, "you already have!"

"Now, Judy—"

"Oh, Peter!"

"Baby," Peter said; "you see any holes in me?"

"Oh, no! Don't give me that one. She's a sly little number. She'd never be so stupid as to—"

She stopped dead, because the headwaiter was already bowing over their table.

"—get caught," she said, staring at him.

"Señor Reynolds? Doctor Gomez?" the headwaiter said.

"Yes?" Peter said.

"His Excellency requests the pleasure of you and your ladies' company at his table," the waiter said.

It wasn't the first time Peter had seen Miguel Villalonga.

But it was the first time after he had met, had got to know Alicia. And now, looking at him, the effect was disquieting. It was as though someone had held that exquisitely sculptured head of hers into a flame, and let it melt a little. Let it run to flesh. Those full lips of hers became negroid in her brother's face, a trifle bluish—the result, perhaps, of his heart condition. They pulled down at the corners under a sparse, mongoloid mustache. Their expression was feline. The sleepy look of a well-fed tiger. But of one that was perfectly willing to kill for pleasure, even after the more normal appetites were sated. His eyes had the same Tluscolan slant as his sister's. But where Alicia's were luminous, Miguel's were lightless. The blackness of the pit showed in them; the night of ice-cold hell. He was only a little corpulent, probably because of an enforced lack of exercise. He was dressed in white, as always; and his dinner jacket was of an excellent cut. He was smoking a long, pencil-thin cigar, letting the smoke curl up past those ice-black eyes. His nails were delicately manicured, tinted with a soft rose-colored polish. On his finger he wore a massive ring of gold.

Looking at Peter now, his nostrils flared in a gesture that was an exact duplicate of Alicia's. So exact that it stopped Peter's breath. And he saw one thing clearly and absolutely and perfectly: Luis Sinnombre was wrong. He might enjoy playing Gray Eminence to Miguel Villalonga, but he didn't manage him. Or deceive him. Or conceal anything from those black ice-floe eyes that they really wanted to see. The boot was on the other leg. Here was greatness. Great evil, of course. But greatness. The one quality which throughout human history has always been totally independent of morality.

Miguel didn't get up, even to greet the ladies. He sat there studying them, until every nerve they had was screaming.

"Miss Lovell," he said at last, "Costa Verde is honored by your presence."

His voice was light, dry. It sounded like the rustle of oiled silk.

"Thank you, Your Excellency," Judith said.

"This," the Dictator said, "is my assistant, Luis Sinnombre. That means, in your language, Miss Lovell, Louis Without A Name."

"Oh," Judith said. "How do you do, Don Luis?"

Luis bent over her hand. Raised it to his lips. Kissed it instead of making the formal gesture of merely pretending to, which was what good manners demanded.

"Doctor, Doña Paloma, please be seated," Miguel said. "And you, too, Mr. Reynolds. Over there, next to my sister. I believe you've already met?"

"Yes, we have," Peter said.

"But *I* haven't met her," Judith purred, "and I'm just dying to! You see, I've heard so much about her—from Peter."

Alicia's doe eyes were stricken things. Wounded unto death.

"Have you?" the Dictator said. "I didn't know they were so well acquainted. But then, you know how it is, Miss Lovell; nobody ever tells me anything . . ."

In the resulting little flurry of laughter, they all sat down.

"Peter, darling, may I have a cigarette?" Judith said.

"Of course," Peter said, and offered her a pack of Chesterfields.

"Oh, not those!" Judith said. "Don't you have any Players?"

Alicia looked at her.

"I do," she said, and held out her gold, monogrammed cigarette case.

Miguel Villalonga raised an eyebrow.

"Odd that you have similar tastes in cigarettes," he said.

"We have similar tastes in a great many things; don't we Doña Alicia?" Judith said.

Luis Sinnombre laughed.

"Women!" he said.

"Don't we?" Judith persisted.

"I wouldn't know," Alicia said. "In men—perhaps, yes. I think Peter is—very nice."

"He is," Judith said. "Oh, he is! You have no idea how—"

"Miss Lovell," Luis said, "may I have this dance?"

Judith smiled at him.

"Well," she said, "I was looking forward to dancing with His Excellency first—if that isn't *lèse majesté*. Is it, Your Excellency?"

Villalonga smiled.

"Not at all," he said. "But, unfortunately, Miss Lovell, thanks to the badness of a would-be assassin's aim, I find myself a cripple. Dance with Luis. He is quite good at it."

"Of course," Judy said, and stood up. Luis took her arm. They moved off toward the dance floor.

Peter could feel Alicia's gaze.

"Peter—" she said.

"Yes, Doña Alicia?" he said.

"Oh!" she said; "don't be so formal. I don't care about my arrogant and stupid brother. Call me Alicia, as you always do."

"Certainly, Nena. Better?"

"Much!" she said. "May *I* have this dance, please?"

Peter looked at Miguel Villalonga. Looked back at Alicia.

"Delighted," he said, and took her arm.

"You know," Miguel Villalonga said, "I have the distinct impression that I have been lied to, about a number of things—"

"You have, dear brother—oh, but you have!" Alicia said; and moved off with Peter toward the dance floor.

The orchestra was playing a cha-cha-cha. Peter wasn't very good at that; but he managed. Then they switched to a slow bolero. He smiled. At boleros, after his years in Spain, he was very good indeed.

He drew her close. Then he felt her wince. Released her.

"God, Nena, I forgot!" he said.

"No," she said; "hold me, Peter. It hurts a little. But not as much as your not holding me does. Oh, Peter, *Cielo*, I—"

"Nena," he said.

"I have never wanted to kill anyone before. But now I do. Oh, how I hate her! Oh how I should love to claw out her eyes!"

"Nena," he said again, "hate's such a futile emotion.

Haven't got time for it. Nor the space. Too full of its opposite at the moment. Overflowing."

"And I," she whispered. Her voice went ragged. "If I could only kiss you now," she said; "if I only could!"

"That makes two of us," Peter said.

But she didn't answer him; and, looking down, he saw that she was crying. He froze.

"No," she said; "go on dancing, Peter."

She danced the way he had known she would. Totally. She was the music, the rhythm, the slow beat, the lazy guitar strumming.

The music stopped. He took her arm.

"No!" she said; "don't take me back! He knows I love you. And he might as well accustom himself. And she. Because now I am going to take you away from her. Oh, Peter, *Cielo*, you cannot belong to such a horrible woman! I will not permit it!"

"*Muñeca*—" he said.

"I will not, Peter! Why—"

The next was a tango. He drew her to him the way you have to if you mean to dance a tango, not fake it. She fitted into him like a second skin. Under the thin stuff of her dress he could feel the gauze and the tape of the bandage. He drew his hand away.

"Put it back, your hand!" she said.

He could feel her trembling. But she didn't miss a beat. He was aware that Luis and Judith were still dancing, and that Vince and Paloma were, too, now, floating hazily and out of focus on the lateral margin of his gaze. But then he forgot they existed, forgot Miguel Villalonga and the ice-cold menace of his gaze, forgot time in the long slow quiver of her clinging to him, the contact unbroken, from below the throat to just above the knee through all that potent sweep, halt, side break, follow-through of the tango, moving trancelike through steps so intricate, so spectacular that the dance floor emptied, Judy, Luis, Vicente, Paloma, and all the other dancers forming a ring watching them, and the orchestra playing one tango after another until finally he noticed it, and quit. The spectators applauded loudly.

"Kids," Judith said, "the management ought to pay you. What an act! Peter, darling, you've been holding out on me. I didn't know you could dance like that!"

"Perhaps he cannot—with you," Alicia said. "It requires a certain—Peter, *Cielo*, how does one say *compenetración* in English?"

"Don't bother," Judith said, "though I must say that a dance floor is hardly the place to indulge in it. A trifle daring don't you think, Doña Alicia?"

"Oh," Alicia said, "you distort my meaning—but no matter. Peter, Amor, we must go back now. I had better start persuading Miguel not to have you shot!"

They all moved back to the table where the Dictator sat, smoking his thin black *puro* and watching them out of his flat basilisk eyes.

"Ah, Reynolds," he said, "you have hidden talents. And so do you, Alicia, my dear. Quite a show. Quite a show. I suspect there have been others I didn't witness. For instance, for Marisol Talaveda to have got aboard the jet for New York, she could hardly have complied with orders. Which leaves me with the unlikely supposition that Luis became sentimental and allowed her to defy me—or—"

"Or what, Miguel?" Alicia said.

"Or— Nothing, my dear little sister. Some suppositions are far too unpleasant to pursue, don't you think, Miss Lovell? One finds oneself in the position of the tired husband who always telephones his home rather than return unexpectedly. Wise, don't you think?"

"Very," Judith said; "especially if my Peter is in town!" They all laughed. Sat down.

"Tell me, Reynolds," Villalonga said, "aren't you pro-Communist? A bit of a fellow traveler, say?"

"No," Peter said.

"Why not?" the Dictator said.

"Because they push people around," Peter said.

Miguel Villalonga laughed. Pleasantly. Wholeheartedly.

"And that, of course, is a terrible crime?"

"The most terrible," Peter said. "Too hard to stop. Starts with a few broken heads in Munich. And ends up in Dachau—"

Villalonga drew in on his cigar. Studied Peter.

"And what, my dear Reynolds, do you think of *my* government?" he said.

Peter smiled.

"I'd rather not say," he said.

"Why not?" The two words were a whipcrack. Peter smiled, even more slowly.

"Because there are ladies present," he said.

Miguel Villalonga looked at him. A long time. A very long time. Then suddenly, abruptly, the Dictator threw back his head and roared.

"My dear Reynolds, a man with your nerve deserves to live," he said. "I like you! Damned if I don't!"

He turned in his chair, his hand raised. Five waiters, two of whom crashed into each other, converged upon their table.

"More champagne," El Indominable said.

"Miguel—" Alicia said.

"Yes, sweet sister?"

"Hear me well," Alicia said. Then she said, very fast, in a kettledrum roll of pure beautifully precise Castilian: "I love Peter. If you kill him, I shall not survive him one hour. No matter how you try to prevent it. Even if you set guards over me, as you have over our loved and respected mother. There is no way you could stop me—any more than you could have stopped me from doing what I have already done."

Miguel's face darkened, congested.

"With him?" he said.

Alicia smiled.

"With—various," she said. "Am I not your sister, brother mine? Daughter of your mother? Have I not blood of a hundred thousand loves in my veins?"

Miguel sat there looking at her. His face slackened. He looked very tired, suddenly, very old. He turned in his chair.

Looked toward one of the policemen standing beside a column. The man hurried over.

"Call my car," the Dictator said. He turned back to the others. "You will forgive a tired old man, won't you? Time I was abed, eh, Doctor? Alicia—"

"Yes, Miguel?" Alicia whispered.

"Would you come with me? Or would you prefer to stay?"

Alicia got up slowly. Took his arm.

"I'll come with you, Miguel," she said.

14.

Now again, when they had got there together—when with one last arrogantly demanding, prehensile, unspeakably expert, long scalding twist, she had hollowed him out from the base of his throat down to his tight-curled toes, drawing the life out of him into the savage thrash and broil and undulant heat of her, achieving total fusion that included not only the red murder in her teeth and nails but her willful and willing self-destruction, rising through the rhythmically mounting chain of chanted prayerful obscenities to the feral, anguished, demented cries that clung in his ears like the negation of all joy; and it (the act of what they both euphemistically called love) over and done with—he returning to life through the slowing breath-storm heart-hammer, saw that she was propped up on one elbow staring at him, the whole of her glistening in the morning light with the rivers of sweat that poured out of her, still staring at him and fighting for breath, and her face tightening suddenly with something he couldn't recognize until he said "Judy?" and she brought her free hand whistling around to smash open-palmed across his face.

And even then he didn't recognize it. But he had been around a good many years by now and his lessons had all been well learned the hard way; she, Judith, having been one of the first and certainly the best of his teachers, so that he knew one thing with absolute certainty: If you let a woman get away with a rebellious or a humiliating act for as long as five seconds flat, you are done.

Knowing that, not having to even think about it, he responded without anger or heat or any emotion whatsoever, simply rolling her out of the bed with a slap whose crushing, overwhelming force was designed to end the matter forever, and did.

He lay there watching her come up on hands and knees, shaking her head from side to side to clear it, jetting the tears from her eyes in a fine spray by the motion; but when she looked up at him finally, tugging that long, livid, rose-silver scar that was his brand upon her, taut by her throat's lifting upcurve, she was smiling.

"So you're a big boy, now," she said. "Took you one hell of a time, but you've learned. Who's been teaching you things? That little mouse?"

"You among others," he said. "Come on, Judith: give. Why the Pearl Harbor-type sneak attack?"

She got up then, stood there looking at him. She was still something. The packaging remained unmatched. What was inside was a different matter. Then once more her face came clear, her eyes bleak with sudden hurt.

"Again," she said.

"Again what?" Peter said.

"That's the second time you've put her head on my body. That's why I hit you. After being so goddam reluctant to play house with me, you top it off by closing your eyes and pretending it was she you were doing it with! Deadly insult, Peter! There's nothing worse. Absolutely nothing at all. I won't be used. I'm me, darling. Judith Lovell, remember? Not a substitute for your little mixed-blood mouse. Though

I have to admire your imagination. Because even if you have played indoor games with her—which I doubt, because in spite of leaving those crummy Players all over the place on purpose so I'd find them, and pawing in my things, I happened to notice the bed was completely unused—you ought to realize she isn't even in my league . . ."

She stopped still, peering into his face.

"Oh!" she said.

"Oh, what?" Peter said.

"Oh, hell. Same bit. We've been through this routine before. Does that untidy smile on your exceedingly unlovely countenance mean what I think it does?"

"Depends upon what you think it means, Judy."

"That she *is* good. At this sort of thing? Better than I, Peter?"

He grinned at her.

"I wouldn't know, Judy," he said.

"You're lying!"

"Say I'm being a gentleman . . ."

"*Pe-tah!*"

"Put your most charitable interpretation on it, baby. A gentleman doesn't speculate about a girl's abilities in a horizontal position. And if he knows, he doesn't admit it—not even to God in prayer. So since there's no way on earth you, or anybody else, could get me to confess to unlawful carnal knowledge of Alicia, any more than I'd ever own up to ever having seen your nicely rounded little tail uncovered by those invitations to rape you usually wear, why not just assume I'm telling the truth when I say I don't know? I could be. Ever think of that?"

She didn't answer him. She clawed in the box on the table, looking for a cigarette. But it was empty.

"In my side coat pocket," Peter said.

She walked across the room toward the clothestree on which he had hung his jacket. He lay there watching her moving in all the barbaric splendor of her nakedness, the burnt-gold sculpturing a little faded by her long stay in the hospital but still unmarred by any white, showing that her body's yielding to the sun had been as total as all her surrenders—and as wanton, surely.

She put her hand into his coat pocket. The wrong one. As she drew it out the pull tilted the clothestree a little. He saw her stare at something. Then her hand moved. But she had the long, singing curve of her back to him, so he couldn't see what she had done. She put her hand in the other pocket and came out with the cigarettes. She shook one out of the pack, stuck it in her mouth with her left hand, all the time keeping her right hand out of sight, pressed, it seemed to him, against the inhollow of her waist. She moved sidewise to the table. Picked up the table lighter, lit the cigarette. Walked over to the window, unfurling the pale gray banner of the smoke behind her.

"Judy, come away from there!" he said. "People can see you!"

She turned now, and he could see the iridescent crystal and sapphire wash that hid her eyes. She came back toward the bed, holding Alicia's photograph in her hand and walking with that tensioned stride of hers that brought "The War March of the Priests" instantly to his mind.

She didn't say anything. She sank down beside him. Lay there holding the photo and staring at it.

"Oh Judas!" she said.

"Now, Judy—"

"She's—absolutely gorgeous. It's what was bothering me last night. Only I was half-drunk and bitchy jealous so I couldn't see it. Takes a long time to see it, doesn't it? She's—so—so unconventional. How long did it take you, Peter?"

"No time. But then I'd known this face for eight years before I ever saw it."

"Now, Peter!"

"God's truth. Remember the National Museum of Archeology? That statue I showed you?"

"My God!" Judith said. "She could have posed for it, couldn't she?"

"A grandmother of hers, forty-nine greats removed, probably did. Judy, please. I'm awfully tired and—"

She looked at him and let that star-sapphire mist become a crystal spill; a luminous steeplechase down the contours of her face.

"Don't worry, Love. I'm not going to behave like a jealous ingénue. I'm not jealous, really. What I am is scared."

"Scared? You?"

"Yes. You're all I've got, darling. And a girl with a face like this could take you away from me. I hate to admit it, but she could. Notice I said a face. The rest of her equipment's merely incidental. If it were only that, I'd send you off with her for a weekend to get it out of your system. Only it's more than that. Much more."

"More?" Peter said.

"Yes. That was the main thing that was bothering me about her, last night. Not the fact that she was committing dry fornication with you on the dance floor—dry, hell!—say clothed. But that hungry look she has when she looks at you. I don't like it, Peter. It's such a total hunger. This lovely little witch wouldn't be contented with merely the occasional loan of your body. She'd want your soul as well. More than your manly talents. She's probably not much good in that department; but very, very long on soul. Peter—"

"Yes, Judy?"

"What would you do to me if I tore this up?"

He looked at her.

"Don't try it, Judy," he said.

She sighed.

"I thought that. All right, I'll put it back in your coat pocket. But keep it out of my sight, will you, please? All tortures aren't physical . . ."

She got up, went over to the clothestree. Put Alicia's picture back into his pocket. But she didn't come back at once. Instead, she stopped by the radio, switched it on. Stood there waiting until it boomed into sound. A man's voice said:

"*Government forces in Orense Province successfully counterattacked the Communist invaders who landed yesterday, proceeding from the Island of Cuba. Although vastly out-*

*numbered, the superb training and self-denying heroism of
our forces enabled them to—"*

Judith switched it off.

"No, baby; for God's sake leave that on!" Peter said. "He's
talking about the War . . ."

She switched the radio on again.

"Oh, Peter," she said, "I'm so sick of wars and killing
and . . ."

"So am I, Judy. So is the world. But this is important. This
is *here.*"

"Oh," she said, "not again!"

"It's never stopped, Judy," Peter said.

"Oh, hell," she said. "Mind if I turn it down a bit, Love?
You listen to it. I'll keep my attention fixed on other things."

"What things?" he said.

"The invaders suffered numerous casualties," the announcer
said.

"This," she whispered, and came back to him; sat slowly
and carefully on the edge of the bed with the studied grace
of motion that came from having had a battery of cameras
trained on her ever since she was seventeen years old, so
that the conscious avoidance of the awkward, the ugly, had
become unconscious and a part of her; then she fitted her
mouth to his with the camera angles uncalculated but right,
because she did it now from habit even after the need for
it was gone, turning her right profile, the better one, to catch
the light, and kissing him with a slow tenderness that
pushed a probing blade into his vitals, seeking (perhaps
consciously) his known and fatal weakness; the pity that
always and dependably unmanned him.

"The Indians of the town of Xochua . . ."

Peter took his mouth away from hers. Sat there listening,
all attention, now.

"Peter," she said reproachfully.

"Ssssh!" he said; "I was in that town once. It was there
that Jacinto—"

*"Under their Chief, Zochao, have flatly refused to leave
the village, threatened on three sides by the renewed flow*

uf lava from the volcano. Although the approach of the lava is very slow, government geologists believe—"

"Peter, turn that goddam radio off! It distracts your attention too much. And I—"

"You what, baby?"

"I—need you, Peter. To comfort me. Cure my sicknesses. Heal all the various places where I hurt—"

"That," Peter said, "is a very large order, Judy."

"I know. Huge. Immense. And terrifying. You aren't afraid, are you?"

"Baby," he said, "I'm scared spitless."

"Our representatives in Washington," the announcer boomed, *"indignantly deny—"*

"Oh, Judas, Peter! Please stop him from jabbering!"

He got up. Started toward the set. Stopped. Stood there. Seeing his face, Judith said:

"Peter!"

He didn't answer her. He was looking at the radio. Judith listened now, heard:

". . . que el brutal asesinato de la Señora Crosswaithe fuera llevado a cabo por agentes Costa Verdeneses. Esa acusación tan ridícula procede de una fuente poca fidedigna, el Señor Timothy O'Rourke, Corresponsal de Life en America Latina, expulsado de nuestro país por . . ."

"Peter!" she screamed.

His knees doubled. Then he was kneeling before the set, whispering "God! God! God!" so low she could scarcely hear him.

She got out of bed. Ran to him.

"Oh, Peter, Love, what is it?" she said. "What is he saying? What could he say to upset you so?"

"Nothing," he muttered. "Nothing that concerns you, Judy—"

"Tell me!" she said.

"They—they just killed somebody I was fond of, once," Peter said.

"But, Peter, I still don't get it," Judith said. "Why should they want to knock off poor old Buckteeth?"

"Judy, please!"

"Constance Buckleigh. Your ex-wife. Divorced from you. Married to H. Rodney Crosswaithe. Mother of his three kids. Why should anybody——"

Peter went on knotting his tie. Said, without looking at her:

"Because that's the only kind of divorce that counts in Costa Verde. Because Padre Pío got the Archbishop's back up and he wouldn't cooperate. Because Miguel Villalonga happened to see the fire burning up his nice, pretty airplanes and turned back. Because Luis couldn't, wouldn't, or hadn't time to call off his thugs. Or maybe even forgot——I wouldn't know. Because there are people big enough bastards to use even love——"

"Peter!"

"Yes, Judy?"

"You aren't making much sense, you know . . ."

He looked at her.

"Does anyone, ever, in this world?" he said.

"Peter——where are you going?"

"Out."

"Out where?"

"Out of here. Now stop asking so many questions. I've got things to do."

"Oh, no you don't, my beamish boy! Where you go, I go. You know, the latest thing: togetherness."

"Judy, you can't. I've got to see Luis. Got a couple of things to say to that boy. I've let what his goons did to me slide, so far; but this——"

"Peter——"

"Yes, Judy?"

"Think. You know, T-H-I-N-K. With that big head of yours. Which even has brains in it. Which even upon occasion, you can use."

"Damn!" Peter said.

"So you go to see that sweet, simple rattlesnake. You talk

things over with Don No-Name Jive. He extends his regrets
for knocking off poor old Connie. Or he denies it absolutely.
And where are you?"

He looked at her.

"Nowhere," he said. "So?"

"So get back out of your things, darling. And let me comfort you. My turn now. I'm good at it."

"Baby," he said, "I'm in no mood for country comforts."

"You never are, with me, any more," she said.

And then the bells rang. The doorbell. And the telephone.
Both of them, at the same time.

"You get the phone, baby," Peter said; "I'll attend to the
door—"

"Why?" she said. "Afraid I'll shock somebody?"

"Judy, for God's sake!"

"Oh, let them ring, Peter! I—"

But he was gone in one long stride, out of the bedroom,
closing the door behind him. It was a good thing he did;
because when he opened the front door, Father Pío stood
in it.

"So," Peter said, "you want me to use my good offices with
Alicia to see that the penal system is modified?"

"Yes, my son," Father Pío said. "I do not know whether
you know it, but it is of a vileness and a cruelty unimaginable. To be sent to one of the so-called Moral Correction Centers is simply a slow death sentence. The Social Re-
education Centers, where the political prisoners are kept—
though that distinction is not always observed—in them,
the sentence is not even slow. Most do not live out a month.
They are literally tortured to death. What I ask of you, son,
is that if the day ever comes when you can marry Doña
Alicia, you inspire her to—"

"Padre—" Peter said.

"Yes, Son Pedro?"

"I can never marry Alicia. Especially not now."

"Why not?" Padre Pío said. "Nothing is impossible with
God. He may see fit to call your wife to a reckoning, or . . ."

"Padre, He already has. Constance is dead. I am a widower."

"Then," Father Pío said, "it is as I told the Arzobispo! Why should we be forced into mortal sin? Leave all matters up to the Good God! He—"

"Padre, I have absolutely nothing against your God—not even the fact that He's nearly always guilty of criminal negligence. I just don't like some of His self-appointed assistants. Luis Sinnombre, for instance."

"Son Pedro, what do you mean?" Father Pío said.

Then Peter told him.

The old man's face was very still and sad.

"You have much right, my son," he said. "There are many things upon which a marriage may be based, but never upon a murdered woman's blood. Strange. You would deny your faith; yet all your moral instincts are sound."

Peter glanced toward that closed bedroom door.

"Are they, Father?" he said.

"Yes," the old priest said. "Now I must go. Bearing with me, I must admit, the burden of a heart heavier than when I came."

"Father," Peter said.

"Yes, Pedro?"

"Do you believe that God has forgotten the use of men of valor? That if a Gideon were to rise now—a Samson, a David, a Saul—or, best of all, a Joshua—to blow down the walls behind which freedom dies, would God condemn his anger? Or, more—if he were to stain his hands with the blood of the wicked, would God turn away from him? Is there forever a condemnation set upon human wrath, however just?"

"I do not follow you, my son—"

"Nor do I follow myself, entirely. A vagrant thought, Father. Perhaps an idle one. Shall we leave the clarions of liberty, the trumpet calls against the oppressors of the people to los Castristas, Padre? Leave the Reds to use men's hunger, anguish, need for their own dirty ends? Or shall we———?"

The old man stood up.

"I cannot answer that, Son Pedro," he said. "I am not wise enough."

"But there must be an answer, somewhere, Father."

The old man smiled.

"There is. Oh, there is. In your own heart, my son. If you were to spend the whole of one night upon your knees, you would be surprised at the illumination there!"

"Peter," Judith said, "we're in for it again."

"In for what again?" Peter said.

"A party. At Doctor Vince's house, this time. Only it's going to be more of the same. His Nibs is going to be there."

"And Luis?"

"Yes. And your sweet Alicia. Ah, it's going to be just ginger-peachy, Peter! Jolly. Bully. Top hole. You know any more outmoded slang?"

"It all is, as far as I'm concerned. Look, Judy, go take a shower and get dressed. A shower, not the tub; I've got things to do, and I don't have two hours to wait."

"What things?" Judith said.

"Feeding you, for one; you're getting downright skinny—"

"Judging from Alicia la Dulce, I thought you liked 'em like that."

"Them, not you. You I like *llenita*, which means well covered. Get going, Judy—"

"Peter, what other things do you have to do?"

"Buy a swagger stick."

"A *whaaaat?*"

"A swagger stick. You know, a little cane, too short to walk with. You tuck it up under one arm. Use it to smite the insolent members of the lower orders. Veddy, veddy U. Or something."

"Peter—come again?"

"Judy, I just told you . . ."

"Oh, no. 'Cause I know you, Lover. You don't smite the

lower orders. You're fairly dripping with liberalism, democracy, and brotherly love. Not to mention the milk of human kindness. Come on, Peter, give!"

"Believe it or not, Judy, I'm actually going to buy a swagger stick."

"I heard you the first time. What I want to know is why."

Peter frowned.

"Hard to explain, Judy. Say it's a symbol. No, a reminder."

"A reminder of what, Peter?"

"The day old Grandpa Ape picked up a stick and thereby became—man."

"*Pe-tah!*"

"The tool-bearing animal. A short extension of one's hairy paw. A stick's a useful object, Judy. You can use it to point with. Or to root out vermin. Judy, will you please—"

"Peter, you're going to do something foolish! I just know . . ."

"When haven't I? Now, will you go bathe? You smell like Saturday night at Susie's."

"That's why I love you, darling. You say the nicest things!" Judith said.

Doctor Vicente Gomez-García's house was in that district of Ciudad Villalonga known as Puerta de Oro. The district was exactly what its name indicated. The people who lived in this section didn't actually have golden doors on their houses; but they probably could have had, if they had wanted to. When he saw the line of Chryslers, Lincolns, Cadillacs, Mercedeses, Rollses, Bentleys, Daimlers lined up before Vince's door, he took a long slow look at the battered Ford he had rented for the occasion.

"Speaking of the Lower Orders," he said, and pointed at the Ford with his new teak-and-ivory swagger stick.

Judith laughed. Tucked the stiff shawl of tulle higher up around her neck.

"Nick the Greek," she said, "and his scarred-up moll. Tell me, Peter—does it show?"

"A little," Peter said. "Don't worry about it, baby. Besides, that scar is the best advertising I ever had. Now all the little creatures just line up, their *bragas* already off—"

"*Bragas?*" Judy said.

"Panties. Scanties. Culottes. Minimum essentials."

"I'll bet. And it may even be true. The way your little Alicia—"

"Judy, can't we kind of, sort of stay off that subject tonight, please? I've got troubles enough."

"Oh, all right, darling," Judith said.

Through the ironwork grille of the gate they could see the lights on in the garden, and the men in white dinner jackets and the women in Paris creations, sitting or strolling around the swimming pool. Actually, the lights were superfluous with Zopocomapetl growing angrier (or, if you accepted Alicia's version, more amused) every night. But they did serve to counteract the baleful red of the volcano's glare. Before he touched the bell, Peter took a long look. Saw the uniformed policemen standing in the shadows. Saw, too, from the width of shoulders of some of the men in dinner jackets, from the paleolithic heads sitting on those shoulders like a boulder on a wall, unseparated by anything remotely resembling a neck, that there were detectives among the guests. Then a little farther off, he saw Miguel Villalonga surrounded by a little group of most respectful men. And Luis Sinnombre turning his fine black subterranean perverse charm on a group of women. But there was no sign of Alicia. No sign at all.

Judith grinned.

"Chickened out on you, darling?" she said.

"Could be," Peter said, and touched the bell.

A uniformed manservant opened the gate for them. They went in and pole-axed all conversation. Every woman in the garden was staring with frank curiosity at Judith, while Vince led the concentrated rush of males toward the gate. For a long moment they were surrounded. Peter had met most of the men at Señor Corona's house. In fact, the Minister of Information and Tourism was among them now. They all laughed, joked, and presented each other to Judith. Then they bore her off, presumably to introduce her to the women, calling back to Peter:

"Take your pick, Don Pedro! There are many girls—"

But Peter reached out and caught Vince by the arm. Leaned close; said:

"Alicia?"

"Inside the house. With Paloma. And my mother. She looked so ill when she came that they took her in hand. Dreadfully upset over something, which I gather is connected with you—right?"

"Right," Peter said.

"Want to tell me what it is?" Vince said.

"No," Peter said.

"Oh," Vince said. "Look, Peter; I don't mean to pry—"

"You're not prying. And I could tell you. Only I think this particular item is dangerous. The kind people get killed down here for knowing."

"Oh," Vince said again.

"Alicia," Peter said; "any way you can arrange for me to see her?"

"Later," Vince said. "*After* you've chatted with our Glorious Leader."

"Hell," Peter said.

"I agree; but one doesn't say it, Peter. Bad form. And dangerous. Incidentally, you've done wonders for Alicia's public image."

"I?" Peter said. "How?"

"That stunt of getting her to make Luis turn all those people loose."

"I didn't get her to do a damned thing. She did it on her own."

"She would. Sweet little thing, really. And she's won over the Social Register by saving Marisol Talaveda. Part of it's bitchy curiosity, of course. The girls are dying for you—or her—to confirm the current rumor that she took dear little Mari's place."

"I'll send flowers to their funerals," Peter said.

Luis Sinnombre stepped out of the shadows, suddenly, and took Peter's arm.

"My dear Peter," he said, "what on earth is this?"

"A swagger stick," Peter said.

"May I see it?" Luis said.

"Of course," Peter said and passed it over.

Luis stood there, holding the slim, wandlike stick with the ivory head. He gave the head a tentative twist.

"It doesn't have a blade in it," Peter said.

Luis laughed.

"I didn't think it did," he said, "but I preferred to make sure. You just might have heard that broadcast this afternoon."

"I did," Peter said.

"I feared, dear Peter, that you might have jumped to conclusions. Erroneous conclusions—just as the New York police did, thanks to your friend O'Rourke."

"Look, Luis," Vince said, "I'd better go see to my guests—"

"No, stay, Vince," Luis said. "I prefer to have this particular conversation witnessed. For Peter's sake. And, truthfully, for mine. Peter, do you believe that I, through agents of mine, had your ex-wife killed?"

"*Dios!*" Vince said. "So that was it! La Señora de Crosswaithe was—"

"My ex-wife. Yes. To your question, Vince. And also, Luis, to yours."

Luis smiled. Handed Peter back the little swagger stick.

"So, believing that, you went out and bought—this?" he said.

"Yes," Peter said.

"Which, as you've allowed me to prove, contains no hidden weapon, and is too small and light for beating a man?"

"Yes," Peter said again.

"Might I ask why?"

"Doesn't conceal weapons. It *is* a weapon. A magic wand. You point it at assassins, and they disappear. Only it doesn't work yet."

"Why not?" Vince said.

"Haven't had Padre Pío bless it for me. That's one of the essential ingredients. One of the two essential ingredients."

"And the other is?" Luis said.

"Truth," Peter said.

Luis laughed easily, gaily.

"Peter," he said, "do you know the details of how Constance Buckleigh Reynolds Crosswaithe died?"

"Yes," Peter said. "I called my paper in New York. And got through. Which meant that you wanted me to know those details, Luis."

"I did. And they were?"

"The killer entered her home during the day. While her husband was at work, her children off at school. He shot her with a Luger. He was a bad shot. The bullet went through her right shoulder. He tried again, and the Luger jammed. Apparently he was unfamiliar with that type of sidearm."

"Go on," Luis Sinnombre said.

"He couldn't get it to fire again. So he hammered her head bloody with the butt. Broke off one of the plastic grips, which is why the police know it was a Luger. But Connie is a tall, strong woman. Ex-tennis champion. He dragged her into the bathroom and tried to drown her in the tub. She revived, got away from him. He followed her into the kitchen and broke a carving knife off in her throat—"

"*Dios mío!*" Vince said.

"But she still got away from him. Ran, walked, crawled to the nearest neighbor's house. She died with her finger on the bell."

"You are very accurate, Peter. Now may I ask you another question?"

"Go ahead."

"Is there anything you know about me—anything you've heard, that would make you imagine I'd hire a clumsy idiot butcher like that one?"

Peter stood there.

"La Señora Crosswaithe lived in the outskirts of Great Neck, Long Island. Daily she drove her husband to the station to catch the Commuter's Special. This, of course, after having deposited the children at school. And your superhighways, my dear Peter, are hideously dangerous. At any intersection, a heavy truck, with its brakes out of commission, say, might have crashed into her Plymouth Valiant Compact, white, matricula 356 GN 175; turned it over; reduced it to one of those lamentable masses of twisted steel and splintered glass one sees so often in the newsreels. That, my dear Peter, would have been the intelligent method of assassinating la Señora Crosswaithe, don't you think?"

Peter stood there. Ran his tongue tip over bone-dry lips.

"Then *who?*" he said.

Luis shrugged.

"How should I know? A psycho, likely. You have so many of them," he said.

15.

The party, as parties do, was gathering speed. Vince had the big glass doors thrown open and people were wandering into the dining room and coming back with plates piled high with cold cuts, salads, shellfish, chicken. Only the serious drinkers lingered in the garden. Among them, Peter saw worriedly, Judith.

He heard her voice soar above the general rumble of male conversation, the glissando ripple of female laughter, glass tinkle, the clicking of silver against fine china.

"Oh no, Señora Corona! I don't worry about Peter—" she was projecting a good line over, getting it past the footlights, her tone not exactly ringing, but full, strong, deceptively effortless—"at least I haven't, up until now . . ."

The dramatic pause, the timing right, perfect, until Sara Martinez de Corona, the Minister's wife, broke it, coming in exactly on cue.

"But now you do?" she said.

"Yes," Judith; "you Latin American girls are so sexy! I kind of, sort of, suspect that down here my Peter has been had."

"By whom?" Sara Corona said.

"Oh, no!" Judith laughed; "that would be indiscreet, Señora! Especially considering present company . . ."

Then Peter saw that Miguel Villalonga was sitting beside her. Luis had moved a little way off. Out of prudence, likely.

"And you, my dear Judith, are the soul of discretion, no?" the Dictator said.

Peter started moving toward them.

"Oh, come now," another woman—a girl really, not long in her twenties—said: "Surely you *know* who she is."

It was all wrong. Wrong and incongruous. Then he looked at the girl. Recognized her. He had been introduced to her at Señor Corona's party. Carmen—Carmencita Miraflores. Daughter of a man he'd interviewed once—Joaquin Miraflores, Costa Verde's richest citizen. Industrialist and rancher. One of the backers of the Standford expedition to Ururchizenaya. And, if rumor were telling the truth, as rumor quite often did, the man who had financed Miguel Villalonga's rise to power, having seen in him a bulwark against the same hungry masses from whom he sprang. But even so, it was only a little less wrong. Carmencita should have known better. The Leader had long since proved his capacity for biting the hand that fed him. For, in fact, chewing off the entire arm. It was he who used the rich and idle aristocracy who had planned to use him; throwing sons, husbands, fathers, into those prisons from which no man emerged alive; converting daughters, sisters, wives into reluctant whores to avenge, surely, their very knowledge of what his own mother had been and was. Then Peter saw that The Leader was drunk. Or pretending to be.

"Oh, yes! I know all right," Judith began.

"Judy!" Peter said.

"Have the goodness to leave her in peace, Reynolds!" the Dictator said. "This is, after all, a Republic, an Organic Democracy. Free speech is permitted."

"For how long?" Peter said.

"As long as it takes to offend me," Miguel said. "And tonight I am in a complacent, even a permissive, mood. Good food, good wine, excellent company. Go on, Judith. Tell us who it is that has had your friend Reynolds."

Judith looked at him. Smiled.

"Your little sister," she said.

Nobody spoke. The silence hummed, smoke-blue, spark-shot, electric. Everyone within reach of Judith's voice had ceased, quite literally, to breathe.

Miguel Villalonga's heavy, bluish lips spread. He smiled.

"Are you now going to define the verb *had*, dear Judith?" he said.

"Are you?" Alicia's voice whispered through the dead-stopped air. "Can you, Judith?" She came toward them out of the shadows by a little door that must have been a service entrance. Now she stood there where Peter could see her, and her face was ravaged. "Can you, Judith?" she said again.

"Judy!" Peter said.

"Don't interrupt, Reynolds! Free speech and women's rights!" The Leader said.

"*Had*," Judith said, her voice a feline purr. "To have possessed—as physically. To have indulged in boudoir acrobatics, horizontal gymnastics, indoor sports, fun and games. All right?"

"No," Alicia said, "not all right."

"Then you deny—?" Miguel said.

"Nothing!" Alicia said, and her voice was quiet. "Nor admit anything either, Miguel. What may or may not have passed between Peter and me is a matter that concerns only us, our consciences, and our God. I say simply that the Señorita Lovell's definition of *had* is not all right; that if she defines possession thus, I pity her. Peter, *Cielo*, I should like to talk with you—away from this panting pack. Would you?"

"Of course," Peter said and took her arm.

"Wait," Judith said. " 'S not fair. How would you define it, Doña Alicia?"

Alicia stopped. Her eyes were luminous.

"How?" she said. "How does one describe white to a blind man, Judith? One says snow, and he thinks of cold."

"Cold, babydoll, is the last thing I'd think of in connection with you," Judith said.

Alicia nodded.

"That I grant you," she said. "But we waste time. Talk between people so different as you and I amounts to the concealment of thought. In my case, now, not even intentionally. I simply cannot say it. It comes out wrong."

"Try," Judith said.

"No," Alicia said. "The effort is too painful. And the subject itself not to be profaned by mouthing over in public, Judith. To me, so total a tenderness was, and is—a sacred thing."

"Alicia." Miguel's voice was heavy, tired.

"Yes, Miguel?"

"You realize that those words amount to a confession?"

"Do they? I still say white is white and you are blind. You and all the rest. Come, Peter, Amor. I have things to say to you."

"No!" Miguel said. "You will say them here, Alicia!"

She stood there looking at her brother.

"Very well," she whispered; then suddenly, wildly, blindly, she whirled and clung to Peter, went up on tiptoe, and kissed his mouth.

"Well, I'll be goddamned!" Judith said.

Nobody else said anything. They didn't even gasp. Instead they measured their breaths out on the dead-still air.

"That, Cielo, is the first of the things I have to say to you," Alicia said. "That I love you. I tell you so in the presence of these witnesses and before my God. The second is that I shall go on loving you for the little time I have left before I die."

"Nena," Peter said. "You shouldn't. I—"

"The third is that this ends here and now. You will never see me again after this night. Oh, Peter, *Cielo*, that that poor woman had to die that way! That she should die like that because of me, never having heard my name!"

"It was not your fault, Nena," Peter said.

"Wasn't it? At least by cowardice, my Love? If I had made it clear beforehand that I should respond to the murder of Señora Crosswaithe by a public immolation, by an auto-dafé in the Plaza de la Liberación, like those Buddhist monks in Saigon, then—"

"They would have prevented you," Peter said.

"They could not have! Any more than they can prevent . . ."

" 'Licia," Peter said.

She hid her face against him, crying.

"Luis!" the Dictator cried. "Do not move, my friend. Remain where you are!"

Luis Sinnombre stood there. Looking at him, Peter saw he showed no sign of fear.

"Reynolds," Miguel said, "what was la Señora Crosswaithe to you?"

"My wife. Ex. Separated. Divorced. Which is, of course, entirely meaningless in the eyes of the Church, and before God."

"My dear Luis," Miguel said, "what a sentimentalist you have become. Furthering young love! Though to call Reynolds young is rather stretching the point. And I—I had gone fishing. Normally, I should not have returned for weeks. Whereupon you would have presented me with—"

"A *fait accompli*," Luis said. "Or, more accurately, an opening toward the Left, Italian style. With a charming, popular young couple for you to hide behind. To lull the canalla into a sort of contentment. And thereby, dear Miguel, avoid the fate of being hanged beside you like the good thief. Though I seriously doubt that either of us shall ever see Paradise."

"Luis, dear brother," Miguel laughed, "I love you. I love the deviousness of your mind. But best of all I love the clumsiness with which you have operated in this case. I was beginning to be a bit apprehensive of your Machiavellian turn of thought. But this crude and ugly butchery is unworthy of you. Ugh! You've put us in quite a spot with Our Great Sister Republic to the North, you know."

"I have not," Luis said. "Someone anticipated me, Miguel. Somebody liquidated the dear lady for reasons of his own. Accuse me of what you will, but this sort of stupidity—no, Miguel. You know me better than that."

The Dictator looked at Peter.

"Reynolds," he said, "is it not possible that you grew impatient?"

"Your Excellency," Peter said, "is it not possible that you and Don Luis have already talked too much in the presence of too many people?"

"Ha!" Villalonga said. "You suffer from the poverty of spirit that comes from living under a system where noses are counted instead of brains and will. I, and to a lesser extent Luis, can say what we will, wherever we will. Who, my dear Reynolds, would dare gainsay us?"

"I might," Peter said. "One day I may point this little stick at you and—"

"Oh, don't talk rot, Reynolds! Tell me, did you purchase your ex-wife's death?"

"No," Peter said. "The season's permanently closed on females, so far as I'm concerned. Besides, what would I have done with Judith, here?"

Alicia tightened her arms about his neck. Peter turned his face away from Judith's eyes.

Miguel looked at Luis.

"Now that's a thought," he said. "Luis, once your matrimonial agency had achieved its object, what did you propose to do with our lovely screen star?"

Luis came over to him. Bent close to his ear. Then the two of them rocked with laughter.

Judith stood up.

"Peter! Will you turn that woman loose and take me home!"

"My dear Judith," Miguel said, "please do not desolate me by leaving. You will pardon our bad manners. Unlike these gentle people here, Luis and I are plebeian, and we have had little home training. Alicia, dear, be so kind as to turn Reynolds loose. Give him back to his rightful owner. And hurry, or I shall borrow that silly little cane of his and beat you with it, in public!"

Alicia released Peter. Stepped back. Then she saw Judith's eyes. Went up to her, took her hand, said:

"Forgive me. I do not like to cause pain—even to you. And I was never a threat, even when I thought I was. I should have known that they would spoil it for me. As they have spoiled everything, all my life. They even grow cleverer. Now they don't even need to blow up airplanes . . ."

"Alicia, dearest," Paloma Gomez said, "I'm afraid you talk too much!"

"What does it matter now, Paloma? Cannot the dying speak the truth? And in one form or another, I am already dead. Since"—she made a wry little gesture with her hand toward Peter's face—"this image will forever blind my eyes to any other, I end tonight."

"Now look, child, don't be a fool," Judith said, not unkindly.

Alicia put out her slim hand, let her fingers stray along the scar on Judith's throat.

"Were you, when you did that?" she said.

"Hell and death!" Miguel said. "I tire of hysterics, histrionics, and melodrama. Alicia, go lie down somewhere. Paloma, dear, put her in a spare bedroom and lock the door. If she weren't my sister, I'd have her shot for spoiling my evening."

"Why don't you, Miguel? I should thank you," Alicia said. Paloma got up, took her by the arm.

"Come along, Alicia. I really do think you should lie down; don't you?" she said.

"Judy," Peter said, "how about a little food to weigh down some of that Scotch?"

"Oh, all right," Judith said, and got up at once.

"Wonder of wonders!" Miguel Villalonga said. "You don't mean that an enlightened North American woman is actually going to obey a man!"

"Oh," Judith said; "Peter's different. You see, he beats me."

"Bravo, Reynolds!" The Leader said. "A pity to have to shoot you, really!"

"Peter," Judith was saying, as she put a pinch of this and that on her plate from the magnificent buffet supper Vince had spread on the immense table, dating back at least to the reign of Juana la Loca, "You think His Nibs means it?"

"I know he means it," Peter said, "only he won't dare."

"I think he's beginning to like you as a brother-in-law. Oh, damn your fatal charm!"

"Which I don't have," Peter said.

"You've got me," Judith said, "and you've got her—and still you say—"

"That's why I say it," Peter said.

Judith looked at him now. From the way she did it, it was probable she saw at least three of him.

"Meaning?"

"Meaning that maybe you can judge a guy by what he attracts, Judy. And I'm getting a little sick of playing snug harbor to shipwrecked dames."

"Oh!" she said. "Y'know what, Peter?"

"No, what?" he said.

"That's the filthy, rotten, nasty, stinking, lousy—truth. So help me, it is! C'mon, let's go back outside, shall we? I'm parched. I need another little drink . . ."

"Judith baby, I wish you wouldn't—"

"Do I sound like a drunken female, darling?"

"No. But you're getting there. Your speech has retreated back to Boston. You're murdering your consonants."

"Am I?" Judith said. "Poor consonants! Come on . . ."

But he had no sooner brought her back to that empty chair

than Vince's *ayudera de cama*—valet—came up to him and whispered in his ear:

"Pardon me, Señor Reynolds, but you are wanted on the telephone."

As he moved away from the little group composed of Miguel, Luis, Paloma, Carmencita, Vince, Sara, Don Andres, he could see they were all very gay. Judith was gayer than anybody. He could hear her talking much too loudly. Her voice was blurring fast now.

He walked through the big glass doors.

The phone was in the oak-paneled library. Peter glanced at the periwigged and goateed portraits of Vince's ancestors, at the rows of books, leather-bound, handsome, the dull gold of their titles glowing softly in the subdued light. He picked up the phone."

"*Camarada?*" a man's voice said. "Camarada Reynolds?"

"If you cut that Comrade bit, you've got it right," Peter said. "Speaking."

"I am a friend of him of the yellow eyes," the man said.

"Fine. Great. I'm so happy for you," Peter said.

"I do not jest," the man said. "Do you like the artificial fires, Amigo?"

"Fireworks?" Peter said. "Where?"

"In the Barrio de la Negra. At the warehouse belonging to him whose company you must endure this night. After that, at the Archbishop's place. We war on oppression and superstition both!"

"Look, friend, I wish you'd lay off the Archbishop. He's a friend of a friend of mine."

"You mean Padre Pío? For that very reason, his life will be spared. And the other?"

"*De acuerdo.* That one I'm for—that one I'm with you. In twenty minutes, friend."

He turned and saw Alicia standing behind him.

"Take me with you, Peter," she said.

"And get you shot or blown up again? Not on your life, Nena!"

"Then take my car. The white Jaguar outside. It replaces

the Lincoln. There is a pistol in the glove compartment. It is loaded. But please take me with you, Peter . . ."

He took the keys from her outstretched hand.

"I mean to take you with me, permanently. But not this trip," he said.

He knew where the Barrio de la Negra was. It was a poor district crowded with slum dwellings and small factories. Also warehouses. Like the one belonging to His Nibs. The Barrio was called *of the Negress* because it had a jet-black Virgin in its oldest church. Tradition held she had been washed up from the sea. She hadn't been designed to represent a Negress; it was just that she had been carved of ebony, which naturally left her dark. Once Tim O'Rourke had tried to buy her from the church with the general idea—inspired by an overdose of Scotch—of trying to enroll her in the University of Mississippi. He had his lead already written: "Ole Miss Rejects the Mother of God!" But the people of the Barrio had a genuine devotion for La Negra. Tim had had to drop the idea and even leave the Barrio in some haste.

Peter did not go straight there. Instead he turned the Jaguar into his own street, went upstairs and got his Rolleiflex and his strobe. He was coming down the stairs when it hit him. He had got out of the side gate of Vince's house, walked through an army of chronically suspicious policemen, and nobody had stopped him. He had got into Alicia's new white Jaguar which, if anything, was even more conspicuous than the Lincoln had been, and the Armed Civil Guard, who automatically should have been watching the parked cars, had been nowhere to be seen. To go farther back, Alicia's behavior, sufficient in itself to have caused any Costa Verdian whatsoever to have shot him dead on the spot, had been accepted by Miguel Villalonga with bored complaisance. Or had it? And, worst of all, Alicia herself had given up far too easily to his refusal to take her with him. He sat there at the wheel of the white torpedo and stared out into the night. Then he gunned the car, roaring through the empty streets, through which that darkest hour drifted with no faintest promise of the dawn.

Looking at his watch, he saw he had time. So he rammed the Jaguar through a series of power-skidded turns, and approached the Barrio de la Negra from the south, in the direction directly opposite from that anyone waiting for him would have expected him to come. When he was close enough, he did still another thing—he stopped the Jaguar, got out, locked it, and started to walk in the general direction of The Leader's warehouse.

He got there. Found the warehouse alone and unguarded. "In this country where they'd put an armed guard in front of a pit privy if it belonged to a VIP," he muttered. Then he moved away from it, walking almost on tiptoe. Even so, his own footsteps were loud in the empty street. He moved back. Stopped. He had the battery pack of the strobe draped over one shoulder and the Rollei hung around his neck. For some idiotic reason—half superstition, really, he had that damned fool swagger stick hung around his left wrist by the little strap it was provided with. And, now that he was still, he could hear noises. They sounded like breathing.

He moved off, stopped. The sound of breathing came from still another place. And with it, the hard clink of metal. There was no doubt about it, the whole square was surrounded by hidden men. So well hidden that even though his eyes were accustomed to the darkness now, he could not see them. So beautifully concealed that this *coup* must have been planned for days.

He started edging away toward what is called in Spanish *una boca calle*, a mouth street, that is, a street opening into the square. But, before he got two meters from where he had stood, he heard those footsteps coming on. He stopped, pointed the Rollei in the direction from which the sound came. Focused it by guesswork and feel, racking the twin lens all the way out, then back again so that a reasonable depth would be acceptably clear.

He waited. The footsteps came on, heavy and slow, obviously burdened. Then he did something that is the kind of thing called genius when it works and idiocy when it doesn't. He opened his mouth, yelled "Halt!" at the top of his lungs. Then he punched the shutter release of the Rollei.

The strobe murdered the dark. For one instant he saw the man standing there, his mouth a round black cavern in the frozen white terror of his face.

Then Peter cranked the Rollei and shot, and shot again, the white repeated lightnings building up recognizable images in his mind.

"Well, I'll be damned!" he murmured. "The pretty sarge who——"

But that was all. The blue-stained dawn coolness broke apart into shattered fragments, flame stabbed, borne in upon him on a rush of air grown solid, impenetrable, the sound a physical impact that rocked him like a double punch to both ears, so that he lay there on the ground with the smoke rising from his singed clothes, where the vortex of the whirlwind that followed or accompanied or even preceded the sound had smashed him down, in the midst of a silent, glare-washed world that dissolved very slowly into renewed darkness, echoes and a stench he couldn't recognize.

He got up from there. Reeled toward the middle of the square, forgetting that it was very probably surrounded, and stood there looking down through the thinning darkness at the Sergeant who had been the active member of the interrogation team, or rather what was left of him. A pair of trouser-clad legs lay in the square; hips, buttocks, a part of the abdomen. Above that nothing, except the slow seep of blackness draining out of what was left. He raised his eyes toward the shattered shop windows. Saw, in the deep-blue fading of the dark what dripped from every wall within a radius of twenty meters.

He could hear the frightened cries starting from all the houses, see the lights come winking on, so he brought the Rollei to sharp focus and washed that shattered, bloody debris of what had been a man in sudden lightnings, cranked the Rollei and fired again, and still once more, hearing the shrill babble of women's voices from the window, the stride of many men, heavy, purposeful, racing in; and lifted his head, making his bitter, irrevocable decision, his choice between evils, crying:

"No, Comrades! The square is surrounded!"

And, whirling, got out of there through a dawn gone hideous with siren scream, racing miraculously unstopped, unarrested, unshot, toward where he had left the car, and getting there, slowing, stopping, coming on with his hands raised above his head now, straight toward the muzzles of those Czech-made machine pistols he had seen before, and recognized from another time.

"No, Comrade, put your hands down. You are among friends," their leader said.

16.

He had been in the makeshift prison a long time. It was the boiler room of an abandoned factory filled with machinery rusting away in the tropical damp. They had placed two guards over him, youngsters in their late teens, armed with the inevitable Sten guns, clearly middle-class by their looks and behavior, which didn't surprise him, because never in all of history have revolutionists sprung from the ranks of the proletariat, for the very simple reason that to upend the world, envy is a more potent weapon than despair. The two guards had sat by the door, looking stern and grave and threatening for almost an hour after the others had gone, making the controlled, underplayed gestures of menace they had learned from old Hollywood gangster films, before they gave it up and started to ask him questions about his adventures in the Sierras; about the now-legendary Jacinto of the

Yellow Eyes; even—with an indirection and delicacy that proved they belonged to the University-student class—about his relations with Alicia. He told them what he could, and also what they wanted to hear—which was usually, but not always, the same thing. He evaded the questions about Alicia with a half-chuckled *"Hombre—"* and a widespread gesture of his hands that left them with the delightful belief that they knew everything, while in sober fact they knew nothing. And they ended up laughing and joking with him, smoking his cigarettes, and winning most of his money from him at poker, which he let them do in the interest of good will.

But now they were both asleep by the door that not merely didn't have a lock on it but whose bolt was rusted solid as well, so that the officers hadn't been able to fasten it with that and had given up trying and left the teen-agers to guard him when it finally occurred to them that the bolt was on the inside of the door anyhow, and hence useless for keeping a prisoner in. He looked at the two youngsters where they lay, sprawled out bonelessly on the damp cement floor, their young faces slack and untroubled. Then, lifting his gaze, he could see through the little iron-grilled window at street level the pale, washed-out, yellowish light of another dawn, convincing himself at last that his big military-type chronometer with the luminous dial hadn't been lying when it indicated that nearly twenty-four hours had slipped over the rim of the world since they had brought him there.

"Baby boys," he whispered in the general direction of his guards, "it's not simple. It's not simple at all. But don't find that out, yet. Enjoy your youth. Go on believing it."

Then Martin, the Second in Command, came through the door. Stood there looking at the guards.

"Look at them!" he said. "Idiots! Dolts! Why——" Then he drew back his foot and sent it thudding into their ribs. They jackknifed, snatching up their burp guns. Then they saw who it was and put them down again.

"You are a brave man, Amigo," Peter said.

"But you, Comrade Reporter, are not, or else you would have been twelve kilometers from here by now!" Martin said.

Pablo, the Commander, stepped through the door.

"I think that is open to various interpretations. Why did you not escape, Comrade Reporter?"

"I like it here. It's kind of cozy," Peter said.

"All right," Pablo said. "We developed the pictures in your camera. You are a remarkable photographer, Comrade. Would you like to see the prints?"

"God, no!" Peter said.

"As you like. You will be pleased to know that the negatives are already on the way to your paper in New York. This publicity is in our interest. That fool even wore his uniform."

"How did you get them out?" Peter said.

"Martin, here, is a skirt-chaser of the first class. One of his latest conquests is a Gringa airline hostess, who now walks spraddle-legged down the passage of the airplane because he keeps her so sore, that she can no longer close those long, beautiful thighs of which your women seem to have the exclusivity. She will deliver them personally to the office of your paper."

"I hope she can get a taxi," Peter said.

Martin laughed.

"Comrade Reporter," Pablo said, "I thank you for warning us that the square was surrounded. But for that, we should have been slaughtered. Another group of Comrades, who, hearing the explosion at the Archbishop's palace—an explosion from which the little Padre Pío escaped by a miracle, for clearly they wished to murder him and blame us for it—rushed out, and all were killed but three. And those three were captured."

"Don't you boys ever learn?" Peter said. "The same thing happened when Federico blew up the truck factory."

"I know. But we are betrayed both by impatience and by hope. In any event, I thank you. But for you, we should all be dead now, or like the three before the Archbishop's Palace, taken."

"Those three are the unlucky ones," Peter said.

"I know. Two of them are friends of mine. I do not like to think about what is happening to them now."

"Nor I," Peter said. "Comrade Chief, would you like to do something about—that?"

Pablo looked at him.

"Why do you ask?" he said.

"I stayed here to ask it," Peter said. "I did not escape in order to ask it."

"Careful, Pablo!" Martin said. "Take care!"

"Comrade Martin, have you ever read the English writer Maugham?" Peter said.

"No," Martin said.

"He wrote something about you once. Or about somebody very much like you. He said: 'He was very suspicious, and therefore an easy dupe.' Think about it."

"I have thought," Martin said. "And it makes no sense."

"What does?" Peter said.

"What could be done about those who have been captured?" Pablo said.

"If you will release me, I will return here at midnight with the information concerning the exact location of the Moral Correction and Social Re-education Centers."

"Why?" Pablo said.

"You have those little Czech-made popguns. Also, doubtless, a supply of Hexogen—or RDX, if you prefer, mixed with TNT in a rubber-compound base. Or, to put it more vulgarly, plastic. I know of no other edifices in all Costa Verde I'd rather see plasticized."

"Why?" Pablo said again.

"You see these scars upon my face? The new ones? The ones that are still pink?"

"Yes," Pablo said softly, "I see them, Comrade."

"I still say it is a trick!" Martin said. "Just as they sent *agents-provocateurs* to blow up their own palaces and warehouses in order to gain sympathy abroad, and to have an excuse to root us out, they could have scarred him thus in order to—"

"He called out," Pablo said. "He warned us. Else we would have been killed."

"All right," Martin said; "but have you not learned with

what a subtlety the mind of this *cabron* of a Villalonga works? Tell me a thing, Comrade Chief of the Band: Why did they not shoot him, afterwards? Or even arrest him? Why did they let him go?"

Pablo looked at Peter. And now he, too, was frowning.

"Have you an explanation for that, Comrade Reporter?" he said.

"No. It puzzles me as well," Peter said, "except that—"

"Except what?" Martin said.

"Their officers may be among those who are laboring under the misapprehension that my friendship with Doña Alicia Villalonga has the approval, even the consent, of The Leader."

"Hasn't it? People in the *barrio* where you reside say that she visits your apartment openly, and that you are her lover," Pablo said.

"People in my *barrio*, like people everywhere, have an excessive fondness for speculating over things they do not know," Peter said.

"They also say that you are influencing her in favor of the humble classes," Pablo said.

"I did not have to influence her. Doña Alicia is a very gallant woman, Amigo."

"Yet," Martin said, "before you came, she did nothing!"

"Before I came, she felt herself alone. Now she feels supported by me."

"So," Martin said, "you would have us believe that The Leader does not approve of your pretensions toward his sister?"

"I have no pretensions toward Doña Alicia; but no matter. The Leader does not approve of me—period."

"And yet you live?" Martin said. "Ha!"

"Amigo Martin, have you ever seen a cat with a mouse between his paws? Do you know what he does?"

"Yes. He releases it. Lets it run. Catches it again. Turns it loose once more. Until he tires of the sport, and then—"

"Exactly," Peter said.

"But to leave you free to walk the streets—"

"In this one enormous prison that your country is, what difference does that make?"

"And Doña Alicia," Martin said; "what are her feelings toward *you*, Comrade Reporter?"

"*Hombre*," Peter said, "the feelings of a woman toward a man are always a matter of speculation, even when they are married. Let us say she does not dislike me excessively."

"She," Pablo said, "kissed you on a public street in the full sight of hundreds of witnesses, including three jeeploads of police. She declared in a loud voice that she had spent the night in your arms. What do you say to that, Don Pedro, Friend of the Poor?"

"That she lied," Peter said. "She was trying to save my life. As I told you before, she is a very gallant woman, Comrade."

And now Martin was looking at him in a new way, a way that was hard to define; then, turning to Pablo, said, with what sounded curiously like joy:

"Ay, yes, Comrade Chief; let him go! You are right. He will return to us. I guarantee it!"

Luis was not in his office. So Peter asked to see Colonel Lopez. He already knew where Colonel Lopez stood. The Colonel was laboring under that very special misapprehension—that now exceedingly useful misapprehension. When Peter walked into his office, his astonishment was plain.

"My dear Reynolds," he said. "I have my entire force scouring the earth for you, and you walk into my office!"

"As big as life, and twice as ugly," Peter said. "Mind if I sit down? I'm tired."

"Of course, of course! Tell me, where on earth have you been?"

Peter grinned at him.

"That information's classified, Colonel!" he said.

"Ah, romance!" the Colonel said, "I wish I had your gifts, my friend!"

"So do I—at least those I'm popularly credited with having," Peter said.

"The evidence would indicate—" Colonel Lopez began.

"Nothing. Like all evidence, it is circumstantial and inconclusive. I seem to have a fatal affinity for either the hurtful—or the hurt," Peter said. "Look, Colonel—is there any reason why you couldn't tell me the location of the Moral Correction and Social Re-education centers?"

Colonel Lopez studied him.

"So far as I know, none," he said slowly. "That you're alive still, and walking the streets would indicate . . ."

"Love that phrase, don't you?" Peter said. "To be honest, Colonel, I'm not at all sure they indicate a goddamned thing. But I would like to know where those torture factories and murder camps are . . ."

"Why?" the Colonel said.

"Life insurance," Peter said. "Want me to make you one of the beneficiaries of the policy?"

"I'm not sure I get your meaning, my dear Reynolds," Colonel Lopez said.

"Fighting fire with fire, Colonel. I should like to take a few dirty pictures. French post cards of what goes on in those places. Thereafter, I get my negatives to a trusted friend in New York. Until such time as I can do something constructive about Alicia, or Miguelito starts to do something destructive about me, those pictures don't get printed in any newspaper. But I want my alleged future brother-in-law to know they exist and what will happen if he starts playing rough. If you'll cooperate, I'll earmark five or six for your protection as well . . ."

The Colonel looked at him. Then very slowly he closed one eye in one long wink. Pointed at the swagger stick Peter was still carrying. Put out his hand toward it.

Silently Peter passed it over.

Colonel Lopez walked over to the wall map of Costa Verde hanging behind his desk. Lifted his hand. Pointed to a place on the map with the stick.

"Why no, Reynolds!" he shouted. "You dare ask me to betray Our Glorious Leader! You dare!"

Peter took out his notebook. Scribbled the name of

the town the Colonel had pointed to. The Colonel moved the swagger stick. Pointed to another place.

"Thing of bad milk!" he screamed. "Son of the great whore! If you did not have the protection of the gracious lady Alicia, I should shoot you myself, and now!"

Peter wrote that name down, too.

"Take it easy with the hard language, Colonel," he said; "I'm only trying to save my skin."

"You've come to the wrong place!" the Colonel roared and pointed for the third time. "Now get out of here, before I forget myself! Forget the protection you enjoy! Save your skin, indeed! You are lucky I do not have it removed from your filthy gringo carcass in strips!"

"Why, thank you, Colonel, I think you're sweet, too," Peter said, and put out his hand for the stick. The Colonel passed it back to him. Peter shifted it to his left hand, put his right hand out. Colonel Lopez gripped it, hard.

"Never try a trick like that again, Reynolds," he said. "You have tried my patience, sorely!"

On the way back to his flat, Peter studied those three names. They were all to the south, in the jungle country. Xilchimocha, Chizenaya, which was said to be near the ancient Tluscolan–Toltec ruins of Ururchizenaya that the Standford Expedition had found nine years ago but which was lost again now, so quickly had the jungle growths covered the trail that the expedition had hacked to it; and Tarascanolla—all three of them Indian villages forming an isosceles triangle whose legs were approximately twenty kilometers apart. The Costa Verde section of the Pan-American Highway would put them within a reasonable distance of Chizenaya, if they dared use it. But the safest way to go that far south would be by air or sea—if there were a plane or a boat available. Of the two, the boat seemed far more likely . . .

Then, suddenly, he saw Alicia's white Jaguar roaring toward him, coming from the direction toward which he was going. She was driving it. Obviously the police had found it where he had left it and returned it to her. As she poured that sleek torpedo past the cab, he could see her face. Even in that fractured instant he could see the anguish in it.

" 'Licia!" he called, but she didn't hear him. Seconds later the Jaguar was a white toy in the distance, murdering space and time, going on.

"Señor," the taxi driver said, "I fear we have not speed enough to apprehend a vehicle of such velocity—"

"I know we don't. Take me to the address I gave you, Amigo," Peter said.

The flat was a shambles. All the ashtrays were full of cigarette butts and the sodden ends of cigars. So was the floor. The drawers of his dresser had been pawed through. The lock on his desk had been broken and all his notes were gone. He grinned. "Don't think you'll be surprised at how much I love you, Miguelito," he said. But he didn't worry about that detail. Any serious reporter knew better than to refer to his sources in writing, even indirectly or in code, when his beat was a dictatorship or the Communist states. He worried about quite another thing: In all that disorder there were no signs of Judith.

He picked up the cigarette butts one by one from the floor; examined those in the ashtray, but none bore lipstick stains. Her clothes hung in the closet beside his own—except the simple, black-sequined, low-waisted imitation of the 1920's she had worn to Vince's party. The cosmetic jars and flasks of feminine allurement stood on the vanity, untouched. The mute rows of slippers beside his vastly bigger shoes. And in the drawers, the diaphanous wisps of negligees, slips, those silken triangles, so tiny that he wondered how even a girl as slim-hipped as Judy got into them, had been disturbed by clumsy hands, of course, but were, so far as he could tell, all there. The plastic envelopes filled with stockings. Garter belts. Bras. All her intimate, personal things. There was no doubt about it. Judith had not come home at all.

He sat down in the big chair and stared out of the window. He sat there a long time, not thinking but rather consciously trying to reject a long list of things he knew about Judith Lovell. Knew beyond the tender mercy of a doubt.

But it had been a long, rough go, and he was, after all, thirty-seven years old. He sank down, down into the black depths of slumber, dreamless and remote. He escaped memory, drowned anxiety, buried fathoms deep under soundlessness the refrain that had haunted him into sleep.

"What am I going to do, now? What am I going to do now? What am I——"

He beat upward through the mindlessness, thrashing the black water into foaming rage; he clawed for breath, for life, for meaning, crying: "Oh, no, Father! I will not call upon You! I will not! I am not beaten yet. I cannot yet bow down, enter the temples of unreason, nor surrender my thinking mind without murdering my integrity—whatever the hell that is—"

He surfaced, wildly, into light. Saw that the pale amber glow washing the windows was another sunset; and turning over, he lay there staring at the winking orange-red of her cigarette's end, brightening, darkening, flaring, as she ate up the smoke in convulsive gulps.

He put out his hand and switched on the lamp by the chair. The light washed over her in a cruel wave. He saw her hair's poorly, clumsily, half-heartedly rearranged disarray; the smear of lipstick that descended a full half inch beyond and below the corner of her mouth; saw her eyes blue-ringed, deep-sunk, lightless, dull; saw the flutter at the base of her throat. Saw the mouth tremble, the lips so swollen as to look negroid; the bruises on her shoulders; and as he raised himself from the cramped, muscle-twisting position he had sunk into in the big chair, he caught full in his nostrils that last intolerable detail: the wild, fetid, feral stench of sweat; not hers, male. He said:

"Which one, Judy? Miguelito? or Luis?"

She giggled senselessly. The sound of it ended in a hiccup.

"Which one of them, Judith?" he said.

"Both. His Nibs is no damn good. Likes to watch. But that Luis!"

He stood up very slowly; what there was in his face got through to her, penetrated the whiskey fog, the long, dull, slow ache.

"Please, Peter!" she said.

"Please what?" he said.

"Beat me," she whimpered. "Break all my bones. Put me in the hospital for a month . . ."

He looked at her.

"No," he said. "You can find your dirty pleasures elsewhere, Judy."

She came to him, her eyes colorless behind a scald of tears. She put her arms around his neck. He brought his hands up and broke her grip. Stood there looking at her, his face utterly weary.

"Go take a bath," he said. "You stink."

"Peter!" she said. "Don't leave me! Oh, Peter, don't leave me, please!"

He stood there.

"I'll die!" she said. "I'll kill myself. I will, Peter!"

His face didn't change. He said:

"This time, Judy, use a gun."

"Peter—" she whispered. She was rapidly becoming sober now.

"Yes, Judy?"

"I won't kill myself. I'll do worse."

"There is worse?"

"Yes, Peter."

"Such as?"

"I'll live."

"Riddles, Judy?"

"No. I'll live and let Luis make of me what he's already trying to."

"He can make something of you that you aren't already?"

"Oh, Peter!" she wailed.

"Oh, hell, Judy. Go get in the tub."

"You won't sneak out on me while I'm in there?" she said.

"Judy, have you ever known me to sneak about anything —ever?"

"No. You're so goddam honorable that you're almost atavistic. Anyhow, come sit on the edge of the tub. Talk to me—"

"We have something to talk about?"

"Yes," Judith said. "Please, Peter . . ."

"All right. But beyond that I make you no promises, Judy."

"Just listen to me. That's all I ask," she said.

When he saw her body, saw the marks of all the various things Luis and maybe even Miguel had done to her, he wanted to puke. But he mastered the impulse. He sat there watching her lolling in the hot, perfumed water, and contemplated the idea that she not only hadn't resisted the nauseating, painful, unnatural acts inflicted upon her, but that she had probably enjoyed them. The idea fitted. Perfectly.

She saw his face. Whispered:

"Please don't be mean, Peter."

"Oh, no," he said. "I mustn't, must I? I must be nice enough to sit here and be buried in it. Up to the eyes. Go on, Judy, speak your piece."

"All right," she said; her voice was very bleak. "You're nobody's fool, so you'll recognize the truth when you hear it. I was drunk when that happened, but drunkenness had nothing to do with it. If Luis were to walk in that door right now, he could take me to bed, here, before your eyes. All he has to do is to beckon, and I'll come running. Any act he demands of me I'll perform, no matter how unspeakably vile."

Peter didn't move.

"Then, Judy, one question: What the hell are you doing here?"

"Simple," Judith said. "I love *you*, Peter. I don't love him."

"And yet?" Peter said.

"And yet, what I said before still goes. All he's got to do is to crook his little finger and . . ."

"Let's skip the recapitulation, shall we? Seems to me that this pure love you feel for me, and not for him, is hardly an article of value, Judith. Since it wouldn't prevent, or cure—"

"Prevent?" Judith said. "Cure? What can be prevented, cured in this world, Peter? Life itself is an incurable disease we always die of. Yes, I'm quoting you. Shall I give you back a few more of your bright remarks? 'There are no answers to anything.' 'No problems whatsoever can be solved.' Like your own pearls of wisdom, sage?"

"No," Peter said.

"Yet you're right. Let's put it another way: Life is a long nausea that starts with a leaky diaphragm and ends up in a maggot's belly. Is that better?"

"No," Peter said.

"No, of course it isn't! There aren't any good or better. There are only bad and worse. And worst, superlative, like me."

She climbed out of the tub. Dried herself with the big towel. Applied a deodorant spray to her armpits. Took down a flask of that hideously expensive *Peut'être* and began to rub it into the pores of her skin. All over.

"Now does my aroma please you, my lord?"

"No," he said.

"Why not?"

"The way you smell now won't wash off, Judith. The decay's internal. Involves the soul."

She laughed.

"That semantic irrelevant!" she said.

"Quoting me again?"

"Quoting you again."

"Then I was a goddam liar. A loud-mouthed idiot. And a fool. Judith—"

"Yes, darling?"

"Put some clothes on. Tonight I don't like you naked."

"Why not, Peter?"

"You look like a Krafft-Ebing case history. Or something out of Havelock Ellis. Say I find the marks left by your excursion into sadiomasochistic sexual gymnastics a trifle unbecoming. In fact, they make me sick."

"Oh!" Judith said.

He got up. Walked out of the bathroom. She came out behind him. Dug into the drawer. Put on panties. A bra. Slipped a thin housedress over her head. Sat down in a chair, looking at him.

"Peter," she said, "tell me something."

"What, Judith?"

"The truth. Look me straight in the eye and tell me: Have you ever slept with her?"

"The best defense is an offense, Judy? Then you lose. I never have."

"Oh!" she said. "Are you going to—now?"

"Apart from the fact that it's none of your goddamned business, I don't know. And it would depend upon her, anyhow. But you can make book on one thing, Judy: One way or the other it will have absolutely nothing to do with you!"

"Oh!" she said again.

"Besides, that's not the question at hand."

" 'There are no answers to anything,' " Judith quoted again. "What is the question at hand, Peter?"

"You. What the hell do I do with you now?"

"Peter—"

"Yes, Judy?"

"May I get up from this chair and come close to you? What I have to say can't be said coldly and from a distance."

"No," Peter said. "Stay where you are, Judith."

"Why? Afraid I might be able to convince you?"

"No. Even though I haven't eaten in God knows when, if I threw up, it still wouldn't be pretty."

"Is it ever? You mean I disgust you that much?"

"Yes, Judith," Peter said. "You disgust me that much."

She bent her head then and started to cry. She cried soundlessly, without any visible motion of throat and shoulders. She sat there and let a flood of tears chase one another down her face. She made no effort to wipe them away. She just sat there like that, crying.

"Oh, hell!" Peter said.

She lifted her head and faced him. Said:

"You're right. It's better that I say it from here. Dead still, without making an act of it. Without even gestures. If I went down on my knees before you, as I want to, that would reduce this to a bad Class B quickie, wouldn't it? And what I'm aiming for is—"

"A sleeper," Peter said—"your Lotus Eaters' term for a picture that unexpectedly achieves great success with small means, reasonable outlay. Right?"

"No. What I'm aiming for is the truth, Peter. So I oppose your question with another one: Do you refuse to save me?"

"Save you?" Peter said.

"Yes," she said. "As Grade B as that dialog sounds. The truth often lacks style, doesn't it? Only you can, Peter. Save, rescue, heal, cure. Maybe even resurrect. In all my life you're the only man who has meant enough to me to be able to work that miracle. To gather up the pieces of me that are scattered all over hell by now. To erase the scars of all too many brief encounters; wash me till I'm whiter than snow like that hymn says. This is very hard. I don't know how to say it. I don't even know the words."

"Huh!" Peter snorted. "So far you're going great, Judy."

"If you leave me, I won't kill myself, Peter. Because I can't lay that burden on your conscience. You do have a conscience, don't you?"

"Yes, I suppose I do," Peter said.

"If I did that, it would be your fault. The rest doesn't matter. It would be because *you* left me; because, having let me glimpse heaven, you kicked me downstairs again. The back stairs: the ones they let muddy female canines creep up from time to time. Wiggling on their bellies, imploring. So I can't depart this vale of wrath and tears leaving you holding a sack full of moral responsibility. No—only half full. But even so, you see what I mean, don't you?"

"Yes," Peter said.

"I thought you would. Peter, may I please, please get up now?"

"Why? Are you stiff from sitting there?"

"Yes. But mainly because I want to come close to you. Awkward to beg for my life sitting way over here. If this script is *nouvelle vague*, Franco-Italian neorealism, I don't like it. I'm old-fashioned. I want to scream, tear my hair, roll on the floor, chew the carpet. You know, like Theda Bara in the silent flickers a million years ago. Only it wouldn't work, would it?"

"No," Peter said.

"So I have to do it your way: quietly. With restraint. But however it's done—any way at all—I'm still begging for my life, Peter. And I don't necessarily mean life as opposed to death. There are other alternatives, you know."

"Such as?"

She got up from the chair and came to him. Stood there very close to him but not touching, not even trying to.

"Such as life opposed to horror," she said.

He stood there, looking at her.

"What am I supposed to do, Judy?" he said.

"Just take me away from here. Just—love me, without even thinking how little I deserve it. I don't. Not at all. I deserve to be beaten into a bloody, unrecognizable pulp and left in a ditch to rot. Think, if you must think at all, of how much I need you. I don't ask justice of you, Peter. What I ask *is* mercy."

He didn't move.

"And if I consent to wear my horns with complacent grace, there'll be no more—of this sort of thing?" he said.

She looked at him. When she spoke, her voice was bleak. As bleak as truth usually is.

"I don't know. I can't promise you that, Peter. You would have to prevent it. For now. Maybe for years. Until I'm cured. If I ever am. Will you take me on that basis, Peter? On nothing more than my awful, helpless need of you?"

He went on looking at her. Then he said it—voiced what was the victory of pure compassion or his own utter, abject, irrevocable defeat:

"Yes, Judy."

And stood there, wondering which of the two it was, as he held the long, slow tremble of her body against him; not only knowing, but knowing he would never know, until the hour he ceased to breathe, think, feel pain.

But she was talking again.

"You won't be sorry, darling! I promise you you won't. . . . Peter, I know you love her. And she, poor thing, she is dying of wanting you! Only you can't have each other, can you?"

"No," Peter said.

"Why not?" Judith said.

"There's a grave athwart our path. With Connie in it," Peter said.

"Oh!" Judith whispered. "I——"

And then they heard the thunderous knocking on the door.

Peter opened it. Luis Sinnombre stood there, surrounded by a herd of policemen. Judith shrank back, all the color draining out of her face. But Luis didn't say anything. Instead he turned to his uniformed Piltdown men.

"Search the place!" he said.

They fanned out, tearing open doors. All the rooms. The closets. They even looked under the beds. Then they came back, saluted, said:

"She's not here, Don Luis!"

"I didn't think she would be," Luis said. "My dear Peter, are you going to be stupid and gallant and Anglo-Saxon and force me to take unpleasant measures, or are you going to be reasonable and tell me where she is?"

"Where who is?" Peter said.

"As if you didn't know! Your little Alicia, who has disappeared. Miguel is most upset. And when Miguel is upset the results compare with Zopocomapetl when it's upset. I hate to be stern, Peter, but with *this* caper, you've put *my* neck in a sling. In the charming Gringo phraseology of our charming Judith here—how are you tonight, my sweet?—come on, Peter—*give!*"

Peter walked up until he was very close to Luis. Stood there looking at him.

"I wouldn't give you the time of day, now, Luis," he said.

"My dear Peter, you don't have to give me anything," Luis said. "What I want, I take. Or hadn't you noticed?"

Peter didn't say anything.

"Come on, Peter, don't be tiresome. Speak your piece like a good boy."

"No," Peter said.

"Why not?"

"Don't like this script. Too Hollywood. No, TV. Anything I could say now would come out wrong. Make me sound like the male lead in one of Judy's pictures. The kind of thing you can't say now without laughing, or wanting to puke. Or both."

"Why don't you have a try at it in your own inimitable style? Your dispatches are first-rate, everyone gives you that."

"All right," Peter said. "I don't know where Alicia is. But if I did, I wouldn't tell you. I was in the hands of your goons for three days before, remember. It's possible, given time, you could break me, Luis. Hell, it's probable. You took a good bit out of me that trip that I haven't been able to put back. That was maybe irreplaceable. But now you'd better kill me, Luis, because, if you don't—"

"If I don't?"

"I am going to kill you. Do you mind if I say that again?"

Luis smiled, said:

"Of course not. But why do you want to?"

"Because I want to say it right, with the proper lack of emphasis. Not because of what you did to Judy. Not because of my previous, or any future, sessions with your persuasion squad. But because noxious insects and poisonous reptiles have to be eliminated. For the general good of society. Because at heart I'm a Boy Scout. My good deed for some future day, Luis."

Luis laughed.

"I don't think I need worry about that, do you?" he said.

"No, but there is one thing you had better worry about," Peter said.

"Which is?"

"Time. The time you could use, tracing Alicia. The time you're going to waste on me until you finally convince yourself that the only reason why what the cleaning woman will carry out in the slop bucket didn't talk while it was all in one piece and could was because it didn't know. So why don't you take your Neanderthals out of here and go do something useful?"

Luis looked at him.

"You know, Peter, you almost convince me—" he said.

"Luis, I don't give a two-peso crib-girl screw about your convictions. What I'm worried about now is 'Licia! Why—"

"Oh, hell," Judith said. "I wish . . ."

"What, my dear?" Luis said.

"That whoever has got her now would feed her to the crocodiles. Or the fish," Judith said.

"Oh, come now, Judy; you'll have *me* to console you," Luis said.

"But I don't want you, Luis; I want him."

"You said that last night, remember? But we waste time. Peter, aren't you—"

The doorbell rang. Loudly. Demandingly.

Luis nodded. One of the policemen went to the door. A telegraph messenger stood in it.

"A telegram for—" he began; then his voice died.

The policeman put out his hand. The messenger put the telegram into it. He didn't wait for anybody to sign anything. He went down those stairs at a run.

"The Organic Democracy," Peter said.

The policeman brought the telegram to Luis. Luis smiled.

"With your permission, dear Peter?" he said, and ripped it open. Read it at a glance. Stopped smiling. Looked at Peter.

"So you were telling the truth!" he said. He extended the telegram to Peter.

Peter took it. Read it. From somewhere very far away, he heard Judith's voice. It made a hateful noise in his ears.

"Oh, Peter!" she said. "What's wrong?"

Peter didn't answer. He started for the door.

"Peter! Where are you going?"

Peter stopped. But he wasn't looking at Judith. He looked at the Head of the Secret Police.

"Luis," he said, "do I have to ask you not to have me followed?"

Luis looked back, and now his dark face was absolutely grave.

"Of course not, Peter. These boys mean business. And they never heard of the Marquis of Queensberry."

Peter stood there, looking at him.

"You could never get there quickly enough, Luis. Never in this world. And even if Miguelito let you off the hook—"

"What, Peter?"

"I wouldn't," Peter said.

17.

As soon as he came out on the street, Peter heard the police sirens. They came from every direction, loud on the warm-soft, feathery, tropical night air. So he knew that Luis Sinnombre was making good use of his telephone, which meant that the head of the Secret Police would be too busy to occupy himself with Judith tonight. The comfort was small; the choice, like most of life's choices, ugly. It was no comfort to reflect that whatever might happen to Judy (through his now deliberate, conscious abandonment of her) did not involve her death; because, considered coldly, it did involve the destruction of her identity; the annihilation of those thousand, thousand quirks of personality that made her the individual she was, and that individual, to him, in spite of everything, curiously dear. That is, if she were not as a person already destroyed. Was she not, even now, one of the walking wounded? How much more was required to force her into the ranks of the living dead? Of that army of Zombies which was the one unique byproduct of the twentieth century; the people who went on living after too much *Angst, angoise,* anguish, *angustia* had stunned their minds into abject dullness, stopped a little above the minimum requirements of vegetal, inert existence, what they had been once pleased to call their hearts?

But he had no time for that. His choice was already made. Any half-stopped heartbeat now, some blundering ape of a policeman might stumble upon that black hole, cellar, stairwell, closet in which they held bound and gagged his life, his joy, his shape of things to come, his hope of heaven— and one short, tearing burst of Sten gun fire would rip out and end time for him, end the remotest possibility of his continuing to support what was very nearly insupportable now.

So he stepped to the curb and flagged down a taxi. The driver's face was frightened. He said: "To where, Señor?" And Peter answered him: "Anywhere—as long as it's the hell away from here!"

Before they had gone two blocks, they saw the police setting up a barricade across the street ahead of them. "Take another!" Peter said; and the taxi driver: "Do not preoccupy yourself, Señor! I have lived fifty years now by avoiding these animals in uniform!" Peter saw that what the police were doing now was to begin a massive, street-by-street, house-by-house, flat-by-flat search. But in a city of nearly half a million inhabitants, their chances of finding one small, frightened, tender, haunting girl-woman, before it was too late, were nil.

But, even so, he didn't go straight to the warehouse. For, although so far he had seen no signs that Luis Sinnombre was having him followed, he knew the Head of the Secret Police too well by now to accept his word about anything whatsoever. He told the taxi driver to take him downtown. Got out, paid his fare; dismissed the cab. Entered Pam-Pam. Came out the back entrance. Took another taxi and directed the driver to The Blue Moon. Got out and went in. The taxi driver would remember that destination as sure as hell.

The substitute madam wanted to stage a parade of naked girls for him.

"I don't like girls," Peter said.

"Well, it is a little early for boys," the madam said, "but if the Señor cares to wait, I'm sure I could procure him a pretty *niño* in no time at all."

Peter sipped his drink. It was strong.

"Haven't time," he said. "Besides, I don't like boys either."

"Then *what* does the Señor like?" the madam asked.

"Horses," Peter said.

"Horses?" the madam said. "Well, that is a little more difficult—"

"And it has to be the kind that sits on grapefruits," Peter said.

"Now really, Señor!" the madam said.

"I make a jest. A bad joke. The kind that are called in my country tales of hirsute canines. Shaggy-dog stories. Truly, Madame, I have no need for any sort of sexual fare. I simply have to kill a certain amount of time. And in a place where it will be remembered that I was there at this hour."

"Oh!" the madam said. "Please don't tell me any more about it, Señor!"

She sailed out of the door like a dreadnaught.

At once a girl came through it. She had been beautiful once. She was still beautiful in a way. But now she looked like what she was. She put her hand out to Peter.

"Come upstairs with me," she said.

"I am sorry, amiga," Peter said.

"Why not?"

"I have not the desire."

"I will awake it."

"Nor the time, so do not bother," Peter said. Then: "Haven't I seen you somewhere before?"

"No. You have only seen my eyes. But in the head of my brother," she said.

"My God!" Peter said.

"Jacinto has told me much of you. Come and we will talk. Upstairs in my room. For you there is no charge. And all the filigrains you may wish. À la Italienne. À la Française. In any position; making use of whatever you will . . ."

"Look, Teresa—"

"How did you know my name? Did Jacinto tell you?"

"Yes," Peter said.

"Poor Jacinto. He comes here often. And always I take him to my room."

"Your brother?" Peter said.

"Why not? Oh, not what you think! You were in that Indian village with him, no?"

"Yes."

"And you witnessed what happened?"

"Yes. You mean he is still like that?"

"Yes. The other girls do not know he is my brother."

"With *those* eyes?"

"They do not look at men's eyes very often. They look at the bulge of their billfolds. They think he is my lover. When he is in my room I scream and shout and beg him to do this and with that and like this. So that they will not know. You see? So that he can maintain his pride."

"Poor Jacinto," Peter said.

"He is very fond of you. He says you are his only friend."

"Odd," Peter said. "I thought he hated me."

"No. Come with me? I would give you great pleasure."

"Thank you, Teresa, but I have to go now."

"But why precisely now?"

"Because I have just seen the detective who was tailing me leave his post, under the impression that I will remain here all night. Believe me, Teresita, it is my only chance. You know how the police are . . ."

"*Do* I? The billygoats! The malformed abortions of filthy mothers! The—"

"Girl-child," Peter said, "not even Spanish has profanity enough. You'd have to invent a new language. *Adios!*"

She bent and kissed his mouth. She was very expert.

"Now you will come again," she said. "I am sure of that."

"Amiga, so am I. In fact, you can depend on it," Peter said, and went out of there wondering if she had a disease and if he had a cracked place on his mouth and if he did whether the disease were the kind one could catch that way. Then he went down the stairs onto the sidewalk and hailed another cab.

He made the taxi driver zigzag over half of town, under the pretext that he could not remember the name of the street where he wanted to go but only how the house looked. He got out several blocks from the factory and walked the rest of the way. But when he got there, he found only Martin waiting for him.

"Pablo would not grant me the privilege of guarding her," he said; "he declares I am not to be trusted around women. He is right. For, although she is of a terrible skinniness, and also of a certain ugliness, the whole of her adds up to a strange sort of excitement. I have known beautiful women who moved me less. No wonder you are so in love with her, Comrade . . ."

"If she has been hurt or molested in any way, you'll see how much I love her," Peter said.

"Oh, do not preoccupy yourself about that. Pablo is worse than an old woman, or a priest," Martin said. "Now come."

They had her in the back room of a country roadhouse just off the Pan-American Highway, in plain sight of every police jeep that went shrieking past. The Edgar Allan Poe principle. The Purloined Letter technique. Hide the body where nobody'd believe you'd dare to. Not that this place looked like a roadhouse, despite its magnificent location. It looked like the Supreme Parliament of all the flies and filth on earth. And probably was.

She was in a back room, her hands and feet tied to the chair they had her in, and a gag in her mouth that just looking at was enough to make a goat heave. She was being guarded by a hundred kilos—roughly two hundred twenty pounds—of mustached, dark-skinned female whose sex could have been discerned by a blind man from fifty meters away. She had her eyes closed—and was trying to close her nostrils too, against the monstrous stink of her monstrous guard.

"Turn her loose," Peter said.

Her eyes came open. Blazed. The way she looked at him hit him in the gut, going through the scar tissue some of the Chinese mortar fragments had left there, along with the nervous stomach that was largely allergic to food.

Pablo nodded. The She Monster moved with surprising deftness, even a certain grace. Then Alicia came up out of the chair and would have fallen if he hadn't caught her, because they had shut off the circulation in her hands and feet by tying her too tight.

The way she kissed him removed any lingering doubts her captors might have had.

He pushed her away. Said:

"Have they hurt you, 'Licia?"

"No," she whispered, "they have been polite, even kind. They explained the necessity of binding me up thus, for fear I might make some involuntary sound. I bear them no ill will, Peter."

"I do," Peter said. "Pablo, the deal's off. I gave you my word I would come back. But you had to use coercion— 'Licia—Nena, what's wrong?"

Her small face went scarlet. Then she smiled.

"You are my man, no? Then why do I have shame? I have been sitting there tied up for hours—and— Oh, Peter, do you suppose that they have an *excusado* that is not of a horrible dirtiness?"

"They have, Doña Alicia, but it is broken, and there has been no water in it for three months," Pablo said; "and if you were to enter it, you would probably faint. I suggest you go for a little walk with Chiquita, here . . ."

When he said *Chiquita*, he nodded in the direction of the female mountain.

"Excuse me, *Cielo?*" she said, still blushing. "I'll be back immediately."

"All right," Peter said, "but don't hurry. I wish to say a few gross words, unlovely expressions, profanities, and even an obscenity or two, to my good friends here."

"Peter, Love, do not be angry with them. They had reasons for what they did. They explained them to me . . ."

"Nena, you go make *pipi* and let me handle this!" Peter said.

"Oh, Peter!" she wailed and fled.

"Look, Peter, I am very sorry, but from sad experience we have learned to trust no one," Pablo said.

"All right," Peter said, "don't trust me. I see you have a telephone in this flyblown Ritz. I will make you one more proposition, my last!"

"Which is?" Martin said.

"That you let Alicia get into the Jag and—"

"Can't. One of our girl comrades, who is about Alicia's size, delivered the Jaguar to the back door of the Villalonga residence before the police were aware that your beloved was even missing. It was too conspicious, Peter; we couldn't afford . . ."

"All right. That's only a detail. Put it this way: When you let me take her into town, I'll—"

"No, Peter."

"Goddammit, Pablo! I told you I'd come back!"

"I know. And I trust you, Peter; but will you live long enough to be able to?"

"They won't lay hands on me," Peter said. "Why—"

"As of last night they might. Your country's military 'technical advisers,' with their helicopters, airplanes, and expensive weapons designed to train Villalonga's 'Defenders of Democracy Against the Red Menace,' have been withdrawn.

One of our friends among the police—for we have friends even there—states that your dispatches, and those of your Irish friend, are credited with causing your government's change of heart. So——"

"I'll take the chance," Peter said.

"But we cannot allow you to, Comrade. We need you, need the information you possess."

"All right. Then have someone else take her home. When she herself phones me here, and tells me that you have delivered her to a place of safety, I will tell you the location of those prison camps, as I promised."

"And you, *Cielo?*" Alicia whispered, as she came back through the door.

"I go with them, Nena; I have to. Part of the bargain."

"Then I go with you!" Alicia said.

"Now look, Nena—"

Martin grinned.

"It would be safer, Comrade," he said; "trying to take her back into town involves risks of a certain vileness—even to her."

Peter looked at Pablo.

"That is correct, Peter. The police are excessively nervous with firearms, as you know very well."

Peter went on looking at him. Said:

"But the camps are far away. And once we reach them the attacks will be of a perilousness viler than the milk of a witch—"

"Ha!" Martin said. "That is a new profanity! Is it from the English, Comrade?"

"Sort of," Peter said. " 'Licia, Nena—"

"Take me with you! You know I am unhappy apart from you! Oh, Peter, *Cielo,* please!"

"Nena—" Peter said. "You might get killed. Hell, we both might."

"I could ask no greater happiness," she said, "than to lie beside you forever."

"Nena, there is too much risk of precisely that," Peter said.

"Is it not better to die quickly of gunshot wounds than

slowly of grief? Look at me, Peter! Since I have known you I have lost six kilos. Six kilos I could not afford to lose. You would like me to end up in a madhouse, locked in a strait jacket, raving and calling your name? I know we can never be married; but I can be yours, and I will! I accept the sin! What pain, what punishment, what hell could be worse than what I suffer now? Oh, Peter, I—"

He held her to him. Said to Pablo:

"How do we go?"

"In trucks. The truck drivers, because they are all cruelly exploited, support our cause. In an hour they will begin to arrive. They will hide us among the merchandise."

"And when we reach the post of control that the carabinieros of the Civil Guard have always along the highway?"

"Then they *are* in the South!" Martin said.

"At Xilchimocha, at Chizenaya, and at Tarascanolla," Peter said.

"All near the highway! Did you hear, Pablo? Stupendous! Marvelous!"

"And when we reach those posts of control?" Peter said.

"They are fixed," Pablo said. "We know where they are. Three kilometers before each one we descend, walk through the jungles until we have passed them. The trucks will wait."

Peter looked at Alicia. She had on a chic sort of a cocktail dress. Her arms were bare.

"Martin," he said, "send one of the sleepy boys into town on the motorbike to buy a mono, a coverall. No, two. One for me, large. And the other of the smallest size they have, for Alicia. Even so, I fear it will be too big."

"Oh, *Cielo, Cielo,* I am so glad!" Alicia said.

Martin looked at his watch.

"I am afraid it is too late for that by now," he said. "All the stores are closed. Still, you are right. That little dress is not suitable for this trip. Let me see—let me see . . ."

"Do not preoccupy yourself, Comrade Second Chief!" said one of the teen-agers who had guarded Peter. "I will procure monos for the Comrade Reporter and his lady."

"How, Joaquin?" Martin said.

"I will steal them!" Joaquin laughed. "I am a thief of the first class!"

"Don't be a fool, son," Peter said, "the streets are crawling with police."

"Ha! You do not know me, Comrade! I will take along Mario to stand watch. When I return I will present the Comrade with a pistol stolen from the very belt of a policeman! And the monos. Is there anything else the Comrade desires?"

Peter looked at Pablo.

"He is crazy, this *niño*, no?" he said.

Pablo shook his head.

"No, Comrade. He does not even exaggerate. He is the best thief I have ever seen. We have found this talent of his very useful in the past. Since he is going to steal the monos, I suggest that you give him a list of other things you may need."

"Just two," Peter said; "a Commando's knife—and a radio. A transistor radio of several bands. But especially of the six-to-eighteen-meters bands, which includes the police broadcasts to their patrols—"

Martin looked at Peter.

"Now that," he said, "is what I call an idea of a certain intelligence!"

And now, men began to arrive. They came on foot, carrying heavy packs. Peter hoped they'd keep some of those packs out of the truck he and Alicia would have to ride in. He knew that the only thing that would make the hexagon-TNT combination, stirred into a thick rubber foam that looked like chewing gum and smelled like marzipan, explode was a spark. He knew that you could hit it with a hammer, drop it, mold it, play ball with it, and nothing would happen; but in Algiers he had seen what it could do when it went off, so his respect for *le plastique* was profound. They had other things, too; knee mortars of Russian manufacture; long tubes that seemed to be bazookas; Sten and Bren guns; even a few heavier, tripod-mounted weapons. So extensive and excellent was their material that Peter turned to Pablo and said: "How?"

"The major offensive will be mounted any day now. We have profited from your Navy's vigilance of Cuba. Now the Russian ships debark material in a cove near the southern tip of the Republic. We have promised to transship it to Cuba, Peter. And we will—once we have used it ourselves!"

"What are you waiting for?" Peter said.

"The Indians. They are becoming more and more dissatisfied with their lot. Almost they are ready to come over to us. They would have before now, if it hadn't been for Padre Pío. Which is why that swine of a Villalonga tried to blow him to bits the other night."

"This I do not understand," Alicia said. "If my brother—and I grant you he is a swine, Pablo—more swine than you know—killed the little Father, would not that throw the Indians automatically into your camp? I speak Tluscola, and I know them well. They are very devout . . ."

"It would, Doña—no!—Camarada Alicia, since you have joined us—but for the fact that your clever brother had it arranged so that the Indians would think it was we who had murdered the little Vasco. Only, he escaped . . ."

"Thank God," Peter said.

"I am grateful, too, though I do not believe in your God," Pablo said.

"*Dios mío!*" Alicia said. "Look at that!"

They looked. And now they saw that Zopocomapetl was vomiting fire, sending a tongue of flame straight up into the heavens for three hundred meters or more.

"Good!" Pablo said. "They will have other things than us to occupy their minds with, this night!"

Then they heard the roaring of the motors on the road. And saw the first of the trucks stop before the roadhouse. The silent men began to load it quickly, but with great care. They took out what the truck already had in it, at first, then loaded their supplies. Put the innocent merchandise back on top of that.

Peter stepped up to the truck driver.

"This of the volcano," he said, "has it caused much damage in the city?"

"No," the driver said. "But the Indian town of Xochua has been wiped out. Very few escaped."

Then, before Peter could say anything, Joaquin and Mario roared up on the motorbike. They had the coveralls, called in Spanish *monos azules*—blue monkeys—with them. The knife. A policeman's pistol. And the radio. It was a damn fine radio. It had FM, AM, and three short-wave bands. It would be very useful.

Alicia lay in his arms inside the truck. The truck was loaded with sacks of cement besides the other material Pablo's band had now added. The sacks were dusty. They made Peter sneeze. But they didn't seem to affect her at all. She had been kissing him everywhere she could reach ever since they'd left the roadhouse.

"Nena—" he said.

"*Cielo?*"

"Cut it out, will you?"

"Why? Do you no longer love me?"

"Yes. Too much. But if you make me explode, I might also set off the grenades that Martin has in his pocket."

"Oh!" she laughed softly. "Peter—"

"Nena?"

"Would you that I do a thing to ease you? A thing smaller than the great thing, I mean?"

"Such as?" Peter said.

"I could touch you. With the hands. Shall I?"

"Hell, no! Who's been teaching you these childish, filthy tricks?"

"My husband. When he was being faithful to me. Because he did not wish to give me a child. Peter!"

"Yes, Nena?"

"Give me a child! Oh, Peter, please!"

"Now?" he said.

"Now! Tell Martin to turn his back!"

"He still has ears."

"I do not care! I will be very quiet. I will not cry out. I
promise you."

"Nena—no."

"Oh, Peter, *Cielo*—I want you so!"

"And I you. But in privacy. And, if possible, in a bed.
Because if we ever do make another little Sinnombre, I
should prefer him born with hands and feet instead of wheels
and a horn and headlights and—"

"Peter, you are crazy, you know? But I am glad you are.
Because if you were sane, you could not love this quarter of
a kilo of bones with a face like a little monkey's—"

"*Hola*, Monkeyface!" Peter said, and kissed her.

"*Cara de Mona.* Strange, when *you* say it I like it."

"That makes two of us."

"Peter—kiss me."

"Nena, let's not start *that* again!"

"I won't. Only kiss me good night. I have a desire to sleep.
In your arms. For the first time. Where I mean to sleep all
the rest of my life."

He kissed her. But she drew away quickly. Said:

"Oh, Peter, what is wrong?"

"Nothing."

"Tell me!"

"No. It will spoil it."

"It *has* spoiled it. So tell me!"

"I thought about—her. Sleeping alone, forever. And her
three children without a mother. And her husband without——"

"*Ayeee!*" she wailed. "But this is not our fault, my love!
All my life I have suffered for other people's sins. Ay, great
and vengeful God! At least allow me one grand glorious sin
of my own to suffer for!"

"Nena, I don't think you need worry about that at all,"
Peter said.

Book Three

WITHDRAWAL
AND RETURN

18.

From where they were now, lying on their bellies in the thick, sticky mud of the mangrove swamp, they could see the camp. It wasn't at Tarascanolla at all, but twelve kilometers away in the jungle itself.

"Like it?" Pablo said.

"Very much," Peter said. "They have given us all the advantages."

"Meaning?" Martin said.

"Because they wanted to conceal these obscenities from the eyes of the tourists, they have placed them in the jungle. Which is excellent for hiding a prison camp, but even better for those who have to attack it. We can approach to within three meters of that murder factory without being seen."

"Come then," Pablo said, "let us go back to the *albergue*, that we may speak of it."

"All right," Peter said.

They moved through the swamp on their bellies. When they were far enough away from the concentration camp, they stood up, started walking back toward the inn.

"I do not understand you, Comrade Reporter," Martin said.

"What is it about me you do not understand, Amigo?" Peter said.

"Your wanting to lead this attack. If I had such a woman

as you have waiting for me at the inn, I should develop such a desire for life that my cowardice would be enormous!"

"You think mine is not?" Peter said.

"Yet you insist upon leading the attack," Pablo said. "Why, Comrade?"

"The reasons are various. And of a nature both simple and complicated—"

"Start with the simple ones," Pablo said.

"Very well. In the first place, your band, Amigo Pablo, unlike that of the brave Juan, afterwards of Jacinto and last of all of Federico, with whom it ceased to be a band at all and became food for the buzzards, is untrained. Of you all, only I have seen warfare. I have seen too damned much of it; but no matter. I do not propose to watch you being slaughtered through your ignorance. You are very brave and very ignorant, which is the worst of all possible combinations. Lacking knowledge of tactics, it would be better if you were cowards . . ."

"Go on," Martin said.

"I used Commando tactics against the Chinese in Korea. I propose to teach you what I know. I propose to take this camp as a demonstration to you of how it should be done. It is not my intention to lose a single man. Thereafter, you, Martin, will take the one at Xilchimocha; while you, Pablo, with me again as Second, will take the one at Chizenaya last of all."

"Why leave that one for the last?" Martin said.

"Because after this one the element of surprise will be gone; and each attack will be more difficult than the last. That is one reason. The other is that the Moral Correction Center at Chizenaya is where they keep the women prisoners, who afterward will be a burden," Peter said.

"Ay! That they be many, and I will burden them!" Martin said.

"Wait until you see what they look like by now," Peter said.

"Comrade Reporter—" Pablo said.

"Yes, friend?"

"You have not said it all. I want to hear the complicated easons as well."

"I do not know how to say them," Peter said. "I am not ven sure I know what they are . . ."

"Try," said Pablo.

"All right. I went into the Korean War unwillingly, unonvinced that there was anything to be served by killing. r even that there were any principles to life at all. I came ut of that war a little changed . . ."

"How?" Martin asked.

"I had discovered a principle or two."

"Such as?" Pablo said.

"That a man ought to have a house. With a garden around . And a fence around that garden. And a gate to that nce."

"These are principles?" Pablo said.

"Yes, Amigo. Because on that gate should be a sign that ays *No Trespassing*. And at that man's side a gun to permaently remove any creature whomsoever who tries to collecvize that garden, or make that man go to church, or interre with his simple pleasures such as getting drunk on Saturay night and enjoying the woman he has inside that house. ook me a long time to get to those principles. If you want to efoul them with big words, you might say that the state made for man, not vice versa. That man comes first. That s cooperation on weighty matters must always be respectlly asked, not required. Or, as Old Abe put it: *of, for,* d *by*. Catch?"

"Yes," Pablo said. "I catch that you're a reactionary, Comde."

"Yes," Peter said. "A reactionary who is going to help you in this football game. But who is going to kick hell out of ou, the first time you start fouling up the things I got into is mild disagreement over."

"Which are?" Martin said.

"I told you. That little house. That little woman in that use. That little vine and fig tree. And that gate that you, e Prime Minister of the Soviet Socialist Republics, the

President of the United States, or Fidel Castro can't come into unless I do the inviting. Which I would, of course. Give you a drink. Talk about baseball, bullfighting, fly fishing. Let the little woman trot out a home-baked cake. Make you very welcome, friend. As long as you are—"

"As long as I am what?" Pablo said.

"A friend. Which adds up to enjoying my company and leaving me the hell alone."

"Those," Martin said, "are very rare principles, Comrade!"

"Aren't they?" Peter said. "Men have been dying for ten thousand years, trying to make them stick."

When they came out of the jungle, they could see the inn. It was a very pretty inn, and almost new. There weren't any tourists in it now because it was summer, and the tourists only came this far south when it was winter and the climate became endurable. The trucks were all parked in the inn's parking lot, under the split-bamboo sunshades. The sleepy-headed teen-agers, Joaquin and Mario, were painting signs. The signs read CLOSED FOR THE SEASON. When they had finished, they would put the signs fifty meters down the road in both directions, and another larger one outside the door, just in case. So far, absolutely no cars had passed, but you never could tell.

Downstairs in the basement, they had the innkeeper and his wife locked up. The wife was a pretty Indian girl of about twenty. She took being locked up with the resignation of the Tluscola to everything. But the man was a heavyset, powerful mestizo of fifty. From his looks, his Indian ancestors hadn't been Tluscolan; they had probably been the dirty, degenerate fisher Indians—who swapped their wives, slept with their own sisters, mothers, aunts, or cousins when female; or when hard up, in the immediate absence of females, with their brothers, fathers, uncles, and cousins, being one of the most completely ambisexual bunches who ever lived. He, Peter saw, wasn't resigned a good goddam. He was ugly. He wasn't to be trusted.

When Peter came up the stairs he could hear Alicia singing. Her singing voice was between an alto and a contralto, though, when she wanted to she could push it up through the coloratura, through the mezzo, and speak it well within the lyric soprano's range. What she sang now was a love song. The words went:

"La primera vez que te vi, me enamore locamente de ti . . ." Which came out clumsily in English as "The first time I saw you, I fell madly in love with you," thus losing all the lilt and magic it had in Spanish and proving again that translation was a thing you should never do, unless you absolutely had to.

Peter came into the room and saw that Alicia had taken off the coverall, and was wearing the cocktail dress. It looked as though she were going to a party.

"How'd you manage that?" he said. "You look so fresh and cool."

"Oh, I am, *Cielo!*" she said. "I had a shower and washed all my things and lay on the bed naked, hoping you would come in so that I could tempt you. Only all my clothes dried within ten minutes, so I put them back on, because there is no lock on the door . . ."

"Nena—" Peter said.

"Oh, Peter. You're covered with mud!"

"I know. I'm going to take a shower now," Peter said.

"Then hurry! And when you're all nice and clean—"

"Nena," Peter said, "no . . ."

She looked at him and what was in her eyes was very hard to look at.

"Peter," she said. "Tell me why?"

"Because," he said, "I did not know you would be with me, and I have brought nothing, no means of taking precautions. And—"

"Peter," she said, "I told you I want a child. Your child."

"Little Peter No-Name. Hell of a thing to wish on a kid, no?"

"Cielo, you are too complicated," she said.

"We can't remedy it, you know," Peter said, "unless you

are willing to accept murder, as the price of a husband. I cannot accept it as your dowry, Nena. It would dirty our lives forever."

She continued to look at him.

"Go take your shower, Peter," she said.

When he came out of the shower, she was sitting by the window. It was already dusk and the sun was flaming down the sky. In a little while it would be dark, the abrupt, no-transition dark of the tropics. And when it was, he would have things to do. He didn't like even to think about those things now. He was wrapped in the big towel; when he looked for the only shorts he had, to put them back on, they weren't there.

"I washed your shorts for you, and your socks, and your shirt," Alicia said. "Ugh! They were of a filthiness unimaginable. So now they are all wet, and you have no clothes to put on and hence are at my mercy—"

"Nena," he said, "there is one other thing—"

"Which is?" she said.

"What we will do at dawn tomorrow is extremely perilous. I must not lie to you. This of your hunger for a child is one thing, but to inflict bastardy and fatherlessness upon him simultaneously is another. Let me then finish this of tomorrow. And that of the next day, and of the day after. I no longer have any faith in my luck. I have used up too much of it."

She sat there, looking at him. Then, very slowly, she got up and came to him. She put her two hands up and let them lie cool and remote along the slant of his jaw. She went up on tiptoe, kissed his mouth.

"If you are killed at dawn," she said, "you think that by noon I shall be still alive? How little you know me, Peter!"

"Nena—you couldn't; you mustn't! I—"

"I could. And I will. Except——"

"Except what, *Muñeca?*"

"Except that—that you leave your life in me. Your image. Your replica, to grow tall and strong as you are and as ugly as you are, and as beautiful. Can you deny me this, *Cielo?* Deny me the only thing that would save my life?"

"Nena," he groaned.

She opened those almond-shaped eyes very wide. Stared at him. Let him peer into the heart of darkness. Then with a brusque, harsh, angular motion that suited her, she bent her head and cried. Angrily. Terribly. Her whole body shook.

He put out his arms, drew her to him.

She hammered at his chest with both her fists.

"You leave me nothing, not even pride!" she raged. "Must I beg you on my knees? Must I? Oh, damn you, let me go!"

He turned her loose. She backed away from him, held him with the black fury of her gaze, executed a swirling veronica of silk and nylon and lace upward and away, hooked thumbs into that triangular wisp she had on beneath, made a brief, curiously graceful contortion through silken downward slither into suddenly renewed bifurcation and stood there, lifting, swelling, puckering, poised, inhollowed, trembling, under the wonder and the worship of his gaze. He saw that she was slender rather than thin. What in French is called *une fausse maigre. Trim* was as close as he could get to it in English. Her breasts were small and high and conical. Her body was champagne-colored, pale golden, except for the wild strawberries tipping the breasts, a tiny blue half-moon under the left one (What was it Luis had said?), and the startling black plume of her sex. And now, bending forward, cringing a little, surrendering to shame, she came to him with a skip and a scamper like a child, plunging into his arms, burying her face to the rough, scarred hollow of his throat.

He lay there, kissing her slowly, gently, tenderly. But she tore her mouth free, said angrily, harshly:

"Do not waste time! Can't you see I want—"

"What, Nena?"

"You. All of you. And without gentleness. That this may hurt enough to kill my shame."

"Nena," he said. "You're talking about a couple of other guys, aren't you?"

"Peter, please!" she said.

He moved a little. Carefully. But she arched all her body like a bow, and lunged forward and upward, closing around him, holding him achingly, sweetly, tenderly, screamingly, scaldingly in an abrupt shunting of his breath, his life into an oblique tangent away from time, before releasing both for him with what was less a motion than a long, slow, unspeakably total caress.

Her voice was at his ear but he couldn't hear what it was saying for the surge and thunder of his blood; then he felt her nails bite into his back and all the gigantic swelling surf-pound mounted up, hung poised unbearably through the long, long, slow-crumbling dikes of will control being exist-ence sense, going now, caving in, being swept away, ex-ploding into utter dark through which there crashed the sudden, sun-bright cymbal of her cry.

She lay with her arm across his chest, crying. Then she sat up, looking at him with startled eyes. She let her finger-tips stray over the whorls and rents and puckers with which his body was covered, lingering longest over the great silver ridge looping around his shoulder into his armpit.

"*Dios mío!* How you must have suffered!" she said.

"I was out most of the time," Peter said. "But I admit it was no fun."

She bent and kissed his mouth.

"Peter—" she said.

"Yes, Infant?"

"Do you—can you—love me? Love a woman so depraved and of such a vileness?"

He smiled at her.

"Tell me," he said, "how many hundreds of lovers have you had?"

She twined her fingers in his hair.

"No hundreds, Peter. In all my life: two. My poor Emilio —and you."

He raised his head and kissed her. When he tried to draw away, her head came downward with his, clinging mouth to mouth; and the sparkle of her crying was cold upon his face.

"Please?" she whispered.

Then crashingly, shatteringly, terribly, they heard that scream.

He was out of bed in one long leap. Snatched up his shorts, nearly dry now, from the edge of the lavabo, and put them on. From the top of the dresser he took the pistol Joaquin had brought him, but then he put it down again; knowing that the one thing no one could do this close to the concentration camp was fire a shot, and picked up the Commando knife instead.

"Peter!" she cried out.

"Quiet, Nena!" he said. "Don't move!" And raced down the stairs.

As he had known there wouldn't be—for Pablo and Martin and the rest had gone, on his orders, to plant those charges of plastic at the places he had indicated around the walls—leaving only Mario, one of the drowsy teen-agers, to guard the innkeeper and his wife—there was no one there.

And, he saw, not even Mario; because what had been Mario, all that gaiety, spirit, courage, had departed, leaving only the broken flesh that had housed him, lying there before the opened door, staring up into the dim bulb in the basement passages from sightless eyes; having now two mouths: his own, opened wide in terror, in pain; and the other, the new one the innkeeper had slashed across his throat, converting the sleep he was so fond of into that deeper dreamlessness from which no man ever wakens.

It was the woman who had screamed. And now she crouched there, staring at Mario's body with eyes filled with tears and horror; lifting up her head, she screamed again:

"Beast! Assassin! Killer of babies!"

Peter slapped her then, hard, across the mouth. Pushed her back into the room and closed the door. But there was nothing to lock it with, because the innkeeper had burst the bolt from the wood, in his bull-like surge through it. Only there was no time to search for a substitute means of locking it. And the woman had hated her husband—he knew that now—was, therefore, no threat. Peter came out into the dark, hearing that gross animal laboring through the brush some meters ahead, Mario's Sten gun in his hands. The innkeeper was no woodsman. He was already floundering, lost. Peter moved in on a long slanting diagonal; closing his eyes, holding them shut even as he ran, until they were accustomed to the darkness.

He saw the man ahead of him now, heard him puffing like a steam engine; but the innkeeper was now only three meters from the road that ran straight to the prison camp, and, once on it, there would be no stopping him. Even now, one burst from the burp gun, one great shout could end it all for them, bring the prison guards pouring out to gun them down, divided as they were, scattered, unprepared. So Peter closed in upon him, did in one unbroken chain of linked motion the things he had been trained to do: hooked his left arm around the innkeepers' throat, tightening it in ferocious jerks until there was no breath in the man with which to cry, at the same time slamming his right knee into the small of the man's back so that it served as the fulcrum of the lever against which he bent the innkeeper in one unbelievably swift motion, so that the spinal column snapped, producing so instantaneous a paralysis that the man's beefy fingers opened, and the Czech machine pistol thudded to the ground; but Peter, having no time to appraise the already fatal results of his attack, brought that long blade in and down in one swift sweep, feeling it bite flesh, sink through that nothing which is a man to reach that quivering bundle of unquiet flesh, his heart; then, drawing it out again, feeling the hot spurting jet follow it; and bringing his left hand up to clamp over the innkeeper's nose and mouth; put the edge of the blade behind the man's left ear and slashed down in one long slant, twelve centimeters long, severing the carotid, making absolutely sure, because that was the

way he had been taught to do it; because what a trained
Commando does in hand-to-hand combat is overkill his man,
massacre him.

He left the innkeeper lying where he fell, pausing only
long enough to pick the Sten gun up, but not wasting time
searching for the blade the mestizo had used to kill Mario
—surely a switchblade and surely concealed about his person now, and surely employed while Mario slept. Automatically, he wiped his blade clean on the dead man's shirt,
and started back toward the inn.

The woman was still in the basement room, weeping and
praying. She seemed unaware of the smashed lock. But all
the same, Peter entered that room, jerked loose a length of
electric wire, and bound her hands and feet with that, biting
it cruelly into her flesh.

Then he went back upstairs and into the bathroom. He
washed the blood off his arms with cold water. Stood there
staring at his own face in the mirror, bent his head and
vomited, the sound of it a long, long racking tearing sound
that went on and on until the toilet bowl was filled with
yellowish bile streaked through with blood. He pulled the
chain and flushed it down. Then he sat down on the edge of
the tub. He sat there until Alicia came through the door,
and saw how his great shoulders shook, saw that his eyes
were blind.

She knelt down very slowly until her slim body was between his knees. Put up her arms, wound them around his
neck.

"Don't cry, Peter!" she said. "Oh, please, my love, don't
cry!"

She took him by the arm, led him back to the bed, lay
down beside him, kissing his eyes, his throat, his mouth.

"Don't!" he said, "for God's love, don't!"

"Why not?" she said.

"I killed him," he said. "I gave him no chance. I killed
him like a dog."

"As he killed Mario," she said.

"You went downstairs! You saw!"

"Yes, *Cielo*. You are much man, but your heart is as tender as a woman's. Sometimes a man must kill. His death was just."

He stared at her.

"You!" he said. "You are—"

"What, *Cielo?*"

"Miguel's sister. After all. With his face. His mind. His heart. Leave me! I cannot bear you now! I cannot."

But she brought her right hand across his face open-palmed, with a sound like a pistol shot, then caught him by both his ears, furiously assaulting his mouth, pushing him over backward, and sprawling atop him, her lips on his—devouring, ferocious, feral, her small hands coming down from his ears to rake along all his body, and now, gripping, biting in, lifting him in a taut bowed arc from the bed, and mounting in one swift equestrian motion, widespread and over and down so that the act was not penetration but engulfment, she dissolved his bones' marrow, melted his flesh, his nerves, his life into the wild thrashing undulant cauldron of her loins, his sense into the sweat-steamed air, made vibrant by her voice rising through a whole minor appoggiatura into what was far more ululation than a cry.

And when the residual heart-hammer breath-storm had subsided, the anguished and agonized fight to drag enough air into laboring lungs to sustain life had been won, he—raising his head and seeing her where she sprawled across him still, boneless and supine like a rubber doll, the whole of her silvered and glistening with the cooling rivers that poured still out of her every pore, her sculptured Assyrian Astarte's head turned sidewise and her mouth blue-bruised, swollen into a negroid caricature of its former warm fullness, opened like an idiot child's—was torn by pity at her aspect of helplessness, despair. He put out his big hand, gone gray and trembling, and stroked the close-cropped black cap of hair, dripping wet now, glued to her skull by sweat, and whispered:

"Nena—"

She came upright then, staring at him. In the lamplight the tears on her face were a golden flood.

"Nena," he said, "I love you. You have taken it away. It is gone."

"Oh, Peter, *Cielo!*" she wailed, and clung to him, shuddering. Then she lifted that wonderful, tragic, tender face, and smiled, all gamine now, her wide soft mouth bisected by her tears.

"We shall name him Mario, this son that we have made," she said. "Do you not find this just?"

"Yes, Nena," he said. "If we have a child. And if it is a son, agreed."

"Oh, Peter! Have you no faith at all?" she said.

First thing in the morning, Joaquin came up to Peter with Mario's machine pistol in his hand. He held the little weapon out to Peter. His voice was rough when he spoke:

"He would want you to have it, Comrade!"

"No," Peter said. "I thank you, Comrade; but no—"

"Why not?" Martin said.

"Because it is a gun," Peter said, "and a gun is useful only for killing people. Hence I have no further need of it."

"You do all right with a knife," Pablo said, "though even that was unnecessary. He would have died of what you did with your hands. You broke his spine."

"Let us not speak of it," Peter said. "Are you ready?"

"Yes, Comrade Temporary Chief," Pablo said; "but one favor, Commander!"

"Which is?" Peter said.

"Let me drive that truck!"

"No," Peter said.

"Comrade, the man who drives the truck will die. And if you die, the little Alicia will go mad. I am sure of it."

"You are sure of many things," Peter said. "Now hear me, so that we do not make a bad motion-picture script of this. I will drive that truck, because of you all, only I can do it and *not* die. I have a great wish to live now. But I have no desire whatsoever to see one of you killed trying to do what only I know how to do. Now let us put all our watches to the same time like motion-picture Commandos, because it is necessary, not to make heroic gestures."

They synchronized their watches.

"We have found it takes twenty minutes for every man to get into position," Peter said. "By then, there will be light enough for you to see to shoot them, instead of each other. You are not to fire until you hear the truck blow up. And then you are to shoot them in the belly, from as close a range as possible, trying not to kill the political prisoners. And speaking of the guards, you are not to allow even one to escape; nor will you accept the surrender of any."

Pablo's face whitened a little.

"I do not understand you, Peter," he said. "Last night, you wept for the man you had killed. And now—"

"I shall weep for these, after we have killed them. But kill them we must," Peter said.

They lay in the brush and waited. They had blackened their faces with burnt corks taken from the wine bottles in the cellar of the inn. They lay there without moving until the truck came down the road with Peter driving it. It came on very slowly until it was abreast of them. Then Peter reached down and laid the heavy, flat stone on the accelerator, double-clutched, slamming the truck into high. As it roared forward, he opened the cab door and leaped. He hit the ground already rolling. The brush swallowed him.

Five seconds later the truck crashed through the main gate and blew up inside the prison yard.

They left the freed prisoners—except, of course, Pablo's two friends, captured before the Archbishop's Palace, whom they took with them—to butcher the wounded prison guards, and roared away in all the trucks to Xilchimocha. They took the Social Re-education Center there in a sharp fight that cost them seven casualties and would have cost them more if suddenly the Tluscola hadn't swarmed out of their sacred town, formed ranks beside them, and carried the walls of the prison camp in mass frontal attacks that cost them more than fifty dead, swarming over those walls and into the camp in one long screaming red mass of fury.

When it was over, Peter sent for Alicia, whom they'd brought with them because he hadn't dared leave her at the inn with the jungle around it filled with brutalized, starving ex-prisoners. They had left her out of range with Joaquin, who had been slightly wounded in the Tarascanolla massacre, guarding her to see that she didn't do anything foolish. But now they needed her, because she was the only one among them who could speak Tluscolan. Here in the South, the Indians' contact with the Spaniards, either as Conquistadores or colonists, had been slight. None of them spoke comprehensible Spanish.

"Camarada Alicia," Pablo said, "ask them why they helped us! Ask them what it means! Because if all the Indians have come over to our side—"

Alicia turned to the Cacique. She made a series of gurgling sounds in her throat, a very pretty drum roll of grunts; a group of clicking noises; a nasal snort or two.

The Cacique returned the compliment.

Alicia turned to Peter, her eyes wide.

"He says that Miguel defiled their dead!" she whispered. "I do not know how or why—nor, I fear, does he. The message came by the drums. You know how that works? They beat a drum in one village and the sound of it—"

"Yes, I know, Nena. What else does he say?"

"That the Tluscola are at war. That they have lifted the hatchet against Miguel, against the government. And that they will never stop until he, and it, are destroyed. Oh, Peter, how terrible!"

"It is," Peter said. "Now, Infant, you go back to the truck. We've got one more camp to take. The women's camp at Chizenaya. And we'll need you there. . . ."

They did not have to take the camp at Chizenaya. When they got there, they saw the white flag flying above the gate. But, in a certain sense, what they had to do was harder.

There were only thirty women prisoners left alive, and some of them had to be carried to the courts-martial on stretchers to give their testimony. Martin argued that the scrupulosity that Pablo and Peter insisted upon was a waste of time. Practically speaking, he was right. When the trials were over, it took the firing squads the rest of the day to finish up the affair. There was not one among the guards who could have been acquitted by the most lenient civil court on earth.

And, to make it worse, with one or two exceptions, they died very badly, screaming and cursing and crying and begging for their lives. The Commander of the Camp had to be carried to the wall. When Peter saw who he was, he stopped the proceedings long enough to walk over, stick a cigarette in his mouth, and light it for him.

But when the Commander looked up and saw who it was offering him this last courtesy, he swallowed the smoke and started to cough and the tears ran down across the faint but still visible scars of the furrows Alicia had clawed into his face the day he had beaten Peter up in the street before his house. Perhaps he remembered that. Or the three days of interrogation he had conducted.

Peter bent closer.

"Would you like to give the commands to the squad?" he said. "It is an honor I offer you for old times' sake—"

"No!" the Captain screamed. "Oh damn you, Gringo! Give them yourself!"

"No," Peter said; "in me it would be unbecoming. In me, it would seem vengeance. Comrade Martin!"

"Yes, Comrade Pedro?"

"Take over," Peter said.

But Martin didn't give any commands to the firing squad. Instead, he walked over to where the Camp Commander sat tied to the chair, with his back toward the squad. He saw how the Commander was crying and straining at his bonds. He smelled the odor arising from the fact that the Commander had lost control of his sphincter and defecated upon himself in his fear. He watched the yellow pools of urine gathering around the Commander's feet.

Then he drew his Mauser and shot the Camp Commander through the back of his head.

The Cacique of the local Tluscola knew where the lost, found, and lost-again city of Ururchizenaya was. So they all went there, as a more or less conscious release from the things they had had to do. Peter took pictures of all of them among the ruins. The ruins were very beautiful. They made Peter wonder if, when the Conquistadores came with the cross and the sword, the world had gained or lost. He was studying the intricate hieroglyphics when Alicia came up to him.

"Let us spend the night here, *Cielo*," she said, "for if the God of my Spanish ancestors is too stiff-necked to bless our union, perhaps there is here another god of my Indian forebears who will!"

So they requested permission—and got it (there was nothing Pablo, and very little Martin would have refused Peter by then)—to spend the night in the ruins of Ururchizenaya. But, at supper, before the others had gone back to the regular camp, Peter caught her looking at him with what was either horrified fascination or fascinated horror.

"Nena," he said, "what passes with you?"

"Peter, will you forgive me if I say a thing?"

"Say it, *Muñeca*."

"The—the executions. You, you commanded some of them!"

"Yes, Nena."

"Why, Peter?"

"I requested the privilege in two or three cases. Where your brother's goons had been especially rough. This disturbs you, *Muñeca?*"

"Yes, Peter, it disturbs me. Not that it had to be done. But that *you* should do it!"

"And yet, the other night, that of the innkeeper—"

"With your hands! With only a knife. And he with a machine gun that could have riddled you with bullets! Oh, but you were much, then!"

"And now I am not?"

"No, Peter. Men tied to posts—I did not watch it; but I know how it is. And I could hear. A silence that stopped my heart from beating, then your voice, *yours!*: '*F i i i r r r r e !*' And all the world breaking in half with the crash of the shots! Oh, no! Oh, no, Peter! This is ugly! This is cruel! Others can do these things, but not my love! Not ever you!"

Across the fire from them, Pablo's young face darkened. He stood up.

"Comrade Alicia!" he ripped out.

"Yes, my Commander?" Alicia said.

"You volunteered for this mission. You are under my orders. And now I order you to come with me!"

"Now look, Pablo—" Peter said.

"I shall return her to you, Comrade. And you will thank me, for if you wed a woman so sadly lacking in discipline, in respect for you, you will regret it. I propose to end this problem now."

"How?" Peter said.

"There is a thing I want the Camarada Alicia to see. I think it will improve her progressive indoctrination immensely. Now, Comrade Sister of the man who caused these things to be done—come!"

When Pablo brought her back again, she came flying to Peter's arms and cried and cried and cried beyond the hope of speech.

"Now I will leave you," Pablo said. "That you rest." Then, to the others: "Form ranks! Forward march!"

"Nena—" Peter said.

"Oh, Peter! Oh, Peter! Ohhhhh! That you had done other things to them than shooting! That you had cut them all over as the Indians do, smeared them with honey, and tied them down upon a hill of ants! That you had burned them alive! That you had killed them by millimeters! Ohhhhhhh!"

"Nena—" Peter said.

"The beasts! The savages! Animals! Assassins!"

"They are dead, Nena."

"I know. Peter, *Cielo*—"

"Yes, Nena?"

"Forgive me! Forgive your stupid one, your idiot, your little fool!"

"My little angel from the sky," Peter said.

"Know what they did?" she wept. "Do you know?"

"Yes, Nena. Let us not speak of it. Let us not spoil this night."

"Ay, no! I shall never forget it; but I will not speak of it. Instead I will take away all the pain I have caused you, and you must take away what I have seen . . ."

So they spent the night in the ruins of Ururchizenaya. Peter took flash pictures of her lying naked in the arms of a hideous idol, pretending to be a human sacrifice. Bathing in the Pool of the Maidens. Kneeling before the statue of the unknown goddess she looked like. The statue was much bigger than the one in the Museum, which was why it was still here. The Standford Expedition had had to settle for the smaller one. This one was too big to haul away.

In the morning, Pablo himself came to fetch them, calling out from a discreet distance. It was a good thing he did, because they were both stark naked and fast asleep in each other's arms. When they had dressed, Pablo told them the news. All night long the radio that Joaquin and poor Mario had stolen at Peter's request had been filled with messages in code on the higher bands. But the government radio hadn't even bothered with such refinements; it was screaming to the four winds for help, crying that Ciudad Villalonga was surrounded by the Fidelistas and their Indian allies.

And, as if to compound confusion, Zopocomapetl had split itself open halfway down one side.

So they got in the trucks, throwing out the useless goods

to make room for the liberated prisoners, leaving those too sick, too hurt, at the inn, under a swearing medical corpsman and two Indian brush nurses, and started north again.

19.

They roared north without being stopped at all. There were no longer any uniformed *carabiñeros* of the civil guard upon the roads. There was nothing on the road, nothing at all. Even the service stations were closed and locked. They had to break into them and work the pumps by hand in order to get the fuel oil into the tanks of the trucks. Over the radio came a confused babble of orders, commands, and prohibitions, depending upon which band it was tuned to. Generally, Martin kept it synchronized with La Voz de Costa Verde, the national radio or Radio Villalonga, the principal broadcasting station of the city itself. The longer he and Pablo listened, the wider their smiles grew. What was going on inside Ciudad Villalonga was barely controlled panic. Strict martial law reigned. The number of offenses for which a civilian might be shot on the spot passed twenty. The Toque de Queda—curfew—had been imposed. Last night, the radio announced, five badly intentioned ones had been shot dead for violating it. Miguel Villalonga's voice, high and hysterical, came over Radio Villalonga, screaming threats to push the barbaric red invaders into the sea. Martial music boomed. There were appeals to patriotism, admonitions to remain calm, but, beyond that, nothing.

Then, suddenly, Miguel's voice came over the air again. The hysteria was gone from it. It was controlled. Perhaps a little too controlled.

"*Due to the vigorous action of one of our patrols,*" he said, "*we have conclusive proof that the Red barbarians plan to exterminate all citizens of the United States of North America who are found within the capital, once they succeed in forcing an entry. This, of course, is entirely in line with the other barbarities they have committed against the people and the holdings of Our Great Sister Republic all over Hispano-America, notably in Venezuela . . .*"

Peter looked at Pablo.

"It's a lie!" Pablo said.

"I know it is," Peter said, "but can you figure out the reason for it?"

"*Therefore, since the situation is admittedly grave—*" Miguel's voice went on.

"Oh, Peter!" Alicia said.

"Quiet, Nena!" Peter said.

"*—my government has decided to put at the disposal of the United States Embassy several of the city's autobuses, withdrawn from the municipal transportation system, to take the personnel of the Embassy and the numerous North American tourists caught here by the unhappy turn of events to places of safety outside the capital.*"

"Still don't get it," Peter said.

"*Each bus will be provided, of course, with an armed escort to protect—*"

"*Ya! Ya!*" Martin said. "You get it *now,* do you not, Comrade Reporter?"

"Poor devils," Peter said.

"Peter, *Cielo,* perhaps I am of an enormous stupidity," Alicia said, "but I confess I do not understand this. Not at all."

"Your sweet brother," Peter said, "wants to make sure that somebody'll save his neck. So, he collects a few hostages. Bargaining points. Either the Marines come in, or——"

"Oh, Peter!" Alicia said.

"They'll be all right," Peter said. "He won't dare really do anything to them. He needs us too badly for that. This cute caper doesn't bother me. What bothers me is—"

"What, Comrade?" Pablo said.

"That your boys haven't taken the city by now. Before we left Ururchizenaya, it was already surrounded."

"He has tanks," Martin said.

"Very few," Peter said. "Five or six which cannot be everywhere at once. And he no longer has an air force, thanks to Jacinto. And your boys have bazookas."

Martin looked at Pablo.

"He is right, the Comrade Reporter," he said; "they should have taken the city by now. Something has gone wrong."

"I hope not," Pablo said.

"And I," Peter said. "But something always does. It is like my stick."

"What stick, *Cielo?*" Alicia said.

"*Muñeca,* do you recall the little stick I had with me at Vince's party?"

"Yes, *Cielo;* but what I do not see is the connection."

"There is a connection. That little stick—it is called a *swagger stick* in English—was a kind of symbol for me. I intended to march into battle with it, like a British officer in the first world war. Directing my men with it. Carrying no other weapon. Being cool and jaunty under fire. Big deal."

"So?" Alicia said.

"I lost it. First trip out. I think it was when I rolled out of that truck. And I didn't even remember it until now . . ."

"Does it matter?" Alicia said.

"Hell, no. It's just funny, that's all. Life has the damnedest way of cutting a man down to size. And men. And nations. And political institutions."

"Meaning?" Martin growled.

"I mean nothing. I simply repeat what I said in the first place: Something has queered the deal."

"A question of luck," Pablo said.

"Don't believe in luck. Do you?" Peter said.

"Well—" Pablo said.

"Look, Comrade, can you remember any important event in your life that was arranged by luck?"

"Well . . . no," Pablo said.

"But you can recall numerous occasions in which luck pinned a fornication on you of the very first class?"

"Peter! Your language!" Alicia said.

"Sorry, Nena. And now I know you'll make a wife. You're already learning how."

"Luck does arrange things," Martin said. "For instance, we cannot have bad luck without Miguel's having good."

"True; but over the long haul it cancels out. And most of the time it's as impartial as all hell. Dirties everybody."

"Peter! Have you no respect for me?" Alicia said.

"None," Peter said. "I only respect women I don't love."

And now, when the volcano came in sight, he could see that the split through which that moving wall of lava poured was on the side away from Ciudad Villalonga. He didn't know what that meant at first, and it wasn't until two hours later that he found out. The line of trucks stopped, ramming together like a stiffened snake; and, as they piled out of them, they could see the long lines of Communist guerrillas reeling past with handkerchiefs over their mouths and noses, and on their flanks, the Tluscolas who had joined them, with nothing over their noses, crying and coughing, too, and farther out, pushed off the road itself by the retreating army, a crowd of civilians with all their goods in ox or donkey carts or on their own backs and heads, crying in the same bitter grief, although some of them at least occasionally had on the uniform of the national Army with the buttons and insignia torn off to show that they were deserters. The donkeys and the oxen cried too, great asinine and bovine tears that looked like blood. And it came to Peter then that what the Fidelistas and their Indian allies and the civilian refugees were retreating from wasn't Miguel Villalonga's all-but-nonexistent army but the volcano itself, so he threw back his head and laughed.

"What passes with you, *Cielo?*" Alicia said.

"Want to bet that if you started downtown on a hot, dead-still day, and forgot to put your panties on, a high wind wouldn't come up?" Peter said.

"Peter!" she said.

"Say that again," he said, and kissed her. "I love you when you say my name in that tone of utter severity."

"Joder!" Martin said, and Peter saw that it had hit him, too.

"Now you see my point?" Peter said. "In the cinema of which you Costa Verdians are so fond, things would be arranged differently, no? In the great pictures in technicolor, Zopo would blow his top all right, but he would bury Miguel Villalonga and Luis Sinnombre beneath a mountain of lava for their sins. But this is not cinema and I hesitate to call it life, for life consists of more than marching up and down and killing people. Yet, here you have your luck, Comrades. And it is both of a vile vileness and of an utter immorality!"

"Oh, Peter!" Alicia wailed.

When she said his name like that, one of the refugees stopped. He had a pack on his back, and was a good bit better dressed than the other civilians. There was something familiar about his face.

"Don Pedro!" he said.

"You've got the advantage of me, Friend," Peter said.

"Your guide, Señor! Do you not remember me? I am Tomas, he who led you across the lava beds up there, the time you were searching for Padre Pío—"

"Now, I remember," Peter said, and took his hand. "Tomas, do you think you could do it again? I, and this lady, must enter the city."

Martin's eyebrows came together.

"Why?" he said.

"Later, Comrade," Peter said. "It is a thing that I and the Comrade Alicia discussed last night. When things are arranged with Tomas, I will discuss them with you."

"I heard the discussion of last night," Martin said; "it made me to achieve an erection."

"Ohhhh!" Alicia said. "How filthy are men!"

"Can you again, Tomas," Peter said, "or has that big crapper up there defecated across all the paths?"

Alicia stamped her foot.

"Peter, if you do not also stop it, I . . . !"

"I have stopped it, Camarada," Peter said, and kissed her. "Can you, Tomas?"

"Well—" Tomas said. "I think so—yes! We should have to procure horses; and perhaps to search out new trails; but, beyond that—"

"Would it be too dangerous for the lady?" Peter said.

"Can she ride?" Tomas said.

"I won the woman's equestrian championship three years in a row," Alicia said; "and I won it fairly, despite all the lying gossip!"

Tomas' jaw dropped.

"Then you are—then the illustrious lady is—" he said.

"Yes. I am Alicia Villalonga," she said. "I suppose by now my carcass is worth twenty thousand pesos so that your troops may have the pleasure of staring at my legs as I hang upside down in the Plaza de la Liberación, no?"

"That will never happen, Camarada!" Pablo said. "I guarantee it!"

"How can you guarantee it, Pablo?" Peter said.

"I am known to all the important members of the Party. I will write her out a safe conduct, detailing her great services to the cause—"

"Services rendered exclusively to the Comrade Reporter, which, if he were a true Socialist, he would share," Martin said.

"Pay him no attention; he is obsessed," Peter said to Tomas.

"I will write this for her on official Party Stationery," Pablo said, "because it seems to me that she and you, Comrade, can become the means of reconciliation among all classes—"

"Shades of Luis Sinnombre!" Peter said. "Write it, then, Comrade."

"No," Martin said. "First the Comrade Journalist must tell us what he discussed with the Comrade Sister of the Ex-Head of the State, besides whether ten or twelve babies comprise an adequate family."

Alicia looked at him.

"I think you are a good boy, Martin," she said; "a good little boy who, to prove he is a big boy, must write dirty words on walls. And I think that when one day you truly fall in love, you will learn there are no dirty words. That, my friend, there are no words at all."

"Then what did you discuss? Besides the babies, I mean?"

"No. First the babies. For, until someone invents a world where idiots like you Communists and savages like my brother have no control over matters, I wish to have twelve babies with Peter. So that even in this universe of monsters, assassins, and madmen, it will be difficult to kill them all."

"I have no wish to kill babies, Camarada. It is more interesting to make them," Martin said.

"Very well. Pablo and Martin, what I discussed with Peter was a way of saving my brother's life."

"What!" Martin said.

"You heard me, Martin!"

"That, no!" Martin said.

"Comrade Pablo," Alicia said, "will you listen to me? You are older than Martin and cooler of head—"

"Speak of it," Pablo said.

"What if I offered you the surrender of the city? To you, personally. And to Martin, as your Second in Command?"

"It is a trick!" Martin said.

"What is today? The fourteenth of August? Ah, yes! There will be a new street in the city. The Avenue of the Fourteenth of August. And at the head of it, a great bronze statue: Pablo and Martin, the Heroes of the Fourteenth of August, receiving the surrender of Ciudad Villalonga from the hands of the Junta of Influential Citizens to whom the Dictator, Miguel Villalonga, entrusted it when he abdicated and fled. A plaque reading: 'By their noble, wise, and generous action in permitting Villalonga and Sinnombre to leave the country in exchange for an unconditional surrender, Pablo and Martin saved the lives of hundreds of brave Socialist soldiers who would otherwise have had to sacrifice themselves in the final struggle—' "

"Boys," Peter said, "I think we better make *her* President. Or at least head of the diplomatic corps."

"Because I can do this thing, Comrades," Alicia said. "He will listen to me. Give me a safe conduct into the city and I will persuade both Miguel and Luis to get aboard a plane. They have money in various banks abroad. And once they have gone, the hard core of murderous swine who support Miguel because they know that they will be killed along with him when the people take over, will run like rats. And when all these other bands of parvenus, Johnnies-come-lately, last-minute revolutionists march into the city they will have to treat with Acting Head of the State, Pablo, and Acting Civil Governor Martin. Because I will make sure that the city is surrendered only to you who are my friends. And thereafter, they *must* accord you the honor and the respect that is your due."

Pablo looked at Martin.

"This makes much sense, what the Camarada Alicia has said."

"Sí," Martin said; "still, there are many thirsting for his blood."

"Look!" Alicia said. "See the people weeping as they pass! Even the soldiers weep! Shall we not, Comrades, put an end to blood and tears?"

"They weep because the vapors from the volcano get into the eyes and—" Tomas began.

Peter kicked him in the shin—hard. Hissed into his ear "Shut up, you fool!"

"And those who have suffered much at his hands may blame us for letting him go," Martin said. "Still—"

"Still, do you want revenge, Comrades, or a new deal?" Peter said. "A chance to build that brave new Socialist world you're always talking about? To prove to me I'm wrong? That Marxism can work? That it is not as much against human nature as I think it is?"

Martin looked at him. Grinned.

"*De acuerdo,*" he said; "now that the so very clever comrades have played upon our vanity and our sporting instincts, both of accord! Let the bastard go! We have more important things to do. And, frankly, Camarada Temptress, with more guile than the Serpent of the Nile, I should like the various children that I have in all the various streets of the city to read in the history books that their father was a great man. We will do this thing!"

"Fine," Peter said. "Comrade Pablo, write out a safe conduct for three people. Better still, write out three separate safe conducts; because once we are in the city, our ways must part, at least for a time."

"Oh, Peter, *Cielo*, why?"

"You don't think you'll be able to talk any sense into Miguelito with *me* there, do you?"

"No," Alicia said, "but——"

"But nothing! Tomas, this of the horses?"

"There is a ranch near here where we might be able to rent or buy some nags, especially if you have some dollars," Tomas said, "but we had better start out at once, before this Socialist Army encamps itself, forgets it is Socialist, and starts acting like an army."

"Meaning?" Pablo said. Tomas came to attention. Saluted. Barked:

"Your identification, Comrade! What, you have no pass from General Mierda? Nor even one from Colonel Pedo? What is this, a pass from Teniente Jodido? Never heard of him. Comrades, take the Comrade out and shoot the Comrade, *por favor!*"

"You've got something there, Tomas!" Peter said.

"I will write you one from our great Russian Adviser the Generalski Ivanovski Gilipollas Maricon," Pablo said. "No, we will come with you to see you catch the horses. You'll come, Martin?"

"Why not?" Martin said, "since this vileness of a volcano has stopped the whole vile war?"

They started out, leaving Joaquin in charge. They left the trucks parked on the shoulder of the road and followed the narrow, winding trail that Tomas pointed out.

"This of the Indians, Tomas," Peter said; "how did they

happen to come over to the revolution? I thought Padre Pío had them sewed up."

"He did," Tomas said, "until the illustrious brother of the august lady made a mistake—"

"Oh, come off it, Tomas! We are all comrades now!" Alicia said.

"Very well. Miguelito made an error. But the fat one. The mother and father of all mistakes. You know what reverence the Tluscola have for their dead?"

"Yes," Peter said.

"It started with the volcano. It has been nasty for weeks now. First it buried Xochua."

"We heard that on the radio," Peter said. "No—a truck driver told us."

"And when the rescue teams dug into the ruins, they found that the dead had been transformed into statues by the ash—"

"This is not possible!" Martin said.

"Yes it is, Martin," Peter said; "I have seen it before."

"Where?" Martin said.

"At Pompeii, in Italy. I have seen bodies two thousand years old, perfectly preserved by the ash. Changed into statues. Gruesome sort of thing."

"It is," Tomas said. "But the cadavers of the Indians were so lifelike that the brother of Doña Alicia—"

"Camarada Alicia," Alicia said. "I am a Red, too, now. Aren't I, Peter?"

"Yes. Red as all get-out. Red as lipstick. Which reminds me—"

He bent and kissed her.

"More discipline, Comrades!" Pablo said.

They all laughed.

"Your brother, Comrade Alicia," Tomas said, "decided to put them in the Museum of Archeology for the edification of the tourists. That did it. In the face of such blasphemy, the Tluscola declared war. Which means the dictatorship is doomed. Not even old Zopo can stop that for very long. Miguel's troops are deserting him—except for those who have committed so many crimes that their lives depend upon his protection. When the volcano cools down again, he will be in a worse position than he is now. Therefore I think he would be wise to take the advice of the Comrade Alicia, and flee—"

"Oh, he will!" Alicia said. "I am sure of that."

Watching her now, where she rode, picking her way across the barely solidified flats of the lava, the steam coming up around the great clumsy bundles of wet rags they had wrapped around the horses' hoofs to protect them from the heat, it came to Peter that she was of those who would do everything beautifully, perfectly, from dominating a skittish horse to holding an infant in her arms. And the way he felt about her rose up and thundered in his chest, and an ice-cold blade of terror entered him slowly, probing for his breath.

Because this was wrong; it contradicted thirty-seven years of experience. For, if there were any one item life didn't provide, it was flawlessness. Or, when it did, on a strictly temporary basis, as if to make more bitter the flawed residue after flawlessness was gone; to increase the insufferability of memory. Of emptiness. Of cold.

He jammed his heels into his nag's flanks. Brought the ugly beast abreast of hers. Reached out and clawed away that mask she had made for herself, with another for him, and another for Tomas out of the torn strips of her heavy Italian silk half-slip. Dragged her into his arms, and almost broke her mouth before the residual terror drained out of him, allowing tenderness to return.

"Oh, Peter!" she said. "Oh, my Love! *Cielo mío*—My Own —what was that for?"

"Because I love you so much I think I shall die of it," he said.

"And I, you," she said, looking at the guide. "Oh, if he were only not here! Oh, if there were only some place where . . ."

"No," Peter said; "not like that, now. I looked at you, and

suddenly I saw our son in your arms. Or our daughter. It was so little I could not tell."

"What was it like?" she said.

"Well, it had lots and lots of hair. Black."

"It could hardly be blond, *Cielo*—"

"And you were feeding it. And I was angry with it and jealous of it for putting its greedy little mouth where only mine has been—"

She bent her horse's head about with one swift, beautifully, perfectly executed pull on the bridle, bringing him around until he was across the would-be, half-eroded memory of a trail, so that her back was turned squarely toward where Tomas rode. Her hand came up, clawed at the topmost buttons of the mono.

"Kiss me there now," she said, and her voice was ragged. "I want you to. I——"

"No," he said. "Tonight. When it is dark. I will order him to sleep apart."

"Oh that it were night now!" she said.

And then, finally, it was night, but it was not dark. Zopo comapetl washed all the sky with orange-red. He sent down little trickling rivulets of fire nosing into their camp. He blinded their eyes, tore at their throats with his noxious vapors.

Nevertheless, they made love.

With a hungry, desperate urgency—as though they knew what was going to happen tomorrow. As if they could read the front page of a newspaper still unprinted.

"I can," he whispered. "Goddam it, I can!"

"You can what?" Alicia said.

"Read tomorrow's newspaper," Peter said.

"What does it say, *Cielo?*" she whispered.

"No," he said, "I can't. I'm not clairvoyant worth a damn. Can't read—"

"What does it say, Peter!" Alicia said.

"It's—it's blank. No. It has the usual things. Movements

of armies. Alarums and excursions. Wars, threats of wars. People mucking up their lives. Only—"

"Only what, *Cielo*?"

"We aren't there. I don't see us there at all."

She looked at him. Then she locked her slim arms around his neck. He bent and kissed her mouth, her breasts.

"No," she said; "no preliminaries, *Cielo*. I do not need them. I am ready now. Enter me. Come into my body. Into my life. And then there will be tomorrow. In one way or another; there will be."

And, when he had done her bidding, when he had entered that wonderful, warmsoft interior tremble, had been caught and held by that absolutely unbearably adhesive cling and scald, which nonetheless had to be borne if he were not to spoil the occasion with too much haste, she was entirely still, completely silent, so long that he did not know when it was that she began to move. But when she did, it was like temple dancers worshiping creation, beginning, life, in slow, sweet, undulant rhythms, so slow, so gently tender that all urgency left him, and they lay together entwined, penetrant, encompassed, making not the usual evasive euphemisms for ugly fact, but very truly love; achieving so complete a sublimation of the basic sexual hunger that the sky was graying above Zopocomapetl when she said:

"Now, *Cielo*, now."

And even then without urgency. He felt her long, deep, internal shudder begin and waited quiescent until it rose to vibrant, quivering near-peak before racing to join her in that momentary shattering of the very stuff of being, that little death, that instant of fusion when they twain became one flesh, when the awful loneliness to which each child of man is born is for that tender instant stilled.

And looking down, he saw her eyes awash, but she was smiling.

"This time, yes," she said. "This time surely!"

It took them all the next day to cross that ravaged stretch where no trails had survived the old gods' wrath, or their laughter. Four times they were stopped by Red patrols; but Pablo's passes were as effective as he had said they would be.

But, coming into the city in the dawn, after another night that had duplicated the one before and, if anything, surpassed it, they were not stopped at all.

The reason they were not was both a tribute to Tomas' skill as a guide and evidence of to what extent Miguel Villalonga had lost his grip on history. From the trail above, Tomas had studied the approaches to the city through a pair of new and powerful glasses. He handed them to Peter. Pointed.

"Down there," he said, "on that side, the eastern side, nearest the sea. Do you not see the gap, Comrade?"

"Yes," Peter said, "but what I do not understand is why there should be a gap precisely there—"

"That sector was occupied by the company of Ernesto Guttiérez. A friend of mine. They were all badly disaffected, so I suspected they might desert. I was correct. They have."

"There are other gaps," Peter said, looking through the binoculars.

"There is much disaffection," Tomas said. "For now it is the volcano and not his army which is saving Our Glorious Leader's mangy hide. Oh, I beg your pardon, Comrade Alicia!"

"It is all right," Alicia said. "I have scant love for my brother, Tomas."

So they had gone down there and passed through the gap in the blue light of dawn. Alicia gave them a lesson in horsemanship by jumping her mount over the barbed wire the troops had left. But when Peter tried it, his nag got so tangled up that Tomas had to cut him loose with wirecutters.

"Which," Peter said, "you just accidentally happen to have, eh, Tomas?"

Tomas grinned.

"To live, I must move about. And there is barbed wire everywhere, these days," he said.

But, once inside the city, it was he again who made the obviously sensible suggestion that had occurred to neither of the others.

"You will dismount," he said, "and take off those coveralls. That is, if you still have clothes on under them. Do you?"

Alicia looked him straight in the eye.

"And what, Comrade Tomas, makes you think we might not have?" she said.

Tomas grinned.

"I thought perhaps you had left them off for the sake of quickness and convenience," he said.

Alicia turned to Peter.

"That we may have a house one day. That we be able to cease making public exhibitions!" she said.

"We have our clothes on, Tomas. Why?" Peter said.

"Because a man and a woman in *monos azules* on horseback in the city would be—rare, Comrade. But a pair of sleepy lovers, in normal clothes, walking hand in hand, are not. Even if the man does have three days' growth of beard. That only indicates their ardor. That they have not wasted time on nonessentials—"

"Tomas, you're a smart man," Peter said, and took out a five-thousand-peso note.

Tomas frowned.

"Do you not have any dollars, Comrade?" he said. "That banknote will not buy a pack of cigarettes, now."

So Peter gave him twenty dollars, which caused him to grin happily. With twenty dollars he could buy almost anything. Including one of the hundreds of luxurious automobiles stalled on the streets because there was no longer any gasoline to run them with, and whose owners' need for hard currency to further their escape was desperate. To such a pass had the Eternal Republic come.

They left Tomas and the horses and went walking hand in hand like children through the city. There was no one else in the streets. No one at all. The silence was eerie. It crawled along their nerves. Their footsteps were gunshot-loud in all that stillness. Alicia stopped.

"Oh, Peter, look!" she said.

A *buitre* was sitting on the cornice of a building looking down at them. Then he saw that there were *buitres*—buzzards—sitting on the roofs of all the houses watching them out of those flat, lightless eyes, without moving those obscene, scaly, bluish-red heads. Others circled above Ciudad Villalonga and above them the *bijiritas*—kites—and immensely high, infinitesimal black crosses against the blue wash of the heavens, the cóndors. Yet in the streets, there were no dead.

"They know!" Alicia shuddered. "Oh, Peter, *Cielo*, they know!"

Peter saw another thing: Miguel Villalonga was not planning a street-by-street, house by house, suicidal defense. There were no barricades, no barbed wire in the streets. Nor any trenches. All the defenses were peripheral.

Then, abruptly, there was sound. It blared from the loudspeakers of a sound truck that crossed an intersection several blocks away. They heard a snatch of words: "*All United States citizens are urgently requested to go to their Embassy in order to be conveyed . . .*"

"So that caper's not working so good, eh, Miguelito?" Peter said.

"*. . . to a place of safety.*" The mechanical, tinny voice came over to them, more faintly now, as the intervening buildings cut off the passage of the sound. They could hear it for a while longer. Then it died.

"Come on, *Muñeca*. We've things to do," Peter said.

They parted in the Plaza de la Liberación. Or started to. "I will persuade him," Alicia said, "you can be sure of that."

"Only I'm not," Peter said.

"Trust me, *Cielo*," Alicia said. "Peter—"

"Yes, Nena?"

"Where will you be, this night?"

"In my flat. Why?"

"Oh—" she said. "Must you stay *there*, *Cielo*?"

"I will go to the Hilton. Is that better?"

"Very much better. If I can, I will come to you—"

"And if you cannot, Nena?"

"I will try to telephone you."

"All right," Peter said.

And loud in the silence, they heard the clatter of running feet. But, fast as they whirled, they saw no one at all.

"How rare, no?" Alicia said.

"Very rare," Peter began; then he heard her whisper: *"Santa Madre de Dios!"*

He turned, followed the lightlocked pointing of her gaze. Saw the two women—the fat female dreadnaught who was the acting madam, since Miguel had locked his mother up, and another nondescript, rather skinny whore—come down the stairs of La Luna Azul with that burden in their arms. Shuffling under its weight, they went around the corner into the Street of the Martyrs of the Faith, which was a narrow blind alley opening on the square. Then they came back again, empty-handed, running. They pounded back up the stairs of The Blue Moon. Even from where Peter and Alicia stood, the snorting, whistling, panting of their breaths came over clearly.

"Oh, Peter, no!" Alicia said, and clung to him. But he broke free of her grasp, and entered the Calle de los Mártires de la Fe. She stood there, trembling. Then she followed him.

He was kneeling there with the woman's head cradled on his arm. She was completely naked, and now Alicia could see the blood pumping out of her through a line of little blue holes that stitched her slim, young body diagonally from left to right, starting from the left shoulder and slanting down across her right breast, which had two holes in it, one of which had destroyed the nipple, almost to her waist. She was trying to tell Peter something, but the blood kept coming out of her mouth and choking her. Peter wiped it away as best he could with his handkerchief.

"Was it Jacinto, Teresa?" he said. "Tell me! Was it Jacinto?"

She stiffened in his arms. Opened her mouth. Vomited up a great rush of blood. Got it out. Said, "Sí, Peter, *cariño*"— and died.

Walking together the rest of the way to the palace, because he did not dare leave her now, Alicia said nothing to him. She simply moved beside him, crying without motion, without sound, her face wet all over by her tears.

Before they were close enough for the guards before the door to distinguish who they were, he stopped. Said:

"Alicia—"

She looked at him.

"Sí, Peter, *cariño*!" she said.

He did then what he had to do. Drew back his hand and slapped her stingingly across the face. She stood there, looking at him. Then with a little, broken whimper, she came to his arms.

"What right have I?" she sobbed. "What right at all? Who am I but one more whore among all your whores? I have not even the strength to forego my little share of you. Perhaps one day you will allow me, too, the privilege of dying in your arms . . ."

"You want me to hit you again, 'Licia?" he said.

"Why not? I have given you that right, have I not? I have become such a thing as a man may beat, no?"

"Nena," he said, "that was for two things: debasing what you are by doubting me. And for mocking the dead."

"Ohhh!" she said, and looked up at him. "Peter, *Cielo*, you mean that you have not—"

"Played indoor games with that poor slaughtered p͏ commercial goods? Hell, no! I'm nobody's Tenor͏ knows; but so far I haven't been reduced to buyi͏ least not yet. I knew her, yes. Her name's Te͏ Jacinto's sister. You know, our pyromaniac frie͏ yellow eyes. And the only reason I knew her ͏ cause I had to hole up in that dump to shake your brother's uniformed apes off my tail . . ."

"Peter, I—now I have too much shame. One day you will tire of forgiving me for this debility of mine, no? Only I cannot dominate it. I have such a fear of losing you! I think —— Peter! What's wrong? You look . . ."

"Get! Go to those goons over there. Lock yourself in your room. Stay there till I tell you he's dead."

"That who is dead, Peter? I do not understand—"

"Jacinto. He said first her, then you."

She smiled at him then.

"I am not afraid, Love," she said.

"But I am! Goddam it, 'Licia—go!"

"Sí, Peter. Sí, Cielo. Sí, cariño of all the wicked, sensual women. Which includes your little Alicia. Who could devour you, now. Who could take you here upon the street. Who—"

"Nena, I've got it rough enough now," Peter said.

20.

When he opened the door of his flat, he saw that he need have neither worried, nor hoped. Judith wasn't there. The flat had been swept bare of her things. The only reminder of her presence was the perfume, *Peut-être*, lingering on, faint but persistent, on the air.

He walked across the room to the mantel over the fake replace his landlord was so proud of. In the grate it had a up of electric-light bulbs, concealed behind plastic logs. flicked a switch, some of the lights came on, but the idn't; then, after a few seconds' interval, the ones een on before went out, and vice versa, with the result that the flickering on and off of the red bulbs made a remarkable imitation of fire. Only Peter, whose hatred of fakery was the nearest thing to a religion he possessed, never flicked that switch. Now, he ran his fingertips over the quite real slabs of flagstone of which the chimney was made until he found the one he sought. He pulled it out, put his hand inside the cavity he himself had chopped behind it, and drew out the Walther 6.5-mm. P–38 automatic that had been the official sidearm of the Wehrmacht's officers in World War II.

It was wrapped in oilskin. He unwrapped it, sat there in the big chair, and cleaned it, although it was already quite clean enough. He slammed home a clip of bullets and set the safety. Then he dropped it in the side pocket of his jacket and sat there thinking about poor Jacinto, whom he didn't hate at all but whom, sometime during the next few hours, he was going to kill. Or be killed by. But it wasn't a thing that thinking about did any good at all; so he turned to the consideration of Judith's absence; what it meant. But what it meant was nothing, or everything. So he got up from there and switched on the radio. The newscaster's voice blared out:

"His Excellency, the Head of the State, this afternoon made a direct appeal to the President of the United States of America, requesting intervention by the Armed Forces of Our Great Sister Republic, due to the extreme gravity of the situation. Previous appeals, made to the useless and cowardly Organization of American States and the Red-dominated United Nations, having been summarily rejected by those groups, Our Glorious Leader decided—"

"Boys, you've had it, haven't you?" Peter said.

"His Excellency pointed out to the President that in view of the known atrocities committed by the Reds, and their open threat to exterminate every North American citizen found within the confines of Ciudad Villalonga when they enter the city, such intervention is entirely justified. Omnibuses of the Public Transportation System are being readied to take United States citizens residing in our capital, as well

*as the numerous tourists caught here by the revolution,
to a place of safety. But Our Generous Benefactor insists—*"

"Horsecrap," Peter said, and turned off the radio.

There was no hot water; but, considering the temperature
outside, the cold water was more than warm enough. He
shaved, bathed, and changed into clean clothes. He stood
there holding the Walther and wishing he had a shoulder
holster; but he didn't, so he cut a flap of oilskin and lined his
hip pocket with it and put the automatic in that. He had
already started toward the door when the door bell rang.

He opened the door. Tim O'Rourke stood there, grinning
at him.

"Now I know I'd better change my brand," Peter said.

"*Hola*, buzzard's breakfast food!" Tim said. "C'mon, let's
go drink to the demise of the Everlasting Republic."

"With pleasure," Peter said; "let's go to Harry's."

"Hell, no!" Tim said. "Too far. No taxis. No gas to put in
'em."

"I know that," Peter said, "only I have to go to Harry's,
Tim."

"All right. I can stand the Marine-type fitness hike if you
can. But why do you?"

"Because we can see the Official Residence from there."

"I've seen it before. Haven't you?"

"Yes. But today I've got a hankering to look at it some
more."

"Why?" Tim said.

"To see who goes into it. Or tries to."

"You're sick, you know, boy; sick!" Tim said.

"There you've got something, Timmie lad; now come on!"
Peter said.

They sat at a table in front of Harry's. Peter kept watching
the Official Residence and fiddling with the Rolleiflex which
he had brought with him in case whatever variety of hell that
broke loose would be worth a shot. There were guards all
over the place. But guards hadn't stopped Jacinto from blowing up the airport. He tried to put himself in Jacinto's place.

Figure what he'd do. Then it hit him. Tonight. When she comes out to join me. If they let her.

He relaxed. Sipped his drink. Grinned at Tim.

"Timmie boy," he said, "how'd you get back down here?"

"Jet," Tim said. "From Miami. You go up, and you come down, and you're here."

"You know what I mean. Aren't you *non grata* and all that sort of thing?"

"Aren't you dead and all that sort of thing? That's what's being said in New York. Little Mari cried her eyes out. Took me all night to console her."

"Come again?" Peter said.

"Just did. Two days ago."

"Tim, let's start all over again. Were you or weren't you kicked out of this country? Declared *non grata*, et cetera?"

"Why, hell no! They love me down here. I respond to The Treatment. Besides, if I were *non grata*, they wouldn't have let me back in, would they?"

"You've got a point there. So you're *grata*. You've come back to help bury the Eternal Republic?"

"Exactly. And to see if the reports of your demise weren't a trifle exaggerated. I thought they were, what with His Nibs' little sister in there pitching for you. By the way, how is she?"

"Great," Peter said.

"And Judy?"

"Don't know. Haven't been seeing much of her lately."

"Thought not. You know, I've been studying your method. Works. Damned if it doesn't! That playing it cool. That, 'Oh, no, dear! I'm not a bit interested in getting into your lacy little scanties. I'm hard to get. *You* make *me*.' Only it works too good."

"Meaning?"

"I've acquired myself a Missus. Legal. In the Church, yet."

"Well, I'll be goddamed!"

"You are, you canine's son. 'S all your fault. But thanks anyhow. Mari was practically a gift from you to me."

"What Mary?"

"Not Mary, *Mari*. Marisol Talaveda. You and Alicia got her

out of this Unhealth Resort. I finally dragged out of her how. Little 'Licia took her place in a bugged bedroom. In which old Great Lover performed in his own inimitable style—"

"Tim, believe it or not, that's just not so."

"All right. I'm gallant, too, now. Learned it from you."

"Oh, hell, skip it. So you married Marisol! You lucky bastard! Sweet little thing. I liked her."

"She liked *you*, brother. Main hurdle I had to get over. You were chivalrous. You were gallant. You were a gentleman. You nobly refused to take advantage of her. So I sez: 'Why don't you forgive him for that? He'll make it up to you the next time, or I don't know Old Ginger Pete!' So she was terribly insulted with me, like dames always are when you hit 'em with the truth. The trouble is they want to turn on the virtue and refuse you. But when a guy turns *them* down, they get anxious. Begin to worry whether they've really got it all and if it's stacked up high enough in the right places . . ."

"Tim the philosopher!"

" 'S God's own truth. Anyhow, she cooled off after a while and let me start squiring her around, mainly because she was lonesome as all hell, and kind of lost in the Big City. Though that helped. Her being up there, I mean. Down here she'd have felt like a Blue Moon babe if she hadn't mourned for that poor bastard Roberto for at least three years. Incidentally, they didn't get along all that hot together—a detail she sort of hid from everybody, including your lil' Monkeyface. Besides which, I speak Spik. At first, all she would talk about was you. But I finally convinced her I wasn't half bad myself, mainly by keeping me paws off her, no matter how much I was tempted. And you know these Latin dames, brother. Invented the word *sweet*. Make all our broads seem like battleaxes. Seem, hell! How'd we manage to grow so many witches, boy?"

"Forgot the first lesson: 'A gong and a woman sound better when hit.' "

"Truth. And all those deep-frozen tails!"

"Tim—out of line, and off the record. You can even poke me one for asking, but I thought that little Mari . . ."

"Was a frosty little number herself? So did I, chum; so did I. And brother, was I ever wrong! So we got hitched two weeks ago. And then Miguelito goofs again, and I draw this caper. Anyhow, thanks, Chum. I promised to find you if I could. Give you what she sent you. So pucker up, Petie! Here's where you get bussed by remote control—"

"Sorry. You know: I use that well-known soap. So I'm lovely. And engaged."

"To Alicia?" Tim said, and started pulling photos out of his pocket and laying them down on the table.

"I think so," Peter said.

"Don't you know?"

"No. Not exactly. . . . My God, Tim, what are those?"

"Oh, these? Hell, I was looking for our wedding photo. Brought you a copy, signed by us both. Must have left it in my other suit."

The sound truck crawled around the corner, blaring. That same old announcement. Tim looked at Peter.

"You think what I think, boy?" he said.

"Depends on what you think, Tim."

"That anybody who takes Miguelito up on that one ought to have his head examined."

"Likewise. He'll get them up in the mountains someplace and then politely inform our State Department that their continued safety requires a little friendly cooperation on the part of the Atlantic Fleet—especially the Marines. But I don't think any of the local contingent of our noble compatriots have suckered in. And there aren't any tourists to speak of. But these pictures, Tim!"

"Took 'em in the Museum of Archeology. Dead Indians. Hence Good Indians. Great, aren't they?"

"They look like they could speak!" Peter said.

"They could, once. Before all that nice thick volcanic ash petrified 'em. You want some prints of these?"

"Lord, yes!"

"Then c'mon over to my place. Got a suite at the Verdian Hilton. All they've got these days. Suites. No tourists." Tim paid the check. In dollars. And almost started a riot, because all the other waiters wanted to force the lucky one who had waited on them to divide. The argument was loud. It was apparent the Costa Verdian peso wasn't exactly being held in high esteem at the moment.

"So you're going to marry His Nibs' sister?" Tim said.

"Wish I could," Peter said, "but there's one damned rough obstacle. You know: that business about Connie—"

"Connie? Who's Connie? Do I know her?"

"My ex, Tim. Luis Sinnombre had her killed."

"Oh, that! Look, Pete; you've got it all wrong! It wasn't— Holy Mary, Mother of God!" Tim said.

Peter followed his gaze. Saw what he was looking at. Said: "So long, Tim. Be seeing you."

Then he crossed the street to where she sat. At a table. On the sidewalk. In front of a rather dingy bar. She was alone. He saw that she was crying. Looking at her now, that was exactly what he felt like doing himself.

"Judy baby—" he said.

She didn't answer him. She went on crying. Her hair was wild. There was a dried trickle of blood at the corner of her mouth. The flesh along one side of her jaw had purpled. There were other marks upon her throat, her bare arms. Looking down, he saw that one of her stockings had fallen about her ankles. She looked like the great-grandmother of all the whores on earth. He put his hand under her chin, raised her bleary, tear-stained face. Her breath reeked of whiskey. Yet, Peter saw, she wasn't drunk.

"Please," she said, "will you order me a coffee? I haven't had any breakfast. In fact, I don't think I've eaten in four days. Maybe five. And I can't make them understand. Besides, I haven't any money . . ."

"All right," Peter said. He clapped his hand. The waiter came. He looked relieved to see Peter there.

"A big orange juice," Peter said. "Two coffees. One with milk, the other black. Toast. Butter. Marmalade. Eggs. Bacon."

Judith shuddered.

"I couldn't, Peter," she said.

"You're going to," Peter said. "Why don't you go into the ladies' room and comb your hair? Wash your face. Pull up that stocking. Here—take my comb."

"All right," Judith said.

When she came back, she looked almost human. Peter held the chair for her. She sat down.

Across the street a *buitre* flapped heavily down from the roof. Came to rest in the road. Sat there staring at Peter, then at Judith.

"Make your mind up, you scaly-headed bastard!" Peter said. "The tender cut, or the tough? Or is it both?"

He picked up a glass from beside his plate. Threw it at the vulture. It rose slowly. Flapped back up to the roof. Sat there, still staring at them.

The waiter came with the breakfast. Judith drank the orange juice. The coffee. Nibbled at a piece of toast.

"Eat, goddam you!" Peter said.

She took a piece of bacon. It was damn good bacon. But she masticated it as if it were crawling with maggots. She forked up a bit of egg yolk, ropy, dripping. That did it. It wasn't pretty. Peter wiped her mouth and eyes with his handkerchief. Threw the handkerchief away. Stood up, put a bill under a saucer; took her by the arm.

"Where're we going?" she said.

"To the hospital," he said. "So Vince can give you the care you need—"

"All right," Judith said. But then she stopped.

And he, turning, in the midst of siren whoop, brake screech, horn blare, heard Luis Sinnombre's voice rising, scream shrill, saying:

"You dirty little daughter of this and that; you thing of bad milk. I this upon the grave of your father. I that into the face of your mother. Take her, Mateo! Throw her into the *coche!*" Then dropping, smoothing, purring: "And *you*, Reynolds? Ah, glad to see you back, Amigo! Juanito! Throw this lump of gringo filth in beside her!"

Peter put his hand down, edging it toward his hip pocket. Then he took his hand away. A Walther was a good gun.

Excellent. But it wasn't equal to a twenty-five-shot Bren machine pistol, which could burn through a clip in three seconds flat. And when seven of those burp guns were pointing, as they were now, the odds weren't even calculable. In fact, there weren't any odds. Luis had it made. He put his hands up very slowly. But he had forgotten one characteristic of the police of dictatorships. A lack of resistance didn't change their procedure at all. Behind him, one of them lifted up a blackjack, brought it crashing down on his head. And, sagging slowly through a sun-bright blaze, through a red sear of pain, Peter heard, as he dimmed out of time and space and conscious being, the soaring, delighted lift of Judith's laughter.

He was on a bus, and his hands weren't even bound. Which made no sense at all. The Walther was gone, though. That made sense. But nothing else did. Especially not that they had left the Rollei slung around his neck. He was aware that he was not dreaming. That the bus was real. It and the people on it. Judith, who was sitting beside him. Tim O'Rourke, a little farther away. Then Padre Pío. Then the American Ambassador and his wife. Then a huge woman whose face looked like Luis Sinnombre's. Looked like Miguel Villalonga's. Looked like Alicia's.

The splitting pain in his head wouldn't let him think. But he didn't need to. The armed guard beside the bus driver eliminated any necessity for thought. Miguel's radio announcement had failed. His sound trucks. So he had gathered up his hostages by force.

That was all right. That made sense. But even his bloody, aching head could get to one highly rhetorical question: What man on earth would Villalonga *not* hold as a hostage when the circumstances permitted murder—as they did now? Now they permitted anything. And the answer, requiring even less stirring of the quivering, doughy mass they had beaten his alleged brains into: One Peter Reynolds, foreign correspondent. Since he was clearly out of his mind, stark raving mad, Peter closed his eyes again.

The bus groaned on. Up a mountain road. The driver was in uniform. He had a pistol in his belt. He wasn't very military, though. He had his shirt open almost to the top of his belt. Peter could see a big hammered-silver cross on a chain nestling against the mat of sweaty black hair on his chest. It was a singularly beautiful cross. Of Tluscolan making, surely.

The bus was filled with people. Most of them American Embassy staff members. They looked worried and angry. The Costa Verdians didn't look worried. They looked like people already dead.

"Judy—" Peter said.

She didn't answer him. She sat there staring straight ahead.

Peter's head ached worse than hell. He closed his eyes. But nothing changed. The bus kept right on grinding up that road.

"Judy—" he said again. Then he saw what she was doing. She was winking at the bus driver. Not at the armed guard, who had his back turned and was already fast asleep. The driver was looking at her in the rear-view mirror. He had it adjusted so he could see her legs instead of the road. The bus driver grinned at her. She grinned back. If you could call that macabre grimace a grin. Then very slowly she pulled her skirt up, inch by inch, opening her legs wide. She didn't have on pants. Peter could see the little golden tuft between her thighs. So could the driver. He was sweating. He braked just in time to keep the bus on the road.

"*Idiota!*" the armed guard said, and went back to sleep again.

"Goddam it, Judy!" Peter said, and jerked her skirt down again.

Then he heard the roar, and that long white flash poured past them in a scream of wind, exhaust blast, motor snarl. He looked at it dully, forgetting Judy, forgetting the bus driver. It took the curve ahead of them in a four-wheel power drift and was gone. The bus driver was still staring at Judy's legs. She was inching her skirt up again. She saw Peter's face.

"It's so hot!" she whined. Then all the air went shrill with the sound of brakes, the driver fighting the wheel trying to keep the bus on the road, and the armed guard swearing at him. There was nothing beyond the edge. Nothing at all. A thousand meters farther down there was a broken jumble of rocks. But they didn't go over. The driver was fighting for his own life. For maybe a chance at what Judy was now showing him again.

He stopped the bus one meter from the white Jaguar drawn up across the road. Leaped out, pistol in hand, screaming curses. The armed guard jumped out, too, his rifle ready.

"Put up your toys, *niños!*" Alicia said.

She got out of the Jaguar. She was dressed in a blouse and skirt. Her long, beautiful legs were bare. Her dainty feet were thrust into sandals. Respectfully, the bus driver helped her aboard the bus. She stood in the front of it, arguing with him. He kept spreading out his hands and shaking his head. Then he shrugged. Put up his hand with two fingers uplifted. Just two. Alicia came down the aisle. Knelt down beside the fat woman. Talked to her, begging and pleading with her from the expression on that tribal face, from her gestures. They were both crying now. The woman stroked Alicia's head.

Tim O'Rourke was sitting in the seat just behind the fat woman's. Tim leaned forward, listening to what went on between her and Alicia. Then he got up. Walked to the door of the bus. Got out. Started to run—upward into a pine wood.

The armed guard knelt in the road; took careful aim with his rifle.

"Stop it!" Alicia said.

The guard lowered the gun.

"Yes, Doña Alicia," he said. "As the illustrious lady wishes!"

Alicia went on talking to the fat woman. The fat woman shook her head. They kissed each other tenderly. Alicia got up. Came on down the aisle. Stopped beside Father Pío. Spoke to him. The little priest got up. They both came to where Peter was. Took him by the arms.

"Come, *Cielo,*" Alicia said.

Peter looked at Judith. She was leaning back against the seat with her eyes closed. Tears stole from under her lids. But her mouth was still fixed in that macabre grin. Peter saw that her legs were bare again. Up to her hips.

"Judy—" he said.

Alicia's face darkened.

"Leave that filthy exhibitionistic bitch and come on!" she said.

But the road, like all mountain roads, looped back upon itself two dozen times. Peter could see the bus getting smaller and higher up each time the straight stretches paralleled the place they had left it. It wasn't moving. It seemed to be waiting for something. That bothered Peter. Alicia had the Jaguar's top down, and the icy blast of the air was clearing Peter's head now. He slung the Rollei from around his neck, handed it to Father Pío. The old man put it down between the seats.

Then Peter saw the pigmy figures swarm down toward the bus from the heights above. Saw what they had in their hands.

"Stop the car!" he said.

"No! No, Peter!" Alicia wept. "I cannot! I must not! I—"

"Stop this heap, Alicia!"

"Peter, no! Oh, *Dios mío!* I—"

He reached down, hauled up on the handbrake. The Jaguar bucked like a living thing. Skidded broadside the road. The motor strangled itself as Alicia's foot slipped off the clutch. In the abrupt, dead-stopped silence, they heard the shots. The ripping stutter of machine gun bursts. The flat, slow, deliberate *c r a a a a c k!* of rifles. The lighter, spitting bark of hand guns. A scream. Another. Then nothing. Nothing at all.

Peter looked at Alicia. She cringed under his eyes. He put his tongue out. Licked bone-dry lips. Said: "You knew."

"Daughter," Father Pío said, "if you knew this, and did not tell me, the sin—"

"You knew!" Peter said.

She sat there, crumpling behind her eyes. Said nothing. Peter went on looking at her. Said:

"That fat woman. Your—mother?"

She nodded dumbly. Then he hit her. Open-palmed across the mouth. So hard that he brought blood. Again. And again, his big hand making the sound of a volley of small-arms fire, jerking her head from right to left to right again until he felt hard fingers bite into his shoulder, hauling him back, and as he whirled, a fist crashed into his face.

He bent, ready to leap. Then he saw who had hit him.

"Father—" he whispered; "pardon—I—"

"Beast!" Father Pío roared, "savage! And what is worst, fool! Look at her! Look what you have done!"

Peter looked down. Alicia lay across the seat. Her face was a mess. She was crying without motion, without sound, in a way he couldn't look at because the loss of hope is a kind of death, but that he couldn't stop looking at either until his own eyes went blind, blotting out her face.

"Nena—" he whispered. "Infant, I— Oh, Christ, 'Licia!"

But she was smiling at him now, her swollen, broken lips bisecting the crystal spillage.

"It is nothing, *Cielo*," she said. "We both have so much to forgive each other for. Yet what is love but forgiving? Since angels and saints don't marry, we must—"

"Skip the rest of this until another time, Nena," Peter said; "we've a couple of rough chores to do right now. So come on!"

She straightened up at once, took the wheel; the motor kicked into life. Headed back up that road.

"My son," the old priest said, "there is a law that fits this case. It says: 'Forsaking all others—'"

"I know," Peter said; "but, Father, I couldn't accept—"

"Who are you to reject Heaven's gifts? Sometimes you anger me," Padre Pío said.

The soldiers were still there, busily engaged in robbing the bodies of their prey. They tore rings from inert fingers, necklaces from still necks. When the Jaguar roared around the bend, they stopped it, raised their guns. But they lowered them again at once. Turned. Got out of there, running— twenty-five well-armed men running from an unarmed, battered man, a girl, and a priest.

Then Peter saw why. They were dressed as guerrillas, but they weren't. He had seen some of those faces too many times now not to recognize them. He looked at Alicia.

She had her head turned. Away from that slaughtered pile, from that boneless sprawl, from that slow blackening collective seep. The shudders raced through her slim body in tidal waves. But she saw his look.

"Yes," she whispered; "what you are thinking, Peter. So that your government would have to intervene. Your Ambassador. His wife. The embassy staff. Judith—who is famous. You, who are too, now. Father Pío, whom all the world loves. And—"

"Your mother," Peter said. "*His* mother!"

"*Ay, sí!* That was the master stroke, *Cielo!* Our poor, bedeviled mother! Who—tell me who, Peter—will believe it was not the Castristas, when The Leader's own mother is found among the dead?"

"Jesus!" Peter said.

"I tried to save her! Peter, Love, I tried! The driver agreed I could save two. I was going to save her—and you. Forgive me, Father, for making you a second choice . . ."

"You were right, daughter," the old priest said. "Your choice was wise . . ."

"But she wouldn't come, Peter!" Alicia wept. "She said she would only spoil my life with you! She tried to put me off by saying horrible things: That it was evident you had a pair well hung, and she could see I already knew it from experience! And that I must keep you worn out in the bed so that I need not fear the blonde vicious one, nor any other, and—"

"Daughter!" Father Pío said.

"She spoke truth, Father! As even you must know! And now—"

"And now let us face a sadder truth, my daughter. Let us go pray for our dead . . ."

"No! Wait! Hear my confession, Father! I am equally an assassin! Because I wanted the blonde one to die! I willed Judith Lovell's death, Father! 'As a man thinketh in his heart, so is he!' And a woman, no, Father? So I am damned, am I not? Am I, Father?"

"What you are, Nena, is hysterical," Peter said. "Now pipe down, will you? I don't have the heart to hit you again."

They knelt beside Isabela Cienmil's body. The dead woman seemed to be smiling a little. Father Pío said the prayer for the dead, then added in Spanish, and aloud: "Receive, Oh Lord, thy servant Isabel—as Thou received the Magdalene, the Woman at the Well, and her about whom Thou wrote pity on the ground, as Thou received her who washed Thy feet with tears and dried them with her hair. Her sins were great; but greater is Thy mercy. For that, and for this her daughter's sake, receive and pardon her, oh Lord!"

"Oh Peter!" Alicia sobbed. "Oh, Peter, *Cielo,* He will, will He not? She was kind, you hear me, kind!"

"*Sí,* Nena," Peter said. "Now come . . ."

They moved down that sickening row. Said a prayer above each one. But when they came to the end of it, one thing was clear: Judith Lovell's body was not there at all.

"Peter—" Alicia said. "You think—she escaped? Oh, I hope so! I have enough upon my conscience now!"

"Yes," Peter said, "little Judy got away all right."

"But how, *Cielo?* How?"

"The driver," Peter said; "the guard. Or both. I think she bribed them with the only coin she had left to offer. And, used and shoddy as that was, it worked. Father—"

"Yes, son?"

"We'd better go back, now. Send someone up here for the bodies."

"You go, son—and you, daughter. I will watch here with them yet a while."

"But, Father," Alicia said; "the soldiers might come back and—"

"I have God's protection, daughter. Is that not clear by now?"

"Yes, Father, it is," Alicia whispered; then: "Oh, Peter, *Cielo*—Tim! Don Timoteo—your Irish friend! He—"

"Is one of the finest alpinists and woodsmen you ever saw. We'll pick him up later—if he doesn't pick us up first. Now, there's no time . . ."

Alicia reported the massacre to Luis Sinnombre while Peter waited for her at the hotel. She was careful not to mention that anyone had escaped.

"I'll send up after them tomorrow," Luis said. He sounded bored. "Don't worry, little sister, cold as it is up there, they'll keep—"

Then he turned and looked at her.

"Tell me," he said, "just what the devil has happened to your face?"

"I-I—fainted when I saw them, Luis," Alicia said. "Fell—rolled down a slope. I-I could have been killed. And I wish I had been!"

"Ah, so? Now where do you think you're going?"

"To church," she whispered. "Peter was on that bus, Luis. And my mother. You find it ill that I want to pray?"

"No," Luis laughed; "pray for me, will you? And for Miguel. I suspect we need it!"

"I shall," Alicia said. "I shall pray that you both burn in hell!" Then turned, already running, and left him there.

Peter was beginning to feel much better, now. Alicia had cleaned and dressed the wound on his head. Fed him cold cuts, cheese, wine, fruit. Lay in his arms while he slept. But the whole time, she continued weeping.

What woke him up was the roar that Zopocomapetl made when it finally committed suicide by blowing itself apart.

Even that steel-and-concrete modern hotel reeled drunkenly under the impact. They could hear above old Zopo's bull bellow, the crash of a hundred thousand windows blowing in at once. The tongue of fire split the sky open. They got up and went to the window. The volcano was gone, leaving only a low truncated hump out of which poured a lake of fire, spreading down toward the jungle, toward the sea.

They saw the jungle take fire, the sea explode. Great geysers of steam rose up. Waves raced outward toward the rim of the world. Then the winds came howling back, bringing the smoke, bringing that lung-tearing vapor.

"Come on, Nena!" Peter said. "Let's get out of here!"

But when they reached the streets, they saw a curious thing: Appalling as the catastrophe looked, it had killed almost nobody. Here and there, a house burned. Farther out, some adobe huts of the poor had collapsed. The greatest number of casualties was among the loyal units of Villalonga's army, guarding the approaches of the city against the Reds.

Who would be months in coming now—if they ever did. Because to take Ciudad Villalonga under those abruptly altered circumstances, they needed the one thing they didn't have—a fleet. All the landward approaches were cut off by the burning jungle, by that lake of fire.

"Nena," Peter said, "I don't know whom your brother knows Upstairs; but whoever it is, he sure takes damned good care of Miguelito!"

She turned to him, caught at his arms, clung to him, shuddering.

"Nena, Infant," he said; "what's wrong?"

"My mother—those people on the bus—they're dead, of course," she said; "but up there, so close to Zopo—" Then she stopped. "Oh, Peter!" she wailed. "Padre Pío! Your—your Judith! Tim!"

"Good God!" Peter said. "Come on!"

She drove the Jaguar expertly up the road that so far was still open, probably because the already opened split in the far side of the volcano had spilled out the major lava flow. Still there was no valid ground for hope—smaller eruptions than this one had wiped out teeming cities within fairly recent history; and up there where Tim and Judy and Father Pío had been—

He put it from his mind, refusing to think about them, about the way they had probably died by now, because it wasn't a thing to think about, because thinking about it was too much, comparable in a way to suffering it, or maybe even worse, since the dead are forever exempt from grief, from remorse, from memory. So, he turned to Alicia, seeing her face bruised, swollen, a dried trickle of blood in one corner of her mouth, which she had been too occupied with him, too oblivious of self to wipe away; but what she was, what she meant to him, combined with the probability of his losing her, so great as to be indistinguishable from certainty, wasn't to be borne either, so when he spoke, all he said was:

"Strange—"

"What's strange, *Cielo?*" Alicia said.

"I have never met a man of Spanish blood who was wanting in filial love. No matter who that man was. No matter who—or even what—his mother was. Never."

"You are right, *Cielo.* That's what makes it so terrible—"

"Meaning?" Peter said.

"That Miguel loves Mama. As much as I do. No, more. There you have a rarity, Peter! My mother, who was a woman of outrageous behavior—who all her life had been a wanton—was lovable. I have loved her all of the little time I have known her—"

"The little time?" Peter said.

"Since I came back from Spain. Before that, that she was my mother was concealed from me—"

She was silent then. And, because where they were now the road was of a vile vileness—in the popular Costa Verdian phrase—he didn't say anything to her. Instead he looked down and behind to where Ciudad Villalonga lay white in the sun. From that height, it appeared untouched. Here and there, smoke rose from burned-out houses, but that was all. Except that between it and the truncated volcano, a lake of fire lay. Beyond that, the jungle burned. The lava still poured down into the sea, exploding it into snowy geysers of steam. The whole thing was weirdly beautiful. Peter reached for the Rollei to take a picture of it, but Alicia bent the Jaguar around a curve and it dropped from sight.

"Nena," Peter said, "you say that Miguel loved your mother, and yet—"

"He has murdered her. Yes, Peter. I think it is because he is no longer entirely sane. And because he has been corrupted by Luis, who never really was. They have, both of them, come to believe their own propaganda. That the Republic could not exist without them. That they are the only bulwark between the people of Costa Verde and complete disaster."

"I agree that changing them for the Castristas will only be swapping the devil for the witch," Peter said. "Still—"

He saw another thing now: that the road was going to be open all the way up, that the already opened split on the other side of Zopocomapetl had taken the pressure off, so that except for several meters of ash, drifted in places as high as snowbanks, there was nothing to block the road. Except for a trickle or two, the major lava flows were away from the road, sliding down the eastern side of the volcano, or what was left of it, toward the sea. And since no major road ran east from Ciudad Villalonga for the simple reason that that was where the ocean was, this road, like all the roads north and west of the city, was safe. But all the roads to the south had been wiped out, effortlessly negating the Communists' very clever strategy of striking from the one point of the compass nobody expected them to, and reinforcing Peter's belief that the basic quality of life was irony— when it wasn't meaninglessness. And then they came around one more curve, and he saw that he was right.

The bus stood there by the side of the road. All the paint had been seared off it, leaving it rust-red and silvery bright. But they could still see the line of holes that had crashed into the side of it, see the spiderweb tracery of the shot-up windows. Beyond, sullenly, fiercely, the pine wood burned, crackling with unholy laughter. The bodies still lay beside it in long rows, where they had been gunned down. And yet, Peter saw, old Zopo had granted them an accidental or maybe even a deliberate, benediction. He had covered them with white ash, had formed them into statues.

"Oh, Peter! Oh, *Cielo*, look!" Alicia said; and he turned, staring at her, because that note in her voice was joy. Then he looked back again and saw Padre Pío stepping gingerly down from the bus itself. His clothes were gray with ash, but he was unhurt. Peter was out of the car at once, gathering the old man in his arms in that great back pounding bear hug that Spanish-speaking peoples call *un abrazo* and which permits men to show a deeper and truer emotion for each other than is possible among colder races; and when he had turned him loose, Alicia, forgetting in her joy that the old man was a priest, kissed him on both cheeks, as she would have her own father.

"Children!" the old man said severely, but his eyes were misty.

"Now will you say that you cannot work miracles, Father?" Peter said; "now do you dare?"

The old man smiled.

"I say only that God still has work for me here below," he said. "The truth is much duller, son. I hid under one of the seats of the bus and prayed. And since I have not enough fat on my bones to roast, I only cured a bit more, making me even tougher and more unpalatable. Now this of the truck, children?"

"Tomorrow, Father," Alicia said; "Peter—"

"Yes, Nena—"

"It was not as bad as we thought, up here. Perhaps . . ."

"We can look, 'Licia; but if we don't find them close to here, we'll have to go back, organize a true searching party if such a thing is possible. What we really need is an airplane. Or a helicopter. Still—"

"Father, wait for us here, will you?" Alicia said. "We shall not be too long . . ."

They walked on up the road, past the burning forest. The heat was unbearable, the smoke clawed at their eyes. And it was no good. This wasn't the way to do it. Even if hope existed, which—considering how rapidly the situation deteriorated with every meter they climbed above the bus— was one big *if*, this was not the way to search for Judith and Tim. What that way was Peter didn't know. He suspected that at the moment, with the woods on both sides of the road burning like the hinges of hell, the way didn't exist. And that when rational search became possible it would be too late. Forever too late. If it weren't already.

"Hell, let's go back," Peter said, but then he heard her gasp:

"Oh, Peter, look!"

A flow of lava had cut the road; five meters farther on, another. Between the two, the soldiers' bodies lay. Their only way out had been into the woods, but the pines had surely already been afire by then.

Alicia clung to him, shuddering. Peter looked across to the low hump that was all that was left of Zopocomapetl. Then back at the bloated tarry horrors that no drop of ash had touched.

"I know they had it coming, but did you have to play *that* rough?" he said.

Then they both heard that faint, feeble voice.

"Petie, boy—"

They turned. A scarecrow reeled toward them. An all-but-naked scarecrow, fluttering charred rags behind it as it came, fluttering strips of skin.

"Tim!" Peter said; "my God, Tim!"

"Mr. Reynolds, I presume? And Doña Alicia? Honored— honored—" Tim said. They caught him between them as he fell.

Alicia knelt there, cradling Tim's head in her arms, and watching Peter's face as he made that choice. The choice he had to make now. The one choice that she less than anyone else on earth could help him make. All she could do was suffer acutely and damnably and agonizingly while he made it. And silently.

She saw his eyes clear; heard him say, his voice rough with pain:

"Help me pick him up, and get him to the car. We've got to get him down faster than all hell—"

Now she was released. Now she could say it.

"And—and Judith, *Cielo?*"

Peter's eyes went sick.

"We *know* he's alive, Nena, and that he won't be long, unless we really pour it on. So what choice is there? Gamble Tim's chances against what we *might* find? Hell no, 'Licia. Now come on!" he said.

But once they had Tim in the car—having had to leave Padre Pío once more because the sports roadster just wasn't built to hold four people comfortably and couldn't hold four at all now that Tim couldn't sit up—and Alicia was slamming it down that road, while Peter held Tim in his arms, Tim woke up and started to talk so slowly, gravely, sadly that it took them some time to notice he wasn't making sense.

"So maybe I was wrong about her. So maybe it didn't matter that she was the easiest lay in the Western Hemisphere and that her heels were shaped like ball bearings and she had calluses on her back from going over on it any time anybody pushed. Pushed, hell—waved. The breeze was enough to send her over. So what? So nothing. So I'm Paddy's Pig from Ol' Malarkey if I know a goddam thing any more. Jesus and Mary! God bless us all. Never a cry. Never a groan. Just that look. All lit up. Like candles on an altar . . . I tell you, Petie boy, she—"

"Tim, will you please for God's sake pipe down?" Peter said. "You're going to need that breath—"

"What on earth does he mean?" Alicia said.

"Who knows? Who even cares? Nena, can you get a little more speed out of this thing?"

"Yes, *Cielo;* but I am not sure I can keep it on the road if I do—"

"Stop it, then," Peter said. "Let me take over."

"All right, Love," Alicia said.

She sat there holding Tim. It was characteristic of her that she wasn't afraid. After her first startled questioning whether any man could do to and with a car what Peter was doing now, she sat there and listened to her heart; and her heart said that Peter could do anything—anything at all. So she sat there smiling while Peter leadfooted the accelerator, slamming the Jaguar into those mountain hairpin turns wide out; power-skidding them, cutting the wheel in the opposite direction from the one he wanted the car to go; and gunning it as they broke loose; showering the very treetops with pebbles from the road; trailing a hundred-meter-long cloud of dust and volcanic ash behind them; double-clutching, dropping into second with a snarl that threatened every instant to tear the guts out of the gear box, then stroking it up again, knifing through the shifts without dropping a revolution on the tachometer, barreling into the straights in one great fine lovely cacophony: exhaust blatt, tire scream, motor thunder, and the wind's long, long tearing.

Then they were down again, and he was pouring the Jaguar through the all-but-empty streets toward the hospital, and getting there, chopping the ignition, jumping out, reaching into the car and dragging Tim out, and carrying him, big as the Irish reporter was, into the emergency entrance in his arms.

While they were waiting for the results of Vince's and the other doctors' examination, the sister who remembered Peter from his daily visits to Judith there babbled away until it came to him that there were justifiable reasons for murder, after all.

"Even now, in the Cathedral, His Excellency prays, alone. And then, within the hour, the procession will come up the street with Don Luis leading the Escort of Protection; and then the Archbishop and then the Image of Our Lady of Compassion, and the Jesus of the Great Power, and then—"

Vince came through the door.

"He'll make it, Peter," he said. "He has fifteen per cent of his body covered with second-degree burns. He'll probably be laid up here two months. But with the new techniques of burn treatment, he'll go home almost as good as new—"

"And then," the sister went on brightly, "they will say a *Te Deum* in gratitude for the salvation of the city, and—"

Peter looked at her.

"Hermana," he said, "who told you this city was saved?" He turned to Doctor Gomez. "Thanks, Vince," he said; "now we'd better go send a telegram."

"To relatives of his?" Vince said.

"To Marisol Talaveda, who just married the lunk," Peter said.

21.

When they came out of the hospital, Peter went to the Jaguar and retrieved the Rolleiflex, which still lay between the seats where Father Pío had put it after Peter handed it to him on the mountain road. As he pulled it out, it came to Peter why they had let him keep it. He wasn't to have been the first of Miguel's victims, but the last. He could hear the announcer's voice now, as clearly as though the man were actually speaking: *"Films found in the camera of one of the victims, the famous North American journalist, Mr. Peter Reynolds, conclusively prove that the attack was carried out by Communist guerrillas, as their uniforms can be clearly seen in the photographs. The government plans to release copies of these remarkable pictures to the international press at the earliest possible moment. This dastardly crime . . ."*

"Son of a bitch!" Peter said.

"What did you say, *Cielo?*" Alicia said.

"Nothing, Nena; come on . . ."

They started walking across the Plaza to the cable office. Then they saw the soldiers. Alicia stopped, her fingers gripping Peter's arm.

"Keep walking," Peter said.

"But Peter, *Cielo*, they—"

"They nothing. They're soldiers, not police. And I'm dead, remember? At least as far as Luis is concerned."

He could feel her trembling; but she moved beside him, head up, staring straight ahead. And more and more soldiers came out of the Avenida McDowell, which led to the Plaza de los Mártires Concepcionistas, where the Cathedral was. From their uniforms, Peter could see that they were units of the crack Escolta del Caudillo, the Leader's Special Guard; but they weren't displaying any of the snap and precision for which they were famous—at least not now. Now they straggled across the Plaza in disconnected groups, talking to one another in low voices; and, in their faces, their puzzlement was plain.

"Peter!" Alicia said; "they should be at the Cathedral, guarding Miguel! I wonder—"

"Ask them," Peter said.

"Oh, no!" Alicia said; "*Cielo*, I-I don't dare!"

"Then I will," Peter said.

"No, *Cielo*! You, no! I will ask them. After all, I am his sister and— Peter, Love, wait for me in that bar. Have a beer. Have two beers. Do not preoccupy yourself. I'll be all right."

He kissed her quickly. Released her arm. Crossed over to the little bar under the archway. Sat there with a cold beer in his hand, almost untasted, watching her talking to the soldiers. He saw one of them indicate her battered face. He could see from the flustered gestures of her hands that she was lying nobly, trying to explain that. They clearly didn't believe her; but, being who she was, they had to take her word for it. Then he saw her coming toward him, downed the beer at a gulp, and stood up.

"Oh, Peter, *Cielo*, they—" she said.

"Gentle down, Nena. Have a beer," he said.

"Peter, he sent them away! He says he no longer needs an escort since he is clearly under divine protection! And when their Captain argued that there were subversive elements loose in the city, he said: 'When the time comes that I must die, I shall die, with you or without, Captain. Who can gainsay the will of God?'"

"He's nuts," Peter said. "A beer, Nena?"

"Yes. But Peter, he has them half believing it. He pointed out to them how hopeless the situation was before Zopo blew up. And now the Reds cannot enter the city at all!"

"The Reds can't. But the typhus can. Malaria. And that new virus infection that causes hemorrhages. In fact, they have. Vince is mobilizing all the medicos. He's afraid we're going to have a triple epidemic on our hands—"

"Why, Peter?"

"Oddly enough, old Zopo seems to have blown his top for his own reasons, not for any special interest in the affairs of men. . . . Ah, here're our beers. Down the hatch, Nena—"

"Peter, I don't understand."

"I know you don't. It's simple. The eruption blocked the Reds and gave your lovely brother a new lease on life. But it also took out the aqueduct that brings the water from the big reservoir high in the mountains to the little one just behind the town. The water supply is diminishing alarmingly. Some of the poorer districts don't have any water now. Vince isn't worried about the hospital, which has its own supply from three artesian wells in the basement, but he is worried by the already noticeable increase in the type of diseases that come from pollution."

"How awful!" Alicia said. "Haven't our poor people suffered enough?"

"Maybe they're all sinners and have got it coming. Now drink your beer like a big girl and come on," Peter said.

"Peter—what about Father Pío? He's up there alone, with nothing to eat and—"

"That's taken care of. I told Vince, who is going to send an ambulance up after him. The problem is finding a truck for the bodies. But now they can wait. Volcanic ash makes a wonderful preservative . . ."

"Now what will we do, *Cielo?*" Alicia said as they came out of the cable office.

"Hole up somewhere until I can figure what the next move is—and if it makes any sense to move at all. I vote that we check into some fleabag. Both Miguel and Luis know where I live and the Hilton's too goddam conspicuous. They're sure to find out I didn't get mine, any minute now. So a cheap hotel, *Muñeca*. In a way, I've given you a perfect disguise. Even a desk clerk who's seen you before would never believe that you're you with *that* face . . ."

"Peter—" she said solemnly.

"Yes, Nena?"

"You mean to go on beating me up every time you get mad?"

"And if I did?"

"I-I'd just have to endure it, then. Because being without you is worse. And you don't get angry very often, do you?"

He drew her to him.

"Nena," he said, "if, as long as we both shall live, I ever lift a hand against you again, I pray that God will strike me dead!"

"No, Peter! Don't say that! I can be terribly exasperating, you know, and—"

"Nena, from here on in, you've got it made. You've got carte blanche to exasperate the living hell out of me twenty-four hours a day. Anyhow, come on. I'd take you to the country, if there were any way of getting out of town; but—"

"But there is not," a third voice said; "so now, Comrade Reporter, the place where you are going to take her is the Cathedral."

"Look, Jacinto," Peter said, without even turning his head.

"Shut up!" Jacinto said. "Be quiet, Peter! I know Teresa died in your arms. And you know I killed her. But do you know why?"

"No," Peter said.

"Just keep walking ahead, toward the Cathedral—both of you. We have a little rendezvous with your August Brother there, Illustrious Lady! I have a little score to settle with Miguel—a score that requires your cooperation."

"Jacinto—" Peter said.

"I told you to shut up, Peter!"

"You will have to kill me first," Peter said. "Pointing that firecracker at me won't be enough. You'll have to kill me."

"You think I wouldn't?" Jacinto said.

"Make sure you don't miss," Peter said.

Alicia didn't say anything. She walked along beside him so close he could feel her taut, fine body trembling.

"Why did you kill your sister?" Peter said.

"Because she was a whore," Jacinto said.

"That wasn't why," Peter said.

"Because it was time to kill her," Jacinto said.

"Not that," Peter said.

"Because she set out to demonstrate to me that the debility which sometimes comes upon me . . ."

"That always exists within you. Do not lie, Jacinto!"

"That always exists within me," Jacinto said. "Yes, Comrade, I must not lie—did not that night exist, or could be cured by a vicious one of her skill—"

"And did she?" Peter said.

"She died, Peter! You saw that, didn't you?"

"Yes. In my arms. But why? For having proved your weakness could be cured, or for not having proved it?"

"For having proved the time is now," Jacinto said.

"The time is now?"

"Yes!" Jacinto said; "yes, Comrade Reporter! The time is now! It has all terminated for me, so it is now. The time to kill. The time to die. You heard me, it is now!"

Inside the Cathedral it was dark and cool. They walked up the center aisle with Jacinto behind them pointing the little machine gun at their backs. The silence swallowed their footsteps. Peter looked at the massive walls, built by Indian slave labor three centuries ago. They would die here and not even the beggar woman sleeping before the door would know it. From within this mass of stone and leaded glass the sound of a cannon would reach the square as a gentle murmur. No one would hear the faint popping of Jacinto's murderous toy.

And then, suddenly, they saw Miguel Villalonga. He wasn't at the main altar. He was at a little side niche dedicated not to the Holy Virgin but to Mary Magdalene. They moved closer, and then they saw the reason for his choice. The good, pure little Mother of God could not be expected to understand or succor a whore's soul—so his reasoning, or his madness, must have gone—but La Magdalena, who had been herself of the bad life, could and would have compassion upon the soul of the departed Isabel, would comprehend this whore's son's, matricide's monstrous grief, accept indeed his monstrous penance—

That penance which held them there, unbreathing.

He knelt before the altar. He was rigid as stone. He had his two arms stretched out in the form of a cross. At his right side and his left two huge candles burned. They were more than a meter tall, and as big around as a strong's man's arm. And Miguel Villalonga knelt there unmoving, with both his hands puffed, ballooning, charred black, resting without the slightest tremor in those candle flames.

"*Dios!*" Alicia wept. "*Oh, Dios mío!* Ay, Santa Madre Querida! No, Miguel, no!"

"Miguel!" Jacinto howled.

The Dictator did not move.

"Miguel Villalonga!"

The Cathedral threw back the echoes from nave to crypt. "*Meeee gwel llll Veeel ya lonnng gaaaa!*"

Still the man kneeling there did not move.

"I am going to violate your sister now! As you did mine! I—you hear me? I am going to . . ."

The candles sizzled from the blood and grease dripping into them. The smell came over and took them in the nostrils. Peter retched.

Jacinto caught Alicia by the arm.

"Lie down, bitch!" he howled. "I—"

Peter moved in, very quietly.

Jacinto hooked a heel behind Alicia's legs and pushed. She went down. He sprawled atop her, clawing at her skirt.

Then Peter was there. He lashed out with his foot. The kick caught Jacinto in the face, rolled him off and away from her. But he kept his grip—in part, and with only one hand—on the gun. But a Sten gun cannot be controlled with one hand.

At his first burst, Peter threw himself flat, down, and under its flare. He heard the tinkle of glass as the lens of the Rollei broke. But Jacinto had both hands on the Sten now; it spluttered, bucked, chattered like a maniac thing. Peter saw those flat yellow eyes. Saw the insane joy in them. But they were not looking at him.

He twisted, looking back in time to see Miguel shudder under the multiple impact; see the black line of holes stitching the back of the white uniform. Miguel bowed to La Magdalena very slowly. Lay at her feet, under her doll-like, vapid smile.

Peter tensed the muscles of his legs. Jacinto smiled at him above the smoking muzzle of the gun.

"No, Comrade; I have no wish to kill you, now. Nor to avail myself of your woman. What good is it now? I have no hatred of you, and he who might have enjoyed the show is dead. So come—"

Alicia sat up, pulling her skirt down over her slim legs. "Where?" she whispered.

"Outside in the square. At the bar in front. I feel devout. I have a desire to see the procession."

"Jacinto—" Peter said.

"Comrade, one word before you do another foolish thing. I know how brave a man you are. So Doña Alicia will walk at my side with the muzzle of this little headache-, heartache-cure pressed against her breast. You hear this?"

There was a harsh, grating click. Another. Louder. The sound of metal being slammed home.

"Yes," Peter said.

"Know what it means?"

"You just put in a fresh clip."

"Correct. Now walk with me like good children across the square and have a pleasant drink with me. Who knows? I may even let you live. At least a little while."

And then they were sitting there at the table with Jacinto between them, and Alicia was holding Peter's hand and looking into his face as though she were trying to memorize it, as she maybe even was. And now the square was filling up with the people come to watch the procession, so many of them that they got between their table and the square, blocking the view. Seeing how Peter was watching them, Alicia leaned forward and whispered:

"Please, *Cielo!*"

He didn't answer her.

"What will it be, Señores?" the waiter said.

"Beer," Peter said; "the blond, not the dark."

"Very well, Señor," the waiter said.

They sat there, drinking the beer. Peter had a hard time making it go down. Then they heard the motors of the motorcycle police come roaring into the square. They stood up. But they still couldn't see anything. There were too many people between them and the Plaza.

Then, in one easy bound, Jacinto was up on the table. He stood looking over the heads of the people with the Sten gun dangling from his hand. No one paid him the slightest attention. In the Glorious Republic, people were all too used to seeing uniformed thugs with machine guns in their hands.

Peter wrapped his fist around the straps of the Rollei's carrying case, eased it from around his neck. Let it dangle. A Rolleiflex is not the lightest camera in the world. And swung well—

Jacinto lifted the burp gun. Fired a short burst over the heads of the crowd. At the first stutter, all the people between forty and fifty years old, all those who had lived through the last revolution, the one that had brought Miguel

Villalonga to power, hit the street face down. The younger ones stampeded, running.

And now, clearly, Peter could see the square. See motorcycle patrolmen throwing their machines flat and diving behind them. See the squad car in which rode Luis Sinnombre, as head of the police, brake to a stop; see the frightened face of the Mayor, who was dressed for the occasion in top hat, frock coat, and hickory-striped pants; and with him the Archbishop in his gorgeous robes; but the Archbishop's face was even more frightened than the Mayor's, which didn't speak well for his faith, and behind them the Mayor's wife in black with the traditional mantilla raised by a high comb in her hair, and at her side the Mother Superior of the Convent, barefoot as her order demanded, and behind them all the Virgins and crucifixions and Saints on the shoulders of the invisible bearers hidden beneath brocaded-velvet-covered stands, quivering as though they were living things.

Luis Sinnombre was shouting at his chauffeur, his mouth a great red cavern in his face. Then coolly, expertly, Jacinto opened fire.

Peter saw the gun stitching holes in the patrol car. It was very curious to watch: there would be a little puff of something, not vapor, not smoke, and the paint would scale off around the point of impact, leaving a little bright silvery ring of bare metal around the inky spot where the bullet had gone in; and the lines of the holes rising, rising until the windows crashed and shattered into intricate spiderweb traceries with holes in their exact middles and the door tearing open and Luis Sinnombre falling out of it, clawing at his holster for his automatic, and the stitching stopping, reversing itself, centering on the man, tattooing into him so that he jerked like a rag doll, slammed back against the car, and held there by the trip-hammer blows of that half a clip that was making ground meat of his belly, almost cutting him in two; and it was then that Peter swung the Rollei.

The camera caught Jacinto on the side of the head and knocked him off the table. He hit the sidewalk and rolled, still keeping his grip on that machine pistol and coming to rest against the overturned table which impeded very seriously his field of fire, making it impossible for him to swing the Sten to the right.

Then, knowing he was going to die if he didn't, and also if he did, the difference being that if he didn't a hell of a lot of other people were going to die with him, having time only to shape in his mind "Forgive me, Nena" but not to say it, Peter raced for Jacinto, slanting to his own left, Jacinto's right, in the desperate, forlorn, idiotic hope that the reduced swing of the gun in that direction would let him get there alive, seeing the flashes linking themselves like the splutter of a newly lighted blowtorch, hearing the sound become one continuous roar; and he, slanting in, clawing for Jacinto's legs, felt a jackhammer hit him in the left shoulder and side and upper left thigh all at the same time, with no appreciable interval between the blows, and he going on, not feeling the pain or the shock yet because they hadn't had time to register, slammed into Jacinto, sending him down, smashing his right fist into the Commando's face again and again, and Jacinto rolling, kicking free of him and diving for the machine pistol he had dropped when Peter crashed into him, and Peter coming up on his knees and Alicia's screams ripping the fabric of sound apart, and Jacinto grinning through the blood and dirt on his face and swinging the machine pistol around toward Peter—

And Peter hanging there on his knees, trying to get up, and Jacinto, out of his vast and icy reserves of pure cruelty, perhaps—or maybe because, being Spanish, being Tluscola, he understood sympathized with, even respected whatever it was that made a man expend the last of his strength in the effort to die on his feet, to treat death with both the dignity and the contempt it deserved, easing his finger off the trigger and watching while Peter struggled there, the sweat popping out on his forehead, his veins bulging visibly in his temples, forcing himself to get up, to stand upright, to die not in an attitude of supplication or of resignation, but rising tall in whatever shreds of valor he had left, whatever tatters of pride, which was a gesture, he knew, maybe even a ridiculous one, but a gesture that had nevertheless to be made because the why and the when of his dying having already been taken care of, there remained only the how to give meaning to it, to give—and now he could think the words without choking over them—honor and grace to his taking leave of a life that had had very little grace, small honor, and absolutely no meaning at all.

So he struggled to get to his feet in the midst of a silence that had the texture and the feel of the collective horror of all the people who watched it, held there frozen by that horror which had, as horror usually does, a hypnotic quality of fascination about it, making them, those who had not already fled, who were picking themselves up out of the gutters into which they had flung themselves, forget their own danger, their own fear, until finally he made it, and hung there swaying, but on his feet, his left arm dangling, smashed in three places by the first burst, a section of his small intestine perforated; a bullet lodged in his thigh; the blood coming out of him in little spurting tendrils, watering the sidewalk with red, and Jacinto still smiling his ice-cold maniac's smile, raising the muzzle of the gun a little; then curiously spinning, whirling as the ball from the Mauser pistol of the chauffeur, who had been driving the now quite dead and even in death nameless Luis, tore into him; and caressing the trigger of the machine pistol which spat just twice before it quit, missing the chauffeur both times, and Jacinto running now, trying to fit a new clip in place of the empty one he had yanked out and thrown away, and the motorcycle police, lying on their bellies behind their fallen mechanical mounts sighting on him and holding down the triggers of their own Bren guns until they bucked empty, and the dancing rag doll caught in that murderous crossfire not so much falling as splattering upon the cobblestones, riddled, cut to pieces, hashed out of humanity even before he fell; and Alicia catching hold of Peter as he, too, started at last to sag, to give, and a dozen other hands helping her, easing him down into a chair beside the table.

And the sirens beginning to shrill along all that street and

Alicia crying in a way that was absolutely insupportable, impossible to listen to, the sinews of her throat cording and those cries of more and less than human grief tearing out of her past the hand she had thrust into her own mouth and bitten to the bone, rising shrill and terrible like the scrape of glass on stone, like the splintering planes of anguish, like the final loss of hope, vibrant, naked, demented, wild, until by pure contagion every woman in the crowd was shrieking along with her, the sound of that collective hysteria racking hearing out of existence until Peter's big, gray, trembling hand came out and quivered on her face and his equally gray all-gone less-than-soundless voice stilled in an instant all their screaming as he said:

"Don't, Nena—please don't cry."

And she, Alicia, dropping to her knees and crossing herself, her contralto warm as sunlight and as deep, soaring up:

"Mother of Jesus, save him! For his life I promise Thee my life in service, in silence, in poverty, among the barefoot ones. I pledge it. I pledge Thee my life. I don from this hour the gray robes of Thy slaves. If Thou wilt save him— Oh please please please—dear little Mother of God! The sin was mine! All mine! I sought him out; I tempted him! Oh, Holy Mother do not take away his life I beg Thee, I beseech Thee, I supplicate Thee—Oh most sacred Virgin, please!"

And some of the women dropping to their knees beside her and praying with her. And some of the men looking at that bloody, terrible hulk still upright in the chair and saying, "*Que cojones!*" which is not quite equivalent to saying "What guts!" in English, but is close enough; and somebody else: "Make way for the Archbishop! Do not let him die without a prayer!" And he smiling then, thinking, and maybe even saying:

"Yes, pray for me, for all the defeated, the lost, the hopeless, the afraid—"

Then, quite abruptly, nothing. Neither time nor place nor even pain.

22.

First, there was pain. It awoke somewhere deep inside him and began to grow. As it grew it whirled in bright-colored concentric circles like a pinwheel at a fireworks display. And all the colors of that pain were tones of red and yellow, whirling there from their epicenter in his middle, then widening, not into a bigger circle but into a parabola, an ellipse that included the whole left side of his body from his shoulder to his knee. The colors grew brighter, and with them the ache, the sear, the bite, the white-hot multiple stabbing. He went rigid, stiffening, his mouth opening, opening.

And hands gripped his right arm hard; there was a slight, tiny, piercing sting, noticeable only because it was so far away from the epicenter of his pain. The whirling ellipse of agony went on. But it had lessened, because he no longer had that overwhelming desire to scream. And now it lessened still more, dimmed very rapidly, the colors fading, the toothed ellipse rounding into a circle, leaving more and more of his body free of anguish, sinking finally to one white-hot coal low on his left side, which dimmed, faded in its turn into a long, slow ache, and through the onrushing dark he heard the staccato trill of a soprano voice saying in Spanish:

"Believe you he will survive all this, Doctor?"

And Vicente Gomez' voice drum-deep, slow-rolling:

"What I believe or what you believe, Sister, has no importance. What is important now is to continue the penicillin and the terramycin against infection, and the plasma against the shock. In about two hours, we will have an analysis of his blood type, which will make it possible to give him the transfusions he needs. Doctor Martinez is working on that now. Since the wrong kind of blood will kill him; and since, among the members of our staff who have not yet fled, Martinez, slow as he is, remains the only one I trust to do even so simple a thing as determining his blood grouping without making fatal errors, we have to keep him alive until that information arrives . . ."

Also, there was place. It was characterized predominantly by tones of white. The vague, featureless beings who inhabited it wore white, too. They came and went, drifting in and out of the timeless fog in which he existed. They did things to him. Many things. It wasn't very clear to him what those things were except that they were all unpleasant. He had the indistinct impression that they were torturing him. Once, in a flash of clarity—which, in his state of timelessness, may have lasted seconds or hours; afterwards he could never tell—he was sure of it. There was a tube in his right nostril. Another dangled from a bottle hanging from an iron stand, downward to his right arm, into which it disappeared through a needle big enough to disembowel an elephant. Various other tubes were attached to his body beneath the sheets, connected to him by a wildly complicated sort of harness. Then mercifully he faded out of clarity once more into dark.

Last of all, there was time. He became aware that his sensations had duration. That the aching of his arm, his leg, but especially of his middle went on and on. He realized that there were periods when the fluorescent lamp over his bed was out because enough light came through the window, and other periods when the windows were black, and the fluorescent lamps made their singing. And now the routine of the things the beings in white were doing to him changed. Other beings dressed in different colors: black or gray or blue or even vivid mixtures of tones were brought into the room and linked to him through pain.

He was not exactly sure how the linking was accomplished, but on his part it involved a hurtful piercing of his right arm. This happened several times. The last time it happened, time and place and pain all meshed, locked into clarity, into awareness; and Alicia's face stared at him with great and brooding tenderness from the opposite bed. He looked at her, tried to smile, gazed down to where her bare arm extended, saw the red blood pumping out of it through a transparent tube which entered a bottle then came seeping down another tube to enter his own through that elephantine needle. He raised his eyes to her face, seeing that she was wearing a curious kind of a headdress, a coif and veil exactly like the ones the nursing sisters wore, except that hers were gray; but, before he could occupy his tired mind with that detail, her warm, tender, wonderful mouth puckered into the shape of a kiss, and she, raising the fingers of her other hand to it, made the gesture of tossing it to him. And then, quite suddenly, it was all right. He was alive, with her warm, gay youthful, renewing blood singing in his veins like wine.

But when she got up, he saw she had on the absolutely damnedest kind of dress. It was gray and shapeless, and belted around her waist with a piece of rope.

And, oddest of all, her feet were bare.

It took him until the middle of the next night to discover that *all right* was an exaggeration. A gross exaggeration. *All right* meant he was going to live, that he had time ahead of him, a future of sorts. But now the lesson that Luis' goons had begun was extended in depth; and he was forced to apply to his continued existence the same logic or illogic that had made him fight his way to his feet in order to die standing tall. Only now it was infinitely harder. Because it was no longer a grand gesture, one brief emotional clawing deep into himself to find the roots of atavistic valor; now it consisted in a long, slow deadly contest with what is any man's cruelest adversary, himself. He lay in the hospital bed, alive now, fully conscious, staring at that dangling electrical push-button called in Spanish, because of its shape, *una pera*—a pear—which would ring a bell and light a lamp to summon the night sister. He lay there ten minutes, twenty, half an hour; then he pushed it.

Because, if he hadn't, he was going to scream his guts out. The sister came, saw without questioning his pain, eased that needle into his arm, and dropped him very swiftly through the bottom of the world into the gray hell of delirium of formless, morphine-bred dreams. The next time he held out for an hour, lying there staring up into the great white eye of naked agony, all his body licked about with flame. He lay there for that hour thinking or not thinking, forming in his brain and with his silent lips a chant that had no words, and that was and was not a prayer which afterwards he could never remember, but which got him through one hour, three minutes, and four seconds, before he pushed that bell.

That night pain came and sat upon his chest. It had weight, an odor—of ether, of disinfectants, of medicines, of various indefinable hospital smells—but it had no form. Silently he continued his fight with it, retreating into that wordless chant of the night before, calling Alicia's face to mind, thinking precisely and profanely upon the details of her body, feeding the feeble flame of sensuality; but that was no good, although it got him through two hours and a half.

He had already reached for the bell when Padre Pío walked through that door with that serene disregard for rules that didn't mean anything—such as visiting hours (aided and abetted in his stubborn effort to do God's work twenty-four hours a day by the nursing sisters on night duty who, defying Vince's orders, let the old priest come and go as he pleased)—that was as much a part of him as his respect for those that did, such as truly loving his neighbor as himself and maybe even a little more.

All night long the old man sat there holding Peter's hand and talking to him gravely, tenderly so that all the air was filled with his raspy, breathy *"Hijo mío"*—"My son"—until Peter fell into a sleep both healing and profound, whereupon Father Pío left him with a whispered blessing and hurried out to visit some other sufferer, some heartsick, grieving widow, some family all too desperately poor. In the morning, to his own intense disappointment, Peter could not recall what they'd talked about, what the old priest had said.

The morning came graying in through the windows and the day sister's rubber-soled shoes came whispering down the hall. She came into his room and stared at him, gave a little choked-off scream, fled.

When she came back, Vince was with her. He stared at Peter in his turn.

"Had a bad night, didn't you? Why didn't you call?" His voice was rough, angry, concerned, armed against his own pity."

"No," Peter whispered; "no calls."

"Why not?" Vince said.

"Oh, damn you!" Vince said, lapsing back into Spanish, which proved if anything how greatly he was shaken: "I will never accustom myself to it—never. If it served for anything, perhaps. But no. It is foolish and wasteful and maybe even bad; but it moves me much. And in my profession, Friend Peter, it is not useful to be moved. Oh, you son of the great whore! Oh, you Yankee unsayable of bad milk, spare me this. I am tired of witnessing useless valor—if valor is ever useless—if it can ever truly be deprived of meaning—"

Peter smiled at him; said:

"Vince—"

"Yes, Peter?"

"Let me keep it. Don't befoul it with words. Say I had—a great night. Great, marvelous, fine, enormous. Yes, an enormous night . . ."

"Why enormous, Peter?" Vince said.

Peter went on smiling, feeling the pain sinking down, down, fathoms deep, withdrawing now, maybe even vanquished.

"Because," he said, "because I won."

Doctor Gomez went on looking at him. And, usefully or not, he was moved. His voice came out harshly, angrily, filled with pain.

"Did you? Does any man, ever?" he said, and walked out.

"Now what the devil?" Peter said; and, probably because

they had been speaking Spanish, he said it in that language, so the day sister understood.

"Oh," she said brightly, "he is afraid that when you find out—" Then she stopped, clapped a hand over her own mouth; whispered: "*Madre mía!*"

Peter looked at her.

"Say it, Sister," he said.

"But—" she quavered.

"Say it!"

Her head came up. Angrily. Proudly.

"Why not? It is, after all, the Will of God, and Doctor Vince, for all his skill, and despite his criminal denial of the teachings of the Mother Church, is but a man; and so are you, even though you were brave; and—"

"Say it!"

"Doña Alicia has—entered the convent. The gray sisters. The Barefoot Ones. She made a vow that if Our Lady would save your life, she would give up her own to the service of the Sainted Mother of God. And in the humblest of the Orders: The Barefoot Slaves of Our Lady. So—Don Pedro! You must not! *Ay, Madre mía!* What have I done?"

"Murdered him, no doubt!" Vince said, stepping through the door. "If I had my way, all you silly religious bitches would rot in hell!"

He bent over the bed.

"Peter—" he said.

Peter didn't answer him. He had turned over, his face to the wall. His eyes were closed. But the tears came out under their lids. Soaked his pillow until they had to change it. They had to change the next one, too. Sometime during the afternoon, the nursing sister noticed that he had vomited up the little food she had been able to get down his throat. By then it was already too late; he had lapsed back into unconsciousness. They had to feed him intravenously. That night, Vince called Padro Pío.

"Look, Father," Vince said; "he is going to die unless we do something. Something that lies outside of my training.

You think the Mother Superior would let Alicia come to see him, if you intervened? Do you?"

"Of course, son. I am sure she would," Father Pío said. "The Mother Inez of Jesus is a very intelligent woman. She knows well when a rule must be bent a little, say in the interest of values that transcend all rules. But speaking of transcendental things, when are *you* going to find time to have a long talk with me, son Doctor? It seems to me that we should examine this atheism of yours scientifically, no? I will borrow your microscopes, flasks, test tubes, and the like to weigh and sort out the reasons you say there is no God!"

"I will give you one," Vince said. "In there, on that bed. That a man like Peter should be dying because of utter nonsense. Sort that one out, Father—but later on, please! Now what is necessary is that you leave this of my conversion for some other time and go talk sweet words to that bald-headed old witch at the convent. Father, believe me; there is no time!"

Father Pío smiled.

"With God there is always time, but in deference to your anxiety—I go," he said.

Two hours later Alicia was there. In her novice's robes, flanked on both sides by two stern-faced sisters of the order. Vince looked at their feet, which were exceedingly dirty from having walked all the way across town to reach the hospital.

"There is a bathroom down the hall," he said; "go wash your feet."

"Doctor," the oldest of the sisters said; "God will protect us and your patient."

"God?" Vince said. "Never heard of him. Go wash your stinking filthy feet before you track a whole epidemic into my hospital!"

"Doctor!" the sister said.

"Or get out," Vince said. "I have a dying man on my hands now because of your irrational tommyrot! I am not of those who suffer fools gladly. You heard me—go wash!"

Alicia's voice was almost under sound.

"Doctor Vince," she said, "is he—is he—?"

Vince looked at her.

"Yes," he said, "he is. When I had him saved. When he was out of it. What we need, my dear Alicia, is a new law, in which murder by superstitious cant is added to the list. Then I'd at least have the pleasure of seeing you hanged for what you've done!"

"Doctor," Alicia said, "I——" Then her voice drowned.

"Oh, hell, Alicia, I'm sorry! But I had grown fond of Peter. Do not listen to me. Listen to your heart. Listen to your God. Your cheap little God you can strike bargains with!"

Then he turned on his heel and marched out of there.

"What a wicked man!" the sisters said.

"No," Alicia said; "he is very good. Many nonbelievers are. Now come."

"Where?" the oldest sister said.

Alicia looked at her.

"To wash our feet, just as he said. Who knows? Perhaps microbes are unbelievers, too."

She spent the night on her knees beside Peter's bed. She heard him raving, heard the things he said. The other sisters left the room lest their very ears be corrupted by such blasphemies. But just before sunrise he quieted. He seemed to be talking to someone.

Alicia got up, went to the bed. Leaned close.

"Judy—" Peter said.

Alicia whirled, her bare feet whispering against the floor. But in the doorway she stopped. Stood there. Bowed her head.

"All right," she murmured. "This, too. All right. Do not take it away. But along with it, a little strength, for favor? What is needful for bearing it. Is it wrong to ask that?"

She went back and knelt beside Peter's bed.

"Judy," he said. "Dead. You're. So stay. Go back. Can't stand—"

"Peter—" Alicia whispered.

"Your eyes. Dead. Ends. All. You said. In a maggot's belly.

Dirt clotting on your mouth. Back. Nothing to say now. All said. Useless. Down there. In the dark. The wet. The ooze. Dead."

"Peter—" Alicia said.

"Back. Leave me. What do you want? In God's name, what? Save me? You? Laugh. Don't make me. Hurts. Hurts like hell. To laugh—hurts. Hurts to cry to cry to cry. For you. Jesus, yes!"

"Oh, Peter, please!" Alicia wept.

"For you. Sure, baby, sure. Sure, Judy—anything. Say it. Yes. Make a doormat out of. Intellectual pride. For wiping. Feet. Say it. Hail Mary, full of Grace, the Lord Our Father Who art in when you come into Your kingdom remember—"

"Please!" Alicia said.

"—one hurt sick lost—idiot baby girl—remember—heal, bind up, shelter, save—"

Alicia bowed her head, whispered: "Yes, I pray it, too. Yes."

"—and wash. It off. All that stuck from twenty-seven years of rolling in it. Wallowing. Sometimes with me. Yes. In the Name of the —— In peace, yes. Rest, Judy, rest. Leave me in peace in peace in peace don't torment me with your new-washed angel's face, your strange saint's eyes! No! Let me die let me die you're gone and blessed and beatified and I couldn't love you hadn't love enough what I had left to 'Licia—"

And now, kneeling there beside him, Alicia ceased to breathe.

"—took it all. So don't. Save. A life I don't want. Can't bear. Don't!"

Alicia leaned close to him.

"Peter, Cielo," she said, "she wants you to live, your Judith. And I—I cannot, unless you do. Please, Peter. It is so small a thing. Even though I can never be yours again, nor you mine—don't leave me! Don't empty the world!"

His eyes were closed; but slowly, painfully, he smiled. And his voice, speaking, had a hint of consciousness about it now, of thought.

" 'S all right," he said. "Outnumbered. All the heavenly hosts. One barefoot angel. One soiled, made-over saint. Too many. Give. Uncle. Towel's in."

Alicia put out her hand and touched his forehead. It was cool. His pulse seemed normal.

She touched the bell. The night sister came. She called Vince. Vince examined Peter.

"Yes," he said at last, "the crisis is past. He will live. And you, what now, Alicia?"

She looked at him. Her eyes were awash, but she was smiling.

"My cheap little God keeps His cheap little bargains, Doctor," she said, "even when they are made in His behalf by His little Mother. So I must keep mine. *Adios!*"

Then, very quietly, she walked away.

Two hours later, Peter woke up. He was very weak, but he was both conscious and sane.

A week later, they rolled Tim O'Rourke into his room in a wheel chair.

"Petie boy," Tim said. "Goddammit, you had me sweating! Couldn't do that to me, you know!"

"Do what to you, Tim?" Peter said.

"Cash in your chips. Mari would kick me out of the flat as sure as hell. Blame me for it. Swear I hadn't taken good enough care—"

"You did your best, Tim," Peter said.

"And so did you, son. Thanks, boy. They told me you made Stirling Moss look like me auld grandmither, bringing me in. Down that road. That road where if you *walk* too fast, you fall off. Alicia told me you never got under a hundred an hour, even on those hairpin bends!"

"Kilometers, Tim. That's only sixty miles. You said that that Alicia—"

"Yep. She looked in on me before she went back to the convent that night she prayed you back out of your grave. Sorry she took that plunge. Damfool trick. I'm a bead-counter myself, but—"

"Let's not talk about it, Tim."

"All right. Have it your own way. I said a prayer or two myself. Of course they probably went up like a lead balloon, but—"

"Thanks, Tim," Peter said. "That chair. That doesn't mean—"

"Hell, no! Tendons are a little drawn, that's all. I'm having baths, massage, and exercise every day. That Doctor Vince of yours is an ace. Harvard Med School. Did you know that?"

"Yes," Peter said.

"Talkative little fellow, aren't you? Fairly running off at the mouth. Diarrhea of the jawbone. Now, look, Petie boy, there're other dames—"

Peter shook his head.

"No, Tim," he said, "not for me there aren't."

"Pete, they just don't take a babe into a convent right off the bat. You know that, don't you?"

"Yes. She has to be a novice for a year before she takes her final vows. So what?"

"So you've got time! During her novitiate, you get notes to her—by the gardener. By the gal day students. Hell, there're a thousand ways—"

"No, Tim, there aren't any ways at all. That was Alicia, and she gave her word. Her slant is that Our Lady of the Mercies, or of the Remedies, or of the Good Happening, or something, came through. Saved this shot-up hulk. So now she has to keep her part of the bargain. And she will, brother! You don't know her . . ."

"Know her well enough to realize you're probably right. You damn fool, you should have married her two months ago."

"Couldn't."

"Why not? Because of Judy?"

"No. Not because of Judy. Tim, tell me—did they ever find her body?"

"No. And they've quit looking. Funny thing . . ."

"What's a funny thing?"

"I've got the damnedest feeling I *know* something about that. That I saw something, heard something— Hell! Probably the DTs . . ."

"You saw or heard something that—?"

"It's tied up with poor Judy. Only it's gone, boy. I must have been playing Joan of Arc at the stake when it happened. Because it's all mixed up with—with fire. With hurting. The trouble is, I'm not sure I saw it at all."

"Saw *what* at all, Tim?"

"Dunno. Judy. She was doing some crazy thing. Not crazy. Odd. Unlike her. Then—"

"Then?"

"Bang! The mountain cut loose. What was that line that Robert Oppenheimer said the first time they pushed that button and dumped the A-bomb on us?"

" 'I am become Death, Shatterer of Worlds.' Shiva. My favorite deity. Because he makes sense. From the *Rig-Veda*, I think. No, the *Bhagavad-Gita.*"

"He had something there. That was what it felt like. I lay down and rolled. But even the ground was on fire by then, so it didn't do much good. It's all mixed up now. I don't even know whether it was before, or after, I heard those shots—"

"After. The lava caught the soldiers who did the job, Tim."

"Say! I remember that! They shot themselves. They were being roasted alive so they took the easy out. And Judy—"

"And Judy?" Peter prompted.

Tim's eyes went blank.

"Damned if I know, chum," he said.

"Tim, if you get out of here first, will you wait for me?" Peter said.

"Sure, Peter! I was planning to anyhow."

"Help me find Judy's body. Give her decent burial. I owe her that much. I—I deserted her, Tim. To go after Alicia. Who didn't need me. Who, as she's proved, was strong enough to go on without me. And now I've lost them both."

"Peter, being saddled with Judith Lovell all your life isn't the sort of thing I'd wish off on a friend of mine. You talk about saving her, protecting her; but, hell, boy, you aren't God Almighty! She'd have gone off the deep end someday, in spite of you. Like I said, what you should have done was to marry little Alicia—"

"And, as I said, I couldn't. Not because of Judith, Tim; but because of Connie—my ex-wife, in case your memory is still as bad as you claim. What kind of life would 'Licia and I have had, when that poor bitch had to get murdered so that . . ."

"She got murdered, all right; but you and Alicia hadn't a goddam thing to do with it. Or very little. The real cause was his secretary. Little blonde bundle of toothsome tail he was shacking up with. So poor Connie was in the way. So he hired this cheap punk. This hophead. The punk got the chair. They gave friend hubby life. Because of the kids. Not to make 'em orphans. Fat lot of good he'll do 'em in the clink."

"You mean that—that Connie's husband——"

"Yes. There was a curious little overlapping of responsibility, though. You and Alicia thought Luis Sinnombre was going to knock poor Connie off. So you could get hitched. Not that he was sold on marital love, but reasons of his own. Goddam crooked reasons, if I know anything about the late, great Luis. Maybe he was, but he never got around to it. And, anyhow, if it had been that character, the gas stove would have blown up or a brick would have fallen off a chimney as she passed by or she would have had a real fatal car smash. Slick. No evidence. No clink. Nobody fried. But you two were being so frigging noble that you sent me up there to warn her—"

"And gave friend husband the idea!" Peter said.

"He'd been entertaining that particular idea for one hell of a long time, Peter. All he had to do was to figure out an excuse. And I handed him this ready-made one on a silver platter. Even made the papers. So he hires a bodyguard to protect little wifie. And it was the bodyguard who—"

"Now you tell me!" Peter said; "now—"

"Tried to tell you before, but you wouldn't let me. No—

it was because Judy showed up and cut us off, wasn't it? Anyhow, he'd have killed her himself, sooner or later. Comes out at the trial that your ex-beloved was a first-class pain in the ass. So this big, bloody obstacle of yours just didn't exist. Connie didn't cross over Jordan to let you chillun go. As I said, you should have married 'Licia two months ago . . ."

"Tim, will you please shut up? Or at least change the subject?"

"All right. Your beardy boys finally got over the volcano, did you know that?"

"No!" Peter said.

"So far they're on their good behavior. Only three anti-Yankee-Imperialist meetings this week. Our embassy hasn't been stoned but twice. Waste of rocks. Zopo busted all the windows out of it anyhow. And it's closed. What with the Ambassador and his wife dead and no recognizable government in sight, I doubt we'll open it. They're dividing up the haciendas. All the peasants are drunk, so nobody's farming anyhow. Food's rationed. Water's rationed. Hell, everything's rationed, except tail. And that might as well be with all the babes from the Blue Moon in uniform with burp guns in their arms playing she-soldiers. Brother, what goes on at night! The whole Red army's got the clap by now. Only us poor civilians are left out, Tomas tells me, or we would be, wasn't for all the hungry little babes who know what the only thing is they've got to sell. Some of 'em from good families, too. Seems Miguelito got that lesson across, if only posthumously—"

"What lesson?" Peter said.

"That most dames are whores at heart. Anyhow, at its worst the Everlasting Republic wasn't in the shape it is now—"

"In other words, a major screw-up?" Peter said.

"You ever see the Reds do anything else?" Tim said.

23.

The first week after he came out of the hospital he wasted; which, actually, was the only intelligent thing to do. But he didn't waste it out of intelligence: he let it slip by in a mood of melancholy, of lassitude; derived doubtless from his body's abysmal weakness but also from too close a contemplation of the appalling emptiness stretching out before him, now. He went daily to the Archbishop's palace to talk with Padre Pío. But the talks did him very little good. Now that the distance between him and death had widened again, the first thing that returned to Peter was the resilience, the toughness of his mind. Try as he would, he could not accept pious platitudes, even from so extraordinary a man as the old Basque priest. He respected Father Pío. Loved him even. But, as he put it: "I can't, Father. It's still the witchdoctor's cave, no matter how pretty it is. And—if you will allow me a couple of big, solemn, two-dollar words—I cannot, surrender my intellect without murdering my integrity. Whatever the hell that is . . ."

"Nothing," Father Pío snorted; "words!"

Peter smiled.

"And the things *you* say, Father?" he said.

Physically, however, his daily walk to the palace was good for him. Since the Communists had come to power, not unsurprisingly none of the oil companies, had stepped forward with an offer to rebuild the refineries the Castristas themselves had dynamited. So there was no gasoline in Costa Verde. Everybody walked. And the distance between Peter's flat and the palace was great enough for him consciously to resist measuring it, for fear that it would discourage him. The walk strengthened his legs, improved his wind. That he was not hungry like everyone else was due only to the fact he had no appetite. The fleet of trucks—which, being Diesel-powered, could run on unrefined crude oil and therefore were not immobilized by the lack of gasoline—went daily into the country and returned almost empty. To the *campesinos* what winning the revolution meant was that they didn't have to work any more. In the provinces around the capital, the young Fidelistas like Pablo and Martin immediately put into effect Chapter One, Verse One of the Revolutionary doctrine: Agrarian Reform. The haciendas were divided up among the *campesinos*. The results were disatrous. Sixty per cent of the peasants lost their crop for the lack of the *haciendado,* or the *haciendado's* overseer, to tell them what to do, the simple things they had been told every day of their lives without ever bothering to think about, remember, or assimilate. Twenty per cent decided to take a holiday in town before settling down to work; and the remaining twenty per cent, the shrewd, intelligent minority, produced almost exactly what they needed to feed themselves and their families.

In Ciudad Villalonga—on the agenda, of course, was a change of name—the water tasted like gasoline because the tank trucks formerly used to carry the now nonexistent gasoline had to be sent up to the big reservoir to bring water into town. On the agenda, too, was a project to repair the aqueduct. There were rallies, meetings, parades without end. Yankee imperialism was denounced morning, noon, and night, until people actually began to believe that there were American-owned businesses in Costa Verde, which, in sober fact, apart from United Fruit—which had closed its doors and sold its holdings long before the Revolution—the Verdian Hilton, and one or two smaller hotels, there never had been; because as a general rule Yankee businessmen are too pragmatic to shovel fleas into a barnyard, which was what investing in Costa Verde (under any of its various caudillos, military juntas, and the rare civilian who reached the presidency in the elections in which each candidate usually polled more votes than the entire voting population), had always been. Even the oil refineries had been Dutch- and British-owned.

These details Peter got from Tim O'Rourke, who was everywhere, happily gathering the materials for a book about the Revolution. They dined together every night. So far, nobody had denounced them as imperialist spies—probably, as Tim had said, because even Costa Verdian ingenuity wasn't up to figuring out what they could find to spy on in a country without an air force, a fleet, or any army beyond a militia armed with light infantry weapons.

"Exploitation!" Tim roared, slapping his knees in pure delight. "Now they're talking about exploitation! Pete boy, you tell me: How're you going to exploit a bastard you can't even get to move? But, speaking about moving, we'd better, chum. Stateside—and fast."

"Why?" Peter said.

"Rumor has it that they're going to import Ernesto 'Rubles' Ramirez from Fidel-land to help 'em get organized. And you know what Rubles' idea of organization is, don't you?"

"Yes," Peter said. "The one thing on which the Extreme Right and the Extreme Left see eye to eye: shooting people. Purges. Spectacular trials where everybody confesses to sleeping with his own eighty-five-year-old grandmother—"

"Funny thing: they've been downright mild. The score's only ten so far; and that damn well had it coming."

"Pablo's influence," Peter said. "Good Joe, Pablo."

"Our good friend Tomas picked up any leads about—Judy?" Tim said.

"Yes. He's supposed to see a type who knows another type who is supposed to have two or three of those ash statues on his place. If one of them is a woman, I'll go have a look."

"Better make it fast, Peter."

"Why?"

"A hunch. You and me, chum, are made to order for Camarada Ernesto. Hirelings of the capitalistic press. Bent on corrupting the workers' innocent little minds. When that boy gets here, I want to be among the absent."

"All right. If what Tomas says is promising, it only means one more day. If not, we ship out. I ought to check in at Doctor's anyhow for physical therapy to re-educate this arm—"

"Not much good, is it, boy?"

"It's seventy-five per cent paralyzed. I couldn't even squeeze a girl with it."

"Saaaay! Speaking of dames, I saw Alicia today; and she had on clothes! I mean her own, like she used to wear. And make-up. Cuter than all hell . . ."

"Did you talk to her?" Peter said.

"Yes. She asked about you."

"And?"

"When I suggested that she come along and *see* how you were, she said a funny thing—"

"I'm listening."

"That she'd better not. That since there was nothing you could do about her anyhow, she'd rather not face you. That it would only make both of you feel rotten—"

"Tim, did you tell her about—Connie?"

"No! Damn my stupid hide! That never occurred to me!"

"The next time you see her, do. You think that she's broken her novitiate?"

"Looks that way. When I asked her, she smiled kind of sad-like and said: 'They decided I was—too naughty to belong to that club, Tim . . .'"

"Meaning?"

"How the hell do I know? That's all the lady said . . ."

And then, in the morning, when he was dressing himself with painful slowness to go look for her, the bell interrupted him. He opened the door with his good hand. Both Tim and Tomas stood there. And just from looking at them, he knew Tomas had found Judith for him; but the expressions on their faces seemed to be more than the occasion called for.

"Tell me," he said, "is she alive?"

"No, Señor," Tomas said.

"Then what the hell? I've already got used to the idea that poor Judy was dead. All things considered, it's probably best. So—"

"Look, Peter," Tim said. "There's one kind of funny detail that—"

"Meaning that she didn't make a pretty corpse?" Peter said.

"Ay, no, Señor!" Tomas said; "she is most beautiful! As in life. The ash—"

"I've seen ash statues before. They're a hell of a lot better than the usual embalming methods. So come on!"

"Pete," Tim said, "about that detail—"

"Well?" Peter said.

"Father Pío's outside in the car, waiting for us. You're a tough-minded old son; but I was—well—kind of hoping that this time you——"

"What, Tim?"

"That you won't spoil it for him. Brother, he's got it made! Like a kid before the tree on Christmas morning. He's already arranged for a glass-sided coffin, set in solid silver and—"

"Tim, you aren't making much sense, you know."

"How can I, when *this* doesn't? You see, Pete—she died in a church. No, in a little roadside chapel. Zopo had knocked the roof off it the same time he buried the town of Xochoa, so she hadn't any protection. She died at the altar—on her knees. And you know these types down here . . ."

"Not to mention a certain son of th' Auld Sod who can swallow his share of mumbo-jumbo if it smells of incense and candle grease and is properly solemn," Peter said.

"So all right. I plead guilty. Call me stupid, but what she looks like right now is what saints ought to and generally don't. Her face—Jesus, Petie—when I kick off, I'd like to have a little of that—that whatever it is, she's got there now."

"Okay," Peter said. "Get on with it, Tim. Time's a-wasting. What's your pitch?"

"Just you keep still, Peter Pan! I'm getting there. Seems one of these weatherbeaten Indian broads up there got separated from her kids—five or six or eight—depends on who's telling it. Wandered into that chapel while looking for 'em. Swears Judy smiled at her. Left, and as soon as she gets outside, her brats sing out, 'Mama!' All twenty dozen of them. Nary a blister among the lot. That started it. So all the Tluscola up there started going to the chapel to pray first—pray to Judy, Pete! Can you tie that one?—before searching for the missing. And since very few people up there got it—"

"The split was on the other side of the volcano, Tim. Ninety per cent of the lava went down the eastern side."

"You see? There you go already. Lord, Pete, didn't anybody ever tell that you mustn't go around unwinding miracles? Bad form, oh, very! The point is that Father Pío and his Indians have got themselves a new saint, boy. La Gringa, they're calling her. Peter, can't you muster up a little charity, Christian or otherwise, and not foul up the deal for them?"

Peter smiled.

"You mean, like lying to them or something?" he said.

"Or like keeping your big fat mouth shut for a change, eh, Petie? I'm for the truth when it adds to the sum total of happiness, boy. Or when it props up that kind of shaky article, human dignity. But when it doesn't—the hell with it, I say! Besides—"

"Okay. You've sold me a bill of goods, Tim. Besides—what?"

"I *saw* her die, Peter. I didn't remember it. No—that's not right. My mind sort of reneged on remembering it. Call me a superstitious lug from the peat bogs of the Emerald Isle, but it's not *all* hokum, boy. The way she took it—head up, smiling—Jesus and Mary, Pete—I—"

"All right, Tim. You've done your good deed for today," Peter said.

Outside in the street there was a jeep waiting. Or rather it was a British Land Rover, which is a four-wheel-drive car considerably bigger than a jeep. It had a covered truck body replacing the original.

"Courtesy of Comrade Pablo," Tomas said. "And the tank is full, Señor."

"Bless him," Peter said.

Father Pío was inside the truck bed. He was on his knees, a rosary in his hand. Peter could see his lips move. So he didn't say anything to the old priest, then.

Again, they went up that road. The bus was still there, bright red with rust now, but the bodies were gone. The Land Rover groaned and whined over the lava floors where the soldiers had roasted alive. They were cold and solid now. That particular danger was over forever.

They went on up, past the stumps and skeletons of the burned pines, until suddenly Tomas, who was driving, wheeled the truck into a trail he had to know was there to see.

They came up to the chapel. Got down from the Land Rover. Father Pío led the way. He knelt down beside—that. Started to pray. Peter moved up the ash-drifted aisle behind him. Stopped. Stood there. When he could see again, he studied Judith Lovell's face.

She had fallen forward, toward the altar. But her head was lifted a little, her chin resting on her left arm. In her right hand she had a cross. The curve of her hand had kept the ash off a part of it, and Peter could see that it was of hammered silver. His mind reconstructed it whole from that detail: an antique, hammered-silver cross, singularly beautiful, clearly of Tluscolan making. Peter looked at that cross. At her face. Said: "My God!"

"See what I mean?" Tim said.

Father Pío went on praying.

Peter put out his good arm toward Tim. Said:

"Get me out of here!"

Tim helped him outside into the clearing before the chapel.

"Pete boy—" he said: "You want to lie down someplace? You look—"

"No," Peter said. "Call him."

"Call who?"

"Father Pío. Tim, I can't. This is too much. I can't."

"Take it easy, boy. Tom—get the Padre, will you?"

"Sí, Señor," Tomas said.

"Yes, son Pedro?" Father Pío said.

"Father," Peter said, "you cannot. It would be a deception. You must not! She was a very wicked woman, Father. Besides the husbands of whom I already told you, there were lovers without number, and vices, and nameless practices and—"

"I know, son. And so does God," Father Pío said.

"But, Father!"

"God has chosen such instruments before, son. You have seen her face?"

"Yes, Father."

"And what is there now, does that not to you outweigh whatever evil she has done, or been, or thought?"

"Father—I am not a believer. Her face—"

"Yes, son Pedro?"

"I cannot accept her face. I'd go mad. Deny my reason—"

"Then deny it, Pedro! And save your soul!"

"Father, I cannot—"

"You, son, are a fool," the old priest sighed; "but, one day—

"I'll wait, Father!"

Father Pío smiled.

"You think that you can outwait God?" he said.

Peter went down the slope toward the burned-out pine wood, following the way she must have come. And then he heard the footsteps behind him and turned. Tomas and Tim had followed him. But Father Pío was still inside the roofless chapel.

"Look, Pete, you're in no shape for hiking," Tim said.

"Not hiking," Peter said. "Looking."

"For what, Señor?" Tomas said.

"Charon. His three-headed pup. Or both of them."

"Señor?" Tomas said.

"I get it," Tim said. "The ferryman of the river Styx. The helldog guarding the gates. Right?"

"In modern guise, Tim. Read bus driver. Read armed guard. Call me the original illegitimate child, but I can't buy sanctity. Too rich for my blood."

Tim stood there, looking at him. A long time.

"All right, Peter," he said. "Come on."

They found them in the little stone-and-adobe hut, roofless like the chapel. The three of them stood there looking at the ash-covered bodies of the guard, the bus driver.

"Charon," Peter said, "Cerberus. Pretty, aren't they?"

Tim found his voice. It was very harsh.

"So," he said, "you win, Peter Pan!"

Peter shook his head.

"No, Tim, I lose," he said.

"Señor—" Tomas said.

"Go get your jeep, Tomas!" Peter said.

"But, Señor—" Tomas said.

"Go get it, Tom," Tim said.

"Sí, Señores, I go," Tomas said.

When they had them in the truck, and were winding up the steep slope toward the chapel, Tim said:

"Look, Peter, there's no proof she shot them. Maybe they killed each other—fighting over her—"

Peter shrugged.

"Peter, for the love of God!"

"All right, all right. So she didn't. So they were struck by lightning. After they stripped down—to take a shower, say. So all she did was rob the dead."

"Rob the dead?" Tomas said.

"That chain around the bus driver's neck. Last time I saw him, he had a cross on it. Hammered silver. Tluscolan."

"The one she's got in her hand now," Tim said. "Peter, goddam it!"

"You think I like it, Tim? You think I couldn't use a nice

long-bearded Father God? Some pie in the sky? A shining miracle or two? You think I like ugliness? Hell, boy, I—"

"Sorry, Pete. Only—"

"Only what, Tim?"

"It's so goddam crazy!"

"What isn't? Tomas!"

"Sí, Señor?"

"Turn this heap around!"

"Around, Señor?"

"Yes. Away from that chapel. Away from that sweet, simple-minded old coot up there. Who's got it made. And who's going to keep it, if I've got anything to say about it!"

"But, Señor—" Tomas said.

"But nothing, Tom!" Tim said, beginning to grin now. "Turn it around!"

When they had got up there, when they had come to that place that Tomas had told them about, where the road edged a precipice one thousand seven hundred meters high, dropping straight down to the sea, and the sea beneath it indigo, the color it takes when it is absolutely bottomless, they lifted the statues down again.

"Hell," Tim said, "seems a pity not to say a prayer—even for these bastards . . ."

"To whom?" Peter said. "Aphrodite? Astarte? Eros? Pan?"

Then he put his good hand, the right one, against them, and pushed. He wasn't strong enough. The others had to help him. They stood there looking down. But he didn't; he turned his back to the precipice, to the sea, to the sky.

He did not hear the sound they made striking the water. The fall was too great. And had begun—since even he had to grant them humanity—and maybe even ended long ago, anyhow.

All the way back to the city, he didn't say anything. But once they were riding through the streets, he said:

"Drop me off at the cemetery, Tomas."

"The cemetery, Señor?"

"Yes. Want to have a little talk with a friend—"

"You," Tim said, "want to talk with a friend in the cemetery, boy?"

"Well, maybe not a friend. With Miguelito, Tim. Who understood sin. And repentance. And expiation. And maybe even sanctity. But then, maybe Judy did, too. And maybe great sinners make great saints. I wouldn't know . . ."

When he had got down from the Land Rover and walked through the big gates, Tomas turned to Tim and said:

"It is better that we wait, no?"

"The hell with that noise, Tom! You take me wherever Doña Alicia lives now," Tim said.

He was still there, sitting by Miguel Villalonga's grave, when she came. She walked very quietly up to him, and put her hand on his shoulder. He turned, stared at her, whispered:

"Nena—"

She was crying so she could not speak.

He got up slowly, lifted her chin with his one good hand. Bent and kissed her mouth. Drew away. Said:

"You—you've come back to me, 'Licia?"

"Yes," she said.

"Mind telling me why?"

"Because you are free, Peter. Tim told me. And I also—"

"You decided there were already saints enough, Nena? There are. Some very rare ones. Especially here of late. But, anyhow—"

She smiled at him impishly, through her tears.

"No, Cielo, I did not decide that. They—they—oh, what is that gringo phrase? Since I am to become a Gringa, I must learn to talk like one, no?"

"No. Talk like my 'Licia. My Nena. You were saying?"

"They indicated to me the door. Kicked me out. Almost literally, they were so mad!"

"Mad at you, Nena? For what?"

She smiled again. But now her mouth trembled. The tears on its upturning corners danced.

"A matter of esthetics, *Cielo*. The great curve of felicity that a woman pushes before her as a token of her lover's esteem is most unbecoming beneath the cassock of a nun. Especially with the enemies of the Church in power. So the Mother Superior thought it best—"

"Good God!" Peter said.

"Already I have no dress I can wear. This one is borrowed. If you were only a little as goatish as other men, and would look at me as they do, you would have seen it by now. But no matter. Come on, *Cielo*. I have to help you pack. Tim talked with Pablo by phone. It is all arranged. Pablo thinks it best we leave now before this terrible one arrives. I agree. I have much envy to see New York. Does one walk much, there?"

"Walk?" Peter said. "Walk?"

"*Sí, Cielo*. My feet hurt, now. I have not worn shoes in so long that—"

He mumbled something so low she could not hear.

"What did you say, *Cielo*?" she said.

"Nothing. Yes. A verse. 'How beautiful art thy feet with shoes, oh Prince's daughter!' I don't remember the rest of it. And it doesn't matter. Come."

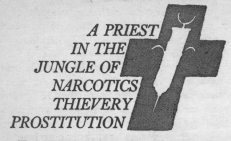

*A PRIEST
IN THE
JUNGLE OF
NARCOTICS
THIEVERY
PROSTITUTION*

"Father Egan is to New York City's narcotic addicts
what Father Damien was to the leper colony on
Molokai; what Albert Schweitzer has meant to
the crude hospital at Lambarene;
what Tom Dooley meant in Laos....
A searing tale you will not forget."
BOB CONSIDINE, *N.Y. Journal-American*

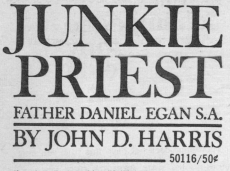

the
JUNKIE
PRIEST

FATHER DANIEL EGAN S.A.

BY JOHN D. HARRIS

50116/50¢

If your bookseller does not have this title, you may order it by sending
retail price, plus 10¢ for mailing and handling to: MAIL SERVICE
DEPARTMENT, Pocket Books, Inc., 1 W. 39th St., New York, N.Y. 10018. Not
responsible for orders containing cash. Please send check or money order.

PUBLISHED BY
POCKET BOOKS, INC.

golfers' gold

AN INSIDER'S
VIEW OF PRO GOLF
AND PRO GOLFERS—
PALMER, NICKLAUS, PLAYER,
SNEAD, VENTURI AND
MANY OTHERS—BY

"champagne tony" lema

WITH
GWILYM S. BROWN

50110 / 50¢

If your bookseller does not have this title, you may order it by sending retail price, plus 10¢ for mailing and handling to: MAIL SERVICE DEPARTMENT, Pocket Books, Inc., 1 West 39th Street, New York, New York 10018. Not responsible for orders containing cash. Please send check or money order.

PUBLISHED BY POCKET BOOKS, INC.

"Uh, guys? Is there a problem?"

Chigger cleared his throat. "No, ma'am. We're just waiting for you."

"Well, don't. I'll be there shortly. You guys just eat."

That was all it took. They attacked the food like ravenous hyenas. No more talk. No more laughter. Just the sound of utensils hitting plates.

She was no Emeril, but the yummy sounds coming from the men made her feel like a master chef. Her pleasure wasn't complete, however. The boss was still missing in action.

Chigger swallowed some orange juice then turned to her. "Ms. Lily?"

"Yes?"

"If you'll pardon my language, this is the best damn meal we've had in ages."

She waved her hand at him. "Aw, shucks. If you think this is good, wait till dinner."

"I don't know that I'll be able to think of anything else."

"You'd better." Cole's voice came from the hallway.

Lily turned to see him walking toward her and her whole being reacted. Her heart squeezed, her pulse jumped, her skin tingled with goose bumps. It was entirely unsettling, and not a little annoying. What was it about him?

"Boss, you're just in time." Manny placed the bowl of eggs in front of Cole's place setting. There were some left, but not enough for seconds. "It was all we could do not to finish it off."

Cole pulled his chair back, his gaze darting to Lily,

then away. "Yeah, well, I had things to do this morning."

Chigger gave her a look that told her Cole was full of beans.

As Cole filled his plate, Lily reached for the pancakes. "I'll go heat these up."

He put his hand on hers, and it was as if she'd been hit by lightning. She nearly dropped the plate. He pulled away instantly, as if he'd been burned, too.

"Don't bother," he said, but his voice was grainy and stiff.

"It's no bother."

He finally looked at her. The contact made her knees weak. This was nuts. It wasn't possible. She didn't know him, she wasn't interested in getting to know him, except for Eve's sake, and she'd made a personal commitment to keep herself man-free for a year.

"Put the plate down, Lily."

His voice was clear again. That smooth, velvet tone swirled inside her head. She obeyed him, not because of his words, but because of the unsteadying effect his voice had on her.

She sat and picked up her fork, although the last thing on earth she wanted was food. But she couldn't just stare at him. She certainly couldn't lunge at him, although the thought of clearing the table with one sweep of her arm and going for it was highly appealing.

He hadn't eaten anything yet, either. His hair was still damp from the shower. His eyes seemed tired, but piercing nonetheless. It wasn't fair for him to be so good-looking. Although she knew her feelings weren't about his looks. Well, not entirely. This, she was afraid, was chemistry. Or would that be biology?

Cole jerked his gaze away and shoved a forkful of food in his mouth.

As he did, she pulled herself together. It took all her will, and all her concentration. So that was probably why she hadn't realized she and Cole were alone. That all the men had disappeared. She hadn't heard a sound.

This was not good.

CHAPTER NINE

DYLAN PICKED UP the phone on the third ring.

"It's me."

He bit back a sigh of disappointment. He'd been expecting a call from an informant about a certain carjacker. But his sister didn't call all that often, so something must be up. "Hey, Ashley. What's wrong?"

"Nothing. Just checking in. Have you heard from Lily?"

"Not today."

"Oh."

"Ash?"

"Yeah?"

"Come on. Spill."

Her sigh traveled over the phone line so clearly he could see her expression in his mind's eye. She'd be leaning back in her chair, head tilted to the side, her mouth in the pout she'd used well since birth. "Out with it."

"It's a client."

"Uh-oh." Ashley worked as a junior account executive with a San Antonio based advertising agency and seemed to have more than her share of problems with male clients.

"I know. Can you stand it? It happened again."

"Is he married?"

"Seven years, and he has two kids. Honestly, Dylan, I don't get it. I don't encourage them at all. Not even a little."

"Oh?"

"Well, maybe I flirt a little. But that's innocent stuff, and anyone would have to be a dope not to realize it."

"So this client is a dope?"

"Yeah, but a rich dope."

"That makes things a little more complicated."

"I know. I really do want his business. I just want him to get any other ideas out of his head."

"You've done it before."

She sighed again. "Maybe it is me. Maybe I'm asking for trouble and I don't even see it."

"Ashley, honey, you're a beautiful woman. You could stand perfectly still and not say one word, and men would still try their best with you."

"I swear, men just make things so complicated."

"Not all men."

"I'd like to meet one who doesn't."

"Me?"

"Nope. You make things complicated, too."

"Hey."

"Come on, big brother. I lived with you for a long time. I know about you and—" She cut off her sentence.

"About me and?"

"Nothing."

"Julie. Is that what you were going to say?"

"Yeah. But that's because my mouth was in gear while my brain wasn't. I'm sorry."

"It's okay. It was true. But now all I want is to see her safe."

"I know, Dylan. Listen, I gotta run, but I love you. And say hi to Lily for me, okay?"

"You got it."

"Dylan?"

"Yeah?"

"Are you all right?"

"I'm fine. Honest."

"Okay. Talk to you soon."

He hung up the phone, wondering if everyone in his family knew about his feelings for Julie. Of course Lily did, but he'd never suspected Ashley had a clue. Great. So they were all probably feeling sorry for him. That was just perfect.

He sat down, looked at her picture, and shook his head. "Where are you?"

DINNER WAS another triumph for Lily. She'd made prime rib, scalloped potatoes, asparagus in brown butter, rolls and her famous peach pie for dessert. The praise made her blush, and secretly wonder if she should have gone to the Culinary Institute of America instead of the Federal Bureau of Investigation.

The only thorn in the crown was Cole. He'd disappeared shortly after breakfast, hadn't joined the rest of the crew for lunch, and when he finally came in for dinner, he was markedly silent and sullen.

She had seen him once, though. She'd been in the kitchen, washing glasses, and she'd caught a movement out of the corner of her eye. Cole. He was by the porch, not on it. And he'd been looking right at her.

She'd thought he would bolt as soon as she met his gaze, but he didn't. He stared at her in a way that made her heat with a blush. It wasn't a sexual thing.

Well, not entirely. It was blatant hunger, and something more. Something that frightened her. Before she could figure it out, he'd turned and walked away.

She'd watched him until he passed out of sight. His straight back, the way he held himself…so proud. It was nuts how she felt about him. As if he needed her. As if she had been brought here for him, not Eve.

He'd never left her thoughts for the rest of the day. And now he sat at the table, quiet, drawn inside himself. There was a fortress around him, and she had no idea how to get inside.

When she'd asked Chigger if he knew what was wrong, the old man had been just as bewildered. He'd said something interesting, however. "Don't you pay no mind to his moodiness. Cole Bishop is one of the finest men I've ever met, and if he's on your side, you'll never have to be scared."

All through dessert she'd thought about that comment. If she trusted Chigger's assessment, then she had little to worry about. Cole would eventually come around. But sometimes friends had blind spots. Perhaps Chigger wanted his boss to be a fine man, and forgave the evidence that he wasn't.

The thing was, she needed to spend more time with Cole. Staying in the house all day while he worked outside wasn't exactly going to get the job done. So tonight, she'd have to make up for lost time. Shake him out of his sullen mood and get him talking.

Cole didn't say his first word to her until he finished the last of his pie. "Thanks." The single word came with a short nod of the head, as impersonal as he could get without just putting a buck on the table. Then he got up and walked down the hallway, his back straight, his shoulders so wide she thought they might touch the walls.

"I sure wish Cole would learn to shut up," Manny said. "Man can talk your ear off."

The others laughed, and she smiled with them, but her preoccupation was such that she hardly registered that they were all looking at her, and that other than the one comment, the lively chatter of a few moments ago had come to a halt.

"Why don't you go on, Ms. Lily," Chigger said in a sort of stage whisper. "We've got dishes to do."

She nodded, touched his shoulder as she got up. Then she walked toward the back of the house to find Cole Bishop.

He was in the last place she looked. The nursery. He wasn't doing anything, simply standing in the room, his arms folded across his chest, his gaze on the empty crib. She knocked, but he didn't acknowledge her. Perhaps he didn't hear her. She stepped inside the room as quietly as she could, torn between pushing him and leaving him to his private thoughts.

For a long time, they both stood silently, Lily leaning against the door watching him. His chest rose and fell rhythmically, almost as if he were asleep. Perhaps he was in some sort of trance. Truly lost in thought. About what? The child he wanted so desperately? The decision he'd made to have that child in such an unorthodox manner?

How she yearned to help him. To bring him solace. Why, she had no idea. A reaction to her own recent pain? A distraction from her own problems? Whatever the reason, it was as real as her heartbeat, and tangible as the door she leaned against.

His childhood, at least the tiny slice she knew of

it, wasn't enough of an explanation for the angst she saw in him. One event, even as hurtful as being betrayed by his father, wouldn't lead to this extreme. What else had occurred? Something to do with Eve, she felt sure. Something tragic, she feared.

"The dinner was a fine one."

His voice startled her, his words threw her off-balance. Dinner felt like a hundred years ago. "Thank you."

"The guys are pleased. But don't worry. You won't have to be here long. I called the agency. They'll start sending out applicants tomorrow or the next day."

"I'm not worried. Besides, I'd want to stay even if you did have a decent cook. This is a trial, remember? To see if you and I—"

He turned on her abruptly, as if he meant to scare her. Or hurt her. Her body tensed, ready to protect herself using whatever means necessary. But he stayed his ground. The only weapon he had was his eyes. The fire in them. But the heat wasn't just about this thing between them. This chemistry. There was anger in his gaze. Accusation.

"Why are you looking at me like that?" she asked.

"Because I don't know who you are or what you want."

"I told you—"

"How do I know you're telling me the truth?"

She blanched. Had he found out about her arrangement with Eve? About her true purpose in coming here?

"For all I know, you could be a scam artist out to steal my money, my land."

She let out a pent-up breath. Her real secret was safe. "I'm not."

"Oh, okay," he said sarcastically. "That convinces me."

"What brought this on? Last night—"

"Last night was nothing." His arms went to his sides and he took a step toward her. "It was a mistake."

"How could talking honestly be a mistake?"

His answer was in his icy stare.

"No matter what you think, I'm not the enemy."

His lips curled into a smile that was no smile at all but a dangerous mask, hiding a rage that simmered just below the surface. "You are. You're everything I'm afraid of."

Despite a shiver of fear, she stepped closer to him. "Why? Why me?"

"You're a— You're after something. Don't tell me you're not."

"Okay. I won't deny it. I am after something."

"I knew it," he said, the words ground out like broken glass.

She almost told him everything. That she was a private investigator, and that she was here to bring him back to his family before it was too late. But then she remembered Eve's face—the desperation and need for this woman to make amends. How could she betray her friend? She hated the lies, but she knew without a doubt that she was doing a good thing. That Cole would thank her in the end.

His right brow rose, urging her to talk.

"Shockingly enough, what I want has more to do with me than you. I'm here about a job. About a chance to change things for the better. And you're not making it very easy.''

His mouth had became a slim, hard line as his lips pressed together tightly. The suspicion in his gaze deepened.

''Why are you doing this, Cole? Why are you so angry? I don't mean just now. I can't understand why you'd be so angry at the world that you need to buy your own child.''

''It's none of your goddamn business.''

''Okay, fine. It's none of my business. But it's going to be someone's business, unless you want the mother of your child to be a moron. The question is legitimate.''

''You want a legitimate question? Why are *you* here? You can have any man, and you know it. You don't need this arrangement. All you have to do is snap your fingers.''

''Is that so?''

''You know it is.''

''I don't know what planet you're from, but down here on earth, I'm no femme fatale. I'm thirty, and I've never had an honest relationship. The last man I was with, oh, he was something. He treated me like a queen, bought me presents, convinced me to move to a different city, get a job I wasn't even sure I wanted. He gave me a gorgeous engagement ring. We picked out a damn china pattern. After all that, after giving him everything, after building my dreams around him, I found out he was married. With two adorable children and a house in the suburbs. Oh, and that ring? As fake as he was.''

Cole winced. A subtle movement she would have missed if she hadn't been staring at him so intently.

"You're not the only person who's ever had his heart broken," she assured him.

"How do you know I had my—" He stopped, closed his eyes for a moment.

"It's damn clear that you're hurting. But it's also clear you're an intelligent man. You have to know that you can't buy someone's love."

"I'm not trying to. I told you. The marriage would be in name only."

"Cole, that's not what I meant. You can't force a child to love you. It doesn't work that way."

"I won't have to force him. I'll give him everything."

"I don't see that you lacked for anything growing up. Did that work?"

"You don't know what you're talking about."

"No? Then tell me. Explain it to me."

He started to walk out, to leave her without explanation, but as he passed her, she touched his arm. She felt his muscle bunch under his shirt, felt his heat. He turned to her, and his gaze burned her once more.

"You need to go."

"All right. I will. But tell me why. Tell me what horrible sin I've committed."

His gaze raked her face. A second later, he'd broken her hold, and it was his hands on her arms. He held her tightly, hurting her. The power she'd seen in him from the first moment scared her now. She felt as if he could crush her. Instead, he kissed her.

He kissed her with all the pain and rage in his heart. Kissed her as if he could kill her with his lips.

She whimpered, and he flew back, releasing her, the shock on his face evidence enough that he hadn't meant her harm. The way he looked at her was more than she could stand. Such confusion, such need. He was drowning, right there in front of her. Drowning in a sorrow she could barely understand.

She touched his face, her palm against his cheek. He stood perfectly still, although she felt his jaw tense. "Who hurt you like this?"

"Don't."

"Don't what? Don't ask? Don't care?"

"That's right. Don't care."

She rose on her tiptoes. "Too late," she whispered. And then she kissed him. Gently. Willing him to feel her compassion. Urging him to take comfort.

His hard shoulders relaxed as he moaned, as his hands moved to pull her closer. She caressed his cheek, his hair. It was a moment of surrender, and not just on his part. Her awareness shifted as she tasted him, as his tongue slipped inside her. This was no act. She wasn't pretending. She needed to understand him. She'd known him two days and it felt like a lifetime. As if the want had always been inside her, dormant until he touched her.

He'd awakened something inside her. What she didn't know was if it would heal her, or break her.

CHAPTER TEN

COLE DRANK HER IN, her scent, her taste, the feel of her body against his. He wanted more. He wanted all of her.

She touched his tongue with hers, and he moaned as much in pain as in pleasure. If she knew what she was doing to him, she'd run as far and as fast as she could go. The urge to punish her for another's sins was almost as strong as his desire to take her. He had to hold on to the part of him that was sane, that told him she wasn't Carrie.

Her hand moved to the back of his neck, and her cool fingers made him tremble. He pressed himself against her, letting her feel his erection, showing her exactly what her touch was leading to.

Instead of pushing him away, she moved her hips.

He tore his lips from hers. "Get out of here, Lily. Get out before it's too late."

Her answer was to pull his head down and quiet him with another kiss.

There was no more strength to fight her. He moved with her until the door was at her back, and then he pressed his hips against her, put his hand on her breast. The feel of that softness beneath him made him hungrier still. Her nipple against his palm was as hard and stiff as he was, even through her shirt and bra.

Leaving her lips, he dipped his head to her neck, to the hollow beneath her ear. He kissed her, nipped her, all the while showing her what he wanted with his body and his fingers.

"Cole." Her breath came out in a sultry whisper. "Cole, wait."

It was only then that he felt her hand against his chest. He lifted his head.

"We can't do this. It's not what either of us wants."

"Speak for yourself," he said, his voice a growl he barely recognized.

She moved to the side, away from him, and he lowered his gaze to her chest. To the stark evidence that he wasn't the only one wanting.

She blushed, which was something to behold. It caused her face to glow with an innocence that made him ache for her even more.

"Someone has to be sensible here," she said. "Sleeping together isn't going to help."

"You're wrong."

"No I'm not. It's a way to escape. To avoid the real issues."

"There are no issues."

"Right." The word hung in the air, flat, filled with disappointment. She turned and opened the door. "I'll get packed and be out of here within the hour."

He stopped her with his hand on her arm. "You don't have to go tonight."

"No?" She met his gaze. "What are you saying?"

He should tell her she could stay until morning. Get a good night's sleep before her long drive. That would solve his problem. He could go back to his comfortable life. He'd continue his search for a more suitable woman. For someone who wouldn't make him need or feel or care. "Stay..." The rest of the words wouldn't come. Because the thought of her leaving was just as upsetting as keeping her here.

"The night? Until you have a new cook? What?"

"I don't know. But we can figure it out tomorrow."

She looked at him for a long moment, then nodded. "All right."

"Lily..."

"Yes?"

He wanted to tell her that he couldn't stop thinking about her. That this spell she'd put him under was pure hell. That he'd never wanted anything as much as he wanted her in his bed. Instead, he said, "Nothing."

Her lips curved into a sad smile. "I think I'll turn in now. I'm pretty tired."

He nodded as he released her arm. The moment she was out the door, he wanted her back. What the hell was going on here? The whole day he'd thought about why she was the wrong one. About why she should leave. He had a hundred reasons. Was it her kiss that made him stupid? That made logic fly out the window?

Maybe he should go to Jessup. See if Noreen was busy tonight. That would help. Or would that only make him want Lily more? *Shit.* It was all wrong. All of it. But he wasn't willing to give up his plan. He *couldn't* trust Lily. If he did, he'd be a fool. Wanting her like this made him vulnerable, though. She could get to him with her body, just like Carrie had. And then he'd be right back where he'd started.

The best decision he'd ever made was to go solo.

To build his own unique family. To eliminate the danger of another woman ruining his life.

So why did he want Lily to stay? Was it just about sex? Or was something far more insidious going on? He leaned his forehead against the cool wood of the door. That was the problem, wasn't it? He had no idea if Lily was telling him the truth or not. He just couldn't see. It was like color blindness, only his problem was woman blindness. The only way to protect himself was to stay away. To send her away.

Tomorrow. Tomorrow, he'd tell her to go.

IN SAN ANTONIO, in a little bar that smelled faintly of wet dog, Sebastian Cooper sat in the darkest corner, milking a vodka rocks as he listened to Bob Seger and the Silver Bullet Band sing about old time rock and roll. In front of him, by the scratched, dirty pool table, a woman prepared to take her turn at eight ball.

She was in her thirties, and the years hadn't been kind. Her blond hair, piled up on her head, looked dry and brittle, especially under the harsh lights illuminating the green felt playing surface. She was the kind of thin that women liked to think was attractive, but most men found unappealing. She seemed all sharp edges instead of soft curves. Her clothes were too short, too small, too vulgar. When she laughed, which was often, she inevitably broke into a fit of coughing.

Her companion, an older woman who provided the hilarity, wore a T-shirt with the pithy slogan, *One tequila, Two tequila, Three tequila, Floor.* Her bons mots were well peppered with curses, one word in particular.

Both women stared at him. The younger with a lusty, if mercenary, gleam, the older through a drunken haze.

Sebastian took another sip of the cheap vodka. It had been a lousy day. He'd gotten a speeding ticket, which meant his insurance was going to go up again. His secretary had quit. Just like that, after four years. She'd given him exactly two days' notice. And to top it all off, when he'd opened the glove compartment to get the registration papers for the car, he'd found Julie's tennis bracelet. He had no idea why it was there. A present from him. Given to her on their first anniversary. She'd cried when she'd opened the box. They'd made love on the living room carpet.

But the discovery hadn't just stirred memories. It had also brought home the fact that Julie might be gone for good. That the police department and Dylan could very well come up empty. While he waited for the motorcycle cop to finish writing his ticket, Sebastian had been forced to acknowledge that possibility for the first time. The revelation hit him hard. She couldn't be gone. Not forever. Not like this. Not when she was so important to him.

He took another drink and his gaze moved to the woman's rear end, which was sticking out prominently as she leaned over the table. Something stirred in him. A dark hunger. He slapped a buck tip on the table and headed toward the blonde. At least he wouldn't be alone.

LILY FINALLY got out of bed at three-thirty. She'd slept, if you could call it that, for a couple of hours, and tried valiantly to go back to sleep, but it was no use. She might as well get something done instead of lying in bed tormenting herself.

To say she was confused was an understatement. Even the pages and pages she'd written in her diary hadn't made things clearer. Cole was an enigma, and her feelings about him were even more of a mystery.

She slipped a pair of shorts underneath her sleep shirt and headed for the kitchen. Although she couldn't precook breakfast, she could do a lot about lunch and dinner. A meat loaf, a lasagna, both could be easily reheated when needed. The cooking would keep her occupied, which would be a very good thing.

The house was dark but she found her way to the kitchen, nearly blinding herself when she turned on the lights. After a brief adjustment, she got to work. First was coffee. Then she assembled the ingredients for both dishes. That pretty much took all the counter space. She measured everything, diced onions and garlic, shredded cheese, put on a big pot of water to boil for the pasta. All the while, she thought about Cole. Big surprise.

Damn, but he could kiss. He'd about knocked her socks off. Even scarier, she'd been inches away from ripping his clothes off and throwing him to the floor.

Excellent detective work all the way around, eh? Sterling. The first thing she'd learned in the academy was not to make it personal. To distance herself from the situation. Getting involved in any way was a danger to both the agent and the civilians. So what had she done the moment she'd arrived? She'd let her curiosity sway her into a shaky course of action. She'd let her hormones lead her directly into temptation.

The water hit a rolling boil, and she put the lasagna

noodles in to cook, then set the timer. After washing her hands, she got to work seasoning the ground beef, which was messy work indeed, since she believed in using the tools God gave her and digging in with both hands.

She was pretty sure her attraction to Cole wasn't about his looks. Not that they hurt or anything, but she'd been around plenty of gorgeous guys, and never once had she wanted to jump their bones within the first fifteen minutes. She hadn't even wanted to do that with Jason.

God, Jason. One thing about fixating on Cole—it made her forget all about that SOB. She stopped kneading. Was that it? Was Cole a distraction? At home she'd been so miserable, so moody and frustrated with herself, but being here gave her a whole new focus. The job, evidently, wasn't enough. She'd needed it to be personal.

Damn, damn, damn. Talk about selfish. Her friend was dying and had asked her to do one thing. Find her grandson and bring him back home. But no. That would be too straightforward for a manipulative creature like herself. She had to pretend she wanted to have his child. She'd completely convinced herself that she had to understand him in order to get him to reconcile with Eve. The whole house of cards could tumble down with one logical breath.

She attacked the meat again, and it occurred to her that she needed something physical to do. Meat loaf didn't cut it. She needed to run or lift weights or ride. Yeah, ride. After breakfast, she'd borrow a horse. Get rid of some of this energy.

The noodles needed stirring, but first she had to wash the gunk off her hands. As she scrubbed, her thoughts went back to that first meeting. She tried to picture what would have happened if she'd simply told Cole the truth. He'd have shown her the door. She felt sure about that, and not just because she needed to rationalize her behavior.

So if her very first instincts had been on the money, where had she gone wrong? When had the situation gotten personal?

The moment he'd touched her—when she'd looked into those dark, angry eyes. Some internal switch had gone from off to on, and that's all they wrote. Biology in action.

She'd seen some documentaries on the Discovery Channel about human sexuality, and one show in particular had been about this very thing. After years of research and study, it was a mystery why one person enticed and another repulsed.

She didn't have a clue what made her want Cole. But want him, she did. Not that she was going to do anything about it. But she had to admit the truth to herself—when he kissed her, he curled her toes.

The sky was getting lighter. It was just past 5:00 a.m. The noodles had a few more minutes to cook, and then she could put together the lasagna. In the meantime, she separated the ground beef for the meat loaf and put it in another bowl. She'd add chili sauce and a few spices, then she could cook both dishes at the same time.

The timer went off, and the next half hour was Cole-free. Her thoughts were on the food, on the menu for the day. But once she put the casseroles in the oven, there was nothing else to distract her. All she was left with was dishes to wash and a head full of doubt.

COLE ATE his breakfast in silence, which wasn't unusual. He also kept his gaze on his plate, which was. Looking at Lily had side effects, and he wasn't well rested enough to handle them.

For the second night in a row, he'd slept terribly, reason enough right there for her to go. On the other hand, the morale of the men hadn't been this high since… Ever. They laughed and ate like each meal was their last, and one hell of a lot of work was getting done. That was good, because he needed them to pick up his slack.

Manny reached for another biscuit, his third, if Cole had counted correctly. "Lily, what are we having for lunch?"

"Meat loaf."

A collective ecstatic groan was heard around the table.

J.T. swallowed his mouthful and asked, "Do you make it sweet? Or spicy? My mom used to make it with ketchup, and man, it was the best. We'd have it hot at night and make sandwiches the next day."

"My mother used Worcestershire sauce." John cleared his throat as he always did when he talked about his mother. "She was a fine cook. She always made fresh mashed potatoes with meat loaf."

Cole chanced a look at Lily. She sat between Chigger and Spence. She'd finished eating, and it was clear she was enjoying the conversation. When she glanced his way, he went back to staring at the remains of his eggs, ham and hash browns.

"Spence, what about you?"

"My mother wasn't much of a cook," he said, his voice so soft you had to strain to hear him. That was

Spence. "But we had a lady who worked for us, her name was Rowena, and she was one hell of a cook."

"What'd she make?" Manny asked, leaning forward.

"Sweet potato pie. Corn bread that melted in your mouth. Macaroni and cheese. Oh, yeah. That macaroni was something else."

Cole, with his downcast eyes, listened interestedly as the men waxed on about their favorite foods. If he'd watched them, he would have missed the reverential tone, the way food was so connected to people they loved. He wouldn't short them a cook again. This was a good lesson.

But he also realized good food was only a part of the reason the men had grown nostalgic. Lily, with that way of hers, made it easy to talk. To confess. Even with that smart-ass mouth of hers, she was still the kind of person strangers would confide in.

He'd told her more than he should have. Damned if he hadn't thought about telling her everything.

"Cole?"

He looked up, and all eyes were on him. Lily must have been calling him for a while, but he'd been too lost in thought.

"What about you? How did your mother cook meat loaf?"

"She didn't." He pushed his plate away and grabbed his hat from the back of his chair as he stood. "Manny, where'd you say those fences needed fixing?"

Manny looked surprised. Tough. It was Cole's ranch, and if he wanted to fix fences, he'd damn well fix fences.

"Out by pasture two."

Cole nodded, then headed out toward the barn. He'd had enough of talking about mothers and meat loaf.

THE HORSE'S NAME was Charley, and Manny had told her he was responsive. Manny had been right. Lily barely had to touch him to get him to turn or stop. He was a beauty, too, brown with a white nose. Charley wanted to run, she could feel it in the quiver of his body, but he maintained his pace. Once she got farther out into the pasturelands, she'd give him his head.

She'd also borrowed a hat and a canteen, and was going to take full advantage of the animal, the day and the hours ahead.

It had cooled down into the nineties. This time of year in Texas, you couldn't expect much lower. She didn't care. The heat felt healing to her, as if something inside had been cold for a long time and was just now thawing out.

She rode past the cattle. Most of them were standing and chewing in the shade of the oak trees, some were lying down, some watching her ride. They were big Black Angus, prized for their beef. They made her think of home. Of her dad. He took such pride in his herd.

At the end of the first pasture, the cattle thinned out, and the countryside became more wooded. The shade made the grass greener, and she suspected there had to be springwater nearby.

She found the fence long before she found Cole. And she heard him cussing long before she saw him. When she did, she reigned in Charley and took a moment, giving homage where it was due.

He had his shirt off. That was just for starters. He was wrestling with a big fence stake, trying to beat it into submission with a huge mallet. His gloved hands made his chest look even more naked, if that was possible. Normally, Lily wasn't a big fan of sweat, but Cole's glistening body made her reconsider. The tension came back to her insides, in the hollow place she became aware of whenever she got close to him.

He swung the mallet again, and she drooled over his muscles. His biceps alone were worthy of a sonnet. If only she had a camera.

His curse jarred her, not because of the word, but because she realized she was staring with her mouth open. Literally. It was kind of embarrassing. Urging Charley forward, she called out a hello so she wouldn't scare Cole. There were no first-aid stations here, and that mallet could do some serious damage.

He jerked around to face her. There was no immediate look of welcome. Instead, he scowled. Somehow it wasn't quite fair that the frown made him more handsome. Hell, he'd be gorgeous no matter what he did.

"What are you doing here?"

"Taking a survey."

"I mean it, Lily. What the hell are you doing? Don't you have work to do at the house?"

She waited until she got a few feet from him, then dismounted. After a quick stretch, she smiled at the shirtless cowboy. "I've already done my chores, boss. Lunch is fixed and ready. Dinner is prepared, except for the salad."

"That still doesn't explain why—"

"I wanted to have a ride, okay? I needed some air."

"You'll get all you need when you ride back."

"Thanks for your concern. But before I leave, I'm going to help you with the fence."

"No, you're not."

She sighed. "Oh, Cole. You're so predictable."

He bristled. "What does that mean?"

"I knew you were going to argue with me. But you forget, I grew up on a ranch. I've fixed fences. I'm not a delicate flower that can't get her hands dirty."

"I don't care. I don't want your help."

"Sure you do."

"Didn't we make a big enough mistake last night?"

She pulled a pair of Manny's gloves out of the saddlebag and put them on. "Here's what I'd like to do. Work now, and argue later."

"I—"

She held up her hand. "I understand your concerns. But for now, let's not think of me as a woman and you as a man, okay?"

"It doesn't bother you in the least that I don't want you here?"

"Nope. So, what's this?" She tapped the rail. "Does it just have to be reseated?"

He gave her a world-class glower, then grudgingly nodded down the way a piece. "We've got about six down, and the wire needs to be replaced."

"Well, isn't that lucky? I happen to be great at replacing wire." She walked over to his horse, a beautiful stallion, and got the wire and tools from the saddle. "Now you be careful with that mallet."

She walked away, knowing he was staring at her, feeling his gaze on her butt. With turnabout being fair play, she had no right to complain, but man, was she self-conscious.

Clearly they couldn't even be in the same county without getting all worked up over each other. Maybe—and this was just an idea, nothing written in stone—maybe they should just get on with it. Do the deed. Begin the beguine. Maybe all this tension between them was just so much pent-up energy that needed to be released, and once it was, they could be around each other comfortably.

She nearly stumbled over some tangled wire and examined the situation, seeing where it would be best to start. But as soon as she began the actual work, she brought back her idea for consideration.

A little bedroom gymnastics might just be what the doctor ordered. Let them both get it out of their systems. Afterward, they'd talk without all this nonsense. All this awareness. Right?

Oh, who was she kidding? He'd have to be the worst lay in Texas for her to stop thinking about him that way. And there was no possibility of that being the case.

Once she got him in bed, she had the feeling it would take the national guard to let him go. The only solution? She didn't dare even think about heading in that direction.

She turned toward where Cole was working, but she couldn't see him. Not in the flesh. But he was there, in stunning detail in her mind's eye.

Work. Just *work*. Hard physical labor. It was her only hope.

CHAPTER ELEVEN

COLE SWUNG the mallet again and felt the vibrations up his arms and into his chest. Damn her. What was she trying to do? Did she want to force him into a corner? Or did she just want to drive him crazy?

Once more, he lifted the sledgehammer above his head, but then he looked at the rail. It was buried halfway to Sunday. He hadn't paid attention, and now he had to dig the damn thing up and start all over.

He cursed for as long as he could come up with fresh words. It was her fault. Everything was her fault. Especially the crazy thoughts that had plagued him all morning.

Putting the mallet down, he grabbed his shirt and wiped his face with it. Even in the shade it was damn hot. She probably forgot to bring water with her. Great. So she'd pass out from heatstroke, and then what was he supposed to do? Tie her to Charley and hope she'd live until the horse got back to the ranch? Like hell.

The thought of water made him aware of his own thirst, and he took care of that with one of his two canteens. He was used to working in the hot sun and he'd come prepared.

Damn woman.

What he needed to do was go find her and talk to her. Give her the speech he'd been rehearsing since last night. She'd argue with him, but in the end, she'd see he was right. This wasn't the place for her. The men would survive on their own food for a few more days. He'd go back to square one, and this time, he'd be much better prepared to find the kind of woman he was looking for.

She wouldn't be beautiful, that's for sure. She wouldn't be mouthy. She wouldn't crawl under his skin like someone he could mention.

When he thought about it, it was probably good that Lily had come to stay. He would never have been able to get so specific about what he wanted until he'd seen what he didn't want.

He took one more swig of water, letting his gaze follow the broken wire fence. It wasn't getting any cooler, so he'd better go get her. The rail would wait.

He put his supplies back on his saddle, donned his shirt, although it was too hot to button it, and hoisted himself on Phantom. The Arabian stallion had been with him for three years, and they'd grown to know each other well in that time. Good old reliable Phantom. No surprises with him.

He set out at a cautious pace, wary of loose wire. Cole relaxed, or tried to. It didn't seem possible with Lily in the same vicinity.

By the time he saw her, he'd rehearsed his speech half a dozen more times. She was on the fourth rail, and as he rode by each of the previous three, he had to admit she'd done a passable job fixing them. At least she hadn't lied about working on a ranch.

She looked up at him as he approached. Her hat shaded her eyes, but her mouth was lit by the sun. He wished he didn't know the taste of her. The feel of those lips.

Forcing his gaze down, he saw how hot she was. Sweat stained her white T-shirt under her arms and down her back. Her bra strap stood out in stark relief. The way her jeans hugged her hips made him too aware of what effect she had on him.

"You done already?"

He shook his head and reached for his second canteen. "Brought you water."

"Thanks." She walked over to him. "It's thirsty work."

"No doctors out here. Man gets heatstroke, he's pretty much done for."

"Well, it was very considerate of you." She unscrewed the cap and tilted her head back to drink. His gaze went to her neck, the smooth pale skin, the hollow at the base. He shifted in his saddle.

She finished her drink, then handed him the canteen. "I'm almost finished here," she said. "Another hour or so ought to be enough."

"Not today. Not with this heat. We'll finish another time."

"I don't mind."

"I do."

She shrugged. "You're the boss."

Damn straight.

"God, I wish you had a swimming pool," she said as she headed over to get her tools.

His gaze moved to the copse of trees dead south. An idea took hold in his head with a pit bull's teeth. He didn't even dismount and help her with the wire. Instead, he became uncomfortably aware of his own clothes sticking to his body. The sweat that made an itchy path down his back.

''Come on,'' he said. ''There's something I want to show you.''

She didn't hurry. Although he was anxious, he couldn't help but notice the care she took with the supplies. He always said you could tell a lot about a man from the way he kept his equipment.

Finally, she handed him those things she'd borrowed, then put her boot in the stirrup and swung her other leg over the saddle.

Before her butt even touched the seat, he'd urged Phantom forward. Lily would follow. He'd give her his speech there, by the spring. After they'd both cooled off a bit. If she hadn't been with him, he'd have taken off every stitch and gone swimming. Even when it was hot like this, the natural spring water kept cool.

Oh, great. Now he was picturing her in the buff. Skinny-dipping and laughing, her breasts buoyed by the water, her nipples hard with the cold. Of course, his body would react too, only in the opposite manner. Another great joke by a fickle universe.

''Cole?''

He turned his head. ''Yeah.''

''Where are we going?''

''You'll see.''

''Just tell me one thing. Is this a good surprise?''

He nodded.

''You know what?''

''Huh?''

''You're one strange son of a bitch.''

He smiled. Yeah, he did know that. But it worked, so he didn't give a damn. He had his kingdom. This parcel of land in Texas that no one could touch. He had his stock and his breeding program. If he was forced to tell the truth, he'd have to admit he wasn't a born rancher, but that was okay. He liked managing the ranch, coming up with new techniques and innovative approaches to raising cattle. Besides, he hired men who loved the work. All in all, he was proud of his accomplishments, even though there was one thing that would make the whole picture perfect.

Phantom must have felt his impatience because his pace quickened as they reached the heaviest concentration of trees. Or maybe he just smelled the water, and his thirst was getting to him. The horse led them through oaks so old they must have seen the world get born. The pointed leaves shimmered in the light breeze, and for the first time since leaving the house, Cole felt some relief from the heat.

Soon, very soon, he'd splash that cold water all over himself. He didn't care if his clothes got soaked.

He'd rather like it if hers did.

Phantom stepped over the carcass of a tree that had been felled by lightning. Right after that, he curved to the left, and a few moments later he brought them to the spring.

It wasn't big. Not like Elm Creek or anything. But it was a good half mile across, and the water was fresh and clean. He could smell it from here, and so did the horses.

"Oh, my God! This is gorgeous!"

"Yeah."

Lily dismounted and the first thing she did was remove Charley's saddle and bridle. "Go on, boy. Get yourself some water."

The kindness surprised Cole. Most of the women he'd known wouldn't have thought of an animal before their own pleasure. He shook his head as he did the same for Phantom.

"What is this?"

"A spring."

"I know that. I mean, this place?" She looked around in pure wonder, appreciating the natural beauty that had always calmed him. This was where he came to be alone. To think. The only reason she was here was that she was going back to San Antonio soon. No one came with Cole out here. Sure, the men knew about it and used it, but they also knew never to bother him here.

Her gaze moved from the blue-green water to the border of thick plants and rocks that made up the shore, then to him.

"This area is called the Callahan Divide, the boundary between the Brazos River and the Colorado Basin. Before we white men came and ruined it all, this was home to thousands of buffalo on their way to the high plains. In fact, the first business out here was selling the bones."

"For what?"

"They were used to refine sugar."

"Excuse me?"

He nodded. "I don't think they use buffalo bones anymore."

"So is this water just for drinking?" she asked, turning back to the spring. Even though he could only see her profile, the look of longing was clear.

"No, we use it for swimming. But we didn't bring any suits."

"Suits? We don't need no stinkin' bathing suits."

"Pardon?"

Her grin lit up her face. "Bastardized line from *Treasure of the Sierra Madre.*"

"I know that. I was referring to the content of your statement."

"Oh. Right. Well, I don't know about you, but I'm wearing underwear. And frankly, my underwear reveals a lot less than my bathing suit."

He could feel his cheeks heat as image after image flashed through his brain like a peep show. Sure, she could get away with underwear. He, on the other hand, wore boxers, and in his current state, there would be no mistaking what was on his mind.

"I don't think so."

"Tell you what," she said, her fingers undoing her belt buckle. "You keep your pants on. I'm going swimming."

"Lily…it's not a good idea."

"Why not?"

"Were you there last night? Or was that just me?"

"Oh, yeah." She leaned against a tree and pulled her boots off, then her socks. "That's easily fixed. Turn around."

"What?"

"Obviously, you have no self-control, so turn around. Don't watch me." As she spoke the sound of her zipper echoed to Kansas and back.

"Very amusing."

"Look, big guy. I'm really hot and sweaty, and I don't have to be. You do what you want."

"But I need to talk to you."

"Great. See you in the water."

Just as he was going to tell her to wait, she pulled her pants straight down and stepped out of them. Her legs. Oh, Lord. Her long, lean legs seemed to go on forever. As his gaze traveled up her pale, perfectly muscled thighs, his temperature rose dangerously, and when he got a load of her pale-pink satin panties, he hurt himself trying not to drool. Of course, his dilemma worsened. It would sure feel better taking his pants off. There was only so much room there. But the tent factor would make a hooker blush. Maybe he should turn around. But he couldn't. Not when she was lifting her T-shirt off.

The material rose slowly. The panties were cut high on the leg and low on her stomach. Her belly button went in, not out, and her torso was what Manny would call "ripped." Slight indents on the sides, with a soft feminine curve up the middle.

He'd been so engrossed with her stomach that he hadn't noticed her T-shirt was gone. But once he saw her bra, it was pretty much all he could think of. It matched her panties. One of his little quirks was that he was a sucker for just that. Women in matching underwear. Of course, if she'd had a garter belt, nylons and high heels, he'd probably embarrass himself right here and now. As it was, the aching in his jeans wasn't getting any better.

Her laughter made him look up from the soft mounds held by the satin material, the outline of her ripe nipples clear and irresistible. But he forced his gaze to her face, and her great big old grin.

"You are so busted."

"Huh?"

"Let's see.... Your mouth has been hanging open since my pants went down. And, uh, Cole Junior there is doing his level best to break out of prison."

He whirled around, giving her his back to contemplate. He *had* been busted, and it was his own damn fault. His cheeks filled with fire, and he cursed his libido, but even this didn't ease the strain of "Cole Junior."

Her laughter bounced off the trees as she headed toward the spring. Even though he shouldn't, he dared a look.

Big mistake. Huge error.

Her panties were thongs.

He groaned as he watched her buttocks. He could pound nails with junior, and that was no exaggeration. If he didn't cool off soon, he might permanently damage himself. Only... "The hell with it," he said, and threw his hat down and wrestled his boots off. His shirt and socks were next, and then his belt buckle.

Lily was already immersed in the water by the time he reached the edge of the spring. He could see her shadow as she swam like a little mermaid. Now was his chance. He undid his pants with care, then slipped them off. His groan was a mixture of relief and pain as he freed himself from the constraint. The moment he kicked his jeans to the side, Lily came up for air. And looked right at him. Her gaze moved down his chest, and he put his hands in front of his crotch.

She laughed out loud. Really howled.

He couldn't get any more embarrassed, so he took his hands away, revealing the Empire State Building in his shorts. Wading purposefully into the water, he didn't stop until he was a foot under.

LILY WENT UNDER, too, just to check that Cole wasn't committing suicide by drowning. She could see him clearly in the water, with his back to her. He moved his arms and legs to keep from bobbing to the surface, but not for long. Soon, he went up, and so did she.

When her head popped to the surface, she pushed her hair back with her hands, her grin absolutely uncontrollable. He was just too adorable for words. So embarrassed. She'd like to embarrass him quite frequently. His cheeks looked so cute when they were pink.

He scowled at her, but she knew his bark was worse than his bite. Such a *guy.* Anger was always first. But the good ones went through the anger until they got to the other side. Cole would find the humor in the situation. Maybe not today. Maybe not this year. But he would.

"You can stop gloating," he said with a growl that matched his expression.

"Not yet. I'm having too much fun."

"So you're a sadist, is that what you're telling me? You like making people uncomfortable, then laughing at them?"

"Not people. You."

His brows went up, and in his surprise his frown disappeared. "Why me?"

"Because you're such an easy target."

"I am not."

"Oh, please. You are so. You blush like a virgin in a bordello."

"You do know that I could drown you out here and you wouldn't be found for a long, long time."

"Right. You brute. You can't even stand the thought that I might get thirsty."

"Can't we just swim quietly?"

"Sure." She dove under again and swam to where he was treading water. Before she could stop herself, she'd yanked the back of his shorts down, taking a moment to appreciate the white butt she'd uncovered.

Then she swam away as he turned on her. She came up at the other end of the spring.

"That was infantile."

She laughed. "I know."

"You're too old for that nonsense."

"Like hell I am. In fact, it's my goal in life to be an eccentric old woman. Pulling down your underwear fits right into my long-range goals."

"I've got some short-term goals that seem pretty doable." He moved closer to her, his body slicing through the water like a seal.

She liked him wet. And truth be told, she liked him hard. She'd been unbelievably flattered at his display of lust, and secretly happy that she had no such obvious meter. She wondered if he knew that she wanted him just as much. That her insides had tightened, and that she had an awful itch that only he could scratch.

She was utterly, completely, wantonly turned on. Her fingers ached to touch him everywhere. Her body felt hollow and hungry, incomplete.

He was getting closer now. She didn't try to escape his revenge. She wasn't going to make love to him, but she sure as hell wouldn't mind some kissing. Maybe even a little touching.

"What is that look about?" he demanded.

"What look?"

He shook his head as he swam right up to her, his body inches from her own. "The one on your face. You look like you're planning something else. Something evil."

"Wicked, maybe. Evil, no."

"How wicked?"

Her smile curved up slowly as she thought of all

the possibilities. In the water, on the bank. Wet. Dry. A plethora of libidinous choices awaited them if only they would get a bit daring. If only he would. She was ready. More than ready.

Cole cleared his throat. ''I brought us here to cool us down.''

''It didn't work.''

He didn't answer her for a long time. His gaze roamed her face, searching for something, but she wasn't sure what. Permission? It was granted, couldn't he see?

Seconds ticked by and he did nothing. Made no move. She couldn't understand what he was waiting for. But she was patient. Honestly, she could wait. It wasn't as if she'd die or anything if he didn't touch her soon.

His hand brushed hers. She didn't even think it was intentional. But it was all the encouragement she needed. She swam to his chest, wrapped her arms around his neck and kissed him until she nearly drowned in pleasure.

CHAPTER TWELVE

COLE HAD to breathe. Her mouth and his were locked so tight he didn't swallow any water, but if they kept this up, they'd both drown. He kicked until their heads were above the water line, then broke away from her. "Come," he whispered. Then, the taste of her still making him crazy with want, he pulled her toward the shore. Testing the depth about three feet from land, he touched the rocky bottom, found a foothold, then pulled her into his arms and kissed her again.

She tasted like cinnamon and artesian water, and he couldn't get enough of her. It was insane, he was insane as he thrust his tongue into the warmth of her mouth, mimicking the act he desperately wanted to do. When her legs wrapped around his waist, he groaned with frustration. But he couldn't do anything in the water.

He headed toward dry land, his hands holding her virtually naked bottom. She had her arms wrapped tightly around his neck and didn't let go until he stopped at a grassy slope by an ancient oak.

Releasing her wasn't easy. He wanted her body next to his. If it were up to him, he would have simply braced her against the tree and taken her right there. His concern for her back overrode his lust, though, and so he shifted until she stood in his arms.

"We don't have towels," she whispered, her gaze fixed on his.

He shook his head. "We don't have a blanket."

She ran her hand down his chest. "Guess we'll have to let the sun dry us, huh?"

He closed his eyes as her finger circled his nipple. "Uh-huh."

"Think we should hang our clothes up in this tree?"

"Uh-huh," he repeated, not caring in the least what they did with their clothes as long as they were off. He was hard again, but this time he knew he wouldn't leave in frustration. He'd be inside her soon. The thought was so compelling he rushed to strip right there, but the moment his fingers had slipped inside the band of his shorts, she stepped back. The problem was, she hadn't stepped away so she could undress. The expression on her face told him that.

"What's wrong?"

She sighed. "I swore I wasn't going to do this."

"Are you kidding me?"

She shook her head. "No. I wish I was. I wish I could just throw you to the ground and say the hell with the consequences, but I can't."

"Is this about birth control?"

"No. I'm on the pill. This is about me. About what I'm here for."

He closed his eyes again, trying like hell to defuse the near crisis situation in his heated body.

"I'm sorry," she said. "It's all my fault. I was an incredible tease, and I should never have done that. I know better."

When he opened his eyes, she had walked several feet away. She'd folded her arms across her chest, and he could see she felt too naked in front of him. "Care to explain?"

Lily struggled to put her feelings into words, but it was difficult. She hardly understood them herself. She wanted him. Oh my, yes. She wanted him like crazy. But the warning bell had gone off. Some part of her had made her pull away.

The fact was, she wasn't that experienced. Jason was only the second man she'd been with. The first had been Michael Kelper, her high school sweetheart, the boy she'd loved with all her heart and soul. They'd done it the night they'd graduated, and it had been horrible. Neither of them had known what they were doing, and she'd come away thinking, "Is that it? Is that what all the fuss is about?" It wasn't until Jason that she understood there was something great about sex. But she'd put off sex with him until she'd fallen for his charm. For his honeyed words. Until she'd been in love.

"Lily? I thought—"

"Cole, I don't want you to be the rebound guy."

"What are you talking about?"

"Jason. I told you about him."

"The married guy?"

"Yeah. The thing is, I didn't tell you this all happened just a few months ago. I promised myself I wouldn't get involved with anyone for at least a year. Only, I didn't count on meeting you."

"I thought we were talking about sex. Not romance."

She sucked in a sharp breath. "Wow. Yeah. That is what we were talking about. Completely. And there's nothing wrong with that. We're both adults, and it's really obvious we're attracted to each other...."

"But?"

She looked at him with regret. Soft longing. "I'll never want to just have sex. I only want to make love. And I can't have that with you."

A dozen arguments came to mind, but he kept his mouth shut. She'd said no. That was the end of that. But he couldn't keep looking at her in her transparent underwear, her body slick and wet.

He walked away, out of the shade. Out of her reach. Not trusting himself to speak. Then he sat himself down and closed his eyes. He'd dry off soon enough, and then he'd get dressed and head on back to the ranch.

"Cole?"

She was close, just a foot away. "Yeah?"

"You had something to tell me, didn't you?"

Now she was next to him on the grass. He didn't dare look at her. Not if he wanted to get the speech right. He ran it through his head quickly. She wasn't the right woman. It was best if she left. As if she needed more proof than her own words. Of course, he'd pay her for her services....

"Cole?"

He opened his eyes. Turned to look at her. She was very close, sitting down, hugging her knees. So beautiful it made him wish he was someone else. Someone who could fall in love. But he wasn't. And it was high time he told her to go. He took a deep breath and let it out slowly. But instead of beginning the well-rehearsed speech, he felt a stillness inside his chest, something he couldn't remember feeling before. The way she looked at him, with a compassion that was completely new territory, made him think crazy thoughts. Like talking to her. Like telling her everything.

She just waited. If she'd said anything, he probably would have recited his canned speech. But she didn't.

"Five years ago, I caught my father in bed with my fiancée."

The words hung in the air. He could hardly believe he'd said them. Not to her. Not to anyone. What had happened between him and Carrie was his own private hell.

"Oh, honey," Lily whispered.

Her tone made his chest constrict. He lay back and stared at the sky, wondering if he'd lost his mind. A few clouds billowed far to the east. Above him was nothing but blue. "We'd been together for two years. Engaged for six months. I met her at a fund-raiser for a children's charity my family supported. Everything about her was perfect. I remember thinking that exact thing the first time I laid eyes on her. She had blond hair, the kind that looks like wheat. Big blue eyes, a warm smile. She wasn't obvious, though. In fact, she made me work at getting her to go out with me. And then she held out for the ring. But that was okay. I wanted to marry her. I was in love with her."

The clouds were getting closer. Or maybe not. He couldn't trust his perceptions from this angle. It didn't matter. The sun was doing its job, drying him off. Lily wasn't hugging her knees anymore. Out of the corner of his eye, he saw she'd lain down parallel to him, but not too close.

"Then what?" Lily asked, her voice filled with that same kindness.

"Then we started planning the wedding. It was go-

ing to be big, and for her it became a full-time job.
She and my grandmother worked together. I kept out
of it.'' He touched the waistband of his shorts. Still
damp, but nothing major. It was time to turn over.

After he was settled again, with his chin on his
folded arms, he wondered if he should go on. He'd
told her more, much more than he'd intended. But
there was something about Lily that made it okay.
Actually, talking to her made him feel better.

''Where was it supposed to be held?''

''At my grandmother's. No expense was spared.
My mother was gone—she was killed in a car accident—and my father, he wasn't around very much.
At least, so I thought. Then, about two months before
the wedding, Carrie told me she was pregnant.''

''Oh, God.''

''Yeah. At first, I didn't think too much about it.
We were going to be married anyway. I didn't care.
But then I went with her when she had her sonogram.
I saw the baby's heart beat. And man, I'd never
wanted anything so badly in all my life. I went nuts.
I started buying him toys and planning his future. I
couldn't believe my luck, to have found this perfect
woman and to make a son with her. It was everything
I ever wanted.''

''Cole—''

He couldn't stop now. The whole thing had to
come out. To be laid bare on the parched earth.
''Three weeks before the wedding, I came home early
from a business trip to Houston. I was a management
consultant then. The man I was going to see had gotten sick. We rescheduled the meeting, and I caught
the first plane out of there. I didn't bother to call

Carrie, but I did get her flowers. Pink roses, two dozen. Her favorite.

"I got home and I saw the light on in the bedroom. So I hid the flowers behind my back and snuck over to the door. I heard something, but I couldn't tell you exactly what. Just that it made my blood run cold. I opened the door, and at first I didn't see who she was with. It was just some man. Some other man. But then he looked up at me. My own goddamn father. He was still—'' Suddenly, he couldn't speak anymore. In fact, he didn't want much of anything except to go back to when he was numb.

"How could he do that?" Lily sat up again. "The stupid bastard. How could he do that to his own son?"

"I don't know. I never asked him."

"But what about the child?"

He laughed bitterly. "Yeah. The boy…"

Lily waited. He'd tell her in his own time. She was still trying to understand what had happened. How a father could do something so despicable to his own son. "I can't…" She didn't have a clue what to say. "Sorry" didn't cut it by half. Of course he didn't trust anyone. How could he? The level of that betrayal went all the way to the core. To the depths of the soul.

So much of his behavior made sense now. Why he wanted no attachments to a mate. Why he wanted a son of his own. What had seemed eccentric and a little nuts only moments before now had a desperate logic.

She longed to touch him. To hold him close and ease his pain. But there was no touch of hers that

could heal him. He'd have to do that for himself.
"What happened to the boy?"

Cole finally looked at her, and it was all she could
do to stop herself from bursting into tears. His expression was so raw, so hurt.

Her brother Dylan was like Cole. For them, love is
everything—unequivocal, complete and guileless. It
didn't matter which facade they used as protection—
Dylan with his sense of humor and his easy smile, or
Cole with his granite mask—they were more vulnerable than they would ever admit.

She said a silent prayer of thanks that she'd stopped
Cole and herself from going too far. Despite what
he'd said, this wasn't just about sex. If it had been,
he wouldn't have told her his story. He wouldn't have
had to turn away from her.

"I'll tell you something. Despite everything, I still
wanted that boy. Crazy, huh?"

"No, not really. I suppose you'd already sort of
fallen in love with him."

Cole nodded, then put his chin on his arm again.
"I knew it was my father's fault. He was such a manipulative bastard, Carrie didn't stand a chance. I
knew she had to be feeling guilty as hell. But I
couldn't stay there, not while I was so angry. I
thought I might kill him."

He grew quiet then, and she could almost imagine
what he was thinking about. She understood betrayal.
Being lied to. Being stupid and naive. What she
couldn't imagine was that betrayal coming from
someone in her own family.

"I went to California for a couple of weeks. I had
a friend in Laguna Beach who lent me his house. I
did a lot of thinking. A hell of a lot of walking. And

the more I thought about it, the more I was sure I could never get past it. Not as far as my father was concerned. I never wanted to see him again. And I wasn't sure I wanted to see Carrie, either.

"My grandmother told me to buck up. To accept the situation and grow from it. To come back and act as if nothing had happened. She said it was my duty as a Bishop to carry on. To raise the child on my own and never speak of the unpleasantness again. I'd never heard her so angry as when I told her no."

The sun finally got to Lily, and she turned over. She was terribly thirsty, but there was no way in hell she was going to move away from him to get water.

"As it turned out, it wasn't over. Not by a long shot. I got a letter from my grandmother about four days before I was supposed to head back. Carrie had lost the baby. She'd miscarried. And she and my father had gotten married in Las Vegas."

Lily had no more words. Everything seemed inadequate. Foolish.

"Eve—that's my grandmother—didn't care for that last bit, and from the last letter I opened from her, the marriage had been annulled. I never spoke to my father again."

"What about you and the others? Carrie. Your grandmother?"

He shook his head. "I did end up opening the last letter Carrie sent me. Turns out the story I'd been given wasn't exactly the truth. There was no miscarriage. Eve paid for the abortion, and she paid for Carrie to disappear. I've never spoken to my grandmother again, either."

"But surely after all this time... She's your only family."

"I have no family."

"But—"

Cole stood, dusted his stomach and knees, even though there was nothing on them. "I think we're dry enough to go back now."

She nodded, and while she should have been thinking of how to convince Cole that seeing Eve was the right thing, despite the mistakes his grandmother made, she couldn't get past her own reaction to his pain. She ached for him, right down to her bones.

She'd grown up so privileged. Her family cared for her with love and tenderness, with enough discipline thrown in for her to have a good future. She'd always been able to turn to her father, her mother. Dylan and Ashley were there for her whenever she needed them.

Oh, she'd made mistakes. Transferring to the FBI offices in Dallas to follow Jason was a big one. Heck, just being with Jason at all had been a mistake. Growing up, she'd committed a hundred minor infractions, and all of them had been dealt with swiftly and fairly. She understood the concept of consequences, and it had made all the difference. She'd always known, deep in her heart, that everything would be all right. It was the fundamental truth about her life.

How could someone recover from a nightmare like Cole's? When the betrayal had come from the people who were supposed to love and protect him? No wonder there was such a wall around his heart. The question was, could the wall be toppled? Was seeing Eve—forgiving her—the one ingredient that might just save him?

She forced herself from her reverie and saw that Cole was already dressed. He was saddling Charley for her, while his own mount stood nearby. She got up and slipped on her socks, her jeans, her T-shirt. Then she found a rock to sit on while she put on her boots. The whole time, she watched Cole. Admired the way he moved, the inherent grace of the man.

She wanted to fix him. To make the ugliness disappear. But she also knew that his plan, while it had a certain logic, would ultimately be the worst thing for him.

Cole needed to work through his anger. He needed to see that his father was sick, and that Cole himself had done nothing wrong. He hadn't deserved any part of that tragedy.

Not that she was the one to help him, despite her wish to. He needed someone trained in this sort of thing. She'd had a psychology class or two, but this was out of her league. The only thing she could offer him was her friendship. And the possibility of helping him reconcile things with Eve.

"What's this?"

She turned to Cole. In his hand, he held the canteen she'd brought from the ranch this morning. "Oh. It's water."

"I can see that. Why didn't you tell me you had your own?"

"Because I didn't want to spoil your gesture. It was lovely of you to think about me like that."

"Lovely. Right."

She pushed herself off the rock and stamped her left boot to get the right fit. "Yes. Lovely. Kind. Considerate."

"Bull." He put the canteen back on her saddle. "It wasn't even about you. I just didn't want to have to carry you back to the ranch."

She approached him as gingerly as if he'd been a

wild stallion. He took a couple of steps back, but then he waited. His gaze wary, his back stiff and straight, he let her touch his arm. "Listen up, cowboy. I know you're not the SOB you pretend to be. Don't worry. I won't tell anyone. But you don't have to get all prickly with me. I understand."

His grateful smile made her feel like a million bucks.

"Lily?"

"Yes, Cole?"

"No offense, but, lady, you're full of crap."

COLE DIDN'T say much on the way back to the ranch. He was too busy wondering what in hell had gotten into him. He'd told Lily things he'd sworn he'd take to the grave. And now she knew. She knew his secrets, and with that came power. Instead of the relief he sought, he'd made himself vulnerable. What an ass. What a stupid miserable ass.

He looked over at Lily. Her gaze was on the trees, the big oaks that made this part of the country famous. That long neck of hers tried to seduce him again. Her smile was just as dangerous.

She made it too easy. No one was that good a listener. He wasn't sure how, but she'd manipulated him. And that was the issue, wasn't it?

No woman should be that close. Especially not someone as cunning as Lily. Oh, man. She made it look real. Her eyes, her voice, the way she touched him. All of it designed with one thing in mind—to trap him.

Maybe this was good, though. Maybe he needed to revise his plan. Just hire a surrogate. Forget the rest. Hire a male nanny. Plenty of kids grew up fine without a mother, as long as they had a father who was there. One who gave a damn.

He realized she was staring at him. Her brows had come down in concern, and her lips curved into a worried frown.

"What's wrong?" she asked.

"Nothing."

Silence. Then, "Okay."

Why did she back off so easily? That wasn't like her. Nosy. That's what she was. Why did she want to know so much about him? Who the hell was she?

He spurred Phantom to a quicker pace, anxious to get home. He'd figure out what to do when he was alone. Away from the smell of her, the memory of her skin.

Damn, he still couldn't believe he'd told her. That he'd laid himself bare. Then he thought about her face. How she'd looked at him. Could that kind of compassion be faked? Of course it could. But what if she wasn't—

No. No way was he going to let himself believe in her. Trust her. He'd already gone too far, and even though that couldn't be undone, he could do plenty to ensure it wouldn't come back to bite him on the butt. If he had to drive her to San Antonio himself, he would. She was gone. Out of his life. Out of his thoughts.

He passed the oak with Manny and Rita's initials carved in the bark, the boy's open declaration of his love. Cole had given him hell for damaging the tree, but Manny hadn't cared. He was crazy in love, and his dreams were as innocent as a sapling. The kid loved the ranch. More than Cole did, he often thought. He wanted to have his own place someday, just like the Circle B, and marry his girl and have a houseful of kids.

Cole hoped he got his wish. That Rita turned out to be the sweet thing Manny thought she was. Cole had to remind himself that there were fine and decent people in the world. Aside from his men, he tended to believe the rest of the human race was suspect. Untrustworthy. Yeah, the brush he painted the world with was awful big, but better to be too cautious than stupid.

There was a chance that Lily was a good woman. That she had only his best interest at heart. But it was a small chance. One he wasn't willing to take.

CHAPTER THIRTEEN

LILY HEADED back to the house from the barn, anxious for a shower and to get to her journal. The ride back had been tense, but she hadn't said a word to Cole about it.

Of course he'd pulled back. Proud as he was, it must have taken everything he had to tell her about his past. About his father. The defenses had come back up immediately, and it was no use trying to convince him that she'd never use his secrets against him.

She'd leave him be for tonight. Then, maybe tomorrow, or the day after, she'd broach the subject again. By then he'd have had time to process what had happened. If only he'd see that talking to her had opened a door that had been bolted shut. With luck, the conversation today would lead directly to a reconciliation between Cole and Eve. More than ever, Lily understood that her task was hugely important. Only it was Cole who needed her success most. It would ease Eve's heart, but it might just save Cole's life.

Manny stood by the door as she walked into the house. He smiled at her in a way that made her feel warm inside. Like she was already a friend. "How'd it go?"

She nodded. "Pretty well, although I didn't finish.

But there's only about two hours more work to be done.''

"That's great. Me and Spence'll go out there tomorrow."

"Did you guys eat the meat loaf?"

His grin broadened. "Yes, ma'am. Made myself a great big old sandwich, and when I finished that, I had another. Chigger ate three."

"Wow. I'm glad it was a hit. Is there any left?"

"Some." He opened the fridge and took out a can of root beer and the covered plate of meat loaf. "Want a drink?"

"Diet, please. I'll just have a sandwich, then I need to go shower."

"So where's the boss?"

"Taking care of Phantom. I think he said he needed to go check on a bull."

Manny nodded, then crooked his head to the left. "You thinking about staying?"

"Maybe."

"For, you know…" He pointed his soda can in the general direction of her stomach.

"Maybe. But most likely not."

"But don't you think—" He looked at the door, out the window, then back at her. "Don't you think it's crazy?"

"A little."

He snorted. "I think it's a lot crazy. I mean, I want kids, too. But the whole damn reason I want them is so that Rita and I can raise them together. So they'll be our kids, you know?"

"Yeah. I do. But everyone's different, Manny. We all need different things."

"If you ask me, what he needs is a good woman."

Manny's gaze and the arch of his right brow let her know just who he was referring to.

"Nope. Sorry. Not me."

"Why not? I know it doesn't look like it, but Cole, he's a good man. He takes care of us like you wouldn't believe. I mean, we have medical and dental, you know? And every Christmas he gives us a piece of the pie, a big old bonus. He never asks too much, and he only gets angry when we've done something that deserves it. He'd be a good husband, I know it."

She couldn't help smiling at his earnestness. "You do, huh?"

He got her diet soda, popped open the top, then handed it to her. "I surely do. People just don't know Cole, that's all. That's why they talk about him. 'Cause they don't know him."

"Who talks about him?"

"Damn near everyone in town. You wouldn't believe the stories. Some say he killed a man. Did you know that?"

"I'd heard something about it. But it's not true."

"Nope. It's not. At least, I don't think so. But if he did, there was a damn good reason."

"Why don't you ask him?"

"Huh?"

"Ask him. Instead of wondering."

Manny shook his head. "Oh, no. Cole doesn't talk about himself. Not ever. He hates it if anyone brings up his family or his past."

"I still think you should ask. You're his friend. You should be able to talk about these things. Rumors don't do anyone any good."

"I know. Rita says the same thing. But I can't. It would be intruding, you know?"

"It could be more like concern. Friendship."

Manny didn't look convinced. "I'll think about it."

"You do that. I have the feeling Cole needs someone to confide in."

"It won't be me."

"Maybe not." She got a couple of slices of bread from the loaf, then scooted by Manny to get the mayo out of the fridge. "Do me a favor and try, okay? Try to be his friend. After I'm gone, I mean."

"I thought you were gonna stay?"

"It's a long shot. I'll probably leave as soon as he hires a cook."

"Oh, man. I almost forgot. I gotta tell him the agency called. Someone's coming out tomorrow."

Lily's stomach took a dip. She didn't want him to hire someone new, and she didn't want to leave. Which was incredibly dumb. For heaven's sake, they were both the walking wounded. And they both needed lots of time to heal.

Anyway, a man like Cole would have a hell of a time trusting a woman, and if there wasn't trust in a relationship, then there wasn't a relationship.

"I'll go catch up with him," Manny said. "See you at dinner. Oh, and thanks again for the meat loaf. Man, you're a *milagro* in the kitchen."

"Wow. No one's ever said I was a miracle before. Thanks."

Manny gave her his Tom Cruise grin, then walked out, slamming the back door behind him. Lily took a sip of cold soda, finished making her sandwich, and headed toward the back of the house and her bedroom, eating as she walked. She felt a bit desperate about her shower. And then there was dinner to put together. She needed to reheat the lasagna and make a salad and garlic bread. But first, her journal. There was a lot to understand, a lot to think about. And a ticking clock. Cole might just want to hire that new cook tomorrow, and then what would she do?

She'd have to talk to him in the next twenty-four hours, that's what.

COLE WATCHED HER all during dinner. She laughed and talked artfully with the others, making even shy J.T. comfortable enough to discuss his childhood, which had been no picnic. She was good. Damn good.

Chigger and Manny kept eyeing him. At first, he thought Lily had told them about his father, but then he dismissed that. It wouldn't make sense for her to do something so obvious. But they were thinking something.

The only thing that distracted him from his watchfulness was the lasagna. It was the best he'd ever had, and he was hungry as a bear. When he'd gotten back, he hadn't taken any time for lunch, grabbing an apple on his way to his office. Luckily, there was plenty, because everyone had seconds, and some had thirds.

Lily made sure their plates and glasses were full, ate her own meal, and managed to swing the conversation around to the topic of Manny's fiancée. But Cole wasn't fooled. He knew Lily didn't care about Rita. She wanted to hear Manny go on about how he loved her. How marriage was his dream, and how he wanted so many kids. And she wanted to see Cole's reaction.

He had none. What Manny did with his life was his own affair.

Finally, the food and the chatter wound down. It was Spence's night to do dishes, but nobody seemed inclined to leave him to it. Even Chigger had a second cup of coffee.

Lily brought the coffeepot over to Cole. She stood just to his left, her body close, but not touching. "More?"

He nodded.

She leaned slightly forward to pour, and that's when she brushed against his arm. He stiffened, his senses immediately heightened. Her scent filled him, not the coffee's. Everything else dimmed as his concentration focused.

She put her hand on his shoulder. Just rested it softly. She'd finished pouring the coffee. It didn't feel as though she had any intention of moving.

He gave no indication that even that small touch had caused a riot inside him. But when her fingers squeezed gently, he let his hand drop below the table. He touched the back of her thigh.

She kept standing there. Chigger told one of his horrible jokes, and the others laughed. Then J.T. brought up the Abilene Rodeo, and with all the jabbering it was a wonder anyone heard anything.

Cole tuned them out. It wasn't a choice. He couldn't hear anything but his own heartbeat. As the seconds ticked by, the reasons for telling her to leave faded. His suspicion felt foolish, paranoid. But mostly, he wanted her. Dammit, all it had taken was a touch.

DESPITE BEING bone tired, Lily couldn't sleep. She couldn't stop her feverish thoughts. She couldn't make Cole leave her be.

It wasn't all that late. Just past eleven. Dylan would be out or at his desk. No way would he be sleeping. She sat up in bed, turned on the light and got her cell phone from the dresser drawer.

He answered on the third ring. "Lily?"

"Yeah."

"Damn, I'm glad it's you. Don't you check your voice mail anymore?"

She hadn't. Not in two days. She'd been so wrapped up in—

"I have some bad news."

Her heart thudded in her chest. Oh, God. Was it their father? Ashley? Or, even more likely, was it Julie? "Tell me."

"Eve had a stroke."

The air left her lungs in a rush as she absorbed the information. "Is she—"

"She's okay. It doesn't seem to be too bad. She was at the doctor's office when it happened. Actually, in the lobby, but they got to her real fast. She has some trouble talking right now, but that could clear up all by itself. They won't know much for a couple of days."

"But she's going to live, right?"

"Yeah. Unless…"

"What?"

"Unless she has another stroke."

"God, this sucks."

"Yeah. It would be a good time to bring her long-lost grandson back to the fold. Give her a reason to fight."

"I haven't brought the subject up yet."

"What are you waiting for?"

"I was waiting for the right time. Now I don't have much choice, do I?"

"I spoke to the doctor. She's gonna need some rest for the next couple of days. He thinks she's strong and that she might end up moving a little more slowly, but that's it. So you take the time you need. It's more important that he shows up, and if you rush it—"

"Right. I'll do my best." She shifted on the bed until her feet were on the floor. "How are things with you?"

"About the same."

"Damn."

"I've been interviewing for the assistant. So far, nothing."

"You'll find the right person."

"Sebastian came by last night."

Lily wasn't bothered by the non sequitur. But she was bothered by Dylan's tone. "Is he doing any better?"

"Yeah. He is."

"And?"

"That's what's bothering me. He is doing better. He looks like he's sleeping, and he's put back some of the weight he lost."

"Why is this not a good thing?"

"Because I think he's decided Julie is gone for good."

She closed her eyes, not wanting to ask the next question. "Do you?"

He didn't answer right away. She heard him breathing. In the background, probably from his computer CD, she heard Erik Satie. "No," he said finally. "I don't. I think she's alive. I think she's in trouble."

"Then you'd best keep looking for her, little brother."

"I will."

"Keep me up-to-date about Eve, would you?"

"Of course. If you'll check your voice mail."

"I will. Good night, Dylan. Tell Dad I miss him."

"Night."

She clicked off the cell phone and put her hand in her lap. The news about Eve played havoc with her thoughts. Aside from the very real fact that Eve was a friend, and that Lily selfishly wanted her to be well, the stroke made everything here infinitely more dire.

Eve might be fine.

She might not.

Cole had to have a chance to talk to her. To make peace. Eve had to see him, to hear his voice and see how strong and capable he was. And it was all up to Lily.

She'd tell him. Tomorrow. Not in the morning, though. After he'd finished work. Chigger had told her the guys weren't going to be there for dinner. They were leaving early, going to a poker game in Buffalo Gap. She'd have Cole to herself so she could talk to him without interference.

She'd have to think long and hard about what to say. He knew she was from San Antonio. Was it so out of the question that she would know Eve? Perhaps she could mention it casually, as if she hadn't made the connection between them.

No. No lies. She'd tell him everything. And then it was up to him. She couldn't force him to see Eve. Ultimately, it was none of her business.

Who knew what had been left unsaid today by the spring? Maybe Cole had even more reason for not speaking to Eve. Something he hadn't told her. But she doubted it. In fact, her intuition made her almost frantic to put the two of them together.

Tomorrow night. Eve would be all right for one more day. She had to be.

COLE SPENT most of the next day on the phone, taking care of business he'd neglected since Lily had arrived. It was a relief to think about cattle and feed and the payroll. To wrap his mind around problems he could solve. Hell, he'd been so happy to be at work again that he'd let the men go into town a couple of hours early. Never let it be said that Cole Bishop wasn't one hell of a boss. Of course, it also didn't hurt that there was no one around to give him a raised eyebrow or a lecherous grin. They all thought he'd slept with Lily. Wouldn't they be disappointed to know the truth.

He turned off his computer at five minutes to four, but only because the woman applying for the cook's job was due. He headed toward the house, wondering if Lily would be in the kitchen.

He'd had lunch in his office, and except for breakfast, he hadn't seen her. He hadn't wanted to. It would only make his task more difficult. The plan was to hire the applicant, regardless of recommendations or suitability, and send Lily on her way. After she was gone, he'd be himself again. Things would go back to normal.

The kitchen was empty except for the intoxicating aroma of baking bread. It made him hungry all over again. With any luck, the new cook would be able to bake bread, too. And peach pie. Lily might even be willing to share her recipes. No. Not a good idea.

He went into the living room, and was pleased to find the scent of bread followed him there. After he put his hat on the console, he got his briefcase and pulled out his employee questionnaire. A sound made him look up from his paperwork, but it wasn't Lily. Disappointment hit his solar plexus with the power of a KO punch.

Dammit. Dammit all to hell. He didn't want to want her. He didn't want to be excited to see her. He didn't want to feel anything for her at all.

The doorbell saved him further torment, and just before he opened the door he was able to pull his focus away from *her*. The woman who smiled at him was in her fifties. Her dark hair was very short, almost a buzz cut, and her eyes were large behind tortoise-shell glasses.

"Mr. Bishop? I'm Virginia Holt."

He nodded, remembering his manners. "Yes. Come in, please."

She nodded, stepped inside, then followed him to the living room. After handing him an envelope, she sat on the couch, putting her large purse beside her.

He found her résumé inside the envelope, and what he read eased his mind considerably. She'd been a cook for several large ranches, including the King Ranch. She'd been at each job for at least five years. The recommendations that followed glowed. "Why did you leave your last job, Mrs. Holt?"

"My daughter got pregnant. She lives in Abilene with her husband, and I wanted to be closer to her. It's my first grandchild."

"I see."

"May I ask how many of you there are?"

"Most of the time, five or six. But at roundup—"

"I know all about roundup. I can cook for six or sixty. As long as I have control over the pantry, you never need to worry about that."

"Good." He sat down, ready to hire her on the spot. But it might worry her if he was too eager. "Do you have any specialties?"

"Like the bread I smell coming from the kitchen?"

He smiled. "Yes."

"You not only get me, Mr. Bishop, you get my sourdough starter, which some people consider worth the price of my salary. I bake bread as well as pastries. I like a varied menu using the local produce. I make sure the food I serve is nutritious, but frankly, and pardon my bragging, no one's ever noticed the nutrition part. They've just asked for seconds."

"Speaking of salary…" They discussed terms, and although her fee was a great deal more than any cook he'd had before, he'd be a fool to let her go. She was everything the ranch needed. She'd even clean up around the house, as long as he got someone in to do the heavy work.

He folded the papers and put them back in the envelope. As he looked up to make his offer, Lily appeared in the hallway. He wasn't sure how long she'd been there. My God, she was so beautiful. But she seemed terribly sad. He wanted to go to her, comfort her. Something was wrong.

"Mr. Bishop?"

He jerked his head toward Mrs. Holt. She seemed perplexed. "Yes? What?"

She cleared her throat. "I was asking about the accommodations."

"Right." He looked back at Lily. She was closer now, although not in the living room yet. She stared at him as she pushed her hair back with both hands. The movement caused her T-shirt to rise so he got the smallest glimpse of her stomach. His reaction was way out of proportion. He'd seen her nearly naked, so why was he so upset about that little flash of skin?

"Mr. Bishop?"

He'd done it again. He turned to Mrs. Holt. She smiled at him, then glanced at Lily. By the time she looked at him again, he'd decided. "I'm sorry, Mrs. Holt. You're eminently qualified for the position, but I'm not sure this would be the place for you."

She shot a look at Lily. "I see."

"I hope so. But if things change, and you're still available…"

"Of course."

She rose, and he walked her to the door. He had to consciously slow down and not shove the poor woman out. Finally, she was gone, and he hadn't embarrassed himself too badly. Lily was in the living room, looking at him with that sadness he'd noticed before.

"Why didn't you hire her?"

"She wasn't really qualified."

"But you said—"

"I don't want to talk about Mrs. Holt."

"No?"

He shook his head. "I want to—"

"What?"

"Nothing. Look, I've got more work to do, so I'd better…" He walked past her, intending to go back to his office and stay there. Already, some part of him was aware of how stupid he'd just been. He'd had the perfect cook and he'd—

Lily stopped him with a hand on his arm. All

thoughts of cooks and work fled until he was left with one word. One thought. One desire.

He turned slowly.

Her lips parted.

And he kissed her.

CHAPTER FOURTEEN

THE DRUG that was Lily flowed through his system, melting his resolve, blurring his reason, threatening his sanity. He didn't care.

He drank her in with his kisses, wallowed in her taste, her scent. As if by their own will, his hands ran down her back, underneath her T-shirt so he could feel her flesh. He groaned as he explored her back.

He felt her fingers on the back of his neck as she pressed him tighter against her lips, until he knew he must be hurting her. But her fingers, cool and long and wicked, slipped into his hair, sending chills down his body. The world could end and he wouldn't care. He wouldn't let her go.

Insanity. That's what it felt like. He was crazy, intoxicated, desperate. He rubbed her with his hips, letting her feel the way she was killing him. Then he forced himself to pull back. "What have you done to me?"

"I don't know. But you've done it back."

"I can't stand it anymore." He opened his eyes, and it surprised him that they'd been closed. Her gaze met his and he saw his own need replicated in her dilated pupils. Her cheeks were infused with a flush of red, as were her lips. Moist, slightly parted, they nearly sent him over the edge.

She stepped slightly closer and put her free hand on his chest. "Look at me," she said.

He did. He couldn't have looked anywhere else if he tried. He stood, mesmerized as her hand moved down from his chest to his waist. Past his belt. Down his fly. Until she molded her hand around his thick, constricted penis.

His groan came from deep inside, a place he'd never known. He'd wanted before, been mad for relief, but this…this was beyond endurance.

"I want you this much," she said, squeezing him gently. "But—"

He kissed her objection away. Kissed her and pressed her hand between his hard length and her stomach.

Then she stepped back, out of his arms, out of his reach. His whole body reacted with despair. They'd already stepped off the cliff. She couldn't possibly want to stop now.

But then she lifted her hand, and when he took hold of her, she led him down the hallway. The entire million steps to his bedroom.

SHE CLOSED the bedroom door and shut out the last of her misgivings. Whatever happened after, she wouldn't regret this. Her body literally ached for him. She wasn't stupid, she knew that making love to him was going to infinitely complicate their relationship, but even so, she knew she was doing the right thing.

Her intuition had been there her whole life, guiding her, warning her. If she'd only listened with Jason, she would have saved herself a mountain of heartache. Her sixth sense had never been stronger than it was right now. She *needed* to be with Cole. It didn't mean things were going to be peachy from now on. In fact, she thought the lesson might be far more harsh than she could imagine. But it was a lesson she had to learn. With this man. Now.

She turned to face him. He seemed electrified, as if there were megawatts of energy flowing just under his skin. What got to her most was that he was waiting for her lead. She could see how much he wanted to just rip his clothes off, but his hands were by his sides. Flexing into fists, yes, but at his sides nonetheless. He wasn't going to make a move until she gave him the go-ahead.

The best way to do that seemed to be with a non-verbal approach. She kicked off her right boot.

By the time she'd taken off her left, Cole's shirt was in the corner, and he nearly keeled over in his haste to remove his own boots.

She didn't blame him. In fact, she felt the same intense need to be naked. To be next to him. No, not even that. To have him inside her. That's what the rush was about. She shivered from the inside out and squeezed her legs together, then dispensed with her T-shirt, which was followed by her jeans.

When she reached behind her back to unclasp her bra, Cole stopped her. "Wait."

She did. She put her hands down as he looked at her. His perusal was thorough. His dark eyes took in her face, then her neck. When he reached her breasts, the examination stopped.

Her nipples were so hard she thought they might poke holes in her bra. She was built more for speed than comfort, so her breasts weren't going to make the front page of any paper. But they were still firm, and dammit, they were sensitive. Right now, beneath his intense focus, she had goose bumps on her goose bumps.

His mouth opened slightly as he stepped toward her. For some reason she couldn't explain, the man still had his pants on. But she'd take care of that. Later. He was going to touch her. With his hands? His lips? Either one was fine by her as long as he did it *now*.

It was his hands. The flat of his palms, to be precise. And they rubbed the tips of her nipples in slow circles. She leaned forward to press his hands to her, but he backed away, forcing her to be still. To let him do it his way. "You bastard."

He smiled. "You haven't seen anything yet."

She moaned as she closed her eyes.

His hands disappeared. "Look at me."

She obeyed. He touched her again.

"Don't close your eyes. I want you to see everything I'm going to do to you."

"And what would that be?"

"You'll find out."

His hands kept circling, and the sensation in her breasts was like fire and ice. The circles got tighter and faster, and it was as if he were winding her up like a toy. Her insides were going berserk. She couldn't shift enough to get any relief between her legs, and she couldn't make him change the pressure on her breasts. Torture. That's what it was. Sweet, incredible torture.

His hands stilled. He reached behind her back, and in one fluid motion undid her bra. Then he moved his attention to the straps, easing them over her shoulders. He hesitated there, rubbing the bare skin where the straps had been. The only thing holding her bra up was her arms, held tight against her sides. He brought his hands down her chest, cupped her breasts, then slipped the bra off.

She had no idea where it went after that. All she could think of was the cool air, and Cole's gaze, on her naked flesh.

"You're perfect."

She grinned. "I'm already a sure thing. You don't have to woo me with flattery."

His low chuckle excited her in a totally different way. "What am I going to do with you?"

"You want that alphabetically?" He moved his hands back to her breasts, and she sighed. "I couldn't help notice—"

But he didn't care what she noticed. His lips stole her words and her breath. He rubbed his chest against her, the smattering of hair just enough to make the sensation fully arousing.

She'd seen pictures of guys built like Cole, all hard muscle, but this was her first experience with one in the flesh, so to speak. It was a little daunting, but she'd manage somehow.

He ran his hands down her back and cupped her buttocks. She still had her panties on, and that seemed to bother him. But instead of doing the sensible thing and ripping them off her, he took a somewhat different tack. He slipped his fingers underneath the leg bands, and then he pulled the material up, giving her a wedgie. But it wasn't like any wedgie she'd ever heard of. This was...

Oh, my.

He gathered the material in one hand, then eased his hand between them, doing the same maneuver with the front of her panties.

As she leaned into his kiss, he moved the material back and forth, rubbing her just enough to make all the other parts of her body jealous.

She moaned, breaking the kiss, focusing totally on her panties. Silly her. She'd always just thought of them as underwear.

Cole pulled a little tighter and rubbed a little faster. And because she was a quick study, she found herself moving, too. A little, not a lot. Putting pressure where pressure was supposed to be felt.

Her breathing escalated and her limbs started to stiffen. But when she closed her eyes, he stopped.

She opened them again quickly, and he picked up where he'd left off. So he wasn't kidding about keeping her eyes open. She didn't mind. As long as he kept doing what he did so well.

The buildup began again. Quick breaths, heat, muscles tightening—

He stopped.

"Hey," she protested.

"Patience."

"My ass."

"Oh, I like it when you talk dirty."

"Cole!"

He stepped back, and she didn't know was what was going to happen next.

He didn't make a move. Not a smile, not a gesture.

"Cole?"

"Yes?"

"Are we staring at each other for a reason?"

He nodded.

"Can I ask what that reason is?"

"You'll figure it out."

"Great. Puzzles. Just what I was hoping for."

He laughed out loud and it made her blush with pleasure. "It isn't a puzzle so much as a game. And it's your move."

"Ah," she said, the light dawning. "I see. Hmm." She tapped her lips with her finger, trying to hide the excitement that filled her with joy and power and a want as real as the one straining the buttons on Cole's Levi's.

Oh.

She took a couple of steps, just enough so that if she wanted to touch him, she could. But she didn't. Not yet. She wanted to get this right. Give as good as she'd gotten.

There was this thing she'd read about. It had always seemed a bit much. But given the circumstances? What the hell.

COLE WASN'T SURE he could keep this up. The waiting, that is. The gleam in her eyes told him his torment would end soon.

She put her hands on his belt and slowly pulled the leather through the loops until she held it in her hands. Then she walked behind him.

He started to turn, but her hand on his shoulder stopped him.

"Hmm."

"What?"

"Patience."

"Smart-ass."

She patted his butt. "That's me."

She took hold of his left wrist and pulled it in back of him. Then she wrapped his belt around it. Next, she got his other wrist, and that, too, she tied with the belt. She made a loop of the leather. He tugged. There was a little give, but not much.

No one had ever tied him up before. While one part of him hated it—hated not being in control— another part of him was almost too excited. If she touched him right now, he was afraid he wouldn't be able to hold back.

"Very intriguing, don't you think?" she whispered, her lips grazing his ear.

"Cute. But not that cute. Come on, Lily. Take it off."

"Patience, patience."

He gritted his teeth as she walked around him, trailing her fingers over his back, his arms, his chest. When she was in front of him again, her fingers moved straight down until she found his waistband.

She pulled him closer, yanking him by the pants. His automatic response was to stop himself, but of course, he couldn't. Another try at breaking free, testing the belt, met with failure.

She had the power, and all he could do was take what she might give. It was completely unsettling. No woman had ever dared try anything like this. He'd made it clear he liked to be in charge.

Until Lily.

Her fingers played along his fly, rubbing his erection through the denim. He shuddered, willing her to get on with it.

She undid his top button. He held his breath.

She undid the next button. He forced himself to stay calm.

She undid all the rest of the buttons. He nearly lost it.

Then her lips went to his chest. As she pushed down his jeans, she kissed him, licked him, leaving a hot, wet trail all the way down his stomach. She paused as she reached the crucial juncture in removing his clothes. She crouched down, her hands on his hips. He felt her lips on his stomach, just below his navel. Another shudder ran through him.

Then she carefully, slowly, pushed his jeans past the point of no return. Of course, Cole Junior sprang to attention. The feel of the air alone was enough to make him moan. And when she touched him with her fingertips, he bit his lower lip, hard, and thought of the pain instead of the pleasure.

She ran her hand all the way down to the base of him, then back to the head. He'd never been this hard, never been so ready. If only she would…

She did. He felt her lips encircle him, the shock of her warm tongue. It was agony. And ecstasy. He wanted to touch her, but the damn belt—

He couldn't believe what her mouth was doing to him. As much as he wanted to impress her with his staying power, he knew he couldn't last much longer. He wanted her too much.

As if sensing his imminent explosion, she stopped her ministrations. She stood up. Smiled at him in that devilish way of hers. Sliding his jeans the rest of the way down, she held them while he freed himself of their constraint. Then she went behind him again, grabbed his wrists and pulled him backward. He didn't want to go. At least not in this direction. The bed was over there, across the room. But she called the shots, and he took one step after another away from heaven. Finally, the back of his legs hit his chair, and she pushed him down. The leather of the oversize club chair was damn cold on some places that were mighty hot. She grinned at his gasp.

"You're a cruel woman, Lily Garrett."

She nodded. "Cruel and mean and just awful. I don't know what you see in me."

"Me, neither."

She took a couple of steps back. What a feast for his eyes. Her long hair, long legs, those incredible breasts. If she didn't hurry—

Her fingers went to her panties, and she made a show of taking them off, teasing him unmercifully with the movement of her hips. Maybe it was a good thing they hadn't gone right to the bed. Maybe he could calm himself down a little. The last thing he wanted was for things to be over in two seconds. He took a deep breath, which caught when she straightened and tossed her panties over her shoulder. She was magnificent. She didn't have much hair. She was mostly bare and smooth and as erotic a sight as he'd ever seen.

She approached him slowly. With each step, he got harder, which was damn near a miracle. So much for calming down. She didn't stop until her legs were against his knees. Then she put her hands on his shoulders, gave him a wicked smile, and lifted her leg, wedging her knee between his leg and the arm of the chair. Using him as a fulcrum, she climbed up so she straddled him.

He had to admit, it was interesting.

He leaned forward and kissed her just below her

breasts. Her scent, clean and womanly, made him curse his belt and her foolishness. He wanted her. Now.

As it happened, he got his wish.

She lowered herself inch by slow inch until his eyes were level with her breasts. Then one hand went from his shoulder to his penis, holding him steady as she continued down.

He couldn't do anything. The way she leaned on him made it impossible to even thrust up. "Lily, let me go."

"No."

"I said untie me, dammit."

"And I said no. Just relax."

He tried to free himself again. It was no use.

"Don't struggle," she whispered. "I promise, it will be okay."

"I—"

"Look at me."

He met her smoldering gaze. And as they stared into each other's eyes, she lowered herself those last inches. He'd never known he could feel this intensely.

She didn't move, even though he desperately wanted her to. But then her silken muscles flexed and released around him. No other part of her moved. She just squeezed him until he thought he'd go insane. Finally, when he couldn't stand it one more second, she rose up, then down, then up again.

She moaned and tossed her head back, her fingers tight on his shoulders. Faster now, taking him for the ride of his life. He struggled with his hands, struggled to move, to thrust, but he couldn't.

She rode him with complete abandon, with utter

control. Watching the ecstasy on her face, he stopped fighting. Stopped trying to make it happen his way. He let her lead him all the way to the most intense climax of his life.

CHAPTER FIFTEEN

LILY SAGGED against him as she tried to slow her breathing. Now that she'd climaxed—oh *boy,* how she'd climaxed—her leg muscles rebelled against her unorthodox position.

What on earth had possessed her? She'd never been kinky. Well, okay, maybe a little kinky. But no whips or chains or anything. So why had she been so determined to tie Cole's hands?

His breathing was still in high gear, too. She needed to move, but he was still inside her and she didn't want to let him go. Of course, getting a charley horse wasn't exactly romance personified, so she grabbed his shoulders again and untangled herself from him and the chair. "Be right back," she said, then kissed him on the nose.

"Hey!"

"What?" she called over her shoulder as she hurried to the bathroom.

"I'm tied up here."

"I know." Then she slipped inside and closed the door behind her. She was asking for it. Oh, yes.

After she took care of the pressing issues, she slowed down as she faced the mirror. Naked as the day she was born, she looked like a woman who had just been most deliciously laid. Her hair was a mess, her lips swollen and red, and her chin and cheeks were pink with stubble burn. The very picture of the joy of sex.

It occurred to her that their sexual frenzy had made them both irresponsible. Thank goodness she was on the pill. At least she didn't have to worry about that.

Her mood a little flattened by that left turn to reality, she washed her face, brushed her hair, and headed back to free Cole.

Good night Irene, he *was* a gorgeous hunk of a man. Sitting in the altogether like that made her a wee bit itchy for round two. Only this time, she wanted his hands unfettered. Yum.

"Are you going to stand there all night, or are you going to untie me?"

"Now, now. Don't get testy."

"I'm not testy," he said, testily.

She moved to the back of the chair while he leaned forward. A few seconds later, she'd untied him, and he stood. While he rubbed his wrists, he looked at her through narrowed eyes. "Mind me asking you a personal question?"

She grinned. "What? You think what we just did wasn't personal?"

"My question is about that, actually."

"Oh, don't worry. I'm not normally that, uh, creative."

"No?"

"I never have been."

"Hmm."

"What's that look for?"

"Nothing."

"Cole. What is going on in that gorgeous head of yours?"

He walked around the chair until he was very close

to her. "It's not that I didn't like it," he said, his voice that husky whisper that sent chills up her spine. "I'm just used to playing a more active role."

"That was the point, silly."

"The point?"

She touched his cheek with her hand, loving the masculine feel of his beard, and beneath that the warmth of his skin. "It seemed the right thing to do. To take charge like that. To let you be on the receiving end."

"I don't like feeling helpless."

"But you're helpless all the time. So am I. So is everyone. There are things in life that we have no control over. But that doesn't mean we can't enjoy the experience."

"Odd time to make a philosophical point."

"I wasn't trying to make a point. I just went with what felt right. But now that I think about it, I understand why I did it."

"Because you wanted to teach me Buddhism?"

"Ha. My goal was as basic as it gets."

He nodded, although suspicion still darkened his eyes.

"Honest." She crossed her heart with her index finger. "I had only impure intentions."

"Okay. But next time—" He stopped midsentence. The suspicion in his gaze turned to worry.

"It's all right, cowboy. I know there isn't going to be a next time."

"I—"

"Well, maybe one more time. For heaven's sake, you just sat there like a lump. I think I deserve one go with you participating fully."

"Hey, wait just a damn minute."

She grinned. "I know it's early, but can I sleep over?"

He shook his head. "No. Absolutely not. We've already gone too far. I should never have touched you. I won't make that mistake again."

"Oh. Okay then." She turned to leave, but he stopped her with a touch. Searched her face with those dark, brooding eyes of his. Then he sighed. "I sleep on the right. And I don't like the windows open."

"You charmer. How could I ever resist?"

Taking her by the hand, he led her over to the bed, then pulled her into his arms. The feel of his naked body made her shiver.

"I can't resist," he whispered. "That's the whole problem."

"Let's make a deal, shall we?"

"What?" he asked, lowering her down to the cool sheets.

"How about if we pretend it isn't a problem, and declare a truce for tonight? Tomorrow, we can pick up our angst at the door."

"You're very strange."

"I know." She punctuated the short sentence by rubbing her hips against him. "But that's beside the point. Do we agree? No past, no future, no ifs, ands or buts. Just pleasure until the sun comes up."

"Very strange, and very beautiful." He kissed her tenderly, then nipped her lower lip. "But I have to admit, from time to time, you do have some inspired ideas."

Lily closed her eyes and let out a soft sigh as Cole's fingers trailed down her stomach.

Being with Cole was easy. So comfortable. The

only fly in the ointment was her lies, but she wouldn't think about that now. Not while his finger circled her belly button, then moved down her pelvis. When he reached the small patch of hair, he lingered there with a featherlight touch. She turned her head slightly on his big down-filled pillow, then grew still once more. The overhead fan sent waves of cool air over her body. It wasn't that the room was hot, but Cole was, and her body and his touched from shoulder to knee. He was on his side, she was on her back. It was perfect. "You know what?"

"What?"

She smiled. "You have wonderful hands." She felt the vibration of his chuckle against her arm.

"I know. Which is why tying them up was such a shame."

She looked at him. "Are you going to keep harping on that? Did you or did you not enjoy yourself?"

"Yes, I enjoyed myself. And no, I'm not going to harp on it. I'm just making the observation that this way can be enjoyable, too."

To illustrate the point, his sly fingers moved down to her soft, bare folds. He petted her as if she were a cat, and he damn near had her purring. But he also made her want him. It was all she could do to remain still. To stop herself from thrusting up, forcing his fingers to do more than pet.

"So soft," he whispered. "So beautiful."

She couldn't help herself. Her hips moved up slightly, just as his finger hovered over the most sensitive part of her body.

"So, that's how it is, eh?"

She nodded. "Oh, my, yes."

He dipped inside her, and continued his slow moves up and down the moist heat.

There was no way to stay still now. Her body fairly hummed with a desire that built and built.

His lips found her earlobe and he nipped the tender flesh, then he swirled his tongue in the soft shell, giving her goose bumps. But a moment later, those same lips captured her mouth in a kiss as gentle as the breeze.

She kissed him back, tenderly, sweetly. A long, languid exploration of taste and sensation. *What he did to her.* It was more than she could ever explain, more than she could even understand. He knew exactly how to kiss her without her saying a word. He touched her with magic fingers. He moved with a masculine grace that stoked a flame deep inside.

As he nibbled his way down her chin, it hit her. This was truly making love. And it was her first time.

His kiss deepened at the same time as his fingers. She moaned in contentment as he thrust into her, then in disappointment as he broke the kiss. But she didn't complain for long. His talented mouth rained kisses down her chin and between her breasts, down farther and farther until he had to shift his body so he could move between her legs.

His warm breath preceded his lips as he pleasured her. He explored every part of her most intimate self, finally centering on the one spot that would send her to the moon.

She gripped the bedsheets, but they didn't hold. As the tension mounted, she reached back and found purchase on the headboard. Her breathing grew faster and more urgent, her hips bucked, but the pressure never wavered. Harder. Faster. There, there, *there*.

Lily cried out as she went over the edge, as her body trembled and her muscles tensed.

Before she could relax, before the echoes of her climax had stilled, he was over her, his weight on his hands, his face above hers. He captured her gaze, and as his expression became a mask of intensity, he entered her. There was no hesitation, no pause. He filled her completely, and she cried out again. He moved with a steady, powerful rhythm, and with each thrust he rekindled her climax. As strong as the sensations were where they joined, they didn't compare with the passion of his gaze or the fire in his eyes. The desire there was so raw, so real she would have trembled without a touch.

It was more than making love. It was a melding of bodies, souls, spirits. There was no separation. No him and her, only them. Only this. Only now.

His eyes finally closed, but only for a moment. When he opened them again, his mouth curled into a grimace, his neck muscles bulged and he rocked the whole bed with his thrusts. He came with a primal cry that touched the deepest part of her heart.

A moment later, after he was drained and she had caught whatever breath she could, he lay down, wrapping his arms around her tightly. His breath and hers mingled, their chests rising and falling, the sheen on her body becoming the sheen on his.

She kissed him all over his face. His eyes, his nose, his lips, his cheeks. And then she let her head fall back on the pillow. Closing her eyes as she struggled back to sanity, she had a moment of perfect clarity.

Something strange was happening here. She was reluctant to call it by name. It was too soon for that.

But she knew that this was different. That Cole was different. She just might be in serious trouble here.

But how could she tell if this was the real thing? Was this what it felt like? This shivering want? This feeling of completion when he was inside her?

Looking at him made her want to cry. She longed to tell him everything. To confess her lie, to show him the road to forgiving his grandmother, to heal him. Heal them both. But if he knew the truth, he'd hate her. And without the truth, there was no hope for them.

How could things have gone so far so fast? There was danger here, for her heart and his. She had the horrible suspicion it would all come to a bitter end. To make matters infinitely worse, she knew that her betrayal was going to be the final straw for Cole. He'd finally lowered the walls around his heart, and tomorrow she'd deal him a killing blow.

Could he possibly believe she had only good intentions? Could he ever forgive her?

She knew the answer to that. Tears came to her eyes, and though she blinked and struggled to hold them back, they fell down her cheeks in fat, hot streams.

If this wasn't love, she didn't know what it was. And if it was love…

What an unbelievable tragedy.

CHAPTER SIXTEEN

THE FIRST THING Cole saw when he woke up was Lily's face. She was fast asleep, her black mane of hair wild on his pillow, her eyelashes brushing the tops of her cheeks, her skin pale and perfect in the early morning light.

What had he done?

She was so beautiful it made him ache. At some point the night before, they'd gotten up and fixed sandwiches to bring back to bed. And then they'd talked...and talked. The way Lily listened— He'd held back nothing. She made him feel safe.

He knew it was dangerous, believing in her like this, but he was tired of being suspicious. Of holding himself apart from everyone and everything.

Lily had given him a push out the door of his exile. She'd ruined his plans, changed his mind about how he would have his child. Dammit, he was in the exact position he'd wanted most to avoid. Being numb was easier. Shutting off his emotions ensured that he would never be hurt. He'd really blown it this time.

Why in hell had she come to his door? Even more puzzling was why he'd let her stay. He'd known right away she wasn't the right one to mother his child. At least, not the way he'd planned it.

Now he couldn't ignore the fact that he'd thought about having children with her. Lots of children.

They'd watch them grow together as a team. Loving them, and each other.

He wanted to touch her. To feel the warmth of her body, the silk of her skin. He wanted to know everything about her. And he wanted her to know everything about him.

So now what? Was he supposed to drop his plans just like that? Ask her to marry him for real? Or should he show her the door and forget he ever met her?

That last thing wouldn't be easy. She wasn't forgettable. Her humor, that sassy mouth of hers. The way her hair shimmered. And now… Oh, man, now he knew what it was to be inside her. To feel her lips on him. It wasn't enough. He wanted more. He could imagine doing everything with her. All his most private fantasies. She'd be game.

He wondered what she fantasized about? That would be interesting. And a little scary. She was so unpredictable. When she'd tied him up—

He felt himself harden as he remembered. It had frustrated him like crazy, but it had also excited him. She could have done anything to him and he wouldn't have been able to stop her. She could have hurt him. But she hadn't.

What was it she'd said? She wanted him to feel helpless. She'd told him he was helpless all the time. It was true, he supposed. He had no influence over the weather, the stock market, the men who worked for him. He was helpless to create the world he wanted, even though he'd sure as hell tried. So maybe she was right. Maybe the thing to do was relax and enjoy life. Let the chips fall where they may.

It would mean being vulnerable. But wasn't he,

anyway? He'd already gone past the point of no return. If she left him now, it would hurt. Hurt like crazy.

He hadn't known her long enough to be feeling these things. He'd known Carrie for months before he'd honestly cared for her. But Carrie had never been so open with him. She'd been guarded, and had made it easy for him to keep his thoughts to himself.

Not Lily. She'd press and intrude and annoy him until he told her everything. Was that a bad thing? He had no clue.

All he did know was that he'd made mistakes before, and he wasn't arrogant enough to think he wouldn't make them again. But some mistakes were worse than others.

He brushed her cheek with the back of his hand. She made him care too much. It was no use trying to kid himself. He'd let her inside. All he could do was pray that she hadn't brought any weapons with her. His heart wouldn't survive another assault.

LILY WOKE with a start. For a moment, she was still in the dream, still being punished by an unseen hand. But the dream dissipated as consciousness took hold. Cole wasn't next to her, and she didn't like that at all. She wanted the comfort of his arms.

She sat up and saw the light under the bathroom door. Heard the faint sound of his shower. Part of her wanted to rush to the bathroom and climb in the shower with him. Even though she was sore from last night, she still wanted him. Wanted him like she'd never wanted anything in her life.

What an ass she was! Such a selfish little weasel. She'd been so cocky, so sure she'd find a perfect solution to this problem and be back at the Double G in a couple of days, bringing Cole with her. A tearful reunion would follow, and she'd move on to the next case.

Right.

She was knee-deep in alligators, and it was her own fault. She'd screwed up big time, and she didn't know how to go about making things right.

She checked the door, listened carefully. The water was still running. She threw back the covers and found her clothes, dressing as she went along. When she had everything on except her boots, she tiptoed out the door and closed it behind her.

Dylan. Dylan would know what to do. He'd help her.

She hurried to her bedroom and closed, then locked the door. Dialing with shaky fingers, she said a small prayer that her brother was home. He was.

"Hey, it's me," she said.

"What's wrong?"

"Oh, everything."

"Want to start from the beginning?"

"Hold on a sec." She put the phone down, went into her bathroom, grabbed the box of tissues, then got the phone again. "I didn't mean for it to happen this way," she began.

"Of course you didn't. What way?"

She settled on the bed and told Dylan everything. No details about last night, of course, but the gist. She explained about Carrie, about his father and Eve. She assured him Cole wasn't a horrible man, just horribly hurt, and now she was going to have to hurt him again.

Dylan didn't interrupt. She heard him turn off his

computer halfway through her tale, and she could picture him as he sat at his desk. He'd be doodling, of course. He always did when he was on an important phone call. Nothing recognizable except for shapes. No names or eyes or little hearts.

She grabbed a tissue from the box and wiped her damp eyes. She felt like pond scum. Worse. "Dylan, what am I going to do? I've messed everything up so badly."

"You couldn't know it would turn out like this."

"But even so, I shouldn't have lied."

"He would have sent you packing the first five minutes."

"Then I should have been clever enough to find a way to make him listen."

"Oh, I see what we're doing."

"What?"

"I believe it's called self-flagellation. You don't need me for that."

She sighed as she scooted back on the bed, going right into the corner, taking her pillow with her. "Come on. Help me."

"I'm trying to. But you have to stop beating yourself up first."

"I don't know if I can."

"Look, kiddo, there's only one thing you can do, and I don't have to tell you what it is."

"Yes, you do."

"Fine. I'll spell it out. You have to tell him the truth."

"About Eve?"

"About everything."

"But—"

"Lily."

She closed her mouth, trying like heck to quiet all the justifications running through her head. "Go on."

"You have to tell him. He'll be angry. Who wouldn't be? But you've been there long enough for him to get to know you. He'll calm down eventually, and then he'll see the position you were in. He may not like it, but from what you've told me, he's a pretty smart guy. He'll see you didn't act maliciously."

"Will he?"

"I hope so, hon. But even if he doesn't, you still have to fess up."

"I don't know if I'm strong enough."

"You are."

"But—"

"Lily, you can. It'll be bad, but in the end you'll be glad you did it. You're not the kind of person who can live with lies. You never have been."

Her tears flowed in earnest now, blinding her, and making it hard to breathe. "Oh, Dylan."

He was quiet for a long moment. "You love him that much?"

Of course. She should have known he would guess. "More than that."

"More than Jason?"

She laughed bitterly. "In one of life's more ironic twists, my being here with Cole has made me very clear about my relationship with Jason. He was a jerk and I was obsessed and love never entered the picture."

"Are you sure?"

"I am now."

"Oh, man."

"You got that right. I'm well and truly screwed, little brother."

"I wish I could do more."

"I'm just glad you're there. Hold on." She put the phone down, wiped her eyes and blew her nose. She was able to breathe a little better when she picked up the cell phone. "So what's going on with you? Anything new?"

IN THEIR MAKESHIFT office at the ranch, Dylan stared at his desk pad. There was hardly a blank space left. He'd have to get a new one. It was impossible for him to sit quietly while on the phone. He was too antsy. "No, nothing new. Nothing but one dead end after another."

"Damn."

"Sebastian wanted to know if I thought we should call the investigation off."

"Are you kidding?"

"No. He's really disheartened. I know he's lost faith."

"What about you?"

"I'm not throwing in the towel. Just because I haven't found something yet doesn't mean I won't find the key tomorrow."

"Good for you."

He picked up the top sheet of his desk pad and crumpled it into a ball. After he'd scored by tossing it in the round file, he picked up his pen again. But he froze when he saw what he'd uncovered. A picture. He didn't remember putting it there, but he sure as hell remembered taking it.

Julie hadn't known. She'd been on her sundeck, soaking up some rays. He wasn't sure, but he thought she might have been asleep. Her hair glowed like a halo and the sun on her skin made her seem otherworldly. He'd been completely captivated. Totally smitten.

"Uh, Dylan? Did you fall asleep?"

He shook himself out of the memory. "No. I just got distracted for a minute. But I do have to get going. I've got an interview in a few minutes."

"Really?"

"You might know her. She's done a lot of volunteering for the Texas Fund for Children. Her name is Carolyn St. Clair."

"I may have heard the name, but no face is coming to mind. But that's good about her volunteering. I like that."

"I've got my fingers crossed."

"I guess I'll hang up then."

"You'll do great, Lily. It's a rough start, but hey, don't all great love stories start that way?"

She chuckled, which sounded odd with her stuffed nose. Dylan hoped Cole Bishop was a smart man. Because a smart man would see that she was a keeper. "Bye."

He hung up the phone as his gaze went back to the picture of Julie. It had been so long ago. Her hair had been short, and she'd thought it made her look too young. He'd thought it made her look beautiful. But then, he'd been in love.

Why hadn't he done something about it? He'd waited, and then it was too late. He'd shared all his hopes and dreams with her, but Sebastian was the one she had loved.

It was a sort of cruel torment to have remained friends all these years. But how could he justify ending his friendship? So he'd gone to Dallas and lost himself in the lives of other people. He'd become someone else, but the real kicker was that he'd still loved her. Even when he barely remembered his own name, Julie had been there. In his thoughts, in his heart.

A knock on the door startled him and he shoved the picture in the folds of the desk pad. The next time he ran across it, Julie would be home. At her home, with her husband. But that was okay. He'd had a long talk with God, and he'd promised that if Julie was safe, he'd never again begrudge Sebastian his happiness. "Come in."

A tall slender woman walked into the office. She was in her twenties, and she was a stunner. Her hair was almost red, but still brown, and it came down to her chin. He liked her immediately.

"Dylan Garrett, I presume?"

He rose and extended his hand. They shook, and he liked the feel of her, too. "Sorry about the office. We're still building the real thing, but it'll be a while longer yet." He indicated the chair by Lily's desk. "Have a seat. Can I get you coffee?"

"That would be great, thank you." She smoothed her slim green skirt and sat down, adjusting the matching jacket before she looked at him again. Her shoes and her purse were the same color. "I only had one cup this morning. Definitely not enough."

"I agree." He went to the pot and got a cup. "How do you take it?"

"Black is fine."

"Fair enough." As he poured her cup and another for himself, he realized he'd already made his decision. Unless the woman couldn't read or had a criminal record, she was it. The assistant he'd had in mind. "So tell me about yourself?"

"I live here in San Antonio. Have all my life. I've been working as an executive assistant for a law firm, but frankly, I'm looking for something a little less formal, if you know what I mean."

He brought the mugs and set them down, then took his seat across from her. "I do. What else appeals to you about this job?"

"I've always thought it would be terribly exciting to work for a private eye."

"You have?"

She nodded. "Yes." Her cheeks pinked a bit, and she had to clear her throat. "I think I'd be good at it, too. I like the details. The little puzzles. I've got one of those brains, you know. I think they call them helicopter brains."

"I don't know the expression."

She took a tentative sip of coffee, then raised her eyebrows with pleasure. "Nice, thank you. Anyway, there are people who have train brains, who follow logical steps from A to B to C. And then there are helicopter brains, who make connections from seemingly random events. Not to imply I can't go from A to B, if it's required."

"That's odd."

She got a panicky look on her face. "What?"

"I understood that."

Her smile sealed the deal.

"You do realize there's going to be computer input, filing, that kind of dull, mindless work."

"Of course. But I'm hoping there'll also be enough interesting work to offset it."

"I think there will be."

"Good."

"So when can you start?"

"Seriously?"

He nodded. "I'll have to check out your references, of course, but if there aren't any curve balls, the job is yours." He told her about the pay, the benefits, working with Lily. Enough information for her to make an informed decision.

When he finished she held out her hand. "I can't thank you enough, Mr. Garrett."

"Dylan," he said, taking her hand. "My father is Mr. Garrett. And he lives here, too. Along with Lily, of course, and the ranch foreman, Max Santana."

"Wow. Sounds lively."

"A little too lively sometimes."

"I can handle it."

He leaned back in his chair, well pleased. She would be able to handle it. And whatever else came her way. He knew it as surely as he knew his own name. Now, if only Lily's problem could be solved so handily...

CHAPTER SEVENTEEN

THE LONG DAY was coming to an end, and for Cole, it couldn't come a moment too soon. He'd forgotten all about his appointment with Jeff Harcourt until he'd shown up at the house. Harcourt was from *The Cattlemen,* and he was doing an article for the monthly trade paper. It was a damn shame Cole hadn't been able to focus properly. The article would surely make him look like a fool.

But he'd done the best he could, considering Lily was waiting for him. If he'd had his way, Cole would have spent the day out by the spring, thinking. Everything was topsy-turvy in his head.

He shook Harcourt's hand, then watched him get into his blue sedan. Once the car had disappeared down the road, Cole headed out for the barn. He wanted to see Lily something awful, but he needed some time. Time to figure out what was next.

He passed Spence, who looked at him curiously. "Aren't you going in to dinner?"

"I'll be there shortly."

Spence shrugged as he went toward the house.

Cole kept walking. Past the barn, past the paddock. He found himself in a copse of oaks, with streams of light peeking in between the leaves. He settled himself on a fallen log, and put his elbows on his knees.

He closed his eyes, listening to a faraway airplane, and then it was just the breeze rustling the leaves.

Things had changed. He hadn't wanted them to, but there it was. She'd been the catalyst, but he'd kept walking after she pushed.

In the shower this morning, when she lay sleeping in his bed, he'd realized he couldn't carry out his plan. He wasn't going to buy himself a son. Not that he couldn't, but he knew now that if he did, he was just asking for more heartache than he could stand.

She was right about that. He couldn't control another human being. Not through money or words or with his hands. All he could do was give his son the best that he had, and whatever the boy did with it after that, well, Cole would have to accept it. No matter what.

It would help if his son had a mother who was strong, intelligent, courageous. Who saw the humor in things. *Lily.* Any child would be lucky to have her for a mother. He'd be lucky to have her for a wife.

The thought nearly rocked him from the log.

He sat up straight, ran a hand over his face. How was it possible he wanted to ask this woman to be his wife? He hadn't known her long enough, and besides, he hadn't even called the detective to hear what he'd found out in his background check. Only a damn fool would want to marry a woman he'd only known for a few days.

He stood up, anxiety making him walk again. This was nuts. He didn't love her. He couldn't. It was too soon. And she was too much of an unknown.

But if he didn't love her, why was the thought of her leaving tearing at him? Why hadn't he hired Mrs.

Holt? She would have been perfect, yet he'd sent her away.

Lily had made him crazy. Certifiable. Making love with her had been a huge mistake. If he'd sent her home yesterday, he would have wondered what it would have been like. As it was, he knew. And that was worse. Much worse.

He'd never felt like this before. Never felt so calm and so excited, all at the same time. He'd never known making love could be so powerful. Before Lily, he'd enjoyed sex. He was a normal man with normal needs, after all. What he hadn't understood was that it could be so much more than physical.

Cole was no philosopher, and he didn't go in for any touchy-feely psychobabble, but dammit, he'd felt something in his soul last night. He'd found what had been missing all his life. He'd found it in her arms. In her body.

But he also didn't want to go off half-cocked. There was plenty of time to see how things would shake down. He didn't have to ask her to marry him or anything that radical. He just wouldn't hire a new cook, that's all. Then he'd see. He'd use his head for once. Think things through.

Good. He felt much better now that he had a course of action. He headed back to the house. He was as hungry as a bear. That's why he was walking so fast. Not because he'd get to see her.

Yeah, right.

LILY FORCED HERSELF to eat a little of the pot roast, but her stomach wasn't happy about it. In fact, her whole body was miserable, especially her heart.

Of course Cole knew something was wrong. All

through the meal he kept sending her these little looks. She'd smiled, trying not to make him worry. She failed at that, too.

Then Manny asked her if everything was all right. She nodded. And burst into tears. Completely unwilling to fall apart in front of everyone, she left the table and hurried to her bedroom. She heard Cole's chair scrape behind her.

Oh, God. This was it. This was the end. She had to tell him now, and see the expression on his face when he realized what kind of a horrible person she was. How she'd lied and manipulated—

She flung herself on the bed and buried her face in the pillow. He'd never reconcile with Eve now, and it was all her fault. She'd botched everything. And the worst of it was that she'd probably ruined Cole's chances of ever finding real love.

She still wasn't sure if she loved him. Everything was so confusing that she couldn't trust her emotions. But she was sure that leaving tonight was going to be terribly difficult.

She'd busted her butt all day, cooking meals for the freezer so Cole wouldn't have to worry for the next few days about hiring a cook. That had been awful, but not half as bad as packing had been.

Her suitcase was in the closet, ready to go. As she was. Damn ugly room. She should feel happy that at least she got to go back to the Double G. She'd get to help Dylan find Julie, and that was a good thing, right?

The knock on the door made her stomach churn. If only there was a way not to tell him the truth. To just leave and never look back.

Coward. She'd made this bed. And now she had to make Cole lie in it.

She got up, wiped her eyes with the backs of her hands, and went to the door. Her hand even found the doorknob. But it took an act of will that was quite nearly beyond her to turn it.

The look of concern on Cole's face started her crying all over again. He pulled her into his arms and held her tight, rocking her back and forth. She didn't even pretend to struggle. Instead, she put her head on his shoulder, wept like a child, and wished for a miracle. Between sobs, she inhaled deeply, knowing this was going to be the last time she'd be this close. She memorized the feel of his chest, the way his arms circled her body, the strength of him. She'd recognized that from the beginning. But then she'd thought it was purely physical. Now she understood how strong Cole really was. How hard he'd worked to become the man his father should have been.

"Honey, what is it?" he whispered. "Did I do something wrong?"

She leaned back. "No. You didn't do anything. It's me. It's all me."

He looked at her with his worried eyes, the furrow between his brows deep, his lips curved in a frown. So beautiful. The best-looking man she'd ever seen in the flesh. She sniffed, knowing it was time. She couldn't put it off any longer.

"Nothing can be that bad, honey," he said.

She closed her eyes for a moment, mustering all her courage. "Yes, it can. I need to talk to you Cole. And I need you to listen to the whole thing."

Cole let her take his hand as she led him to the bed. She stood as he sat, and from the way she paced, he had a sinking feeling this wasn't the female trouble he'd first imagined. This was serious.

She sniffed again, grabbed some tissue from a box by the bed, blew her nose, then stood in front of him. Her shoulders were back and her head held high, but he could tell she was damn nervous. What in hell?

"Cole, I—"

"What?"

Her face paled right in front of him. In fact, he thought she might pass out, but she didn't. She cleared her throat, touched her diamond necklace the way he'd seen people touch a cross and spoke again. "Cole, I came here under false pretenses."

The vague feeling of foreboding shifted into something far more concrete. Damn it all to hell. It *had* been too good to be true.

"I'm not a secretary at Finders Keepers. I'm one of the investigators. And I was hired by your grandmother."

"What?" His grandmother? What the—

"Eve is very ill, Cole. And she hates what's come between you. She wants to see you before she dies. She wants to say she's sorry."

Cole stood up and walked to the other side of the bedroom. He couldn't look at Lily right now. Not when he felt this kind of anger boiling inside him. He couldn't be sure what he'd do.

It had all been lies. His family had done it again. Only this time they'd hired the woman who would stab him in the back. The only thing missing was Lily telling him she was pregnant.

"Cole?"

"Your timing is off, Lily. If you'd waited a while,

I probably would have asked you to marry me. And then you could have had a really big laugh.''

He heard her gasp, then the bed frame squeaked. When he turned, she was on the bed, her head in her hands, her shoulders shaking with her sobs. His first reaction was to go to her. To comfort her. Then he remembered. ''You're good,'' he said. ''I've got to give you that. I believed you.''

She looked at him, her eyes red-rimmed and filled with shame. ''I came here to do something noble. To try to help you and Eve make peace. I only lied because I didn't believe you'd listen to me.''

''It would have been nice if you'd given me a chance.''

She stood up. ''Come on, Cole. I'm not trying to justify my actions, but you and I both know if I'd said Eve's name that first day, you would have booted me right out.''

''And now I'm supposed to be grateful? I told you what she did. You know, and you can still ask me to see her?''

''People make mistakes. Even people you love. She loves you, Cole. She doesn't want to die with this bad blood between you.''

''She should have thought of that when she paid off Carrie.''

Lily sighed, then sniffed. ''I don't want you to feel guilty,'' she said. ''Later. When time has gone by, and Eve is gone.''

''I won't feel guilty. I won't feel anything.''

''Now you're the one who's lying. I know better. I know you feel everything. Too much. You were hurt, Cole, but now it's time to end it. To at least listen to her.''

"Why? She'll just lie. Everyone does. Oh, she'll say the ends justify the means, but it'll still be a pack of lies."

Lily winced. "Don't blame her for my mistake. I should have done this better. I didn't know how."

"So you figured the best way to go about it was to climb in my bed? That as soon as you spread your legs I'd agree to anything?"

She jerked back as if he'd slapped her. "You can't believe I made love to you for that."

"I can. And I do. You forget, I've had a lot of experience with women like you. Women who use the bedroom to get what they want." He slammed a hand against the wall but it did no good. The rage was just as strong. "I can't believe I fell for it again. After I swore I wouldn't. After I built my entire life to protect myself from women like you."

"Cole—" She put her hand on his shoulder and he jerked away.

"Don't."

"Cole, I know I've hurt you. But I promised myself I would tell you everything, and so I'm going to."

"There's more?"

She nodded.

"Go on. Make my day."

She wept a little more, wiped her eyes with the crumpled tissue, then looked at him again. "The thing is, I didn't plan it this way. I never meant to— Oh, Cole. I think…I'm pretty sure…that I'm in love with you."

Cole felt as if a knife had been plunged into his chest. She was worse than anything he could have imagined. She made Carrie look like a Girl Scout.

"I'd be obliged if you would be gone by morning," he said, struggling to keep his voice calm.

"But—"

He didn't want to hear one more thing out of her mouth. He threw open the door and walked out. He kept on walking. Out of the house, out to the barn. He saddled Phantom and then he took off. He wasn't sure where he was going. He didn't give a damn. He just needed to get the hell away from Lily and her lies. Damn her for making him feel again. Damn her to hell.

LILY WASHED HER FACE, then folded her towel and put it back on the rack. Nothing of hers was left in the bathroom, or in the bedroom. It was as if she'd never been there.

She turned off the light and got her purse and her suitcase. The emptiness and ache inside her made walking difficult, made breathing difficult. She'd done so much damage. Hurt him so badly. She deserved everything she'd gotten.

But that didn't make leaving any easier. So much had affected her in the short time she'd been here. The guys. Manny with his cursing and his love for the work and Rita. Chigger, such a courtly gentleman, so sweet. J.T., Spence, John. They'd all treated her with complete respect and offered their friendship freely, no strings attached. She'd miss them. Miss the talk at the table, the jokes, the compliments about her cooking.

She turned off the light in the barren little bedroom and headed down the hall. Cole wasn't in the house. No one was. She would leave in the dark, without a word, in shame. It fit. There should be no tearful goodbyes. She'd lied to them all.

In the living room, she stopped and let her gaze travel over the drab furniture, the unadorned walls. She'd decorated the place in her mind. Several times, in fact. While she'd been cooking, she'd put some paintings on that wall, added a rug, brought in some plants.

The tears threatened again, and she couldn't let that happen. She'd cried too much tonight, and she had a long drive ahead of her. Besides, there would be many, many more opportunities to weep after she was home.

She walked out the door, closing it behind her. Closing it for the last time. Leaving her heart behind as she headed to her car.

CHAPTER EIGHTEEN

COLE TURNED OFF his computer and headed toward the kitchen. Mrs. Holt was making pork chops tonight, and he'd always been fond of them. She was a good cook, everything her résumé had promised. But she wasn't Lily.

The two weeks since she'd left had been hell. The work got done, and the bills got paid, and the sun rose and set, but Cole wasn't part of it.

None of the men had asked him what happened. They never even said her name. Which was good. Now, if he could just get her out of his head, things might have a chance of getting back to normal.

He'd given up his dream to have a child. No more searching, no more planning. He understood and accepted that he had no judgment when it came to women. No radar that told him good from bad, lies from truth. He couldn't trust himself worth spit.

The thing he regretted the most was making love with her. Sleep had become a rare commodity. She plagued him in his dreams. The memory of her body, of her kisses, of her scent snuck up on him and made his insides tighten with hurt and want. Crazy, huh? That he still wanted her. After everything she'd told him. It made no sense.

He'd thought a lot about his grandmother, too.

About when he'd been a kid, playing in that big old house of hers. How she'd slip him hard candy when his mother wasn't looking. How she'd listen to him for hours as she sat at her secretary, writing notes and grocery lists, paying bills. She never chased him out of the room. Not like his father had.

He'd be the first to admit there had been good times. But that didn't change the way things had gone down. Eve had hurt him almost as much as his father had. What more was there to say?

He supposed there was one good thing that had changed since Lily had left. He'd stopped blaming Eve. He'd stopped blaming anyone but himself. He'd come to see the pattern of his life, and he'd figured out how to deal with it. Everyone he'd loved had betrayed him, so he wouldn't love anyone. Simple. Clean. Safe. He'd keep to himself. And his men. He'd work. He might even try his hand at writing some articles. But he'd never expect anything again. Not from another living soul.

So what if there was no laughter at the dinner table? It didn't matter at all that the silence of the night drove him crazy. He'd adjust. In time, the ache would leave. The want would stop. It had to.

COLE DIDN'T MEAN TO SPY. He was just rinsing out a glass at the kitchen sink when he saw Manny dressed up in a suit and tie, his hair combed, his shoes shined, looking like a man on his way to the chapel. Which wasn't that far off. A moment later, his girl Rita was heading toward him, and she, too, was dressed to the nines. Her long dark hair swayed down her back, and her dress, a soft blue, clung to her body in a way that would make any man swallow hard. The way they looked at each other...

His fingers hurt and he glanced down to see that he was squeezing the glass so hard it was about to shatter. He put it down, determined not to look out the window again. But he did. He watched Manny touch Rita's hair, a tender caress. Then they kissed, and a pain like fire lit up in Cole's chest.

He had no business envying Manny. Wishing things could have been different. But...

Damn, it had been three weeks since she'd left. He should have felt better by now. He should have stopped dreaming about her every blessed night.

The thing that kept gnawing at him was remembering that first day. How he'd been talking on the phone while she stood there looking so beautiful it took his breath away. He'd had to consciously harden his heart and his voice so she wouldn't suspect what she'd done to him just by showing up.

If she'd brought up Eve that afternoon, if she'd told him the truth about why she was there, he knew for a fact he would have shown her the door. He wouldn't have listened to another word.

It didn't excuse the lies. Or did it? He wasn't sure anymore. He wasn't sure about much. Only that he missed her. And that his life felt as empty as the walls of his house.

Manny took Rita's hand, and they walked off toward their car. Cole watched until they disappeared from view. He tried to work up his anger, to hide in his self-righteousness. It didn't work. He didn't have the energy anymore.

She'd been wrong to lie. But maybe, just maybe, she hadn't meant to hurt him.

LILY KNEW something was wrong. Not just with her emotions, but with her body. And it terrified her to think what it might be.

It was almost a month since she'd walked out of Cole Bishop's life. The worst month she could ever remember. Dylan had helped. He'd been wonderful these last weeks. Really a sweetheart. He hadn't said a word about her crying fits, or her dour mood. He'd been patient and kind, and he'd tried his best to make her feel better. But he knew there was nothing in heaven or earth that would fix the hurt inside her. Time, they said. But what did they know?

She opened the paper bag from the pharmacy and pulled out the package. A home pregnancy test. Just looking at it made her knees weak, and she sat down on the edge of her bed.

She'd been on the pill. She couldn't be pregnant. She hadn't missed taking any, not one. The only reason she thought she might, just *might* be...was because of an article she'd read about drug interactions. It seemed the kind of antibiotics she'd taken could sometimes lessen the effectiveness of birth control pills. She could hardly see the scar on her hand from that dog bite. It didn't seem possible.

But she was two weeks late. She'd never been late before. And dammit, she couldn't stop crying. It was ridiculous. Anything set her off—commercials, movies, even a tender word. She'd just get to weeping and sometimes it felt as though she would never stop.

Of course, the work had suffered. If it hadn't been

for Carolyn, everything would have gone to hell in a hand basket. She'd been great, never prying, but always willing to listen. Lily was lucky. Her whole family supported her, tried to convince her that this mess wasn't her fault. But she knew better.

She kept remembering the look on Cole's face. The hurt, the disbelief, and finally, the rage. As icing on the cake, she also had the memory of Eve's disappointment lodged in her brain. Eve had said it was all right, that Lily shouldn't blame herself, but that was just kindness talking. There was no one else to blame, and everyone knew it.

It was no use putting this off any longer. She had to know.

She hadn't let herself think about what she would do if the test was positive. Of course, she would keep the child. There was no question about that. But her secret shame that she could barely own up to herself, let alone talk about with her brother or sister, or anyone, was that part of her wanted to be carrying his child. It wasn't right, and she had no business thinking about it, but she couldn't help it.

It would be part of Cole. That alone made her hope for a plus sign on the indicator. Could she possibly be any more selfish? No. She'd reached the apex, the absolute summit of self-centeredness. She wanted this baby, even though she knew how it would wound Cole. In his eyes she'd be just like Carrie. But the thought of not having even a part of him made the rest of her life seem such a lonely proposition.

She got up and walked slowly to the bathroom. Locking herself in, she read the directions and went about the rather undignified process of finding out what her future was going to hold.

COLE COULD HARDLY believe he was standing on his grandmother's doorstep. Just driving up to the place had filled him full of conflicting emotions. The good times—damn, there had been so many—overshadowed by a depth of betrayal he didn't even know how to express.

Maybe this was a mistake. He should just turn around. Go back to his new life, his safe life. But how could he? Lily had changed everything. She'd told him things he didn't want to know. Like the fact that Eve was sick. Dying.

He'd sworn never to speak to her again, so why was he here? What did he hope to accomplish? That was the thing. He didn't know. Did he honestly think he would find peace here? That he'd learn how to sleep again? To stop beating himself up for every decision he'd ever made? Was it as simple as seeing his grandmother?

Simple, but not easy. Years of anger held his hand at his side, instead of letting him knock on the door. How large these doors had been as a child. The whole house had seemed gigantic, full of places to hide and places to explore. He'd loved it here, once.

Despite his misgivings, he knocked. Maybe no one would answer. Then he could go home, knowing he'd tried his best. He waited, his heart pounding hard in his chest, his hands damp, but not from the humid air. No one came to the door after five seconds, ten seconds.

He knocked again after a full two minutes.

This time, the door swung open. A woman he didn't know smiled at him.

"Can I help you?"

He almost said no. "I'm here to see Eve Bishop."

"Is she expecting you?"

He shook his head. "I doubt it."

"Your name?"

The woman was attractive and, oddly, barefoot. Things had certainly changed around here if the help didn't need to wear shoes. "I'm her grandson. Cole."

Her eyes widened and her mouth dropped open in an almost comic double take. He might have laughed if he could've found anything funny about it.

"Come in, Mr. Bishop," she said, stepping back quietly so he could get by her. "Oh, she'll be so happy. Stay here, please. One moment." She hurried down the hall, but stopped after ten feet. "Please, wait." Then she turned and ran.

Cole wasn't going anywhere. Not yet. He'd come this far, he wasn't going to back out now. But that didn't mean everything was going to be all hunky-dory with Eve. The facts hadn't changed. No matter how old she got, how sick, she had done what she had done.

His gaze fell on an old pitcher atop a mahogany console table. They had both been there all his life. Nothing fancy or ornate, but simple and elegant. His grandmother's taste in a nutshell.

A wave of nostalgia hit him hard, and a hundred images fought for preeminence in his mind. The smell of the soap in the downstairs bath. The sound of tennis shoes on the white marble. His mother's laughter drifting down the staircase.

If only—

"Mr. Bishop."

He looked up to see the maid standing by the library door.

"Please."

He started across the foyer, and every step brought more memories. And more tension to his gut. He paused as he reached the door, knowing it was his last chance to make a clean break. And then he walked into his grandmother's favorite room.

Everything looked the same. The dolls, the portrait, the carpet, the lace doilies. Everything but Eve. She'd gotten so old. So frail. Seeing her holding on to her cane, tears spilling over her wrinkled, nearly translucent skin, propelled him forward. He needed to touch her. To make sure she was real. To stop time.

"My baby," she whispered. "My Cole."

He wrapped her in his arms, forcing himself not to squeeze too hard. She was so tiny. Like a little bird. His eyes burned and he blinked the heat away, then stepped back to really look at her.

Her eyes had paled, but her strength was still there. Her determination, her courage. And her stubbornness. "Hi, Grandma."

She smiled, and it lit up her face. "Lily said—"

He nodded. "I know. I wasn't going to come. But I figured it was time we did some talking."

She stepped back and ushered him to the couch. After he sat, she did, too, although with her it took a shaky moment. Finally, she was in her wing chair, her white hair pulled up on her head, her cardigan sweater buttoned and her cane resting on the cushion. He wondered how long it would be until the maid brought tea. Eve had always been crazy about tea time.

He didn't have to wait long. Even before either one of them could figure out how to begin, the door opened, and the barefoot woman brought in a tray. The next few minutes were devoted to the old ritual. Eve remembered how he liked his tea. Well, how he drank it. He was a coffee man, but he wouldn't complain today.

She handed him his cup.

His gaze followed the maid until she left the room and closed the door. "That's different," he said.

"Angie? She's very nice. Patient."

"I remember when the help had to wear uniforms."

His grandmother smiled ruefully. "One of the advantages of growing old is that foolish notions can be left by the wayside."

"It really doesn't bother you that she doesn't wear shoes?"

"No. It doesn't. She hates shoes. But she always offers to wear them when company is coming. I don't insist. If her bare feet offend, well, then, that's too bad. Angie has made my life bearable these last few years. I don't know what I would have done without her."

Cole felt shame rise in his gullet. His own flesh and blood had to be taken care of by a stranger. But then, hadn't Eve done that to herself? Hadn't her actions dictated the outcome?

She studied him with her pale eyes, focusing on her face. "You look more like your mother now."

"Do I?"

She nodded. "But I see your father in you, too."

He didn't like the comparison. "I'm nothing like him."

"No, I suppose you're not. I assume you want to talk about what happened."

She never was one to beat around the bush. And neither was he. "Yes, I do."

"It was a sorry mess," she said. "A tragedy of selfishness and greed."

He put his cup down, not at all sure he could keep his hands steady enough not to spill the hot liquid all over her couch. "It didn't have to end badly between us."

"Cole, I did what I did because I loved you. I didn't want to see you in any more pain."

He opened his mouth, but he stopped himself before the torrent of vitriol escaped. After a deep breath to compose himself, he asked her the question that had bothered him for five years. "How could you possibly believe I wouldn't want my child? No matter what Carrie did, it wasn't the boy's fault. There was no excuse for terminating the pregnancy. None."

Eve's lips quivered, but instead of falling apart, she sat up straighter. "I didn't realize you knew about that."

"I got a letter from Carrie. She told me you paid for everything. A nice tidy ending for a messy business."

"I did use my money to get rid of her, and I'm not sorry for it. Not a bit. She was a convincing one. Playing you against your father like that. It still makes me angry."

"But that doesn't justify—"

She held up her hand. "I have very real doubts that what Carrie told you was the truth."

"You just admitted as much."

"I admitted to paying her to disappear and never come back."

"And the child?" Cole's hands were wet, and his head pounded with the worst headache he'd had in years. What compelled him to hear the details? Couldn't he just let it go?

"I'm sorry to have to be the one to tell you this. I would have thought Carrie would. She was looking for ways to hurt you, and this would have been the capper."

"What are you talking about?"

She looked away for a moment, up to the portrait of herself as a young woman. Then she faced him, met his gaze. "The child wasn't yours, Cole."

"What?"

"The child wasn't your son. He was your brother."

He knew the instant the words were out of her mouth that she was telling the truth. Holy god, he'd known it somehow, on some level. It wasn't his child. It had never been his child.

"And for the record," Eve said, her voice a raggedy whisper, "I didn't know she was going to use the money to have an abortion. She'd agreed to give the child up for adoption. I found out after."

He tried to think of something to say, but his thoughts were too jumbled. What struck him hardest was the waste. The waste of a new life, the waste of his love, and the waste of all those years he'd spent in anger. He'd blamed everyone for his stupidity, and he'd focused his hurt on the one person who had never shown him anything but love.

"I'm so grateful I got to tell you these things before I die."

"You're not—"

"Yes, I am. But not today. Today I get to visit with my grandson. I get to hear all about his life. I get to put my hand on his arm. I'm very lucky, don't you think?"

He rose on unsteady feet and crossed to the big wing chair that held the small woman sitting so tall, and he got down on his knees in front of her. He took her wrinkled, delicate hands in his own and he kissed her. "I'm such a fool."

"No," she said. "We all made mistakes. You were hurt. I knew that. I should have found you then. Made sure you understood. But I was stubborn."

"I can't believe that everything I've thought for all these years—"

"It's all right," she said, moving her hand to cup his cheek. "The important thing is that you came. That you're here now. That you've given me a chance. Bless Lily Garrett."

At the mention of Lily's name, Cole rose.

"She didn't think you would come," Eve said.

He nodded. "I wasn't going to."

"What changed your mind?"

He went back to the couch and sat down again, still reeling from the earthquake that had shaken his righteous anger. "She did. She made me think about things I'd been too stubborn to face. She changed everything."

A slow smile lit Eve's face. "She did, did she?

Well, why don't we heat up that tea of yours while you tell me how.''

THE PHONE CALL had come a week after Lily had taken the test. Eve had asked to see her. There had been no explanation, just the simple request. Lily had, of course, said she'd come. But now that she was at the old mansion, she hesitated before getting out of her car.

So much had happened. So much she didn't understand. Big questions remained, and she was trying her best to figure out how to handle it all.

Her hand went to her stomach. She wasn't showing at all yet. In fact, if she hadn't gone to the doctor and had it verified, she hardly would have believed it. Cole's baby was inside her, and these last few days she'd been struggling to decide how to tell him.

She'd left two phone messages, but he'd never called her back. She supposed she didn't blame him. If he didn't call her back by the weekend, she'd have to go out to his ranch. Perhaps that was the best course anyway. This was the kind of news that needed to be given in person.

She got out of the car and climbed the steps to the door. A few moments later and she was once again following the barefoot maid to the library. Eve had the tea service on the cart next to her chair.

"Come in, Lily."

As Lily moved closer, she noticed a subtle difference in the older woman. A shine to her eyes, and some pink in her cheeks. No sign at all of her stroke, except perhaps a slight droop on the left side of her mouth. "You look wonderful."

"I'm feeling well, thank you."

"I'm glad." Lily kissed her cheek, then sat across from her. "And I'm glad you asked me to come by."

"Good." Eve poured, remembering how Lily took her tea. "I want to ask you some questions, if you don't mind."

"Of course not."

She handed Lily her cup and saucer, then folded her weathered hands on her lap. "I'd like to know what happened between you and my grandson."

Lily put her cup down quickly, wondering what she should say. "I'm not sure what you mean."

"I think you do. I think you and he got to know each other when you were there. It would mean a great deal to me to hear what he's like. We really haven't had a chance to talk about that."

Lily's shoulders sagged with relief. It was foolish to think Eve could possibly know about the baby. Or that she'd even guess she and Cole had— "He's terribly handsome," she began, wanting to paint the picture just right. "But you know that. I see now, he's got your eyes."

Eve smiled as she leaned back in the big wing chair. "Go on."

"He's got himself a temper, that's true, but the men who work for him respect and admire him. He's a fair man who pushes for excellence, but he works harder than anyone else."

Lily took a sip of her tea, then she smiled. "He's also got a wicked sense of humor, although he doesn't particularly want people to think of him that way. In fact, he tries to hide a lot. His kindness, his tender side. He puts on a gruff, no-nonsense scowl and thinks no one can see past it. But of course, everyone who knows him any length of time does.''

''You did.''

''Yes, ma'am. I think I saw those traits that first day. He tried to scare me away, but there was something more to it. A challenge. I wanted to spar with him, and if I do say so myself, I gave as well as I got.''

''I imagine you did.''

For a long moment, Lily's gaze went back to Cole's ranch, to the stubborn son of a bitch who'd stolen her heart. ''He wasn't easy. Not ever. I think it's because he's so afraid of being hurt. He'd be the last one to admit it, but he cares so deeply about people, it makes him feel vulnerable. He was shattered by Carrie and—''

''And?''

''And I didn't help any.'' She should stop. She was telling Eve too much. But from the look in the older woman's eyes, Lily could tell she wanted all of it. The good and the bad. ''I betrayed him, too, Eve, and I've never been more sorry. I was a fool, and I took all his old pain and made it fresh again. I wish I could take it back.''

''So what you're saying to me is that he cared for you.''

''Pardon?''

''You said it yourself.'' The old woman leaned forward again, a faint glimmer in her faded eyes. ''It's when he cares deeply that he can be hurt.''

''I suppose, but—''

''If I ask you a question, will you give me an honest answer?''

Lily wasn't sure she should say yes. But, heaven knew, lying had brought her to this sorry state. "Yes, ma'am."

"Are you in love with him?"

She closed her eyes for a moment and put her hand on her stomach. The second she realized what she'd done, she picked up her teacup, hoping the gesture wasn't noticed. Eve waited patiently as the old clock in the corner of the room counted out the seconds. "Yes, Eve. I'm in love with him." Tears welled again, which should have been impossible. But now she understood that there was a never-ending supply of tears. Enough for a lifetime. "I can't stop thinking about him. How I felt when I was with him. It was exciting, you know? My tummy got all quivery when I heard him walking down the hall. And when he touched me—" She stopped, afraid she'd said too much already.

"It's all right. I'm beyond being shocked. I figured you two had found the bedroom."

Lily felt her face heat. "It wasn't tawdry, Eve. It was—"

"Magic."

Lily froze as she heard the voice behind her. Low and deep, smooth as fine whiskey.

Eve smiled. "I believe you know my grandson."

Lily couldn't speak at all. She'd never wanted anything more in her life than this moment, and she was terrified if she said a word it would all disappear.

He walked across the carpet slowly, then moved in front of her. Her gaze traveled up his long, jean-clad legs to that big shiny belt, to the expanse of his chest and the blue-and-white western shirt he wore. She lingered on his hands. They held his hat nervously, moving round the rim. She'd saved the best for last, of course. She tilted her head up until their gazes met.

The thrill that coursed through her body was electric. He smiled at her, and that was all it took. She pushed herself out of her chair and the next second she was in his arms, and his hands were holding her tight, and his lips covered hers in fevered kisses.

"Lily," he whispered, then he kissed her some more. "It's been hell without you."

"I know," she said. "I haven't slept or been able to work. Cole, I'm so sorry. I've never been more sorry about anything in my life. I'd rather cut off my own arm than hurt you—"

He stopped her with his kiss, and she knew she'd been forgiven. But there was still one more thing to confess. One more truth to lay at his feet.

She pulled back and stepped away. "Cole, I—"

He shook his head. "Hold on, okay? Because I have a couple of things to say, and if I don't say them now, I might not have the nerve to say them later."

She nodded, noticing his hat on the floor. He'd dropped it when she'd jumped into his arms.

"I'm still not crazy about the fact that you lied to me. But I also know I would have shown you the door if you'd mentioned Eve. So, while I would have hoped for a different way, I can understand why you did what you did."

"Cole—"

He held up his hand. "I'm not through. I also did a lot of thinking about my family. About what I've been through, and what I've done with it. I'm proud of my ranch, but I don't love it. Not the way I should.

Not with the kind of passion that makes for a truly contented life. I've cut myself off from my past, and that includes all the good things, too. I've taken myself out of the game, and that's left me bitter and hard, and I won't do it anymore."

He stepped closer to her, so she could see the passion in his expression. "I'm giving up the ranch. Leasing it to Manny and Rita with an option to buy. I'm going to concentrate on my other business ventures. The things I do best." He turned around, looking at the far end of the room, where his grandmother stood, tears falling down her cheeks. "We've had ourselves some good talks," he said, his voice low and full of emotion. "Grandma has decided that I should take over the Texas Fund for Children. I've agreed. I'll be the new executive director."

Lily's heart thudded against her chest. Did that mean he'd be here? Live here in San Antonio?

His gaze came back to her. "I want to thank you for helping me see the truth. For pushing me up against that wall. If you hadn't, I would have kept my anger as my only companion. Probably for the rest of my life."

"Can I say something now?"

He shook his head. "Nope. Not quite. There's still one more thing I want to say." He took another step toward her and captured her trembling hands in his. "Lily, I've missed you. More than I ever dreamed I could miss another soul. I've missed that sassy mouth of yours. And your eyes, and the way you cock your right brow when you think I've said something stupid. In the past month, I've learned a lot about myself, but the one big truth, the fact that covers it all, is that I love you.''

Now that he was giving her the chance to speak, she couldn't. She had such a lump in her throat and her heart was beating so fast and hard. She wanted to leap into his arms. To make this the perfect moment of her life. But she couldn't make her mouth work. No words would come out.

''Cole,'' Eve said, ''I think Lily is trying to tell you something.''

''You have any idea what it is?'' He spoke as if she weren't right in front of him.

''Yes, I do. I think it has something to do with the night you two had a roll in the hay.''

He looked at his grandmother, then back at her. The scowl she'd come to love was on his face and the look of confusion was in his eyes.

''She's right.'' Lily's voice sounded high and a little squeaky. ''It does have to do with that night.''

''What?''

''Well, remember that bandage on my hand? When I first got there?''

He nodded, his brows moving down another half inch. ''So?''

''Well, see, I was taking antibiotics. For the dog bite. But what I didn't know was that, sometimes, certain antibiotics can reduce the efficacy of birth control pills.''

''Pardon me?''

''I'm pregnant, Cole. I'm sorry. I only found out two days ago, and I left messages on your machine to call me. I was going to drive out to the ranch this weekend to tell you because I didn't want to keep any secrets from you."

"You're pregnant?"

She nodded. "We're pregnant."

He blinked a few times, his face growing awfully pale. God, if he passed out, he'd take about ten Victorian dolls and an antique tea set with him.

"You want to sit down?"

He ignored the offer. "We're pregnant? Are you sure?"

She nodded. "I've been to the doctor. He says we're due in eight months."

Cole seemed a bit wobbly, but he made it to the couch. He sat down and put his elbows on his knees. He stared at the floor for a long time.

Lily grew a bit concerned, and evidently so did Eve, because she came over to where Lily stood.

"Cole?"

He didn't acknowledge his grandmother at all.

"Cole, do I need to call you a doctor?"

That got him to look up. "No, ma'am." He stood and took a step toward Eve. He grasped her small shoulders in his large hands and kissed her on the cheek. "You're gonna be a great-grandma," he said.

"Isn't that something."

Cole just stood there while a dopey grin overtook his face. Lily could see the child he'd once been. "It sure as hell is."

"Will you do something for me, son?"

"Anything."

"Ask the woman to marry you before she faints."

Cole blinked. Then laughed. He kissed Eve again, then let her go. He approached Lily slowly, still smiling like the cat who ate the canary. "You need to know something."

"What?"

"I was gonna do this before you told me."

"Do what?"

He took her in his arms and kissed her hard. "Ask you to be mine."

"Your what?" She had to hear it from his lips before she would believe it. "Surrogate mother? Wife in name only?"

"God, no." He squeezed her tighter. "I want you to be my wife. My companion. The mother of our children. I love you, Lily, and I want to grow old by your side. So, will you?"

She kissed him, and the tears from her cheeks made him all wet. "Yes, yes, yes. I will. I love you forever, and I'll bear your children, and I'll give you hell when you need it. But no matter what, I'll love you. Absolutely. With all my heart."

"Then it's settled."

She nodded.

His gaze on hers grew very serious. "You woke me up, Lily. You taught me how to feel again. How to love. And I'm grateful to you."

She smiled. And then she kissed him. And she knew, in that way she had, that this was the best thing she'd ever done. And that they would be together for the rest of their lives. They'd have a houseful of children, and laughter and joy and pain and everything else that came when two people joined together in marriage. She saw her future, and it was in his arms. Her intuition was never wrong.

TRUEBLOOD, TEXAS *continues*
next month with
HIS BROTHER'S FIANCÉE
By Jasmine Cresswell

Emily Sutton is up to her ears in the final plans for her lavish society wedding when her fiancé informs her that he can't marry her. So she assumes Jordan Chambers, her fiancé's black sheep brother, is offering to save her from the embarrassment of being publicly jilted in order to salvage an important business merger between their families. But Jordan's not motivated by family at all. What he's always wanted is Emily, and he's not about to squander his only chance.

Here's a preview!

"I THOUGHT IT might be a good idea if we got married tomorrow." Jordan made the suggestion with a casualness that would have been entirely appropriate if he'd been suggesting that she might like to try out a new recipe for brunch on Sunday.

Emily clutched the back of the nearest chair. *Jordan had asked her to marry him.* She was quite sure she'd heard that. Unless she was hallucinating. Was she? She felt her mouth start to drop open again, and she hurriedly closed it.

The study was not a good place to be alone with a Chambers male, she decided. First Michael had called off their wedding for no reason at all. Now Jordan was suggesting something even more totally crazy. So crazy, in fact, that Emily felt a spurt of genuine alarm. She hadn't been serious in suggesting Jordan and Michael were suffering from the onset of insanity. Maybe she should have been.

"I don't think marriage would work out too well for us," she said, trying to keep her voice soft and nonthreatening. She even managed a small, reassuring smile. When dealing with lunatics, it was best to be gentle. "Thanks for asking, Jordan, but if you remember, we don't like each other. I have this quaint, old-fashioned dislike of men who sleep with other men's wives."

Jordan might have lost his mind, but his vision remained acute, and his physical coordination excellent. In three quick strides, he crossed the room and pulled her away from the door, spread-eagling his body between her and her escape route.

"Sorry," he said, sounding sincerely apologetic as he pocketed the key. "But I really need you to listen to my proposal."

"I already had one of those from Michael," she replied tightly. "I believe I'm a little burned out on proposals from the Chambers men."

His gaze narrowed. "*Proposition* might be a better word in my case. I'm offering a face-saving deal, Emily. You owe it to yourself to listen. Marry me tomorrow, and the joint business venture between my father and yours can go on as planned. Marry me tomorrow, and the ceremony will probably be over before half the guests even notice that you're exchanging rings with the wrong brother—"

"Thanks again for the generous offer, Jordan, but before we get carried away, let's remember there's one teensy-tiny problem with your scheme."

"What's that?"

"Half the guests might not notice that I'd married the wrong brother, but I would." Emily spoke more harshly than she'd intended, mostly because for a few insane seconds, she'd actually found herself considering his proposition. She was surely hitting a new low to contemplate accepting Jordan's proposal just because it would provide a groom for tomorrow's ceremony.

Jordan shrugged. "It wouldn't be a lifetime sentence," he said. "We can have the big, splashy wedding our parents planned, and then, in a few months, we can get a quiet, civilized divorce.''

"Divorce is never civilized," Emily said. "It's a heartbreaking betrayal of promises."